CREDIBLE THREAT

Eric James Fullilove

ISBN: 1492206156

ISBN 13: 9781492206156

To my family and especially my sons

C O N T E N T S

CHAPTER 1

At 6:00 a.m. that day it was raining. Mook nervously listened to his crew working in the house, moving around, the clink of cups on the glass coffee beaker. Mook dragged on his Chesterfield and blew smoke out between sips of coffee as he sat on the porch, listening to the rain pattering the roof and the wind whispering in the elms on the property.

Rain. And fog was creeping through the backyard of the stately house they were occupying. The rain worried him because they might not get the job finished, and he doubted they would be shuttled to Houston for another try. Too many people were involved already, and moving them would just add to the total.

The screen door behind him whined and creaked as the springs stretched open and then pulled tight to slam the door shut again. Mook didn't turn around because he knew it was the kid standing behind him. The kid didn't take coffee, apparently, and he would probably stand there until Mook told him what to do about breakfast. The ache in his chest was accentuated by the rain, and it was cooler than it would be in the afternoon. Mook stubbed out his cigarette and went back inside. The kid followed him without a word.

They still hadn't spoken as Mook laid the bowl and the chocolate cereal on the kitchen table, the hard thud muffled by the pad underneath the vinyl tablecloth that had pictures of yellow daisies on it. The kid silently got a spoon from the drainer next to the sink and poured Cocoa Krispies into the bowl. Mook was refilling his coffee cup when the kid closed the fridge door and slopped milk onto the cereal until it was a brown mass. The rest of the crew ignored him as the kid scraped the chair out, sat down, and quietly began eating.

"You checked out?" Mook asked softly. When there was no response, Mook turned and faced the table. The kid had his face in the bowl, slurping up milk and cereal as fast as he could. He was a gangly fifteen, with black hair, just over six feet tall and maybe a hundred and sixty pounds soaking wet.

"You checked out?" Mook asked him again, trying to keep the irritation out of his voice. Mook was not quite as tall as the kid and still had the rugged cigarette-ad good looks of a fifty-something man. As much as he wanted the kid to be OK, having him along was not his idea of a good thing. The men were scattered in the house, working on weapons. They were here on a hunting trip, not to baby-sit some teenager who should, by rights, be more concerned with high school football and girls.

The kid looked at him and nodded, and Mook calmed down. This kid was going to be armed this afternoon, sporting a Remington 700 bolt-action long gun. That made him as lethal as any of the men in the house, and it was important that his weapon be checked out.

Mook took a deep breath as he smelled the gun oil and the stink of wet people; he heard the sound of rain, the squeak of oilcloth on the barrels of long guns. His crew was cleaning their weapons, and the sound of rain on the roof was like gunfire—unless you knew the real thing with an intimacy that Mook couldn't deny.

Mook tried to imagine what the gunfire would sound like: the muzzle flash and the explosion of gas and high velocity slugs, the sound of it echoing off the buildings, the startled reaction of the men and women on the street. He closed his eyes and listened to the rain, imagining the sound of gunfire in the pattern of the drops as he reached for his cigarettes, imagining how it would go if the damned rain ever stopped.

On the kitchen table was yesterday's newspaper with a three-inch headline:

President Kennedy in Dallas Tomorrow

And it was dated November 21, 1963.

Too bad the paper didn't say anything about the rain, Mook thought.

***

Juan was complaining about his stomach as Mook flipped open the paper and looked again at the map of the president's motorcade route.

"S'what you get for messing around in those nigger spots," Mook said to Juan, his mind more focused on the newspaper.

"Fook you, Mook. I do what I want. Girl said she made the chicken just for me."

"Yeah, with last month's lard, I bet," Mook said, and they all laughed nervously.

"Hey, I still got some in the fridge, you want some?" Juan said, and the kid spoke up from the kitchen table with his face semi-buried in his third bowl of chocolate cereal.

"No, you don't. I threw it out. Smelt somethin' fierce." The kid's voice pitched up like he was uncomfortable speaking around adults.

"Juan, don't be sick today. *Don't.* Now all of you shut the hell up, I'm trying to think," Mook ordered, irritated. He looked at the map in the newspaper for the thousandth time and figured it would all be over once the motorcade turned onto Houston Street. Juan would be in the "patsy nest" with a spotter and would have an easy shot as the cars traveled up Houston Street before making the turn onto Elm. Billy would be in the Dal-Tex Building, which sat perpendicular to the Book Depository on Houston. He would have an oblique shot as the motorcade came up Houston, but a great shot from the rear, once the motorcade turned onto Elm. Billy was the first layer of insurance, because should the country not yet need a new president once the motorcade turned onto Elm, Billy would make sure that it did.

That left the kid, who was nominally a backup and would be with another spotter who they would meet as they were getting into position. After much head scratching, Mook had placed the kid out of the way on the grassy knoll overlooking Dealy Plaza. He would have his gun, but his spotter would be there to slit his throat if he got out of hand. Mook was scared that the kid would spook the hit with an early shot, and kid or no kid, prodigy or no prodigy, before that happened, his shadow would put him down on a single coded command.

Of course, Mook thought, the grassy knoll was an impossible shot at a moving target with a long gun. Let's face it, he'd told Raoul, Rex the

Wonder Chimp couldn't throw a banana into Kennedy's car under those conditions. A lethal shot? Give the shooter a bazooka, and maybe your percentages rose to fifty-fifty from the very, very low single digits.

That's why the kid was there. *Why waste a real shooter?*

Mook would be on the street watching, and he would be in touch with the teams via a newfangled radio that looked way too small to work effectively. Juan, and certainly the kid, would have earpieces that would allow them to listen to the communications. Billy, the one he trusted the most, would be by himself and would be miked up.

"Mook, lemme ask you a question." Juan was squat and big-bellied, and the way he talked, the word came out sounding like it was two—*quest-tionne*.

"Yeah," Mook said, finally giving in to the urge to light the cigarette between his lips.

"We start shooting at this fooker, and all hell gonna break loose. Car gonna speed up, polices all around gonna start shootin'…"

Mook just shook his head. "Nope."

"Whatchou mean, nope?"

Mook sighed out a cloud of smoke. "You won't have to worry about that. None of it."

"How you so sure?"

The truth was he wasn't sure of a goddamned thing. None of it—the weather, the assurances that he'd received, the rushed feel of the plan—gave him any sense of certainty. FUBAR (military for fouled up beyond all recognition)—that's what this deal was, with too many people and too many loose ends and a goddamned kid, too.

They'd been gaming several motorcade route possibilities for a month before getting confirmation that the Book Depository option (so named because it was the most plausible Oswald patsy route) had been selected. Their window was severely limited by the patsy, and someone on the inside had pushed hard for this particular route. Now Juan wanted to know how he could be so certain that the predictable reaction when shots began raining on the president wasn't going to happen.

Well, he wasn't sure. Besides, no plan of action, no matter how screwy, survives the first encounter with the enemy, Mook thought. *Especially when the enemy is one of us.*

"Because I am," he said, with more confidence than he felt. He took a drag. His chest felt like a burned-out barrel as the smoke hit it and made him want to choke.

"All you have to do is take the shot once the cars turn onto Houston. 'Viva Cuba Libre' and all that crap, OK?" Mook continued. Maybe, if they were lucky, they would hurt someone before the damage-control boys swept in and killed them all.

"OK, but my stomach is pretty fooked up."

"Nobody ever said the rifle was the only lethal weapon you'd be carrying today, asshole," Mook said, and they all laughed to break the tension as Juan made to lift his leg like he was going to cut loose with some killer wind.

The kid mumbled something while they were laughing that Mook didn't catch.

"What'd you say, kid?"

The kid looked at him with those piercing blue eyes of his and said, around a mouthful of cereal, "It's stopped raining."

And they all looked out the windows and saw that the little bastard was right.

***

The president woke several hours later that day in Fort Worth, Texas. As they were preparing to board Air Force One, John Fitzgerald Kennedy asked about the weather in Dallas.

"Clear and sunny now," he was told. He nodded, thinking about the bubble top on his limousine as they boarded Air Force One.

They flew thirteen minutes to Dallas's Love Field, and the president looked up at the bright sunshine as he descended the mobile steps. They were greeted warmly at the airport, and Kennedy was relieved because he'd been told to expect a hostile crowd.

He stopped to shake hands while his limo was being prepared. He came to a decision and told a Secret Service agent to make sure they got rid of his limousine's damned bubble top. It wasn't bulletproof anyway, and they might as well enjoy the sunshine.

One of his Secret Service agents glanced at his watch.

It was approaching 12:00 noon. In Dealy Plaza, Mook and his people had walked in from various directions, many from the rail yard just above the grassy knoll under a "police" escort. Witnesses would later remark how well dressed the rail yard "bums" were and how difficult it was to get a look at their faces.

Mook ended up on Main Street, carrying an umbrella, even though it had stopped raining hours ago. His first call was to Juan and his spotter, to make sure that they'd placed the patsy rifle and the evidence. He'd laughed when his handlers told him, "A Manlicher Carcano? What a piece of crap." The man who gave him the gun had laughed too—a good joke, but not so funny when you thought about what it meant.

Assassination by committee and lowest-common-denominator decisions.

A cheap patsy rifle.

A spic with mob connections as the number-one gun.

Somebody's kid writing it all down for the school newspaper for a headline right under the honor society announcements.

But even a non-shooting idiot like Lee Harvey Oswald could be lethal in this setup, Mook thought as he looked at the Texas School Book Depository and the way Houston led right up to it before the hard left turn onto Elm. The motorcade would first execute a slow right turn from Main onto Houston, slowed by the motorcycles and cars fronting the president's Lincoln limousine and the sharpness of the turn.

If Oswald only had a clue about what was really going on.

Mook raised his binoculars to look over the rooftops and saw a single Dallas Police sharpshooter. He waved at the man, who waved back.

At Love Field, Kennedy had just finished shaking hands. It was 12:05 p.m., and the president's party climbed into the cars for the motorcade into Dallas proper.

***

The kid was in position, waiting behind a retaining wall along the grassy knoll of Dealy Plaza. They'd walked in from the railway tracks, just as nice and easy as you please; his rifle in a long box that he kept perpendicular to the ground near his leg. No one seemed to notice or care that he had a box, because they were bums, and bums carried things in and out of boxcars and rail yards.

They were moved along by a cop or someone wearing a cop's uniform, and he wondered how many real cops and how many phony cops were in Dallas that day. He also wondered how many of them would die afterward; he wasn't stupid.

They'd told him he was being groomed for bigger and better things. His father had trained him in guns, specifically rifles, since he had been able, and he'd developed and displayed a gift for shooting at an early age.

And Daddy always talked about the com'nists and the dirty reds and the liberal pinkos coming to get the good cit'zens of the You-Nighted States, and Daddy had friends who talked the same way. That's why they had guns: to defend the Constitution. They had guns to defend the rule of law. The kid had been taught about guns, because he was going to defend the Land of the Free one day.

Daddy was the law in their town, and in a small town in Texas, the cop was something bigger and more important than just someone directing traffic and giving out parking tickets. His daddy was Respect, his daddy was Order. His daddy was the center of a young son's universe, and the son's ability to shoot gave the father the right to brag about him to everyone who would listen to the insufferable man with the tin star and the big ego. They would suffer until they saw the kid do his thing, and then they would whistle low and be impressed because the kid *was* something special, and word spread.

There were days when his father went on trips and took the kid with him, and more people with guns and uniforms talked about the Jews, or the Kennedys, or the nigrahs, in almost the same breath as stories about killing deer or hunting game. His father would put his arm around the kid and brag about him some more, telling the crowds who'd seen him shoot that he wasn't no nigger lover, and them Kennedys better watch out for this kid, should he get them in his cross hairs.

On one of those trips, men had come for him, gathering first around his father. They told the kid they were grooming him: that he was a shooter and they were grooming him to take his place as a patriot working to save the country. His father's chest stuck out with pride, even though he was never going to see his son again—that's what they said, and the kid had a hard time believing that his father would give him up so easily, cause or no cause.

But he had. *Just get with the crew and understand what it's like; look around at the tactical situation; understand that once the limos make the first turn that someone is going to die in a triangulated field of fire.*

"You're just insurance, kid," the thin man with the razor bumps and the cheap aftershave that had to burn said. "I seen you shoot. If you have to pull the trigger, then something serious will have gone wrong, but that's OK. You see him still breathing, I want you to kill the sumbitch, OK? You'll be lookin' at a nice flat trajectory, nice easy pulls—bam, bam—then get the hell out. And I mean way the hell out, 'cause this one's just to get you used to what the action is like, and the targets don't get any bigger than this one, understan'?"

"Yes, sir," he'd said. His father had explained to him that this was the right thing to do, and that settled it as far as the kid was concerned. He wasn't sure if his father really believed it, though, because Raoul, the man with the cheap aftershave, had argued with his father just before taking him away. The kid had even seen Raoul pull a pistol, unheard of around his father, unthinkable in his father's house.

"Good," Raoul said. "You met Mook, right?"

"Yessir."

"OK, Mook is not real happy about having you along for the ride. Insists this isn't a training op. But Mook knows this is his last job, and he knows how to take orders."

"Why is this Mook's last job?" The kid had asked, ignoring the dark implication that there would be other jobs like this for him.

"'Cause he's got the cancer, kid. Docs give him six months at the outside."

"Why...why not get someone else?" the kid had asked, even as he recoiled at working for one of the others.

"Because six months from now, Mother Nature takes care of the cover-up for us, at least in Mook's case."

"Cover-up?"

But Raoul had just looked at him for a second. "Don't worry about that, kid. Just do your job, then get out clean, OK? We'll have someone pick up the rifle, too."

The kid had hesitated because he knew he shouldn't ask too many questions. "Why pick me? I bet you got plenty of people who can pull a trigger."

And Raoul had shown him the big Colt Python pistol that he carried. "'Cause you can shoot, and we need your daddy to do something for us, kid. This is how we work. He won't back down if he knows you're with us, understand? So you just do your job, and maybe you catch some action to boot."

***

A little after noon Mook checked the teams by radio, annoyed at the static and interference he was getting.

"Sal, how's the kid, over?"

"Little punk's cool as hell, Mook. Probably crap his pants once it goes down," Sal replied.

"Right," Mook said, knowing that the kid could hear everything. He switched channels to contact Juan's radio man.

"Yeah, Mook, we got a little problem."

"Don't give me that crap," Mook whispered fiercely. A woman in the crowd looked at him and the umbrella he was carrying even though the sun was shining brightly. Mook forced a smile at her and pulled credentials from his pocket.

"Secret Service, lady. Everything's fine," he yelled, waving his ID. *Now get the hell outta my face.*

"Juan's been in and out of the bathroom, man. He looks like hell. And I don't want him puking all over the place 'cause I'm not stopping to clean it up, over!"

Gawd. "Then stick a couple of fingers down his throat and make sure he gets over it, OK? 'Cause if he's not in position when the time comes, I'll kill the bastard myself, do you copy?"

"Nine by nine, boss man. Out."

Dammit! he thought, but he forced another smile at the woman checking him out.

***

At ten minutes after twelve noon, the kid saw a man climb onto a concrete pedestal with a Super 8 movie camera and study angles of the motorcade's approach to Dealy Plaza. Abraham Zapruder, just in front of and to the left of the kid's position, decided that he could film the motorcade's progress just fine from where he was standing. Zapruder, who would die in 1970, checked his camera and waited.

The motorcade had begun with fanfare. President Kennedy was waving to the crowds, seated in the back seat of the Lincoln with Texas governor John Connolly in front of him and his wife, Jackie, to his left.

The crowds were friendly for the most part, and the president smiled at his wife and smiled to the crowds. She would later say, though, they were focused more on the crowds to the right and left of the car and not on each other.

Shortly before reaching Dealy Plaza, there was a commotion in front of the motorcade, and a man who appeared to be having a seizure fell down. The president and Mrs. Kennedy watched as the man was placed in a nearby ambulance and driven away, never to be seen or heard from again.

It was 12:20 p.m.

***

"The ambulance is rolling," Mook heard in his earpiece. He looked at his watch.

They had five, maybe seven minutes, before the motorcade reached the plaza.

Mook extended his umbrella, and the woman next to him looked at him like he was crazy.

The kid heard the commotion from the crowd and the loud exhaust notes from the motorcycles first, long before he saw anything, and his pulse quickened. He pulled the rifle from under its blanket and flicked the safety off, even though he knew it was unlikely that he was going to have to shoot anything. He looked at Mook and saw the umbrella extended—that was the "get ready" signal.

He looked at the radio guy, who was well behind him to keep curious passersby away from the spot where he was set up at the retaining wall in the shade of a tree. He heard the squawk of the radio in his ear just as the first motorcycle became visible on Main Street and began turning onto Houston. He looked at the people in the crowd in Dealy Plaza, at the office buildings and all those windows that ringed the plaza; he saw the pigeons chasing stray crumbs, and Mook with his umbrella raised, even though the weather had cleared hours ago.

He heard another burst of static, then Mook's hypnotic voice, scratchy through the radio distortion. Mook was saying, "We got the go-ahead. Take him, take him, take him…"

He watched as the presidential motorcade slowly turned into Dealy Plaza, ringed by office buildings and windows, a sniper's paradise that no president before or since has ever been subjected to. He steadied the gun at his shoulder and let his breathing slow, and slow, and slow…

CHAPTER 2

Mr. Nellin brought a cheap transistor radio into his second-grade classroom and turned up the volume. The students had wondered what the commotion was about; Nellin tuned the radio, trying to get CBS News locked in clear enough so that the class could hear it.

Richard Whelan, a skinny, silent kid who typically sat in the back, was worried that some calamity had befallen his parents. He was sitting at his scarred wooden desk, a folder with his item for show-and-tell hidden inside. He was embarrassed because he had forgotten his bus tickets and didn't have a way home. His father, a doctor, usually dropped him off at school in the mornings on his way to his hospital rounds, but in the afternoons he was trusted to take the long bus ride down Chancellor Avenue by himself, past Al's Barber Shop where he got his hair cut. And if something had happened to his parents, then who would come pick him up? It was a long walk home, he thought, but if he had to, he'd do it.

"Something's happened," Mr. Nellin said, his voice choked. "They're saying the president has been shot."

The static cleared, and Whelan and his class heard the voice of Walter Cronkite, the anchor for CBS news on television, describing what had happened in Dallas.

"The president has been rushed to the hospital, and we don't have any word as to his condition. There are rumors, however, that President Kennedy has been gravely wounded. We will bring you the details as they develop. For those of you just tuning in, let me repeat, shots were fired at

President Kennedy's motorcade some ten minutes ago, at approximately 12:30 p.m. in Dallas, Texas…"

A hush had fallen over the classroom, and Mr. Nellin, a rare white teacher in a mostly black Newark, New Jersey, classroom, was visibly shaken. Someone knocked at the classroom door, and Nellin answered it, brushing what looked like tears from his eyes. Whoever was outside had sharp words for the second-grade teacher who was telling children about the violence that was in the real world outside of the classroom. It may have been Mrs. White, the principal, who was making the rounds and telling the classes that they were awaiting word from the board of education about early dismissal. She had been none too happy to hear the tinny transistor radio blaring in Nellin's class.

Young Richard Whelan heard none of it as he listened to the reporters and Cronkite, whom he trusted, talk about the possibilities of the young president's survival. Surely his father, one of the most prominent physicians in Newark, would be called to Dallas to save the president's life. Whelan didn't think about the incongruity of having a Negro physician flown to Dallas to save the commander in chief. After all, his father knew Martin Luther King and had gotten him the quotes from a King speech that he'd been planning to use for show-and-tell.

Surely, young Richard Whelan thought, he'd be walking home that day in new shoes that pinched his feet because he didn't dare call his mother and ask her for a ride home. Not when important things were happening.

As they listened, some of the girls began to cry, and Mr. Nellin suggested that they put their heads down on their desks and close their eyes. He had lowered the shades and turned down the lights so that those who wanted to tune out the voices on the radio could more readily do so.

But it wasn't long before Cronkite, sitting in front of the hot black-and-white television camera the networks kept for times like this, came back on the radio and reported that President Kennedy was dead.

This wasn't possible, Richard thought, because surely his father could have saved the president. Maybe his father hadn't gone, he thought wildly; maybe they'd found the yellow booklet of his bus tickets and realized that he would have to be picked up from school.

The other students were now visibly crying, and Mr. Nellin's lips were working as young Richard Whelan looked around his classroom and realized what he'd done. Nellin was saying silently, "Oh, my God," over and over again, and Justine, one of the few white girls in his class, was hugging her dolly. Whelan wanted to go over to her and say that he was sorry, but he couldn't muster the courage to approach the girl. The other kids in the class teased him because they thought he liked her.

Now his father would surely be there to pick him up in the big Chrysler that he drove, and Whelan imagined how angry his father would be with him. It would start with his dad being slow to open the passenger-side door, and then Richard would barely have enough time to scramble aboard before his father slammed the big car into gear and drove off, weaving through the traffic down Chancellor Avenue, all the while listening to the news radio station that he liked, which would no doubt be talking about the Negro physician who had let the entire world down because his son had forgotten his bus tickets that morning.

His father would glare out the windshield, saying nothing, leaving Richard alone in his shame that he had yet again *failed to live up to expectations*. "The Negro isn't like other people, son," his father would say, "and we aren't like other Negroes."

So the president was dead, and it was his fault because his father, whom Richard idolized, could not be in Dallas to save the president from an assassin's bullet.

Mrs. White came to the door and saw the distraught classroom and the distraught teacher and said loudly but kindly that school was being let out early. That any students who needed to call their parents should come to the principal's office, where she would make the calls herself. The bus companies had been notified, and the big yellow school buses would be here within the hour, making their regular stops.

But all Richard could imagine was Mrs. White's horror, after she had dialed the ponderous black phone and held the huge receiver to her ear and heard that this little boy in front of her had effectively killed the president, and why didn't she give him a whipping on the whipping machine rumored to be in the basement this very second?

Yes, and then he would have to wait in shame until he boarded the big Chrysler and bounded down Chancellor on the way to Avon Avenue, bouncing over the railroad tracks with the white walls flashing and the block-long hood too big to see anything but sky over. He imagined the big car bottoming out on the railroad tracks and the soundtrack from

the wicked witch in the *Wizard of Oz* playing in his head—do do do do
do dooooo, do do do do do dooo—and Richard decided that he would
walk home and save his parents the trouble of coming to pick him up.

Yes, he decided, he would do his penance right there and then, cause
no more trouble, and walk home, even though he didn't realize that it
would take him three hours or more in his new and already aching shoes.

Let them bleed, he thought, as he shoved his books into the body of
the scarred wooden desk and let the top drop.

Let his feet bleed.

CHAPTER 3

Sunday Morning, August 21, 2011

Richard Whelan's Porsche was flying down I-95 with Hendrix's "Manic Depression" blaring and the sun glinting off the windshield. He was in a cruising gear with nothing but the music and the hum of the tires on the pavement keeping him company, even though Bettina Freeman was sitting in the seat next to him.

She had been completely silent throughout the trip. Not quite sullen, not quite depressed. Richard didn't know what to think of her moods these days, although he knew in his heart of hearts what caused them. She was tall, elegantly dressed for church in a blue veiled hat that seemed too old for her and incredibly classy at the same time.

She crossed her pretty legs. Her pantyhose stretched, and he couldn't help but steal a glance at her legs under the proper length of her conservative Chanel suit.

It was amazing that she had been his "girlfriend" for nearly a year, and he still didn't know how to read her. They slept together regularly, like two elements of the periodic table drawn together by their physical properties, but neither of them was comfortable with it. Their sex was turbulent and disturbed, just like the first time, when they'd practically assaulted one another.

Of course, the fact that the world was going to hell in a hand basket didn't help them, or anyone else, either. It had been five weeks since the Secret Service had come under intense criticism for allowing gate crashers to actually greet President Obama at an official event. Whelan was Secret Service. He'd worked the protection detail once upon a time, and while he had some sympathy, he'd become increasingly concerned about what he saw as unacceptable lapses in the president's security.

In fact, he'd thought about approaching POTUS (the president of the United States) himself. That wasn't done, of course, and it would be especially awkward given the racial politics of having a black president approached by a black Secret Service agent who wasn't in the right swim lane to merit the privilege. Some of the assholes he worked with had already been doing the chitlin jokes about how Whelan and Obama were going to be high-fiving and hanging out on the basketball court trading outrageous dunks—isn't that right, *bro?*

But he'd been following the internal investigation for the past five weeks, and it just didn't ring true to him. They were basically going to hang it on Michelle Obama's staff for not adequately vetting the list with the Service prior to the event, but that was such a mind-blowing cop out that Whelan couldn't believe it. They didn't dare go after the president's appointment secretary who had planned the event, because she was too powerful and would be the first to point out that security screening was the province of the Secret Service, so if anybody was to blame, it had to be the Service. So they were going to whitewash the thing down to a misdemeanor, and some junior aide to Michelle O., who probably wasn't even there, would be identified as the weak security link. Someone with no power, someone who wouldn't even be mentioned in the executive summary that would be glossed over in a meeting with the president.

And the president would be told that all was well, and that would be that. Neither he nor the first lady had been in any danger, and the Service would play up the fact that this was benign if embarrassing, and O'Shay, Obama's chief of staff, would kiss a little ass, and the incident would fall off the president's radar and everything would blow over.

Which was what concerned Richard Whelan the most. The long gap between credible threats against POTUS from anything less than a motivated terrorist group had allowed complacency to creep into the protection detail's attitude. So warning signs—like these yahoos who'd actually shaken hands with the president at a function they hadn't been invited to—were going to be explained away, only to surface later, when something serious did happen, as *warning signs that were missed.* Since he didn't know how to get anyone to focus on what he was seeing, shame on him for being the same obsessive asshole that he'd always been. And shame on Bettina for being a high-ranking government official who'd stepped in front of the latest Whelan relationship train wreck.

So, when in doubt, go to church. Bettina had presented it to him yesterday as a demand—that they go to Bethesda to her Baptist church so he could finally meet her parents—and Richard knew not to debate it with her.

Richard downshifted at the exit coming up, careful not to sling the Porsche through some of that "driver stuff" that he was prone to do by himself as he took the off ramp. He was not a devout churchgoer, per se. He went infrequently, even though he enjoyed it whenever he did go and invariably seemed to get something out of the music or the sermon.

New Visions was a progressive, upper-middle-class black church with a brilliant pastor and a connected congregation. Whelan was not surprised as he parked his hot rod in a lot filled with Caddys and Mercedes Benzes nestled together with the more than occasional Buick and unidentifiable rust bucket.

He unfolded his six-foot, one-inch frame from the driver's seat, straightened his suit jacket, and opened Bettina's door. There was perhaps a hint of a smile underneath the veil of her hat, although he couldn't really be sure.

They arrived inside just before the choir processional came down the center aisle. Bettina waved at someone who waved back, and she dragged Whelan by the hand until they got to a pew near the front that held Bettina's parents, well turned out and dignified. They ended up sitting with Bettina's father to Richard's left, her mother to his right, and Bettina next to her mother on his far right.

Mother Freeman put her hand on his arm. "Has she told you?" she asked, and Bettina hissed "Mother," who ignored her.

"Told me what?" Richard asked. But Mother Freeman was hushed into silence by her daughter, who would not meet Richard's gaze.

"So, Richard," Father Freeman intoned, just before the congregation was waved into standing by the pastor, "you must join us for brunch after the service."

And Richard Whelan, who had faced death a couple of times, knew the true meaning of fear. Something was up, and he didn't have a clue what it was.

The service started with a hymn, "Just As I Am," and Richard wondered if the pastor had created the service just for him. He stood next to Bettina's parents and sang:

Just as I am, without one plea,
But that Thy blood was shed for me,
And that Thou bidst me come to Thee,
O Lamb of God, I come, I come.

The service moved quickly, although Richard didn't really hear much of what was being said. He stole glances at Bettina, but she refused all eye contact. At the same time, he could feel her parents sizing him up, and he wondered what, if anything, Bettina had said about him.

The preacher stood and began reading from the Bible, Isaiah 40, and he read:

The voice of him that crieth in the wilderness. Prepare ye the way of the Lord, make straight in the desert a highway for our God.

Every valley shall be exalted, and every mountain and hill shall be made low: and the crooked shall be made straight, and the rough places plain:

And the glory of the Lord shall be revealed, and all the flesh shall see it together: for the mouth of the Lord hath spoken it.

The reverend closed the Bible and looked at the congregation. Whelan listened intently as the preacher spoke.

"The Spirit sent Jesus into the desert for forty days, where he spent time with the animals, being tempted by Satan.

"I'm always intrigued about people who make claims about who they are and what they believe. None of us know who we really are until we're put to the true test, until we're thrown into the fire of real-life circumstances. As long as we are suffering under the reckless illusion that we are the center of things, we cannot know God. Some people go through their whole lives without ever being made to face their limitations.

"Without coming to terms with what we're really made of, we find it easy to pass judgment on others whom we consider fainthearted. We find it easy to pass judgment, even though we cannot know how we would behave under similar circumstances; how we would act if forced to choose between two equally unattractive options. Because, until we know, until we've been tested, it's too easy to pass judgment on others.

"And despite its bitterness, we should all hunger for a desert experience. We should all want to be tested so that we may come face to face with what we cannot do alone. Only when you find yourself with your options spent, with your prodigious skills woefully inadequate, only then can you know the indescribable joy of total reliance on God; only then can you understand what it was that Jesus found in the wilderness."

"I really like this pastor," Bettina whispered.

Richard nodded, engrossed in the sermon. Bettina managed to stifle a chuckle, laughing because the great Richard Whelan was under the spell of a man of God.

Richard was thinking about his dad and about how affluence was supposed to be enough to get the American dream, and what a lie it had become when his dad had strayed. His parent's divorce had been bitter and long overdue, and, if anything, it felt like Richard and his sister had been through this desert experience that the preacher was talking about. Only he didn't feel that he'd come out of it renewed, or even with any sense of understanding about why he'd been forced to deal with it. His family name had been revered and respected when he was growing up, yet there hadn't been much warmth in his parents' household. You cannot give what you do not have, someone had once said, and the Whelans had not had a single degree of temperature to spare for warmth. He looked at Bettina Freeman and thought about commitment and affluence and felt like he was doomed to repeat the unhappiness of his past and of his parents. He was of an age where he was well past due—too old to have never been married and not be gay, but with the scarcity of eligible single men, not out of the picture, by any means. He was in his mid-fifties, and Bettina was twelve years his junior. At his age he didn't want a desert experience. Not now. Not with Bettina, or anyone else.

And then it was over. They stood and made their way out of the chapel, Richard conscious of Bettina and her parents and whatever secret was in the air. Bettina took his arm, a surprising show of affection, as they gathered outside of the church. Mother Freeman, feisty at five-foot-six with a pulled-back bun of gray hair and high heels, looked at them for a moment.

"You'll meet us at the diner," she said. It was not a question.

"We'll be along, Mother," Bettina said, still lightly gripping Richard's arm.

Mother Freeman nodded. Bettina's father shook Richard's hand, grasping it warmly, and then bussed cheeks with his only daughter.

Bettina tugged his arm toward the Porsche in the parking lot.

"What was that all about?" Richard asked her sharply.

She turned toward him and lifted the veil from her face. She studied his face for a second, and he could not read her expression.

"I'm pregnant," she said, and to Richard Whelan, it seemed as if the world had shifted on its axis and fallen out of orbit.

***

Later Richard returned to his townhouse in Georgetown after dropping Bettina off, thus ending a strange and strained morning with her and her parents. Her parents already knew about Bettina's bombshell revelation. They had looked at him and spoken to him as though it was a foregone conclusion that the two of them would get married and parent their grandchild.

It was equally implicit that, naturally, Richard would simply go along with all of this, just as he would go along with ordering the same thing everyone else was having for breakfast at the rather upscale diner that Bettina's folks had been going to for Sunday brunch since dirt.

Continuing their pattern, he and Bettina had said virtually nothing on the trip home, and he couldn't tell whether she was upset at his lack of enthusiasm or mindful of the turbulence that her revelation had caused him. Why hadn't she told him sooner? Why would she tell her parents before she told him? What was that look that she had given him when she told him?

Pregnant. That meant that he was going to be a father, and Bettina was pushing the age envelope for motherhood.

It also meant that their relationship had permanence, whether they stayed together as a couple or not, because they would always be parents.

Brilliant loner that he was, did he think he was father material? Had he ever thought of one of his relationships as permanent? Was there any woman who could give him more than tears as he exited the relationship, because leaving was the only thing that he was good at in relationships?

Could he give a woman more than tears for once? *Did you ever think of it that way, Mr. Brilliant Loner?*

Permanence. Attachment. Commitment.

Is there more that you could give as a father? As a husband? Could you stay on the ground long enough to change a diaper or read a nursery rhyme?

A baby. Why hadn't Bettina told him?

The answer was self-evident.

She doesn't think you're father material or husband material.

Doesn't think you can open up and let her in, much less a kid. That's why the long silences, the awkward behavior. She doesn't think she's important enough, that you would sacrifice everything for her or your child. She doesn't want to be a part of the same strategic equation that governs how you live your life. Thanks, Richard, but Bettina Freeman doesn't want to be a loss that gets cut based on the next quarterly review, or the pretty girl down the street, or the next crisis in his all-consuming job.

Thanks, but no thanks—that's what she's thinking.

And who am I to blame her for thinking that way?

A father. Whelan could remember being a college student and his father's growing dismay over the way his career was progressing.

"Why are you wasting your time on political science?" His dad was a physician and therefore had "real world" skills.

"It's what I'm interested in," Richard had replied, defensive and resentful.

"You can't go to med school majoring in that. You need chemistry, math, the sciences."

"Dad, I don't want medicine. I know we've talked about it, but I don't want it."

"Son, you need to listen," his father had said in that voice that Richard hated, the voice that said choice was out of the question.

"Medicine is an honorable profession for a black man. Your grandfather was a doctor, and he handpicked me over your aunt to carry on as a doctor. Your sister—"

"My sister isn't going to do anything but make babies, Dad. I don't see why I should be penalized because of her mistakes."

"It's not a penalty," his father had said, raising his voice. "Politics is a sleazy business, Richard. There is no place in it for someone with your skills."

"Dad, this is a new day, and the new way suggests that I can do more things than follow in your footsteps."

"Into politics? What's next after undergrad with a degree in political science? What can you possibly do?"

"International studies."

"What?"

"I said, *international studies.*"

Doctor Whelan shook his head.

"You're a sophomore at Harvard University, son. Most whites would kill to get to where you are. You have a chance to go to Harvard Medical School! Why throw it all away?"

"I'm not throwing anything away. I'm going to do what I want, not what you want, Dad."

"You're making a mistake."

"It's my life."

"And you're throwing it away."

"I don't see it that way."

"At least let me connect you to some of my friends, people who can give you advice about what to do to enter politics."

"I'm not interested in elected office."

His father had looked hard at him.

"What are you afraid of, Dad? I'm doing what you always say—I'm making something of myself. Why isn't that good enough?" Richard had yelled.

His father had stopped and looked away for a moment.

"You think I'm afraid?" he had said, sounding shocked.

"Of course you are. The world is changing. I'm not limited the way you were."

Alfred Whelan had shaken his head. "The world is never going to change that much, son. You young people don't understand that some things never change."

"Dad, have you forgotten the civil rights movement?" Richard asked softly.

Alfred Whelan had looked down at the carpeted floor as if remembering something painful.

"Have you forgotten that King was killed?" Richard's father had said, his voice rising. "That two Kennedys were killed? You were just a child, but I remember it, Richard. And I am telling you that politics is no place for you."

Richard shook his head at the memory. He had traded politics for law, and ultimately law enforcement, which was even lower on the totem pole than politics to his father.

And now you're having a child; *you're* going to be a father. Time to grow up. Time to put away the toils of your misspent youth. Maybe you'll be better at it than your dad.

Maybe my child won't have to be as perfect as I had to be. Maybe my child won't have to live with the stigma of being exceptional and not good enough at the same time.

A postal truck pulled up opposite his door just as he was fitting his key in the lock. Sure enough, the woman ambled out of the truck toward him, carrying an Express Mail package and a flat envelope to go with it.

Richard, looking at it, noticed that the package was rather large for the Postal Service—a long, fat cylinder with a label that bore his name, but no postage of any kind that he could see.

"Express mail?" he asked as the carrier approached him.

"Not exactly," the carrier said. "A guy flagged me down outside of the processing center and asked me to deliver this to the address marked. Gave me a hundred bucks," she said, smiling.

"This your regular route?"

"Yes sir, when I'm driving on Sundays making Express Mail deliveries."

Richard's warning instincts shoved thoughts of Bettina to the background. Parcels were heavily screened at the post office, so someone who wanted to avoid the security measures could have put anything in the tube—anthrax, a bomb, anything.

He took the package and the flat envelope, feeling the weight and heft of the cylinder in his hand. This was totally weird, he thought. It felt like the package contained a rifle, or a weapon of some kind.

Richard thanked the carrier and went into his townhouse. He laid the package down gently on the kitchen table. He looked carefully at the envelope that had come with it—it was just his name and address, nothing more on the front. He turned it over and squinted at the tiny ballpoint ink printing on the back of the envelope. It said:

> I know what you're thinking, that this is a bomb or something. Open the envelope first, read the note, then open the package. DON'T CALL THE FBI AFTER YOU READ THE LETTER—IT WON'T DO ANY GOOD.

Well, if it is a bomb, Richard thought as he tore open the envelope, whoever did this will have succeeded in blowing me up.

The envelope contained a photo, a reproduction. On the back of the picture, in the same neat block handwriting as was on the envelope, Richard read:

> WE KILLED JFK IN '63; THEN KING IN
> '68 AS A WARNING TO BOBBY.
> OBAMA IS A DEAD MAN AND
> SO ARE YOU.
> THIS WILL BE YOUR ONLY WARNING.

Richard turned over the photo. It was a blurry image, probably lifted from a reproduction of the famous Zapruder film of the assassination of JFK in Dallas. Kennedy's head appeared damaged and thrown back against the headrest of the Lincoln limousine he'd been riding in. Under the warning, also scrawled in ballpoint pen, were the words:

> I WAS ONLY A KID

So was I, Richard thought, remembering that day ages ago in Mr. Nellin's class. Then he opened the other package.

***

Frank Moynihan was in his den, sipping a beer and watching a basketball game, when the phone rang. He had been cradling a photo in his hands—not gripping it by its edges, but just letting it rest lightly on the tips of his fingers. As he sat up in the La-Z-Boy, carefully placing the photo on the coffee table next to the recliner and the beer a good distance away from it, he noted that it was his private line that was ringing, not the hotline from his office in the White House. Now sixty-three years old, Moynihan had been the head of the Secret Service for the bulk of George W. Bush's presidency and all of Barack Obama's.

He finally snatched up the phone on the fourth ring.

"Yeah."

"Frank, Richard Whelan."

"Yeah, Richard. What's up?"

"Don't sound so enthusiastic. I got a weird package in the mail. I think you might want to take a look at it."

"Weird, you say?"

"It's a threat, Frank. But it's a really strange threat."

"Against who?"

"The president."

"You think it's credible?" he asked after a moment's hesitation.

"I only worked the detail for a year, Frank. I don't know. And given the internal crap with the gatecrasher investigation, maybe this isn't the best time for someone to suggest that the president is at risk. But you better take a look at this yourself, because you aren't going to believe it."

"Gimme your address again," Moynihan said. Protocol would be to open a file and have a team go out and debrief Whelan, but he didn't want to go too official just yet.

"You coming yourself?" Whelan asked again after Frank pondered the situation in silence for a few beats longer than was polite.

"Yeah, I'm coming. Be there," he said, thinking about the address and calculating distance and traffic issues, "in thirty or forty minutes."

"Good idea," Whelan said and hung up. Moynihan winced.

Moving quickly through the house, Moynihan gathered his weapon, a light jacket, and his car keys. He called his office, telling them that he would be reachable on his cell phone for the next forty-five minutes and giving them Whelan's number as a backup if they needed to reach him. He debated again the merits of having one of his people meet him at Whelan's address, but he didn't want to take any chances. Not right now.

He glanced at the photo he'd laid on the coffee table, then swept it into a file and into the wall safe.

Whoever was sending him these things apparently had lots of footage of the head of the United States Secret Service in less-than-savory situations. But the kicker had come about five weeks ago, with the note:

WE'RE GOING TO KILL HIM, AND YOU'RE GOING TO HELP

superimposed over the presidential seal. The meaning was clear and unambiguous: someone wanted to assassinate the president of the United States.

Jesus. This was how you did it when you assaulted the presidency, Frank thought. You compromised as many assets as you could, any way you could, and you made your move at the right time.

He left his house and locked the door.

CHAPTER 4

Sunday Afternoon, August 21, 2011

B ettina Freeman entered her house and put on a tea kettle. Perhaps I should call Richard later, she thought, although she didn't know why. They weren't clicking as a couple, and now she was pregnant.

As she debated what to do with Richard, Bettina wondered why she hadn't told him before the scene at the church. Their relationship was like a river between them; it seemed they met in the middle for sex, and little else, because the current was swift and the water was too deep.

Perhaps this would bind him to her forever. She hated herself for thinking that way: typical ghetto playa hater, corralling her "baby daddy" with a screaming infant. Richard would love thinking that he was bound to her by dirty diapers. Well, this was war—this relationship was a war, and if it took a child, then, well...*dammit*. What was she thinking?

That perhaps she wanted a piece of Richard and herself to survive this deep water between them, because her love and whatever he was feeling would not?

There, she'd thought it. Their relationship couldn't survive because they were simply screwing, not talking; not emoting, just rolling around in the sack, because neither one of them could get past their history, both with others and with each other.

So, yeah, she was pregnant with Richard's child. Boy or girl, it would be beautiful, and she would love it. Love it the way she wouldn't let herself love Richard, because Richard would either leave or die or disappear into some unfathomable mystery wrapped up in national security.

She picked up the phone to call him and apologize but got a busy signal. The story of my life, she thought, shaking her head.

She thought about the first time she and Richard had tried going out and the baggage that had prevented them from staying together. She'd been afraid of how much she felt for him and had tried to deny it. Her mood swings had confused him, and her criticism had deflated him. The legacy of her parents was the firm belief that most men weren't good enough for her, and Richard had to fall into that category so that she wouldn't be hurt if he walked away.

And she was still playing the bitch because she was terrified of Richard and what her feelings meant. Not telling him about her condition, the long silences—she was replaying the past and all the mistakes she'd made the first time they'd dated, because she still felt the same way about him and she still wasn't sure what he felt about her.

So, Bettina, she thought, either you figure it out or walk away, child or no child. Figure out what you feel, Tina, because you can't control him, but you can know yourself.

***

Frank Moynihan arrived at Richard's townhouse within a half hour of getting his phone call. Whelan greeted him at the front door with a cup of coffee in his hand.

"Sorry to bother you, Frank, but I thought it was important."

Moynihan shook his head. "Not a problem. What exactly do you have?"

Richard brought him inside to the living room and showed him the envelope, recounting how the postal carrier had been handed the package.

Frank read the print on the back of the envelope and then smirked.

He then looked at the note on the back of the photograph and then slowly turned the photo over.

"Recognize the picture?" he asked Whelan.

"JFK, Dallas, Zapruder film, right?"

"Right. Although I'm surprised you're not more of a conspiracy theorist, Richard."

"Why do you say that?"

"Because this is the famous frame from the Zapruder film, purporting to be the kill shot to Kennedy's head. What the conspiracy theorists say proves that Oswald wasn't alone, if he was involved at all."

"Do you believe that?" Whelan asked.

"If you watch the Zapruder film frame by frame, you can tell a lot about the sequence of the events that took place that day. Kennedy is hit several times, but the fatal shot appears to throw his head back, which means he would have been hit from the front, not from the Texas Book Depository, which at that point was behind the president's limo."

"I suppose Kennedy is the textbook case for the Service."

Moynihan shook his head. "Not really. Too many things went wrong that day that would never happen today." Moynihan paused and reread the note.

"So this person claims to be the second gun. And when you opened the other package...?" Moynihan said, his voice trailing off into a question.

"This came out," Whelan said. He produced a Remington 700 bolt-action rifle, which Whelan gripped with an oilcloth so as not to get his prints on the gun.

"Serial numbers?" Frank asked.

"Filed off."

"Still, we should be able to tell from the basic design when it was manufactured."

"Possibly," Whelan said.

Moynihan shrugged, looking at Whelan, who clearly expected more. "Is there something I'm missing here?"

Whelan looked at him in disbelief. "Aren't you going to track down the postal worker, see who gave her the package, and test the ballistics on the weapon?"

"For what?"

"To try and tie this to the Kennedy shooting in Dallas."

Moynihan shook his head. "This is such an obvious fabrication that you have to look at it a little differently, Richard."

"How so?"

"We need to eliminate this kook from consideration and get on with our lives. Easiest way to do that is to prove that some aspect of the weapon postdates 1963."

"Why do you think this person is a kook?"

"Because an adult in his twenties at the time of the shooting would be in his seventies by now, Richard, far too old to be a handpicked assassin."

"But the note on the photo says he was a kid."

"Yeah, but think about it: a kid as part of some vast shadowy conspiracy to bring down the government? Why? For what purpose? And even a teenager would be in his early sixties by now. So, in order for this note to be true, whoever 'arranged' the Kennedy, and apparently, the King killings, also killed Bobby and now has somehow risen up from the ashes to get Obama? Not exactly what I'd call a credible threat."

"Even you have to admit, Frank, that there is a groundswell of emotion against the president. Particularly because he's black."

"Yeah, and if I shared with you the idiotic crap we see every day from the protection detail, it would either make you laugh or cry. Gun nuts in the Klan, Aryan Nation gangs in prison, white supremacists in Idaho. Hell, you'd think these guys had a manual and a 'Kill Obama' convention going on. But the 'load up the pickup and come to DC to get the darky president' crap is just that—crap."

"And so is this. Some wacko trying to scare us into action just for the satisfaction of shaking up the bureaucracy."

"There have been lapses in the president's protection, Frank. What do you say about those?" Whelan asked, determined not to let his boss off the hook.

"That they have nothing to do with this nonsense, Richard. And those lapses haven't been anywhere near as significant as the press has made them out to be. In fact, I'm not sure why you're even bringing those up."

"I just fear that this comes at a bad time. It's been a long time since the Service faced a significant threat to the protectee. And the lapses that we've seen suggest that the Service has gotten slack in the interim because it's been so long since there was a significant threat to the presidency.

That's why this is so significant—if any of this is real, it's playing into the Service's complacency because there hasn't been an assassination since 1963, and no real attempts since the Reagan shooting."

"It's standard operating procedure to open a file on this. And that's what I'm going to do. But I'm not chasing ghosts. This rifle was probably manufactured in the mid-1980s and looks old because it is, just not *that* old."

"Are you going to tell the president?"

"No. Not until and unless this proves to be more significant than what I see now."

"He has a right to know, Frank."

"Not unless it's credible, and even then, the man has enough on his mind."

"So what are you saying—that you wouldn't tell him even if you thought there was a serious risk?"

"Not unless the risk was grave or involved a threat to his family, which this clearly does not."

Whelan realized that Moynihan was not going to budge, and honestly, he couldn't blame him.

"Do you believe that Oswald acted alone in 1963?"

Moynihan paused and then shrugged. "That's the official party line."

"But do you believe it?"

"I don't have an opinion."

"C'mon, Frank. Surely you have an opinion."

"There are lots of people who don't believe Oswald acted alone. But the alternative is too far-fetched to believe. In order for what the conspiracy types say to be true requires some massive, organized secret governmental force that coerced the Warren Commission into looking the other way. Conspiracies that are successful are by their nature small."

"True, but you've heard the saying—history is written by the winning side. JFK lost, and, if it was a conspiracy, the conspirators won, and the ability to rewrite history came with the victory."

"So you believe the note and the rifle and the rest of it?"

"I never said that. But I don't think it's a crackpot, no. Not necessarily. But like I said, I'm not the expert, Frank. I only spent a year on the POTUS protection detail. That's why I'm going to leave it to you. Take the note and the rifle and the rest of it and have at it, OK?"

Moynihan carefully placed the rifle back in the cardboard tube and slid the photograph back into the envelope.

"Careful with that, Frank. You might be handling a little bit of history," Whelan said.

CHAPTER 5

Dallas, November 22, 1963, 12:25 p.m.

M ook saw the president's motorcade turn onto Houston Street from his vantage point on Main Street. As the president's limousine made the turn, he began counting down to when the shots would begin cascading from the buildings where his people were hiding. The limo was now in the perfect place, with the best view and angle to kill the president from the Book Depository.

One one thousand, two one thousand, three one thousand—take the shot, god-dammit!—four one thousand, five one thousand...

When the voice squawked in his ear, he nearly jumped, mistaking the noise for the expected gunshots. His stomach turned over when he heard "Mook, no joy on the shot! Juan's sick as a dog! Mook, do you read, we got no shooter..."

"Billy!" Mook hissed as he switched channels. Billy was in the Dal-Tex Building. Wrong angle for the patsy, and who knew what evidence they would leave behind if Billy took the shot from the side while the limo was still on Houston.

"I'm on him, Mook!"

Mook took a deep breath. If he said the word, Kennedy would die right then. But...

Seven one thousand, eight one thousand, nine one thousand...

"Hold your fire, Billy. Repeat, hold your fire until the limo makes the turn onto Elm; do you copy, Billy?"

"Damn, Mook, I just about pissed my pants! Where the hell is Juan, over?"

"Juan's down. Billy, I need you to take him down once the limo makes the turn; do you read?"

The first motorcycles in front of the president's Lincoln were just reaching Elm. *Thirteen one thousand, fourteen one thousand, fifteen one thousand...*

"Why the heck you want me to wait, Mook?"

"Once they turn, the angle won't be any different than it would be from the patsy nest."

"Yeah, but they won't be able to see the car from there, dammit!"

The first motorcycles had just turned onto Elm Street from Houston. The president's Lincoln would make the turn in less than thirty seconds.

"I know." Mook clicked to a new frequency, fighting back the sense that it was all slipping away. I'm going to kill that Cubano ass wipe with my bare hands, he thought darkly, seconds ticking away in his head and windows of opportunity closing rapidly.

"Yeah, this is Sal."

He watched in horror as Kennedy's limo proceeded slowly to the left turn onto Elm Street. He reached up and wiped away a single bead of offending sweat rolling down his cheek. He was running out of options.

Fuck me! Rex the Wonder Chimp might be my last chance.

"Sal. Have the kid get ready."

***

It wasn't cold; he was thankful for that. Little Richard Whelan checked his pockets for the fifteenth time to confirm that he didn't have any money. He watched the green Chancellor Avenue bus wheeze past him in a cloud of black diesel smoke.

Clutching his folder for show-and-tell, he began walking. His school was next to Weequahic High, a school he would never attend because the plan was to put him into prep school as soon as possible but no later than the sixth grade.

He zipped up his windbreaker and made it two blocks before his feet began hurting, but he didn't care. He didn't dare call home collect, because he was not going to disturb his mother. And he certainly wasn't going to face his father and admit that he'd forgotten his bus tickets.

So he would follow the bus route, which wasn't the most direct way to go, but he was a second grader and it made sense that the bus route would get him home with certainty. There were big kids leaving the high school, laughing and talking jive. I guess everyone got the early day because of Dallas, he thought, and he fell in behind a group who seemed to ignore him for the first block or so.

Now, he would have to explain what had happened to his lunch money, besides having spent it on lunch. It had to be something catastrophic, he thought, because the president was dead and it was a day for tragedies of all kinds.

Richard liked building models, and part of the reason his parents had had him tested was because he was rather precocious for a second grader. He built models made for teenagers with ease, mostly airplanes, secretly wishing one day that he could fly planes for the air force. His mother always cluck-clucked over the glass of scotch she always seemed to be holding, and then she and his father would exchange some look that seemed to mean everything to them but meant nothing to Richard. He could say that he had tried to buy a big model, maybe the Mercury space capsule model, but had gotten gypped somehow, so that he had nothing to show for it—no money, no model, not even any glue.

He could say that, he thought, as the explanation as to why he'd walked home, because the place where he bought most of his models was on the way home, but easily three quarters of the way on the bus route.

So, yeah, maybe they would buy that.

Or maybe they wouldn't care. He hated to admit it, but it was a real possibility that his parents wouldn't care that he'd walked home. The president was dead, and they admired Kennedy, or so he thought from what they said when they talked about politics. Kennedy was dead, and maybe the Russians would be launching nuclear missiles at them from Cuba. He remembered that he'd written an essay about the Cuban missile crisis in his first-grade class, saying that he didn't want to die in a nuclear fireball. His teacher had called his parents, and they'd had several whispered conversations about his writing. Soon after, his parents had had him tested. The results indicated that his IQ was off the charts, and for some reason this worried his mother.

His father had been impressed for a minute or two, then had gone back to being preoccupied with his patients and the rest of his life that took place in the office they had in their house. Richard was left with both a profound sense of otherness and isolation, a wall of glass that only he could see surrounding him. His older sister was distant and regarded him as a utility to be used and abused as she saw fit, and the freakish nature of his IQ had not helped his standing with her. It also hadn't helped that his sister was a failure, making progress toward nowhere with all possible haste.

And so, from the inside of his glass bubble, it was perfectly natural to come to incredibly flawed conclusions, for the genius of his intellect to lead him rapidly down a path that survived with such obvious flaws because he had no easy points of external reference combined with a gift for connecting the dots between adult things in the real world.

For example, Richard knew that his parents liked Kennedy, because Kennedy was a *Friend of the Negro*, at least according to his father, and that had been important in the South during the unrest of the freedom marches. This was a concept that didn't make sense to Richard, because they already were free—*duh*—but his parents declined to explain it to him when he had asked. The only clue that kept turning over in his head was that when he thought about being handsome or being Superman, he would look in the mirror and couldn't recognize the face that stared back at him as being either. Everyone on the television was white. If Kennedy was the lynchpin between today and a better tomorrow, and Kennedy was dead, would Richard's face ever appear to be handsome or heroic in the mirror? And if the answer was no, at least to his tortured, little-boy logic, would anyone ever care that he'd walked home?

"Hey kid, you followin' us?"

It was one of the big kids that he'd been trooping behind. There was a girl with two guys, and they looked tough, like Weequahic High kids.

"Nope. I'm just going home."

"You live down here?"

"No. Near downtown."

"Downtown?" the girl squealed, her voice high-pitched. "Damn, nigga, you always be walkin' home like this?"

"No. The president got shot."

"The who? Got what?"

"The president is dead."

One of the males looked out over his sunglasses. "So you walkin' home? To downtown?"

Richard Whelan nodded. It made perfect sense to him.

The girl looked down at him.

"What does a kid like you care about the president?"

Because if my dad had been able to go to Dallas, he would have saved him. But I forgot my bus tickets, Richard thought, but, of course, he couldn't say it.

CHAPTER 6

Sunday Afternoon, August 21, 2011

C huck O'Shay, President Obama's chief of staff, was in his White House office catching up on his reading. The various Sunday morning talk shows were muted in the background, although O'Shay was intimately familiar with the guest lineup on each of the programs. *Meet the Press*, for example, had Tea Party Congressional leaders debating the latest budget maneuvering by the White House (and predictably decrying it as being inadequate and un-American) and discussing ways to block additional spending.

The show he was waiting for, though, was *Washington Capital Week*, an obscure cable show that had landed the governor of Wisconsin as its sole guest. This was someone that O'Shay and the rest of the president's strategists had decided to keep close tabs on, because the polls were beginning to suggest that Governor Nugent could contend for the Republican nomination for president. Of all the possible Republican opponents in the upcoming election, Nugent seemed to have the most positives among voters, the least negatives, and the best head-to-head polling against the president. But it's all easy before you get to the national stage, O'Shay thought. And this, to O'Shay's knowledge, was Nugent's first Washington show of any import.

O'Shay checked his watch, picked up his remote, and tuned into the all-news channel. He bent down to continue reading until he heard the familiar theme music and then glanced at the placards and heard the voice-over announcing today's guest. Nugent was a dark, swarthy man with brown hair and hazel eyes. He smiled as the red "on camera" winked on and nodded at the invisible television audience.

This week's guest commentator announced that the governor had an opening statement. O'Shay looked up, thinking that this could be either very good or very bad, and turned up the sound.

"I'd just like to say for the record that I cherish the American way of life. That's a statement that will resonate with many of you and be completely alien to others, because I don't believe that our elected representatives understand what it means, and even if they did understand it, they wouldn't—couldn't—hold it in the same esteem that you and I do," he said, looking directly into the camera. "We don't need gimmicks or slogans or grandstanding. We don't need one face for the unions and another face for business, one stance for Israel and another for the West Bank, one standard for some schoolchildren and no school, and hence no standards, for others. We can only build, preserve, and rebuild our nation based upon principals that we stand for, and things that we like about ourselves. We cannot, we must not, give into the notion that our time has passed or that our sun has set, nor can we afford to be ignorant that the world has changed and continues to change. I do not propose to be all things to all people, just a leader that the American people can follow and respect, whether they agree with a particular stance or not. It's time, my fellow Americans, to put our differences aside and understand that the nuance of political positions is a thing of the past, and that we can't afford to posture any longer if we are to create the kinds of resources we need to protect the baby boomers who made this nation great. Make no mistake about it; I want us to look in the mirror every day not to recover our stature but to acknowledge it. We haven't lost a step in the global economy, and if we smarten up, we never will."

This guy's no dummy. O'Shay scrawled a note on his notepad to mention the broadcast to the president when he saw him. In fact, he decided, he might as well pick up the phone and ask the White House communications office to save the recording of this segment of the show so the president could see it for himself.

O' Shay watched as the commentator fed the governor a couple of very soft lobs that Nugent cleanly smacked out of the park. Significant,

O'Shay thought, because the Republican machinery appeared capable of at least getting this guy a sympathetic ear inside the Beltway.

Capable and willing. They had a contender board with likely Republicans and a quick synopsis of pros, cons, and positioning. Depending upon the outcome of the budget battles, the Democratic money was betting on an improving economy and rising employment to make the president immune from any of the current Republican frontrunners.

And, O'Shay and everyone else were licking their chops, waiting for a certain ex-governor from Alaska to wade into the fray. Palin was incredibly shrewd but had such catastrophic poling negatives that current wisdom was that Obama would win a second term in a walk if she were the nominee.

And that was effectively the problem that the Republicans were facing. Romney hadn't energized the faithful the last time around, Huckabee was feeling too "evangelical religious right," and the more people that jumped in, the better the president liked it. The midterm elections were one thing, but most incumbents got spanked during the midterms, and the sting was fading as Obama continued to make progress and avoid catastrophic errors. No, for every Republican contender, the Democrats had what they felt was a fairly convincing bucket of paint with which to label them, labels that the public would recognize as accurate but short of demonization.

And while O'Shay secretly wanted to run on an antiracist, anti-Republican platform and tie the two up with the conservative news media and call it a day, he knew Obama would never play in that arena. Obama never played the race card, even privately, but many of his staff did because it just seemed that all the egregious crap that Obama had been through had to be seated in racism. Someone had screamed at him during a speech, for example, and O'Shay sometimes wondered whether there wasn't a conspiracy of good ol' boys with gun racks in the back of their F-150s wanting to take a potshot at the first black president.

Well, he thought, what happens if it looks like Obama is going to win a second term? Maybe a credible contender from Wisconsin was just what the doctor ordered to prevent the crazies from doing anything stupid...

Elsewhere

Phillip Stone sat in his study alone with a television remote and two slim files sitting on the burnished walnut of his one hundred and fifty year-old desk. He watched Governor Mike Nugent handle questions like a pro while managing to avoid most of the obvious traps Republicans fell into with the voting public. He affirmed, rather than accused, and he was positive about the past and the future without being defensive. The screening process had identified Nugent sixteen months prior, when it had been clear that Obama would make significant gains in his legislative agenda and Stone's private handicappers had decided that the economy would rally enough to elect Mr. Obama to a second term.

Stone was the ultimate connected kingmaker in the Republican Party. Few people even knew who he was. He had several hedge funds, which had a bunch of highly profitable portfolio companies that cranked out either household-name products or solid red, white, and blue profits, and in many cases, both. Most of his money and therefore his power was hidden, because he didn't care to appear on lists of wealthy people, finding the process both adolescent and barbaric at the same time. And he wanted nobody to know the genesis of his wealth.

Nugent launched into a diatribe about the lack of accountability in Washington, and Stone muted the sound. He turned to the first slim file on his desk, which was a highly summarized view of Mike Nugent's weaknesses that would or could be manifested in a run for the highest office in the land. As he looked at the one-page summary, he reflected that there was always something in these files, it seemed, some level of bad judgment or bad karma that made all of these people either better or worse bets in the race. Nobody was clean—nobody who had taken a breath and wasn't a virgin was ever clean—so you looked at the one-pager, and you either chuckled or cringed, but you put on your big boy pants and you made a decision. Money and time and agenda were all at stake, and one hoped it was just a matter of time before the planets aligned and your team got to go to the Super Bowl.

Besides, Stone thought, whatever was in the file made them controllable, within reason, once they got to the big dance. The only question was the risk of exposure of whatever levers were in the file.

He stared at the photograph pasted into the Word document and moved on, closing the file.

He thought long and hard before looking at the other file again. He was adamantly opposed to Obama getting a second term in office because he honestly felt that the man was bad for the country. Full stop. Yes, he was black, but that was almost beside the point; the world was always going to be run by people of power and influence, and this whole change/grassroots /up from slavery thing that Obama seemed to have going for him was too populist for people like Phillip Stone to stomach. That Obama had figured it out because he was black had occurred to Stone as well, and the notion reaffirmed his view that the power club was better off small, exclusive, and generally white. He knew rich black men and found them as nearly pale as he was, but that just affirmed his view that more for the masses was a waste of time and resources. Besides, he thought, the wealthy blacks were not, and could never be, all the way on the inside of the power base that ran things. They were not, and could not, be part of anything bringing about "meaningful change," because meaningful change was regime change, and that was never pretty and never easy. No, the world was too dangerous, too unstable, for true regime change, and no black man was going to stay in the vicinity of the exclusive club for long. He didn't care how many black entertainers lined up behind him, he didn't care how many liberals lined up behind him, he didn't care how much Internet traffic his sites were likely to get as the campaign began heating up. The business elite, the real power base, hated Obama. Once again, full stop. The guys who really controlled lots of money and didn't care about the stinking *Forbes* lists viewed Obama as too radical for their tastes, and (and this was a truly fatal combination, Stone thought) immune to influence. There was precious little in Obama's one-page file. Health care reform? Pull out of the Middle East? Was the man serious, or simply demented?

That left the third file. He and others had begun the wheels turning on that one too, because they didn't get a warm and fuzzy feeling about Republican chances to unseat the populist/communist/Muslim/black Democrat. Palin was capable of energizing the base but at too high a cost. Everyone else was simply boring, too boring to overcome a down-tick of two percentage points in the unemployment rate in the months leading up to the election. That's what his people were forecasting, and Stone felt that it was going to happen no matter what. Happy, employed, stupid people won't change horses, not with the power of incumbency behind the messaging.

Phillip Stone sighed and pulled on a pair of latex gloves. Nugent is a dark horse, he thought, and Obama—hell, forget Obama, the rest of the dumb-assed Republicans might blow Nugent up.

His father had cautioned him about the contents of the file folder in front of him. The contents were just as bad for democracy as any international threat to American sovereignty—that's what his father had told him. The pages within the thin manila folder were over fifty years old and worn with even the infrequent handling they'd been given during that time, because no one who knew of the existence of this file had dared to make any copies of what it contained.

Even he, Phillip Stone, had pulled the folder out of its secure vault only twice, each time wearing latex gloves as much to prevent smearing the ink and the images contained on the pages as to prevent leaving prints.

The label on the file had been scotch-taped in place, and the tape was peeling and yellowed. The label underneath looked as if it had been typed on a typewriter. The label read "Operation Silent Night," and stapled into the inside of the folder was the impetus for the greatest military operation ever conceived against a civilian government—a memo from then President Kennedy, authorizing the withdrawal of troops from Vietnam, against the wishes of the Joint Chiefs and then CIA Director Alan Dulles.

The first page of the file was a handwritten note that sketched the initial stages of the plot to kill JFK. It was handwritten because the author had been afraid that some misguided soul in J. Edgar Hoover's camp could have identified a typewriter and pointed the finger at him. Handwriting analysis was virtually unknown in the early 1960s.

That first handwritten page contained five bullet points:

- Lyndon Johnson does not need to know until after the fact. As the beneficiary of the op, Johnson will be told at the most opportune time to secure his cooperation, because the cooperation of the new president is crucial.

- A scapegoat must be identified and maneuvered into position.
- A "scorched earth" doctrine will protect the conspirators and will be applied ruthlessly. If it is dead, it cannot be questioned. If it is sealed, it cannot be independently reviewed. If it is troublesome, make it either dead or sealed.
- One coordinator will pull together the operational details and will be the first casualty under the "scorched earth" doctrine once the operation is terminated.
- The contents of this file are to be the sole record of the activities of the conspirators in order to preserve the capabilities developed should the need arise again to force a change in the civilian government.

Stone turned the page. There was a head shot of a man in military uniform but no other identifying notations except for a name scrawled in ballpoint pen on the back of the black-and-white photograph—*Mook*.

CHAPTER 7

Sunday Afternoon, August 21, 2011

Alan Christiansen, director of the FBI, put the phone down and sighed. Richard Whelan wanted to talk to him and had made vague hints about national security. He knew Whelan well, knew the kinds of things that he'd done working for the Secret Service. Whelan was one of the ones that Christiansen thought he could talk to when he needed to bridge the bureaucratic chasm.

But that didn't make Whelan any less of an odd duck. He was way too skilled an investigator to be knocking around the Secret Service, and he had made a name for himself not for being on the president's protection detail but for a series of big scores working alongside the Treasury and taking down a series of huge money-laundering schemes.

And Whelan knew his way around a gun, if the stories were correct. Alan Christiansen had gotten his intel from FBI hostage rescue grunts, the most gung-ho shooters outside of the military in the federal government.

Whelan had been in a legendary gun battle in New York State that had been immediately hushed up because of the delicate nature of one of those deceased, and the matter was now sealed and accessible only on a need-to-know basis. That's what his shooters said. The truth, according to a few indelicate hints dropped by none other than Obama's chief of staff, Chuck O'Shay, was even hairier than the stories.

So if Whelan wanted to see him, Alan Christiansen would clear a tiny bit of airspace out of his busy day tomorrow and set himself up to listen.

But that still didn't make Whelan any less of an odd duck, he thought. Something about him wasn't all there or wasn't all accessible. It had limited his career, even under a president who had met him and recognized the vast intellect lurking under the suit and the shoulder rig that most likely carried a very well cared-for Browning pistol.

No, Whelan had refused to be moved away from the Service for bigger and better things. Had politely closed the door on the president of the United States and stayed as kind of a number two in Frank Moynihan's well-respected Secret Service.

He wondered if it was the action. He'd seen that in FBI agents, guys who were so gung ho to kick 'em down in bad-guy land that they had no lives other than to sit around in cop bars shooting the breeze about things they'd done and lived to tell. One of them had described it as the ultimate in adrenalin rushes as Christiansen had hustled him out of the FBI as a danger to himself and others. If Whelan was one of those, it probably wouldn't end well. The question was whether he was a good enough friend to ask him about it, and the answer to that question was no.

Which meant that probably no one was. Well, wait, that was harsh. Christiansen had no clue about whether Richard Whelan had a different side that he would never see because he, Christiansen, was white. Whelan could have a whole crew of upwardly mobile African Americans who sat around on occasion and talked shop and gave each other advice. Could be that he was seeing only the portion of the man that he presented to the professional world, and there was a completely rich backstory that he had no clue about.

Maybe it was all true.

But Alan Christiansen doubted it.

***

The phone rang. "Bettina, hi."

Richard waited for Bettina to say something, but as usual, she took a few seconds to read the implications of everything he said and the way he said it.

"I was wondering if we were going to talk about things. You were silent after church," she started.

"Bettina…"

"No, wait. Listen, I understand that I dropped a bomb on you, and the way I did it was totally unfair. I just wanted you to see the way things could be between us—my parents, a family, and a child. I'm sorry about the way it came out and the way I've been acting. I want to blame it on hormones, but we really just need to talk."

Richard glanced down at the table and at the copies of the photograph and the note from the purported assassin. Moynihan had allowed him to make copies on his home copier before taking the documents and the rifle away.

The old Richard would have been churning away at the mystery. Since his last major money-laundering case, Frank Moynihan had let him drift a bit and find his own way. The last thirty days had been good, he had to admit, but he knew that Moynihan had his hands full and would be looking for him to get back in the saddle as soon as possible.

But she's pregnant. When had he ever slowed down for a relationship, anyway? Never? Wasn't that sad?

And could he really do it? Be a father, a husband, maintain a home and a relationship and a demanding profession? Could he?

Brave new world. Maybe it was time for him to put away the toils of his misspent youth.

Yeah. He believed it.

"Why don't you come over?" he said, still eyeing the copies on the table before forcing himself to turn away. "There's something I want to talk to you about as well."

***

Richard talked to Alan Christiansen frequently and during most of those talks, there was nothing much to talk about. While he was waiting for Bettina, the phone rang again. It was Christiansen returning his call to ask if Richard had time to talk now.

"Sure, Alan. But I need to know if you're sitting down."

"Yeah, why?"

"I just handed my boss something of an artifact of history," Whelan said, letting the suspense build a bit.

"Let me guess. You were visited by aliens who have been trapped in Area 51 so long they're applying for political asylum."

"Not quite, but perhaps equally bizarre."

"Hmm. Are you going to spill, or am I going to have to guess?"

"I received a weird package and note this afternoon when I got back from church."

"And you told Moynihan about it because. . .?"

"Because someone threatened the president. And me. With a twist."

"Was it a real threat?"

"I thought it merited checking out, but Moynihan didn't seem to think that much of it. And I have to admit, it was a little far-fetched."

"How so?"

"The writer claimed to have been the second gun in Dallas nearly fifty years ago," Whelan said.

"Really? That's bizarre. An adult participant in 1963 would be in their late sixties or seventies by now," Christiansen responded.

"Yeah, but he covered that by claiming that he was just a kid in 1963. If he was a teenager, he'd be in his sixties by now."

"And still a shooter? What's he been doing for the last fifty years? Bagging groceries at the Safeway and polishing his rifle?"

"I don't know."

"And why now? Why you? If someone wanted to kill the president, they would have done so already. We profiled this in the run up to the election, and our conclusion was that the threat maxed out in the first ninety days after his election. So if someone is thinking about going to that particular dance, it seems a little late to me," Christiansen said.

"True, I remember the Fibbies sharing that intelligence with the Service. But let me ask you something. What do you think about Obama's election chances now?" Whelan asked.

"They improve with every improving economic metric, particularly on jobs."

"Correct. Which means, if this holds any water, it's about denying the president a second term. That's what I'm talking about."

"And why would this be a threat against you?"

"I don't know. I'm not that significant," Whelan said.

"Well, before we let this one get away from us, you realize that this is probably baloney. There was no second shooter at Dallas, and even if there was, this unsub isn't him." *Unsub* was FBI speak for unknown subject.

"I keep telling myself that."

"There's a 'but' in your throat as big as all outdoors. But?" Christiansen asked.

"Spider sense."

Christiansen laughed. "Well, you have been known to have a golden gut."

"Unfortunately."

"So Frank is going to make some fairly innocuous inquiries that will go nowhere, and that will be the end of it, right?" Christiansen asked, trying not to sound too hopeful.

"Not exactly. That's why I called you."

"And now I'm truly frightened."

"I didn't tell you what the note said. Not exactly."

"OK."

"My point is that it mentioned Martin Luther King as well," Whelan said.

"And as conspiracies go, tying that one up with Dallas would be a lulu. Which still begs the question, why come back now? Someone getting the band back together?"

"Maybe. I agree it doesn't make sense, unless—and this is a big if—unless it's already been done once. If Dallas was a conspiracy, then it's possible that someone is looking to dust off the manual. Because someone has read the tea leaves and thinks Obama isn't a one-term president."

"Then why warn you?" Christiansen asked.

"I admit, I have trouble with that one. But the way the note was worded, I think the shooter is the one who sent it to me."

"Now I'm thinking I should have a detox team go over there and try and figure out what you've been smoking, Richard. Who even knows who you are? Particularly among seventy year-old assassins?"

Just then the doorbell rang. "Alan, I've got to go. I really called because I want a huge favor, but I don't want to talk about it over the phone. Can I come by tomorrow?"

"Sure, if you can get to FBI headquarters, we can talk about it over lunch. I'll have my admin clear out a time and call you."

"Famous last words, Alan. Thanks for listening. I hope you won't regret it."

Whelan hustled to his door and undid the locks. Bettina came in and bussed his cheek. Richard threw his arms around her and hugged her, wanting for once to break through the reserved façade that had developed between them in the past five weeks. He swept her up in his arms and carried her over to the couch.

"Whew, Richard! Be still, my heart."

"Can't do that. It's beating for two."

Brave new world.

Misspent youth.

"Very funny. You could have damaged our baby with that show of affection."

Her saying it that way silenced Richard for a moment.

"Boy or girl?" he asked.

"Do you have a preference?"

Richard shrugged, thinking, *I would prefer not to bring a child into the world right now. Not like I'm exactly ready for the responsibility.*

"That shadow that just passed over your face says it all, I'm afraid."

"What'd you expect? We're not even married. Our relationship is… different. And we're pretty old to be expecting. Do you think we're ready for this? I don't, and nothing is going to change that in the short run."

"But nothing's going to change the fact that I'm pregnant, Richard."

"You aren't considering abortion, then."

Shocked, she stared at him. "I'm not killing our child, Richard. Don't ask me to."

"I'm not asking you to. I'm relieved that we don't have to struggle through that because I'm not a fan of killing defenseless kids. I know about a woman's right to choose, and I'm not the one who's going to swell up like a balloon, so I generally keep my mouth shut about it. But kill my kid? Uh-uh. No matter how inconvenient Buster's appearance on the scene is going to be."

"Inconvenient?" she asked, her tone implying her dismay at his choice of words.

"Yeah, inconvenient. I'm in a high-stress job, and you are a highly placed and very desirable State Department wonk. They don't exactly have a 'mommy track' at State, last time I heard. And then we have to think about your parents and marr..." Whelan stopped in midsentence, and it was all he could do to avoid turning away from her.

"The word turned you to jelly, huh?"

"I plead the Fifth." *Do you love her? Can you say that, even to yourself? Or are you just going along, because you need to Do the Right Thing?*

"And you should have seen your reaction when my mom called you out in church. I thought you were going to have a coronary."

"Because I knew something was up. Nice touch, adding in the pressure of meeting the parents and your father looking at me like, so, are *you* the dude that knocked up my daughter?"

She pushed against his chest, shoving him back into the seat cushions. "Hey, Superman, I thought you could handle it."

He reached over and kissed her, and when she responded, it turned into an even longer kiss.

"We have a lot of things to work out," Richard said.

"Yeah, like how you made Buster by jumping me without a condom."

Richard sighed. "It was the heat of the moment."

"If I hadn't wanted it, we wouldn't have done it."

"Oh, yeah? How exactly was Lois Lane going to fight off Superman when the Man of Steel wanted some?"

"Kryptonite scissors. You would have been the Soprano of Steel, and your nuts would have ended up in a jar of formaldehyde in the Fortress of Solitude."

Bettina saw the photograph on the table and picked it up, recoiling. "Ugh."

"I was going to tell you my news."

"That disgusting photo is news?"

"Sort of. Someone sent it to me. It's a photograph of JFK being assassinated in Dallas."

"I know what it is. Who sent it to you, and why?"

"Someone claiming to be the second gun in Dallas that day. Someone claiming that they're going to assassinate President Obama and...me."

"You?"

Richard nodded. Bettina snatched up the copy of the note from the killer and began to read. A minute later she put the note down, frowning.

"What was in the other package?"

"A rifle."

"A sniper rifle?"

Richard nodded. "It had the requisite scope on it, yeah. It could have been. Although I didn't want to examine it too closely because I didn't want my prints to get on it. But you know I know guns, and that gun certainly looked the part."

"But that doesn't mean it was real. A gun is a gun, right?"

"Right. And the president gets threats every day. Nothing unusual there, either."

"But?"

"But no one sends a threat to someone obscure in the Secret Service. At least the nuts don't."

"So you think it's real?"

Richard shook his head. "No, I didn't say that. I think it merits checking out."

"What are you going to do? You're not on the presidential detail. It's not your job to do anything."

"Start at the beginning if I can get a little help. He claims Kennedy, Martin Luther King, and Bobby Kennedy. Throw in Malcolm X, and you have all the infamous assassinations of the sixties."

"But that was all fifty years ago."

"Right. But I have to start somewhere. I won't spend much time on it, I promise."

"You better not. You need to start boning up on ring bling, Dad."

"Very funny, Mom," Whelan said, thinking, she's right. I'm going to have to pop the question...

The White House

Frank Moynihan was in the White House, which was just as well, because he'd asked O'Shay if he could get a minute or two with the president, and O'Shay had directed him to come in and they'd talk about it. He'd arrived in his office with Whelan's "gifts" in tow and managed to stow the items away in his office, when O'Shay's summons had brought him to the White House residence.

Obama was dressed casually, and Michelle and the girls were not around, it seemed. Just as well, Moynihan thought, because Michelle would tear him a new one if he upset the president while the girls were around. Obama guarded that aspect of his life more fiercely than he'd ever seen an occupant of the Oval Office do, and it was touching in a way. But beware of Momma Bear if someone PO'd Papa Bear. Michelle was no joke.

As always, Obama was watching sports in the residence with a tray with a sandwich and a beer on it and a thick folder of reading material. The few times he'd been in the residence on a Sunday to meet with the president alone he'd been like this, working and relaxing at the same time.

"Do you want anything, Frank?" President Obama asked, and Frank Moynihan deferred. He'd told O'Shay what he was going to say on the way up to the residence, and O'Shay had told him to make it quick and to the point.

Which usually wasn't possible in these situations.

"Mr. President, I'll get right to it, as I know there's a full slate of baseball games on, and word is you've bet the national debt on the Nationals," he started, and that elicited a patented Obama smile.

"Unfortunately, what I'm going to tell you is not great news, but I will say that this is very preliminary and is probably nothing. Richard Whelan, my number two in the Service, received a threat against you today."

"Credible?" O'Shay asked.

"Not particularly. In fact, the only reason why I'm bringing it up is because of the president's upcoming schedule and the open-air speech on the Lincoln Memorial, as well as the potential impact on the first family. We will try our best to run this to ground, but depending upon developments, we may want to revisit Mrs. Obama's schedule and the level of her protection as well as the children's. I know you hate changing their protection scheme around, Mr. President, but it's been awhile since we've made a random switch, and I think this is a good excuse."

'But, Frank," Obama said, thoughtfully, "what is it about this one that brings you to me?"

"Two—well, really, three things. First, the nutcase sent in a rifle. That's significant because of the second reason—he claims to have been involved in Kennedy's assassination. And Martin Luther King's. And lastly, he threatened Whelan. Which makes this an outlier, and outliers concern me."

"I'm sorry, you said the person—"

"Unsub, Mr. President. Unknown subject."

"Unsub, then, claims to have killed Kennedy? We haven't done anything to Social Security, Frank," Obama said, smiling, "so I don't think there's a gun club at the local old folks' home that's going to have it in for me."

"Very true, Mr. President; that part of it doesn't hold any water. But who threatens Secret Service agents? Who would even know Whelan's name?"

Obama shrugged. "So you want to talk about the Lincoln Memorial speech."

"Yes, sir, Mr. President. I'd like you to reconsider an open-air venue at this time."

O'Shay chimed in. "But you realize, Frank, or maybe you don't, how important that speech is? And how significant the symbolism? Within days of the anniversary of King's 'I Have a Dream' speech? This is going to be seen as the beginning of the campaign, and for the president to speak from the Lincoln Memorial is going to be memorable."

"I understand, Mr. President. We already have significant security plans in place, and we're upgrading and updating all the time. But this is likely the only window that someone looking at your public schedule is going to have for at least six or seven weeks. I don't like coincidence, and I don't like oddball threats."

"Why would anyone warn you about a prospective attempt on my life, Frank?"

"I don't know. Arrogance, maybe? I know this is a lot to ask, but I don't like this. Sir, please at least think about what I've said."

"OK, Frank. Although some Annie Oakley senior citizen with a howitzer isn't exactly a big deal unless she gets up close and personal. And I trust you and your team to prevent that from happening."

"Yes, Mr. President," Moynihan said. He nodded to O'Shay and turned and left.

Obama looked at O'Shay. "What the hell is eating him?"

O'Shay shrugged. "He's paid to be paranoid, sir."

Obama picked up the remote control and turned to a baseball game. "He's doing a heckuva job right now, then. If you have a minute, I'd like to refine this week's schedule, Chuck. I need more prep time for the speech on Friday," the president said, and he and Chuck O'Shay settled in for a solid hour or two of work.

CHAPTER 8

Dallas, November 22, 1963, 12:27 p.m.

"*Sal. Have the kid get ready.*"

The kid had owned the rifle since he was ten years old. A Remington 700 with a scope that he'd zeroed on tiny targets at impossible distances. When Sal cupped his hand to his ear and he didn't see the president dead or dying as the motorcade turned onto Elm Street from Houston, he realized something had gone wrong. Mook's words in his ear began to make sense.

Sal tapped him on the shoulder. "Mook says to get ready."

He was already prepared, having relaxed his breathing and tightened his muscles. He had the gun propped up on the wall bordering the grassy knoll, and he sighted down the scope at the president's car, first picking up the governor of Texas, John Connolly, then Mrs. Kennedy, in her trademark pillbox hat just as the Lincoln made the turn onto Elm. He began swiveling the gun to pick up where he thought the president would be as the car moved toward him on Elm. And that special something that made him an exceptional shooter kicked in—he could see the trajectory that he'd have to move the rifle in to take his second shot, a shot that he knew he would have to take while working the bolt action of the rifle.

An impossible set of shots.

"Billy, this is Mook. Weapons free, take the shot."

Billy was in the Dal-Tex building and so keyed up he thought his head would burst. That damned Cuban was going to get them all hosed with his runny crap. He'd been ready to take Kennedy down when the cars were on Houston. Now he had a better angle, but the motorcade was moving away. He nearly pulled the trigger while he was aiming at the lead motorcycle cop and panicked, letting his finger go completely slack, then he tensed again as he realized that he'd lost his focus.

"Where the hell is Juan?" Mook hissed into the radio as the first shot echoed off the office buildings. He didn't dare look at the president because he didn't think that first shot, coming so soon after he'd given Billy the go-ahead, could have been accurate. That left him with Juan and the kid, and, he imagined, Billy, who would be frantically working the bolt action of his weapon.

"Mook, Juan's got no joy. There's a tree branch between us and the car, and it might be too far by the time they clear the obstruction."

Jesus. Mook wiped the sweat from his forehead. This thing was slipping through their fingers faster and faster. He was now left with only the kid having a clear, flat trajectory, even though having the kid take the shot completely queered the patsy theory.

And the kid had to make an impossible shot at a target moving across his field of vision with the wrong kind of rifle...

FUBAR. First things first, though.

"All units, weapons free. Take him down!"

***

The teenagers that Whelan was walking behind were passing a brown bag back and forth and laughing. Every once in a while, one of the boys would point to Richard and then point to the brown bag, but the girl always shook her head.

"Hey, kid," one of them finally said, and the four of them came to a stop.

"Willie," the girl pleaded, "don't."

He shook her off. "You thirsty, kid?"

Whelan looked into his face. He was wearing cheap black frame glasses with medium lenses in them, and Whelan could see no hint of guile in his eyes.

"Yeah," Whelan said, "a little."

"You want somethin' to drink?" Willie asked.

"Willie!" the girl said, but Willie shushed her.

"What is it?" Whelan thought to ask. He was too shy to be around big kids, but they were now in a questionable neighborhood, and Richard's route following the bus was about to require that he make a right turn into what looked like a tough block. It looked tougher now that he was going to have to walk through it as opposed to riding through it on the bus.

"It's grape juice," Willie said, and the other male teenager laughed.

"Oh," Whelan said, but he finally suspected that they were trying to have fun at his expense. "I don't like grape juice."

There was a Newark police department cruiser rolling silently toward them.

"Willie," the girl whispered urgently, "hide the bag. Cops!"

"Damn, Tammy, why din't you say something?" Willie asked, irritated. They all stopped and paused as the police cruiser drove slowly past them, and when they saw the brake lights come on, the teens began to panic.

"If they gets out, I'm not stickin' around," Willie declared.

"It's just a little wine, Willie," the other male kid said.

"These crackers up here bust you for anything, Johnny. And I mean anything."

The doors to the cruiser cracked open, and two white cops emerged. One of them was cradling his nightstick.

"Afternoon, kids," the cop on the driver's side of the car said. Suddenly the teenagers were looking at the ground and shuffling their feet.

"Afternoon," the group managed to mumble. Richard Whelan was staring at the scene as if he wasn't a part of it.

The two cops ambled up, one of them smacking his nightstick lightly against his palm.

"On your way home, kids?" the driver cop asked softly.

"Yessir," Willie answered, keeping the brown bag close to his leg. "Just walking home, sir."

"Um, hmm. I bet," the other one said, and Richard could see that the pocket of his uniform shirt had the name Stevens on it.

"You little pickaninnies know that the president was killed today?" He was also talking softly, smacking his nightstick into the palm of his hand.

"What's a pickaninny?" Richard Whelan asked.

CHAPTER 9

Sunday Evening, August 21, 2011

P hillip Stone had taken a break to get a sandwich and returned to reading the "Silent Night" file. The next photo in the folder was Lee Harvey Oswald.

He turned the photo over and read what had been written in ball-point pen on the back of it.

Russian "defector" working for CIA
Ex-marine, gives him some skills with weapons
New Orleans/Cuban connection
Credible?

Behind Oswald's picture was a copy of a dossier prepared by either the CIA or the FBI. Stone couldn't tell which. There was a sheet of lined notebook paper stapled to the back with a single question:

Will he stand up to scrutiny? Killed "resisting arrest"?

Then there was a typewritten critique from someone apparently unconcerned about being traced. Stone began to read.

The principal problem is the local authorities and too many loose ends. We need a local PD that we can feed the patsy to as the killer within minutes of the attack, and we need very few questions asked as to why the patsy is the killer. Scorched earth should be applied to the patsy as quickly as possible, unless he's not coherent enough to shed doubt on his guilt, but what local PD is going to buy eliminating him? This is a no-go as far as I'm concerned, unless we get the patsy and the president in a place where we have friendlies.

There was another dossier in the file of an anti-Castro activist who was rejected as being too unstable and not, therefore, a "reliable asset." A dissenting opinion cited the connection between the mob and the Cuban dissidents and the ill-will Kennedy had inspired in both groups.

The single telephone on his desk rang, and Stone picked it up.

"Yes."

"The president is planning to go ahead with his speech at the Lincoln Memorial. What do you want to do?"

"Tell the asset that he needs to make his move now. Moynihan?"

"He knows which side his bread is buttered on."

"Will we be able to pass the Secret Service deployment plan to the asset before the event?"

"Yeah. He's ready if you're still talking about the same asset. But this is short notice for this kind of op, sir."

Stone turned to the last photo in the file. It was a grainy picture taken in Saigon, and it showed only a skinny Marine grunt with a sniper rifle in one hand and his other arm around a Vietnamese prostitute. The photo was dated January 1968 and labeled simply, "The Kid."

"I don't care about notice. We have a piece on the board, and we're going to play it. So, yeah, I'm still talking about the same asset. Make sure he's still ready."

***

Monday, August 22, 2011

Richard Whelan stopped in to see FBI Director Alan Christiansen intending to discuss the assassinations in the 1960s. Christiansen greeted him warmly.

"So what deep dark secrets did you want to look at today, Richard?"

"The FBI archives."

Christiansen had been playing with a pencil and promptly pulled a pad of paper toward him.

"What are you looking for?"

"Alan, this might be difficult. I'm looking for evidence of a myth."

"This have anything to do with the package you got yesterday?"

"Yeah, it does. The writer mentioned Kennedy and King in the same breath. One of the more persistent myths about Martin Luther King's death has always been J. Edgar Hoover—his hatred of the man and the surveillance that King was under."

Christiansen's pencil was poised above his pad, but he hadn't written anything down.

"There's also the long-standing revelations about the FBI's efforts to infiltrate black militant organizations in the sixties under its Cointelpro operations."

"And you want access to those files?"

"Without the Freedom of Information Act censorship."

Christiansen put his pencil down on his desk. "Why not start with Kennedy in Dallas in '63?"

"Because the conspiracy theorists have already raked over that ground in books, movies, you name it. King is different."

"Because he was black?"

"No, there was less attention paid to his assassination. And because of the times. In 1968, the country wasn't ready to treat King's death as importantly as the others. And Bobby Kennedy was killed within months of King's death. I'm gambling that no one has ever successfully examined those files from the inside, with anything close to an objective point of view."

"What do you intend to do with anything you find?"

"I'm not sure."

Alan Christiansen shook his head. "Richard, I can't let you go on a shopping trip through the archives. Those were...dark times, and what's in those files could damage the Bureau."

Whelan looked at the FBI director closely.

"Jesus, Alan. You know something, don't you?"

"I'm a twenty-year veteran of the Bureau, Richard. When I came in, Hoover was still an untarnished legend. In many parts of the Bureau, he still is a legend."

"And?"

"And…there were rumors twenty years ago when I signed up. Rumblings. Talk about the way things 'used to be.'"

"When the FBI and Hoover ran roughshod over the darkies, is that it?"

Christiansen shrugged. He knew he had to wait Whelan's temper out. "It was a different time."

"And I see we haven't forgotten. Still have a Confederate flag somewhere in the archives, Alan?"

"That's unfair, and you know it."

"Is it? Why protect the past? Why not confront it?"

"For what? So you can bring down the FBI?"

"You, of all people, think this is about me and my ego?"

"No, Richard, I don't think it is, at least not now. But if you find something…this wild goose chase you're on will do more than disturb sleeping dogs that should stay asleep. And for what? A fairy tale?"

"But what if something *is* rotten in Demark, Alan? Let's put it on the table—what if there is a shadow power structure that doesn't want a black man to remain president? Look at all the unprecedented insults that Obama has had to deal with already."

"So, the true nature of the country rises up and kills him? Based upon some crazy loon who sent you a picture and a gun? Are you serious, Whelan?"

"Alan, if it's so crazy, why not let me see the archives? Indulge my racial paranoia and shut me up. That's all I'm asking. Let me see the files."

Alan Christiansen shook his head and shrugged. Whelan turned and walked out of his office.

As he watched Whelan walk out in a huff, he honestly couldn't blame him. Then he picked up the phone and dialed an internal number.

"Archives."

"This is Christiansen. I need something from the 'lost' Hoover section."

"Sir, I'll need you to come down personally and sign for whatever it is, since that section doesn't officially exist."

"I understand."

"OK—what are you interested in?"

"Cointelpro."

"Cointelpro. Got it. I'll call you when we've retrieved the material, Director Christiansen."

***

The White House, The Same Time

Sam Redburn headed President Obama's protection detail. He was meeting with Frank Moynihan about the president's speech.

"You don't think the president is going to change his mind about making the speech, do you? Any threats that I don't know about?" Redburn asked, a purely rhetorical question.

"None," Moynihan replied.

"OK, then here's the preliminary plan." Redburn was short, only five foot nine, and stocky. He was a good, solid agent who had risen to the top of the ranks. They were standing over a mockup of the Lincoln Memorial and its surrounding grounds.

"Because of the openness of the grounds, we're going to cordon off the memorial area out to a distance of three hundred yards in every direction. The perimeter will be hard, enforced by roving security teams with dogs. We'll have several entrances set up with metal detectors and agents wanding every single person that comes in."

"Parks Service have an estimate on the expected crowds?" Moynihan asked.

"Not yet. I don't know officially why they seem to be having trouble coming up with a number, but I'm getting some backchannel about them not wanting to predict anything, given that there's a counter rally being planned by that guy from Sky News."

"Need me to make a phone call?" Moynihan asked.

Redburn shook his head. "Let's give it a day. Besides, the crowd estimate isn't crucial in an op like this."

Moynihan nodded, although he made a mental note of Redburn's comment. If there was an inquiry later, every decision would be minutely examined. He'd make sure this one was flagged if it turned out to be critical.

"What about the roundup?"

"We plan to start tomorrow. We should have every nutcase and mental patient who's ever threatened Oracle under lockdown and/or surveillance by no later than Wednesday." Oracle was the Secret Service's code name for President Obama.

"Wednesday? What if Oracle decides to move it up?"

Redburn shook his head. "I'd strongly advise him not to, Frank. The Lincoln Memorial is bad enough. The only saving grace is that it's pretty open ground. There's no place to take a shot within a mile of the place, literally."

"A mile out isn't out of the question, Sam."

"But then we're talking about a professional hit, Frank. There's nothing on the threat boards that remotely suggests that the president is a prime target."

"Doesn't matter. Given the feeding frenzy in the media about Oracle these days, it could be some good old boy that gets off a lucky round. Make sure the perimeter is fully checked out a couple of times before the president speaks, and use your judgment as to whether we need to post people at some of the more opportune places."

"I'll keep you informed."

***

After leaving FBI headquarters, Richard Whelan went to see Bettina in her offices at the State Department. As undersecretary of state specializing in Asia, she was extremely busy because of the region's growing importance.

"She in?" he asked Bettina's administrative assistant, who nodded as she spoke to someone else on the phone. She waved him into Bettina's office.

Bettina was also on the phone, gesturing with her hands as she made her points.

"I understand, Minister, but your last three requests for additional assistance are with the Congress and the president. Yes, I understand how critical your situation is, but my hands are tied without either an executive decision or some action by Congressional leaders. If you want the number of the Senate majority leader, I'd be happy to give it to you so you can plead your case directly to the leadership. Yes, I will keep you informed." She looked up to see Richard standing there and smiled.

"But I'm afraid I have another meeting. Thank you, sir. I'll do what I can. I promise."

She hit the disconnect button and went to Whelan and gave him a hug.

"This is a surprise. Did you go into the office?"

"No. I went to see Alan Christiansen."

Bettina pulled back and looked at him. "Oh?"

"Wanted to look at some old files."

"And?"

"He said no. Not surprising."

"How old?" she asked suspiciously.

"The sixties."

"Hmm. You asked to look at the FBI's uncensored dirty laundry?"

"Yup."

"From the most difficult period in recent history?"

"Guilty again."

"Because of the package you got?"

Richard shrugged. "Why not?"

"Still restless, Superman?"

"Restless? Is that what you call it?" Whelan couldn't keep a trace of anger out of his voice.

"It was a package, Richard, probably sent by a kook. It wasn't the Bat Signal." She started to retreat, feeling him tense, but then pulled him closer.

"I've got a bad feeling about this," he said, and she could sense his restlessness.

"I figured that already."

He's pulling away, avoiding conflict instead of resolving it, she thought. *Not gonna work this time, Superman.*

Bettina began nibbling his ear and then stuck her tongue in it. What was that song? I'm not going to surrender, something like that.

Richard tried to pull away, but she held him close. "Make love, not war, Superman."

It was Richard's turn to pull back and look at her.

"Where's the real Bettina, and what have you done with her?"

***

At FBI headquarters, the archivist called Alan Christiansen when the Cointelpro files were ready.

"It's one box," the archivist told him on the phone.

"Is that all of it?"

"All we've got. Yes, sir."

"OK."

When he returned to his office, he shut the door and told his assistant not to disturb him. He took off his suit jacket and rolled up his sleeves, then spent a few moments going through the files to see how they were organized. A third of the box was labeled "KING" and rubber-banded together.

Christiansen took a deep breath and pulled a thin folder from the group. It was labeled "Birmingham" and consisted mostly of newspaper clippings. Near the top of the file was a clipping of a front-page story in the *Birmingham News*:

JURY TO PROBE NEGRO'S LIE

Birmingham, Alabama, August 22, 1963

The controversy concerning Roosevelt Tatum's statements implicating Birmingham Police in the bombing of minister A.D. King's home continued today in the aftermath of Tuesday's bombing of Negro Attorney Arthur Shore's home.

US Attorney Macon L. Weaver maintained in an exclusive interview yesterday that Tatum's "false charges" that two policemen bombed the Negro minister's home in May resulted directly in the violence of Tuesday night's bombing.

Now, Birmingham Judge Allgood has stated exclusively to this reporter that he will ask a grand jury to consider charges against the Negro Tatum, who falsely alleged that Birmingham Police bombed A.D. King's home last May. It appears likely that the Negro Tatum will be indicted under Title 18, Section 1001 of federal law for making false statements to the FBI.

A.D. King is the brother of the notorious Martin Luther King.

Attached to the clip was a piece of J. Edgar Hoover's notepaper with a couple of terse notes:

X-Ref to Silent Night-
JFK vulnerable in the South/

Attached despite Justice Dept inst. and federalization of Nat'l Guard

Will Pres visit Birmingham?

Christiansen looked at the date—August 1963. Three months before Kennedy was assassinated.

He turned to his computer and began pulling up Internet articles about that period. Birmingham had been a tinderbox with bombs exploding on a regular basis. Two weeks after that clipping, the infamous Sunday school bombing at Birmingham's 16th Street Baptist Church had occurred, killing four little black girls. FBI agents had been spectacularly unsuccessful in finding suspects for any of the numerous bombings that had occurred in Birmingham that year, although it was clear from the "Hoover File" that FBI agents had been instrumental in setting up the "Negro Roosevelt Tatum" for lying to the FBI in the case; "lies" that were not investigated because they implicated Birmingham police in a bombing.

As he continued researching the period, he began to understand the context of the handwritten notes. The Justice Department had instructed the US Attorney (apparently this Macon Weaver, who declared that the falsehood perpetrated by Tatum had resulted in more violence) not to prosecute Tatum. But Tatum had been prosecuted and convicted.

And the escalation of the bombings had led Kennedy to federalize the Alabama National Guard. But the bombings had continued, and Tatum had gone to jail for implicating the police in a bombing.

Christiansen sat back in his chair, thinking about what the note writer had meant. What was "Silent Night"? Why would there be interest in whether the president would visit Birmingham? He looked at the notes again:

JFK vulnerable in the South

Three months later, the president was killed in Dallas.

Which was also in the South. It just wasn't Birmingham and the Deep South.

Which gave him a chilling thought—was Silent Night an operation designed to kill the president, searching for a location?

Will Pres visit Birmingham?

Or would Dallas do?

CHAPTER 10

Dallas, November 22, 1963, 12:30 p.m.

braham Zapruder filmed President Kennedy's motorcade as it passed through Dealy Plaza. He saw the cars make the slow turn from Main Street to Houston and from Houston to Elm, the later turn requiring the motorcade to slow to less than ten miles per hour.

Five minutes earlier, at 12:25, Carolyn Arnold had seen Lee Harvey Oswald in the second-floor lunchroom of the Texas School Book Depository, four floors below where "his" rifle would be found.

"All units, weapons free! Take him down!"

The kid was humming to himself when Sal raised his hand to his ear in response to Mook's yelled instruction. He was humming a Hendrix song, "Manic Depression," and the kid heard the first shot within a second of when Sal's hand went to his ear. He thought for a moment that his singing had somehow gone out on the radio net and triggered the shooting.

Too quick, he thought, and he was right. Billy, in the Dal-Tex building, had jerked the trigger and missed the car completely.

Zapruder's hand jerked, blurring his film.

The kid, sighting down the sniper scope, saw Kennedy pause at the first gunshot and then resume waving at the crowd, apparently not realizing that a shot had been fired. Texas Governor John Connolly did realize that a shot had been fired and began yelling "No, no, no, no!," making Mrs. Kennedy turn to her right.

The kid let out a breath. His locked position flexed a little and the muzzle of his rifle dropped slightly as he squeezed the trigger of the big Remington.

To his left, Abraham Zapruder jumped again, blurring his film. Kennedy was hit in the throat by the kid's first round, and the president brought his hand up toward his face to cover the wound.

On Main Street, across from Elm, Mook could tell that the first shot had missed, and then The kid opened up, and he saw Kennedy reach for his throat.

All units, weapons free, Mook thought. *Hit him, hit him again.* Mook could see the Secret Service agent driving Kennedy's car turn to look quizzically at the president, and Mook saw Kennedy's Lincoln begin slowing as the driver inexplicably took his foot off the gas.

Car's gonna speed up, polices gonna be shooting...

And then the limousine cleared the trees obstructing the view from the Book Depository, and Mook heard Juan finally open up. This shot sounded like an explosion because he wasn't expecting it.

Juan's shot drilled Governor Connolly in the back, blasting through his chest before existing from under his right nipple. One of the frames of Zapruder's film would show the governor's jacket forced slightly outward by the exiting bullet and obscuring the view of the governor's white dress shirt.

On the grassy knoll, The kid was working the bolt action of the Remington.

"Tally ho!" Mook heard in his headset as Billy fired a second time from the Dal-Tex building, this shot hitting Kennedy in the back from behind, a wound that was far too low in the president's back for the Warren Commission. Because it was shot number four, Billy's shot was one too many for the single-assassin theory. This shot became the so-called magic bullet that inflicted several wounds on both the president and Governor Connolly because no other shot could have been fired from Oswald's weapon in the time that had elapsed.

On the grassy knoll, The kid had worked the bolt and settled himself again in a matter of seconds. In the sight, Jackie Kennedy was leaning toward the president, realizing, apparently, that he had been hit. The kid looked through the scope, humming again.

He recalled Raoul, the skinny guy with the cheap aftershave that had to burn, telling him *if you have to pull the trigger, something serious will have gone wrong, but that's OK. You see him still breathing, I want you to...*

His finger tightened on the trigger.

Kill the sumbitch, OK?

Have some death, he thought, and the shooter's mechanics took over. He squeezed the trigger; the hammer dropped, and time seemed to slow...

Zapruder jerked a final time, but he kept the camera running and focused on the president all the way through frames 310, 311, 312. And the shell that had leapt from the barrel of the big Remington found its target—313. The president's head exploded—*have some death*—and Kennedy was thrown backward, and a portion of his skull landed on the trunk of the car.

The kid worked the bolt of the rifle again but realized as time sped up again, *he was done.*

The motorcade picked up speed toward the underpass, and John F. Kennedy's soul departed this world for someplace else.

CHAPTER 11

Monday Afternoon, August 22, 2011, Near the Lincoln Memorial

H e was no longer a kid. His hair was graying, but he was still trim, his eyes still sharp, even if he felt the fatigue of his years. Under a baseball cap and behind sunglasses, he surveyed the National Mall, paying particular attention to the Lincoln Memorial, where Lincoln sat in stately repose. A presidential speech at the Lincoln Memorial—he began to wonder where exactly the podium would be set up and which podium the president would use.

He looked away into the distance and tried to imagine a bullet whistling into Lincoln's lap, but the only thing that he could visualize was Mook's voice in his ear, the view from his scope in Dallas, and the sound of gunfire echoing into the canyon at Dealy Plaza.

All units, weapons free. What had those words cost him over the years? Could it be calculated? Why had they let him live, when everyone else was long dead? He asked himself that question all the time, even though he knew the answer. "They" let him live because they weren't quite sure where he was, or who he was, and they needed him for jobs like this. If he was bitter, it was because he'd lived to tell; if he was resigned to his fate, it was because he'd been so spectacularly successful as a killer at such a young age.

Have some death. At fifteen, he'd done the unthinkable, and he'd become the most notorious murderer in the universe. For nearly fifty years, he'd lived with the images of Dallas in his head and the cold sweat that bathed him late at night when he thought about it. He'd hoped that the memory of the next kill would blot out the memory of the last kill, and he'd lost count. He wasn't an ideologue, and he wasn't a religious man. What he did wasn't morality, it was just physics. He was just an empty vessel, a killer.

Why had he taken those shots so many years ago? He'd asked himself about the seconds, really, that had elapsed when it had become clear that the plan had gone awry. Could he have said no and lived?

Probably not.

But he hadn't been thinking about survival when the time came. It was a job, he had a skill, and he had executed what many believed had been an impossible shot at a moving target. He was following orders. Kennedy wasn't the president; he was a target, a ballistics problem.

And the gateway to a very private hell. The number of shooters who could have successfully taken not one, but two shots at Kennedy's limousine from his position was what—maybe one? Two?

None?

On the National Mall, the only possibilities for a sniper's nest were well over a mile away. An eighteen-hundred-yard shot was possible with the right weapon and the right shooter, and had he still been "The Kid," he would not have hesitated. To put a bullet in Lincoln's lap would pass it through the president's skull, a long-distance death whistling in from heaven or hell or wherever he was set up, peering through a tactical scope and a set of cross hairs.

Lots of things to consider with that kind of distance. Like a bullet-proof podium. The bullet would arrive spent, still capable of doing horrific damage, but it would stop dead if it hit a Kevlar-lined podium. And from a significant distance, he would be aiming well above Obama's head to account for the distance the bullet would drop as it flew toward the president.

A stiff enough wind would make it a no-go. Unless he was going to hit the son of a bitch with a fifty-cal, and that heavy a weapon carried its own difficulties, even though all he had to do was touch the target with one of the rounds, and the target would not likely get up.

Too far away, too stout a target, too big a gun. And too little time to pick a better venue, because the president's schedule wasn't conducive to a "live to tell" shot for weeks and weeks, and the money was anxious for the hit to occur. So he had to find a way to put a bullet into Lincoln's lap and live to tell about it.

And maybe the memory of this one would blot out the memory of the first one.

CHAPTER 12

Richard Whelan had been summoned to Alan Christiansen's office at FBI headquarters by an early-morning phone call.

"I owe you an apology," Alan Christiansen said.

Richard frowned. "Why?"

"Because I looked at a little tiny sliver of Hoover's legacy."

"And?"

"It scared the living daylights out of me."

Whelan looked at the FBI director closely. Alan Christiansen would not meet his eye.

"Does this mean I get to look at the files?"

"As long as we do it together. I need to understand what's there before it gets out."

"I'm not in this to dredge up old secrets, Alan."

"You may say that now, but if what I looked at is any indication, this stuff could be dynamite. And dynamite has a tendency to explode."

"Based on what you looked at, where should we start?"

"With Martin Luther King, in Memphis. Your letter writer said he was involved with King's murder, didn't he?"

Whelan nodded.

"Then let's start with Memphis in 1968."

***

Frank Moynihan asked Sam Redburn to update him on the plans for the president's security detail for the Lincoln Memorial speech.

"We've decided to sweep the rooftops an hour prior to when Oracle takes the podium. We think that should be sufficient."

Moynihan nodded. "Which podium?"

"The Hard Shell. Oracle doesn't seem to mind it, and the White House communications office says that it's likely he'll be using a teleprompter. We can attach the prompter to the podium at the very last minute if need be."

The Hard Shell was a Kevlar-reinforced podium covered with the seal of the president of the United States. Small-caliber bullets would likely not completely penetrate the molded, reinforced plastic shell. Larger calibers would, in theory, be stopped by the Kevlar.

"Good choice. How many agents in total on the detail that day?"

"Seventy-five, in total. Fewer, probably less than thirty, during the event. The bulk of the difference is Sven's advance team sweeping the area."

Sven Mikklesen was another of Moynihan's trusted agents. Moynihan would get the timing of his sweeps of the area from Sven.

***

Chuck O'Shay called Moynihan to ask about the preparations for the Lincoln Memorial speech.

"Everything's going well here. How's the president?"

"Great. This speech is going to mark the turning point in the campaign before the campaign begins. The Republicans are on the run, and he's going to revitalize the base in a way that's going to leave the other guys receding in the rearview mirror," O'Shay said. "He's wondering if you still think there's a bogeyman out there waiting to get him."

"I think the protection plans for the Lincoln Memorial are solid, and we're going to zip up Washington in a baggie to reduce the risk. Is that more like what Oracle wants to hear, Chuck?"

"Well, is there a risk or not?"

"There's always a risk. Will Oracle call off the speech if we get something that checks out?"

"He's counting on you to keep him safe."

"Then we'll make it so, Chuck."

There was a moment of silence as O'Shay considered Moynihan's words.

"Just keep me in the loop, Frank."

"Always, Chuck, always."

When Moynihan closed his cell phone, he was not surprised to wipe away a sheen of sweat from his forehead.

***

Richard Whelan sat in an empty office adjacent to FBI Director Alan Christiansen's office and contemplated the box of files in front of them. He was not sure that he really wanted to peek into the past this way, but Christiansen had piqued his curiosity, as had the mysterious author of the message delivered to his door on Sunday.

"Should we divide them up?" Whelan asked Christiansen.

The FBI director shook his head. "I'm not looking at any more of this stuff, Richard. It turns my stomach, and I'm not sure that I want to know any more than what I've already read. I'm just going to ask that you discuss with me anything significant that you find, and that nothing leave this office, OK?"

Whelan nodded, his stomach tight.

"I'll send in coffee," Christiansen said as he retreated to the door.

Richard's father had been a well-known local physician and staunch member of the New Jersey NAACP, who had expected his son to follow in his footsteps. He'd made trips into the South during the freedom marches and had met King, although Doctor Whelan would later say that he didn't agree with what he called King's "aggressive" tactics. If his father suspected that they were all under intense FBI surveillance, he never said. But what would his father have said about the notion of Obama as president? Would he have believed for a minute that America was "post racial," as the pundits had said after the election?

Probably not. Alfred Whelan was a skeptic who hadn't bought King's "I have a dream" rhetoric and wouldn't have bought Obama's "change" rhetoric. But at least Obama had succeeded in climbing to the pinnacle of power, and Alfred Whelan would have respected that.

Richard reached in and took one of the manila folders. *Have we come all that far in fifty years?* he wondered.

CHAPTER 13

Dallas, November 22, 1963, 12:45 p.m.

The kid walked quickly from his concealment point toward the rail tracks as Kennedy's limo sped off to take the dead president to Parkland Hospital.

Damn, did he just kill someone? Did he just blow his head off? He had the rifle in the box. He still had the rifle, and people were screaming and running, and cops were everywhere. There were people behind him, curious people, but out of nowhere, guys in dark suits had appeared on the grassy knoll behind him. They said they were Secret Service agents, and they warned people away from the area, even though some of the bystanders were convinced that shots had come from the grassy knoll.

He still had the rifle. His shadow, Sal was nowhere to be seen, and he didn't want to ditch the rifle and have it be found by the wrong person.

Where was Mook? The kid certainly didn't want to hang around. The president of the United States was dead, and he'd probably fired the fatal shots. Whoever these people were, they had the power to put a team together to kill the president, and had no doubt that they would kill him because of what he knew.

That meant that he was going to have to disappear. Raoul, the guy with the bad shave and the strong cologne, had told him he was being groomed, but the horror of what he'd done made him sick. Just like that, he dropped to the ground and emptied a gut full of Cocoa Krispies into the greasy scrub next to the tracks, and the curdled milk stench smashed into him so hard that he heaved until there was nothing left.

He was just a kid, he didn't know anything, and he didn't want to die. They were going to kill him, they were going to kill them all—Mook, that chain-smoking bastard, and Juan, the asshole who missed the most important day of his life because he was taking a dump. *Damn them, damn them, damn them.*

He wanted to disappear, but there was nowhere to go. He began walking slowly through the rail tracks, carrying the gun in the box, wondering when someone was going to come for him, but no one ever came.

***

Doctor Alfred Whelan was watching the news coverage of the assassination of the president of the United States and reading with a feeling of dread. His nephew had participated in the freedom rides and the organizing down in the rural South, where the early national news was blacked out and censored, where people disappeared and reappeared hanging from tree limbs, their bodies desecrated in unspeakable ways.

But we live in the North, he thought, knowing that if they—whoever they were—could kill Kennedy, then no one and nothing was safe.

His wife came in, drinking more often than not these days, wondering if he'd called the police about Richard. Richard, whom they trusted to take the bus home all by himself, had not come home, even though the school had been dismissed early and hours ago.

He nodded. She was silent, angry, and drinking, and he wondered what he'd seen when they married. He wondered why he didn't still see the same things, why he wasn't attracted to her anymore. He also wondered how much she knew about his other life.

The phone rang, and his wife picked it up.

He heard her suppress a sob and then call out to him.

He stood, scattering the paper that he'd had in his lap, and went to the phone, expecting the worst. His wife would not meet his gaze, and he paused for a moment to steel himself before taking the heavy black receiver.

"Doctor Whelan, I'm the precinct watch commander in the Central Ward," the white-sounding voice on the phone said.

"Have you found my son?" Whelan said softly.

"No, sir. Two patrolmen did stumble on him at Central Avenue, but he refused to accompany them. I think he's planning to walk the rest of the way home."

"How is that possible?" Whelan asked, his fear swiftly replaced by anger.

"He refused to accompany the officers, and there were other juveniles present. My patrolmen didn't want to start...an incident."

"So a second-grader just walked away from two armed police officers? Is that what you're telling me?"

"Doctor, your son was apparently quite determined not to get into the patrol car."

"Hmm. So where is he now?"

"We don't know. As I said, he's walking home—"

"Then find him and follow him, Officer. You'd do that if he lived in the North Ward, wouldn't you?" he said and hung up.

"Why didn't they bring him home?" his wife demanded, but Alfred Whelan simply turned away from her and went back to the television set.

Cracker policemen, he thought. He'd been among the NAACP leadership that had condemned Martin Luther King for his incessant protests and had endorsed the movement's statements praising the Birmingham police.

And so his son had avoided the police in a northern city, and Kennedy was dead, killed in a hail of bullets in a southern city. He sat there and watched the television, confident that his son would walk through the door any moment, and not at all certain that he understood what Dallas really meant.

Aboard Air Force One, November 22, 1963, 2:45 p.m.

Lyndon Baines Johnson had taken the oath of office aboard the plane and then retreated to the private cabin that had been used by JFK earlier that day. He was a tall, jowly man, and he laid his Stetson in a facing chair and sat back while two of his aides scurried around. One of the communications stewards knocked on the cabin door, and LBJ sent an aide go see who it was.

"So?" LBJ asked when the aide returned from his whispered conversation.

"Mr. President," the aide said, and despite the grim circumstances, LBJ barely suppressed a smile, "there is a radio telephone call from the adjutant to General Taylor of the Joint Chiefs of Staff, a Sam Titus."

"Can't it wait?"

"Sir, this person indicates that he has several people with him."

"Fine. Can we put this on speaker in here?"

"Uh, sir, the communications person said that this phone call was for your ears only."

"OK. They going to put it through here?"

The aide nodded, because the white light on the handset was already blinking.

LBJ nodded, and the aide showed himself out.

LBJ picked up the handset.

"Hello? Who is this?"

"Mr. President," the voice on the other end began, "that's not important. I have with me CIA Director Alan Dulles, FBI Director Hoover, and Cyrus Wilson of the Secret Service."

"I heard they caught the guy who did it, son."

"That's not exactly the reason for the call, Mr. President."

LBJ looked at the handset, puzzled. "Then what is the reason for the call, son?"

J. Edgar Hoover spoke up then from seemingly far away. "You're going to have to appoint someone to investigate these tragic events, Mr. President."

"But they have this Oswald in custody already, Mr. Hoover. I'm assuming there will be a trial."

Dulles cleared his throat and then said, "We don't think a trial would be in the country's best interests, Mr. President. We think an impartial investigation, run by people with credibility with the public, will help the nation heal."

"So what the hell do you propose doing with the lunatic who did this, gentlemen?"

There was a lengthy silence. Then Sam Titus spoke up.

"Sir, before we get into all that, there is the matter of National Security Action Memorandum No. 263, dated October 11 of this year."

"Am I supposed to remember every single piece of paper that Kennedy issued from the White House, dammit?"

"No, sir. It's just that this piece of paper approves the withdrawal of one thousand US military personnel from South Vietnam."

Johnson was silent as the import of what he was hearing became clear. "I'm beginning to get your drift, Titus, and I'm not sure I like it."

"Sir"—this was Alan Dulles—"we know that you support the Joint Chiefs' position that South Vietnam is a critical domino in the entire region that cannot be allowed to fall to the Communists."

"Good Christ, man, Kennedy isn't dead three hours yet, and you want to talk about reversing his policies!"

"Sir," Titus said, "we want to make it clear that the nation shouldn't suffer the loss of two members of the executive branch in one day, and the tragic loss of Air Force One—with all hands—would be viewed as a disaster and an opening for the Russians."

"Fuck, sonny," LBJ hissed, "Are you threatenin' me?"

"Mr. President"—this was Hoover—"with all due respect, nobody threatened Kennedy, and that son of a bitch is dead, and that's a damn shame. We just want what's good for the country."

"And a trial of this nut who shot the President—"

"Not in the best interests of the country, Mr. President," Titus said smoothly. "An impartial commission, with the investigation handled jointly by the CIA and the FBI, is, we feel, the best way to uncover the… truth."

"Jesus Christ, you people are insane. Director Wilson, what does the Secret Service say about these lunatic ideas?"

Wilson had been completely silent through the entire exchange.

"President Johnson, all I can tell you is that my sources tell me preliminarily that Kennedy's car came to nearly a complete stop once the shooting started."

"Which means what?"

"That an accident involving Air Force One would be a very tragic, but entirely possible, occurrence." Wilson stopped, cleared his throat, and then added, "Sir."

***

"A pickaninny," the cop named Stevens said, "is a little ignorant nigger, just like you are, boy."

"Why you gotta say that to a little kid?" Tammy said, starting to get upset at the direction the situation was taking.

Stevens turned to her. "Is that your little brother, bitch?"

Willie stepped up to the cop's face. "Ain't no bitches here, honky." Richard could see that he'd changed his grip on the contents of the brown bag so that he could more easily swing it as a weapon.

"I bet this little bitch likes your nigger dick, asshole. Now if you don't want to go down to the precinct, you had better back off," Stevens said, retreating a step and placing his hand on the gun in his belt.

"What the hell are you—" Willie started, and Johnny came up beside his friend.

"Willie, no. It's OK. Fahgit it," Tammy said.

"I ain't afraid a no cop," Willie said, taking an ill-advised step forward.

Stevens drew his gun. "Then I guess you ain't afraid to die, either, boy," he said as he cocked the .38 police special and pointed it at Willie. The driver cop, whose name was Booker, reluctantly drew his gun as well.

"I thought you said the president was dead!" Richard screamed. The second-grader stepped between the policemen and the teenagers. The cops noted that he was clutching a manila folder.

"What's your problem?" Booker said, taking a step back, trying desperately to defuse things.

"The president is dead. My teacher played it on the radio. That's why I gotta walk home," Richard said through his tears.

The cops looked at each other, as did the black teenagers.

"What the hell you talking about, kid?"

"It's all my fault," Richard Whelan said, trying to wipe his face. "I shouldn't have left my bus tickets home." Sheets of paper were slipping from the manila folder onto the cold concrete sidewalk.

Booker and Stevens exchanged a guilty glance.

"Your name Whelan, kid?"

Richard managed to nod through his tears.

Stevens cleared his throat. "Your parents called the police, worried about you, because you weren't home yet."

"I'm walking home, sir," Whelan said.

"No, I don't think that's a good idea," Booker said. "Let's get in the car, and we'll take you home."

Booker looked at Tammy, who was staring at him. "His father's a doctor," he said by way of explanation.

"You mean a house nigger," Willie said, under his breath, but Whelan could hear it.

"I can walk, sir," Whelan said, and he marched through the tight knot of teenagers and cops without looking back.

CHAPTER 14

"Find anything interesting?" Christiansen asked Whelan.

"I'm only on the background stuff," Richard Whelan said. "They called King 'Zorro,' and according to these files, did extensive surveillance on him."

"Interesting, but not conclusive."

"Hoover appears to have been too smart to keep anything conclusive in his files. But there is one tantalizing reference."

"To who?"

"Someone named Holloman. He was the chief of police in Memphis when King died. Former FBI agent."

"And what's the reference?"

"Just a note on Hoover's notepad. It says 'Tell Holloman that Raoul says the package is ready.'"

"Raoul, you said."

"Yeah? Why?"

"James Earl Ray claimed that a man named Raoul was the one who supplied him with money and instructed him to travel around the country. He said this Raoul character was CIA from New Orleans."

"Is that where they met the first time?"

"I don't know."

"But wasn't there supposed to be a New Orleans connection with Kennedy's assassination?"

Christiansen shrugged. "I'm not sure. I don't think so, why?"

"I just remember that from somewhere," Whelan said.

"It was the film *JFK*, I think. The DA in New Orleans tried to make a case that the killing was a conspiracy and that the conspirators were in New Orleans," Richard said, snapping his fingers.

"It's not like Oliver Stone was making a documentary."

"Doesn't matter. Garrison, the district attorney, was a real guy, and I'm sure he was in New Orleans. So there is a JFK link, even if it's just a coincidence."

The two men were silent for a while, and Richard picked up another file.

"Interesting. This one has ballistics info from the bullet they took out of Martin Luther King."

"What's the date on that?"

"That's what's interesting. It's dated fairly late—wasn't Ray's trial in 1969?"

"Don't know, but it'd be pretty easy to find out."

"Especially if this is from after the trial. If it is, why would the FBI test the bullets after Ray was convicted?"

Christiansen shrugged. "Confirming that Ray's rifle did it?"

"Maybe, but if this is what it purports to be, then the rifle they mailed to me can be tested against this data."

"Your shooter said he killed King with the rifle he sent you?"

"He says he killed both Kennedy and King. Seems like a stretch, but maybe we can get Frank to run some ballistics tests on the rifle I gave him," Richard replied.

"That would be a stretch," Christiansen said.

Whelan used the office phone to dial Moynihan's number in the White House. The call went to his voice mail.

Several Hours Later

The Kid was hanging around the Vietnam Memorial, taking etchings of guys he'd known and guys he'd heard of. He was in the 1968 section and saw the name he was looking for:

Lance Cpl Wilton P. Stiles

Stiles had died in Vietnam in 1968 during a trip into the hell of the A Shau Valley—the Valley of Death—right around the time of the Tet Offensive and the shocking implications that the Vietnam War might not be winnable the way it was being fought.

The Kid stooped down to take an etching, and his *Washington Post* fell open. There was an article about maintenance being done on the Statue of Freedom atop the Capitol building dome and the scaffolding that shrouded the statue. There was idle speculation that the Secret Service would have sharpshooters in the scaffolding for the president's Lincoln Memorial speech, but the Capitol was two miles away from the spot where the president's podium would be set up. If the writer had known anything about guns, he would have realized that it was an impossible shot, and any sharpshooters stationed that far from the president would effectively be out of the game.

The Kid had considered the scaffolding as his shooting perch for Friday's speech, but the distance complicated the ballistics and the choice of weapon. It was a little too far for a Barrett fifty-cal, and he didn't want to risk hitting the target and giving him nothing more than a minor wound.

He had been thinking of aborting the attempt when one of his sources had come through with what he was looking for—a bigger-bore, Russian-made son of a bitch, and it would take down Obama from the Capitol. And there was one available, although he had to see it to make sure that it was the real deal.

With just a few days before the speech, he didn't like being unsettled on a weapon, but he was getting pressure to get this job done, and the pressure of a hit of this magnitude was heavy on his shoulders. He was already spending all of his spare time trying to figure out how to get the weapon up into the Capitol dome and onto the scaffolding surrounding the Statue of Freedom, and he had yet to figure it out.

There was always the possibility that the Secret Service would have agents in the scaffolding, as the *Post* was speculating, which naturally complicated things.

But he'd worry about that when the time came.

He finished his etching. Wilton P. Sikes had been a sniper, working the A Shau and other godforsaken places—just a regular guy who happened to be in the wrong place, at the wrong time, in '68.

Whelan met Bettina near the Vietnam Memorial after leaving Christiansen's office. She kissed him playfully, and he drew her close to him in an embrace.

"How's the conspiracy theory, Superman?" she asked.

"Slow, dusty work. I need sustenance."

"OK. I have just the place," she said, and they started walking toward a hot dog vendor. Richard stole a glance at her and found her radiant, more radiant than he'd ever known her to be.

Too bad I can't take the credit for it.

"OK, Superman, sustenance with a capital *S* coming up," she said brightly, turning to the hot dog vendor. "Four with the works and a couple of cold waters."

Richard looked at her as the vendor piled sauerkraut, onions, and chili on top of four hot dogs. "Four?" he asked.

"For me, yeah, Supe. I'm eating for two. If you want some, order your own," she said, laughing.

"Good God, the Thing That Ate The Mall," he said, stepping away from her in mock horror.

She laughed, and Whelan cracked up too, unable to hold it back any longer. He flashed on the potential between them, the happiness and the joy of having a family with her, of settling down. And yet, he looked at Bettina and wondered—if she wasn't pregnant, would he be forcing himself to think of their relationship as something that would last forever?

***

The Kid finished his etching and was about to walk away when he spotted Whelan and Bettina Freeman walking, hand in hand, twenty paces away. He adjusted his glasses and the baseball cap a little lower on his head and paced them for a little ways as they headed for the hot dog cart.

He gripped the etching as he overheard Bettina say, "For me, yeah, Supe. I'm eating for two."

As he watched her tuck into the hot dogs, it dawned on him that she was pregnant. He turned away, looking down so they wouldn't notice his interest.

Bettina was still a very pretty woman, he thought.

And he was a lonely man who was going to grow old, comforted only by his secrets.

CHAPTER 15

New Jersey, January 1968

Alfred Whelan kissed his wife good-bye and started his hospital rounds. He dropped his son Richard off at the private middle school he attended in Elizabeth and continued to Beth Israel in Newark. He was debating seeing his car dealer because the big Chrysler New Yorker that he drove was getting a little long in the tooth. His practice was doing well, and he could certainly afford it.

The problem was his wife. Mabel was on him about every penny that he spent, because she knew about Sylvia and the child that he'd had out of wedlock.

He would go to Brooklyn this afternoon to pay them a visit. His son, Marcus, was developing into a fine young man, but Whelan had no illusions that his families would ever spend time together. No, he'd committed the cardinal sin, and it made him no better than the nigger on the street, pimping the future of the race for the pleasure of whoever had the money to take advantage of it.

He'd met Sylvia Blaze because she was involved in the NAACP at the national level. She was a fine-looking woman, intelligent and worldly in ways that had intrigued him. They'd had a drink at a conference in Philadelphia at the Adam's Mark Hotel on the Main Line—and then had woken up together the next day.

Even through his guilt, Whelan didn't regret his involvement with her. He'd done the right thing, supporting her and the child when the child came, and doing his best to keep it a secret from Mabel. His excuse was that Mabel had no interest in what he called the Negro Movement; she was content to be the bourgeois wife of a prominent Negro physician and participate in Jack and Jill and whatever else came along. They summered at the Jersey Shore; they had two cars and a big house—bigger since they'd moved away from Newark after the riots last year, in 1967.

Sylvia was no slouch. She was a nurse, an expert in the things that mattered to him, and concerned about the future of black people in America; in short, she was the wife he should have married.

But he was stuck with Mabel, and he was stuck with Richard and Sunna, who, as a teenager, already had the stink of failure all around her.

As he piloted the big Chrysler through the streets of Newark, he reflected on the upstanding public life that he had as a prominent New Jersey physician with the store-bought wife with good hair, a nice figure, and a cold heart, and the secret life that he had with Sylvia, which was the only place that he was truly happy. As long as Marcus kept his nose out of the streets, it was this part of his double life that made him the most happy.

Near Beth Israel hospital, he pulled the big car to the side of Chancellor Avenue near a bus stop and a pay telephone booth. He took the bag of change from the glove compartment (his excuse to Mabel was that he always had to make calls from hospital pay phones) and went into the booth and closed the door. He put some coins in the slot and dialed a number.

"Hello?" Sylvia answered, and Alfred Whelan's heart soared.

Saigon, January 1968

The Kid came upon the officer going through his footlocker and was about to kick his ass—screw the consequences—when the man stood up and he recognized him. His blood ran cold as ice as he saluted, watching the man with the phony captain's bars smile behind a half-assed salute.

"What can I do for you, Captain?" he said, hoping maybe he didn't recognize him.

"Long time no see, soldier," said the man he knew as Raoul. "We were worried about you."

"And now you've found me." The Kid sniffed but couldn't smell the cheap aftershave. Just as well. It would attract bugs and VC in the boonies.

"That's correct." Raoul held up a photo of him, holding a sniper's rifle, with his arm around a very pretty Vietnamese prostitute.

"Pretty girl," he said, and something slimy coiled in The Kid's guts.

"Can we go someplace and talk?" Raoul said, and there was nothing that he could do to say no.

They went to the base PX, and The Kid ordered them a couple of Cokes.

"Whatever happened to Mook?" The Kid asked. Raoul just looked at him over the cigarette hanging off his lower lip.

"Mook was sick. He died a couple of months after Dallas."

"Yeah, I remember you saying that. You didn't help him along any, did you?"

"Me?" Raoul seemed genuinely surprised. "I don't get involved in that phase of the ops, Corporal."

The Kid's father had died shortly after Dallas as well, shot to death with his own gun while sitting in his marked police cruiser. The only reason The Kid knew about it was because one of his buddies was from Texas and the case was mentioned in a letter from home. He'd never dared contact his father after that day in Dallas. He couldn't decide whether he was disgusted or appalled that his father had let him get caught up in it.

"How'd you find me?"

Raoul shrugged. "You joined the military and started shooting up the A Shau. Next time take a lower profile."

"Are you military?" he asked.

Raoul shook his head. "I just have many friends. I take it you like the uniform."

"Pretty high rank. Aren't people suspicious of you?"

Raoul sucked on his cigarette and smiled. "The regulars think I'm Company. The Company idiots think I'm DIA. Anybody gets too curious, I tell them I'm recruiting for a bush run in Laos, and they all get the hell out of my face."

"Who do you work for?"

Raoul just shook his head. "You want to keep drawing breath, you should never ask that. I work for the government, the real government, not the sideshow that everyone thinks is democracy."

The Kid just sipped his Coke. "So why are you here? To kill me like you killed Mook?"

"I didn't kill Mook. We got a job for you, Kid."

"Dallas was a fluke. I shouldn't have been there."

"Dallas was the new world order. You were there because we were grooming you for bigger and better things. We made an investment in you, Kid."

"Whose world order are we talking about, Raoul? The CIA's? The FBI's? MACV's?" MACV was short for the Military Assistance Command—Vietnam.

Raoul shrugged.

"That was a long time ago. I'm not the same person," The Kid continued.

"No, you're this lance corporal character you made up to enlist as an underage kid in the US Marines. It took some very pissed-off people five years to find you, sonny, and in the end you became an accomplished sniper."

"I'm not that good."

"Bull. Word around Central Command is that you undercount your kills by a factor of three to one. That means you make this Hathcock guy look like a pussy. You have a gift, Kid. And you can't run away from it; you can't avoid it."

Carlos Hathcock was a master sergeant who was rapidly becoming a legend as a Marine Corps sniper.

Because I'm still running away from that day in Dallas. "I don't want to be consumed by your ops, Raoul. I'm not Mook."

"You remember Juan?"

The Kid snorted. "Yeah, that asshole. Whatever—"

"I cut his throat and fed his balls to the coyotes. Goddamned screwup."

The Kid hesitated, remembering that day in Dallas and hating Raoul for bringing it to the front part of his brain.

"Well, whatever you're peddling, Raoul, I don't want it."

The Kid rose up to go back to his bunk.

"Wait," Raoul said. The Kid shook his head.

Raoul tugged on his sleeve. "We can do this hard, you know."

The Kid tore his arm from Raoul's grasp.

"I'm a killer, Raoul, you know that. You must know I'm a dangerous man."

Raoul snorted. "Do you have any idea what the carnage was like in Dallas, Kid? Juan botched the hit, which meant a whole lot of people had to die because they saw things they couldn't be allowed to talk about. Do you have any idea what it took to manage the ballistics evidence alone? So you think anybody gives a damn about killing you? Do you think for one minute that someone couldn't reach out and snuff you like an ant? You can run, Kid, but you cannot hide. You can only die. So just hear me out, OK? Five minutes, Kid. Might save your life."

It wasn't as if he could simply escape. They knew where he was. They knew who he was pretending to be. He'd tried to lose the memory of Dallas in the hills and valleys of the A Shau, the kills piling up like cordwood around him, long, long rifle shots that made him seem like a force of magic, shooting from the middle of nowhere. But someone had admired his work. Someone had become interested. Were they military? he thought, and then he remembered the way Kennedy's limo had slowed almost to a complete stop while he'd worked the bolt action of his Remington rifle, the rifle that he'd left in the same box he'd carried it away from the scene in, tucked away in a corner of his aunt's attic. *The limo driver had nearly screwed up his mechanics on the second shot…*

No, they weren't military. Not just military. Kennedy's limo had slowed almost to a stop. Could that have been part of the plan?

And he flashed back on Juan asking Mook that morning about the cars speeding up and the "polices" starting to shoot, and what had Mook said? A simple no.

Don't worry about it.

Raoul was looking at him intently, and he recalled that Raoul had just caught himself in a lie, because he'd said he didn't get involved in operations, but then he said that he'd cut Juan's throat. He looked at the slight, smiling man in front of him and wondered if he could snap his neck somewhere behind a barracks and walk away from this horror and get his life back, even if his soul was a lost cause.

But Raoul simply pointed at his chair, and The Kid sat back down.

"Bobby Kennedy is going to run for president," Raoul said simply.

The Kid shrugged. "Good for him."

Raoul shook his head. "He wants to find out what happened to his brother that day in Dallas." And he wants to understand why we can't seem to win in Vietnam, Raoul thought, but he didn't say it.

The Kid became alarmed. "That's not my problem, pal."

"Relax. But you understand that the people I work with would rather he didn't begin running his own investigation from the White House."

The Kid shrugged. "I'm not shooting another Kennedy."

Raoul smiled. He had him.

"That's OK. We're going to send Bobby a little message first. Maybe encourage him to change his plans."

"Being that I'm a shooter, I guess that leaves me out."

"No, being that you're a shooter, it means we have a message we want you to send."

"I can't just disappear."

"We could arrange a million-dollar wound, get you stateside and discharged quickly."

"I don't miss stateside."

Raoul pulled the photo of The Kid and the prostitute out of his pocket. "Pretty girl," he said, and something in his smile again uncoiled that snake in The Kid's guts. "I had her last night."

And The Kid nearly reached across the table to snatch the man's life from his chest, but Raoul parried his first grab and then settled into his seat. "She's a prostitute, Kid. Get used to it."

"Who's the target?" he asked, suddenly afraid that what Raoul was saying was true.

"Let's just call him Zorro," Raoul said and took another drag of his cigarette.

CHAPTER 16

Georgetown, Tuesday Evening, August 23, 2011

B ettina Freeman finished checking her voice mail account at her office in the State Department, walked over to the couch, and curled up with her head in Richard's lap.

"Anything significant happening?" he asked.

"Nothing new."

"No news is good news."

"Not quite. Right now, all news is bad news."

"So I'm right."

"No, the absence of news is even worse news."

Richard pulled back to look at her. "Are we having a pregnant hormonal swing?"

"No. Damn."

"What?"

"Now I want some ice cream or something."

"No doubt with pickles."

"Don't give me any ideas."

"You keep up like this, and the kid's going to think he's been basted in his mommy's stomach acid."

"You mean she."

"I mean whatever."

"Funny. Moynihan call you back yet?"

"Not yet. And certainly not in the last five minutes since you last asked me."

"I'm an emotionally fragile, pregnant woman. Sarcasm is equally likely to produce tears or homicidal rage."

"Why are you so interested in Moynihan?"

"Why not? Something to keep you busy, digging through the archives looking for evidence of the Trilateral Commission."

"Now who's being sarcastic? Besides, I already have one of their secret, three-pointed hats."

Bettina guffawed. "Oh, so you're a Trilateralist? That explains a great deal."

"Including crop signs, no doubt."

"Uh-huh. Especially crop signs."

They chuckled together.

"Do you really think it's possible?" she asked as their laughter subsided.

"What? That the long-lost killer of Kennedy and King is contacting me from beyond the grave?"

She nodded, watching him closely.

"I don't know, Bettina. I don't know. It would be the granddaddy of all conspiracies, and it begs too many questions. How did they get LBJ to go along? Or was he in it from the beginning?"

"Because LBJ secretly hated Kennedy and King?" Bettina said.

"Enough to kill them both?"

"He became president," Bettina responded.

"He led us into a disastrous war."

"Maybe *they* led him into it."

"Maybe. But who's they?" Whelan asked.

"How paranoid are we?"

At that point the doorbell rang, and they both jumped.

"Plenty," they said in unison. Richard got up to answer the door.

It was Frank Moynihan.

He and Richard shook hands. "You got my message, or is something up?"

"Message. We haven't really looked at it yet. Thought I'd let you know that we've delivered the gun to the FBI labs for any testing they want to do with it."

"You still don't think there's anything to this guy?"

Moynihan shook his head. "With the president speaking at the Lincoln Memorial in three days, I have other things on my mind."

"How is Oracle these days?"

"On fire, I hear. Things are turning his way. This speech is supposed to harken back to the '08 election."

"Wow. That will be something. Obama in full voice again."

Moynihan shrugged. "I tried to warn him off, Richard. But he's just expecting the Service to step up and handle it."

"Not that tough to secure the memorial, right? Who's running the protection detail these days?"

"Sam Redburn," Frank said.

"He's a decent guy from what I've heard. I thought Perkins was next in line?"

"You've been liaising with Treasury too long, Richard. Perkins hates Obama. Redburn rotated in once Oracle picked up an attitude he didn't like."

"Wow. Redburn, huh? Not much of a creative thinker, right? You must be all over him."

"No, I think it's time to let him run the show."

"Really?"

Moynihan nodded. "Yeah. I can't do everything, and if I meddle, it sends mixed messages to the team, and then stuff begins to fall through the cracks."

"Hmm. OK, if you think that's wise. Do you want me to come back from the Treasury assignment? It's in a quiet phase anyway."

"No. Stay with it. It's good career visibility for you, Richard. And I can handle your ghost killer."

"OK, if you're sure. I'll let Alan Christiansen know the rifle is at their labs," Whelan said.

"Yeah, although wouldn't it be something...Still, the memorial is a bitch of a shot," Moynihan said.

"How so?" Bettina asked.

"The fact that it is open space makes it a crowd control problem, but, thankfully, not much of a sniper problem."

"Oh?"

"The nearest high ground is the Capitol building, and that's too far for a shot," Moynihan replied.

"Not even a heavy weapon, like a Barrett fifty?" Richard asked.

"Too far for one of those, even. Plus, a sniper would have to get a weapon up high enough to take a shot. Not easy."

"You called my anonymous guy 'my ghost.' So you still don't regard him as a real threat to the president?"

Moynihan shrugged. "We're taking all the usual precautions and then some. C'mon, ballistics from the sixties? Sam Redburn is good; he'll make sure all the angles are covered."

Richard was mildly surprised at Moynihan's last statement. "So you're really not getting involved in the security for the event, Frank?"

"I'm involved, but I'm trying to take more of a backseat, let my people do their jobs. And speaking of which, given the note that you received, do you want to do Secret Service protection?"

Bettina chimed in. "Are you serious?"

Frank turned toward her. "Absolutely."

"You don't think it's much of a threat, remember?" Whelan said.

"Correct. But you obviously do. So I'm offering, in case you have a case of the willies."

"No thanks. I'd feel pretty weird, and those guys would never let me live it down. Let's just play with the evidence and see what comes out. Like you said, it's probably nothing."

After Frank left, Bettina looked at Richard closely.

"Something's on your mind," she said.

"Yeah, something about Frank just doesn't sit right. The Service hasn't made many mistakes *because* of his meddling style, not the other way around."

"So what are you thinking?"

"I dunno. I mean, he looks OK and says all the right things. But if there was some huge conspiracy to bring down President Obama, wouldn't they have to get to him to have any kind of chance of pulling it off?"

"Damn, Richard, isn't that a pretty big leap?"

"Yeah," Whelan said, and kissed her lightly on the cheek. "It is a very big leap, kind of like believing monsters are lurking under the bed."

Bettina reached over and touched him in a certain way that was always guaranteed to lead them in a certain direction. "I think," she whispered, "that it's been too long since we've been monsters in the bed."

C'mon, Richard, he thought. *Say you love her, at least to yourself…*

***

Moynihan drove back to his house in the dark, ruminating about the day's events. Redburn's planning was solid, if, as Whelan pointed out, not particularly creative. He'd already passed the preliminary Secret Service planning data to his contact through one of his many drops around the Washington area, and now he just had to wait it out. Whoever was behind this was not going to let him off the hook, even after this, he thought.

He wondered whether this was really about race. There were plenty of people around who hated President Obama because of his race, but they would never own up to it. But the way they treated him made it really clear that they didn't respect him—didn't view him as worthy of the office or the power. So that was race, certainly, in the same way a black man, in the eyes of racist whites, could never be smarter than a white man, Obama couldn't possibly be qualified to be president. Unless he had somehow transcended race, which is what some people wanted to believe, at least in the beginning.

Still, the president had inherited a boatload of problems. Depending upon your point of view, you could view him as lucky for having ridden out the down cycle in the economy just in time to get reelected, or you could give him credit for pursuing the banking industry bailout and everything else and having saved the United States and the global economy from a more perilous meltdown. Moynihan thought it was likely a combination of the two. But now the country was worrying about being broke, and Obama refused to get deeper into the Middle East, despite the provocative sea changes in Egypt and Tunisia and others. He wondered if the gun nuts were the ones advocating another entanglement in the Middle East, like Iraq and Afghanistan, just to keep the production lines going in the weapons factories. That would be ironic, although it was equally likely that Big Oil had the money to force another administration into acquiring more reserves the military way. Were those guys color-conscious?

Maybe if the color was green, he thought. Hell, that was what had gotten him in trouble, a couple of pictures with people interested in what he knew about Treasury investigations into counterfeiting and money laundering.

People interested, he thought, and willing to pay.

If it was the money people, either the arms dealers or Big Oil, he could sympathize with the insatiability of their need. He had plenty tucked away because he'd developed such a lucrative practice of selling information about the government to the right people in exchange for suitcases filled with cash. There was no reason for him to have been so stupid as to get caught on camera like some asshole rook, but he certainly had.

So they effectively owned him. At first, the silence had been deafening. He alternately lost sleep over it and convinced himself that they had somehow forgotten about him.

Whoever they were.

Racists wouldn't have the kind of cash to pull this off, he thought. He was putting his money on Big Oil.

CHAPTER 17

New Jersey, January 1968

Alfred Whelan was watching the evening news with his family when the phone rang. His wife answered and held the phone out to him.

"For you," she said, and he ignored the chill in her voice and took the phone.

"Alfred, Roy Wilkens," the familiar voice said. Roy Wilkens was the head of the NAACP. Doctor Whelan, active at the local level, had eventually been "noticed" by the national leadership.

"Roy, how are you?"

"Fine, Alfred, fine. Listen, have you been watching the news? The anti-Vietnam protests?"

"Yeah, it's on now. CBS has a story about some college kids. Flower power, or something like that."

"Hippies," Roy said, and it sounded like *Lepers*. "But that's not the reason I called. I'm concerned about King."

"You mean the antiwar stance?"

"I mean he's gone and pissed off LBJ, Alfred, with all his talk of the moral high ground and how the war is wrong. The man is some kind of a black hippie, and he's going to set things back worse than the Panthers and SNCC put together."

"You think the president isn't happy with King and the Southern Christian Leadership Conference?"

"I know he's not. You ask King about the White House, and the Mouth from the South gets mighty quiet. You ask Abernathy about it, and he defers to King. Nobody else in SCLC knows a damn thing, so if they aren't saying anything, nothing's happening. And that's a problem."

"How so, Roy?"

"King's gonna continue the protests and the marches and pushing southern whites in ways the movement doesn't really need right now. Hippies on college campuses, Negroes in the streets of Birmingham. What's next, Indians riding into Washington on horseback, demanding a new treaty? White people, even the ones who support the movement, are getting concerned that we're caught up in the same law-breaking that the hippies are, and they don't want to bring forth the wrath of LBJ."

"The president has been and continues to be a friend of the Negro, Roy. That kind of talk is just scared white people talking," Whelan replied.

"Maybe so, Alfred, but there are still people whispering about how Johnson got to be president in the first place. Mighty convenient that Kennedy was shot in LBJ's home state."

"You don't think—"

"It doesn't matter what we think, Alfred. Our supporters are watching us, and they are watching King, and they are watching the gun nuts, the Panthers, and that punk Huey Newton. You've seen the posters, haven't you?"

Roy was referring to the poster showing the head of the Black Panthers sitting in a high-backed chair holding guns. It was a best seller.

"Yes, Roy, I've seen the posters. And the rhetoric is poisonous. But I agree, King isn't likely to fade into the sunset of having a dream. And SCLC can still cause trouble."

"We don't need to see any more news shows with fire hoses and guns in Alabama, Alfred. I want to know that I can count on you to talk to SCLC if I need you to."

"Of course, Roy."

"I may want you to see King. In person. You can do that on a moment's notice?"

"Naturally, depending upon my patients. There might be the odd surgery that I have to do, but generally, I can get away for a few days, if necessary."

"Good, good, that's good to know. What do you think about the war, Alfred?"

Doctor Whelan hesitated. Was this a test, or was he expected to speak freely?

"I think," Whelan said cautiously, "that the war is tearing the country apart. The president's best shot is to get the North into a peace process that's going to produce a cease-fire."

"But it's not our fight," Wilkens said definitively. "This is tearing white America apart, and we should stay the hell out of it."

"I don't know about that, Roy," Whelan said, instantly regretting the thought as soon as he voiced it. But he decided he might as well go ahead. "There are plenty of Negro boys dying in that war. I'd hate to think that they're dying for nothing."

"Might be the only hope for some of these kids, though," Wilkens said, "a career in the military. Better than the ghetto, better than the streets in Detroit, or Watts, or Newark. Get the boys out of the cities and away from the no-account, doo-wop lives of street hustlers and make them into something, put some iron in their spines. I bet most of them come back as better men, credits to the race and not an embarrassment."

"Unless they don't come back at all, Roy," Whelan said softly. "A lot of them don't come back, or they come back damaged."

"It's a war, Doctor. The movement must not be a casualty of people like Doctor King. That's all I want to accomplish right now."

"OK, Roy. I'm ready."

Saigon, January 1968

Ming knew not to take any other customers after ten, because The Kid was likely to show up and be difficult if she was with someone else. The American seemed to have a crush on her, and she used it to get things from him, like chocolate and American cigarettes, things she couldn't get from the other GIs.

One of the ironies of the war was that she had plenty of Communists as clients, men who slipped into and out of the capital of South Vietnam with ease and many who had families or supporters near the city. Ming didn't care, although right now she preferred American dollars in order to get American goods, but the Cong still had their needs too.

She was getting bored hanging out in the Shine Bar, looking at her watch and reaching for her pack to pull out another cigarette. It was just before nine, a slow night. As she put the cigarette to her lips, someone else's hand proffered a lighter and nearly cooked her face with four inches of blue flame.

"You must be just back from action, soldier," she said without looking at the man. The lighter had fried the tip of her cigarette instead of simply lighting it, so she concentrated on getting a draw out of it.

"Not exactly," Raoul said. "But I am looking for another good time."

Ming regarded him coolly. This one, she thought, had better pay more. "A good time not cheap."

Raoul ever-so-briefly flashed an impressive wad of cash. "Then I'm looking for a great time, honey."

***

An hour later The Kid showed up at the Shine Bar, looking for Ming. The bartender greeted him warmly, recognizing him as a regular.

"Hey, Quon. Where's my girl?"

Quon placed his usual beer on the scarred wooden bar before responding. He was short and fat, and wore an eye patch that The Kid thought was an affectation.

He also had bad breath. "She leave while ago. Not come back yet."

The Kid was all of twenty years old and had yet to work through his issues with Ming's profession, especially since she'd been his first experience with sex, even after having been in country for three separate campaigns. Since he loved her, or thought he did, he assumed that she loved him. Or, at least, he hoped she did.

Still, she was usually waiting for him in the Shine. Raoul's appearance had rattled him enough that he felt compelled to ask.

"She leave with someone?" It was time to grow up.

"Yeah. Offic'a."

Officer. Raoul rummaging through his stuff, showing him a picture of him and Ming, telling him that she was a pretty girl.

He slammed his beer back down on the bar and took the back stairs, two at a time, up to the rooms where the girls worked.

"Ming!" he started calling as soon as he got to the top of the stairs. There was a black dude leaving one room with a silly grin on his face, from the sex or drugs, The Kid didn't know.

"Ming!" He could hear whispers behind the flimsy screens and thin doors and the grunts of couples in the throes of the act.

No response. He began throwing open the doors and pulling back the screens, breaking a few right off their hinges, revealing blacks and whites and Asians in tangles of sheets, some of the men reaching for gun belts and service revolvers. But no Ming.

"Ming!" he screamed, because she should be in one of these rooms— he wanted her to be in one of these rooms, screwing some big black stud. Just as long as she was alive, he didn't care, he didn't care, dear God, please let her be in here somewhere, with another man...

As if he could pray for anything.

Or she could be with Raoul. Yeah, he could even accept that—that she was having sex with Raoul. Or maybe sharing a cigarette after sex, with that look on her face—the look that hurt him the most when he stumbled in on her with other guys just afterward—like she somehow liked it with these other men. Dammit, he could even take that look on her face if she was with Raoul, if she was alive...

"Ming!" he yelled. He stumbled into the last room at the end of the corridor and stopped cold.

There was blood everywhere. Ming was naked on the thin mattress that lay on the floor, her throat slashed from ear to ear, the blood black against the blue-and-white stripes of the mattress and leaking onto the floor. She'd fouled the mattress as she died, and he turned away from the stink of her bowels. He began backing out of the room, thinking about being careful about not getting her blood on his boots. The thought was funny for a second—he was in the middle of a war and worried about being accused of murder.

As if he could pray for anything...

He was frantic as he searched for Raoul. He tore through the base— looking, walking fast with a .45 cocked and locked at his side—his eyes so wild that people were looking at him and pointing.

He came upon Raoul coming out of the latrine, and Raoul greeted him with a broad smile. The gun came up, and The Kid snicked the safety off and moved closer, placing the barrel of the weapon on Raoul's forehead.

"Tell me," he hissed, "tell me that it wasn't you."

Raoul smiled and wiped his hands on his pants.

"The MPs are going to investigate, once they find the murder weapon."

"You have ten seconds, maggot."

Raoul shrugged. "The murder weapon is going to be a ceremonial knife with the name Lance Corporal Wilton Stiles engraved on a plaque on the handle. Wilton Stiles is the name that you enlisted under, isn't it, Corporal?"

"Shit."

"Yes, as in deep, and you're in it."

"Why? Why did you do it?"

"I told you. We have a job. I can get you out of the country and take care of everything."

"I'm not going to do it!"

"Then listen, because pretty soon you're going to be hearing the high-pitched whistles of the military police coming to arrest you. You'll end up in an ARVN jail, because the Marine Corps won't want any part of you after they examine the body and what you did to the poor girl. If you make it to trial, it'll be a miracle."

"I loved her!"

Raoul pushed the pistol away from his forehead. "She was a prostitute, Corporal. And now you need a ticket back to the world, and I'm the only shot you have. You will come back with me, and you will take this assignment."

"But what about the murder? What about Wilton Stiles?"

Raoul shook his head. "The Stiles identity is as good as dead. Leave everything behind, and come with me right now."

"But—"

"Right now, Kid. You don't have any choice."

"All because you want me to kill this Zorro person?"

"Because we want you to send a message to President Kennedy's brother. Now let's go."

CHAPTER 18

The White House, Wednesday Afternoon, August 24, 2011

Michelle Obama was watching her husband while maintaining a conversation with the wife of an Argentinian diplomat. The president was listening to a high-ranking member of the French government bending his ear about something, and she could tell that her husband was too polite to show his boredom.

He probably wants a cigarette, she thought. He'd given them up over a year ago, but she could tell that he wasn't completely cured. He never said anything to her about it, because he probably knew that she knew, and it was one of those things that they had tacitly agreed would remain unsaid. She allowed it because she kept track of such things, the itemized list of things they didn't talk about, and by her reckoning it was still small enough to be manageable. Manageable, she thought, because she still had a firm grip on where her husband lived inside of his head, and she knew that she and the girls still occupied significant portions of that real estate.

As official meals went, Michelle thought, this one was probably a B-minus. Middle of the week, Camp David coming up if the speech went OK, not a big deal requiring much more than the president's presence in an appropriately tailored suit. They were both always briefed about protocol the morning of such an event, and today that meant that there was no one here who required special handling or preparation.

That also meant that the president was gauging how much of the brief he had left to discharge based upon his job description in these affairs, hence the choreographed seating and the French diplomat now bending his ear. Oh, how much he must want to check the Blackberry right about now, Michelle thought, because he's only here to listen, not to engage. So Barack gets two purple hearts today—one for resisting the arrest of nicotine, the other for not pissing off the diplomat by being rude with his cell phone.

Just then the president looked at her and nodded. The movement was so slight that his conversation partner never noticed it, but in the language of their marriage, it conveyed several messages:

How are you?

I'm fine.

Is the wife more boring than the diplomat?

We don't think like that.

True, but my guy seriously begs the question.

We gonna talk later?

The president didn't know it, but Michelle kept a pack of Marlboro Lights in her purse in case of emergency. She monitored his moods and the climate and the amount of toxic waste the president had to slog through to make sure that her man was OK. She had a short list of events that would trigger her handing the pack and a lighter to the president. French diplomats were definitely not on the list.

So, Barack, you're on your own.

She carried the pack because her husband would be resolute about maintaining his resolve even as his throat got dry with desire for nicotine. He wasn't particularly hooked, wasn't even an everyday smoker back when he'd indulged. But she thought that there might come a time when it would benefit the free world if the man indulged himself, resolve or not.

And then the luncheon was over. The president had a call to take afterward, so Michelle stood alone in the receiving line, bidding the guests good-bye. Barack hadn't confirmed, during their brief glance, whether they were going to talk later or not.

She certainly hoped they were.

***

Richard Whelan called his half-brother on his cell because he needed to talk, and it had been awhile since he'd pinged Marcus.

"What's up, bro?" Marcus Blaze answered. "Recognized the uptight-assed phone number on caller ID."

"Very funny. I was just wondering whether you had some time to grab a cup of coffee between pissing off prosecutors all over the district."

"Aw, hell, Rich, I ain't pissing off anybody who isn't just about naturally pissed off anyway. If we're gonna hit a Starbucks, you be buying, my brother."

"Me? You're the one making the big bucks, Mr. Ambulance Chaser."

"Yes, my brother, but since you never call me 'less you want something, the caffeine is on you. And if you get to the spot before me, I want a grande mocha with whipped cream."

Marcus Blaze walked in, his expensive suit dripping off him like liquid cloth. He set down the alligator briefcase and accepted the steaming cup of coffee gratefully.

"See, I knew you'd get here first. You being Supercop, and stuff."

"What, being Shyster to the Stars just naturally slow you down or something?"

"Nope. Just makes me cooler than you, bro." Marcus chuckled and sat down at the tiny table that Richard had secured in the rear corner of the store.

"So what's on your mind?" Marcus asked.

"Am I that transparent? No 'hey, how you doing' small talk, just, 'yeah, what you want?'"

"When's Tina due?" Marcus said casually.

Richard Whelan did a double take. "You know?"

Blaze shrugged. *She sleeps with you, bro, but she talks to me.* "She told me right after church the day she told you."

"Hmm. She tell you anything else?"

Oh, that she's confused and scared, but you probably have to pick that up on your own.

Blaze shook his head.

"Satisfied?"

"Yeah, I guess so."

"So you were asking me about…" Blaze said, smiling.

Richard smiled too. "About Dad."

Blaze's expression clouded. "We haven't discussed the man in years, Richard. Why now?"

"Curious. How much did you know about him and the NAACP? About him and Martin Luther King?"

"Well, you know that's how he and my mom met. At a convention or something. Dad was up there, for sure, and my mom always talked about how tight he was with Roy Wilkens."

"Did he go see King before he was killed?"

"Yeah, of course. You didn't know?"

"He hinted at it, but he wouldn't talk about it around my mother."

"Because he used those trips to come see his other family." Marcus reflected on how weird that must have been and what being in his father's other home must have been like. Marcus had been the apple of his father's eye, going into law, staying part of the black community, and achieving material success, but not marriage. In that regard he was just like his half-brother—gun shy.

But poor Richard, with his prodigious skills and his failure of a sister...

"And that's why my mother hated talking about it."

And a drunken, pissed-off momma. Marcus nodded. "Makes sense. What's with the sudden interest in history?"

"Doing some research into assassinations."

"Oh, you planning one?"

Richard laughed and shook his head. "No. But someone is, I think."

That stopped Marcus in midsip. "Obama?"

Richard looked around and then gave his brother a "neither confirm nor deny" look. "I've been popularly mentioned as a target, too."

"What, the rednecks pick your name out of a hat to make it worthwhile?"

"I don't know. This one is weird—feels different from an idle threat."

"Oh, crap. I hate it when you get 'feelings.'"

"Yeah, it really sucks, 'cause I'm usually right."

And right then Marcus Blaze had a premonition of his own, and it was so strong it made him shudder.

Someone is going to die. "You need anything, you let me know, bro. OK?"

"Sure, Marcus. Sure."

***

Alan Christiansen was charging through his to-do list in midafternoon when he got a call from the FBI labs. The technician on the other end of the phone was noticeably nervous talking directly to the FBI director.

"Sir, we completed the tests on the firearm delivered from the Secret Service."

Christiansen waited, expecting that the tech would talk him through his conclusions.

Finally, he asked simply, "And?"

"It looks to be a match against the reference work that you, um, supplied, sir."

Christiansen sat up straight in his chair.

"How sure are you?"

"Reasonably sure, sir, although a clearer copy of the reference markings on the bullets from the crime scene would make me happier, but we've worked with worse. This rifle and the rifle that fired the shots in the reference case are one and the same. Sir."

"Do you understand what you're saying, son?"

"Yeah, this King person was killed by this rifle."

"How old are you?"

"Twenty-four, sir."

That explained it. The technician was too young to remember Martin Luther King's assassination. To him, it was just another name—King, M.—on a case file.

"I'm coming over to the labs. I want this information on a complete lockdown. Don't make any notations, make no entries into the case-tracking database."

"No problem, sir, because I already tried and was told there wasn't an active case number, anyway."

Christiansen hung up and dialed Richard Whelan, who answered on the second ring.

"It's Christiansen. What else came in that package with the rifle?"

"A note."

"Where's the note now?"

"I turned it all over to Moynihan. Why?"

"The rifle checks out with the ballistics tests done on the bullets in the Hoover file. Unless this is some sort of paperwork snafu, that rifle checks out as the gun that fired the shots that killed Martin Luther King."

***

Elsewhere, at the same time

Phillip Stone was working on the numbers, something that he liked to do because it kept him close to the business. He and his group of investors, if that's what you'd call them, were the classic insiders. They had knowledge that wasn't in the public domain and would never be in the public domain. They could move the markets; they could make strategic investments; they could make as much money as they wanted to by mining the riches of information that landed at their feet each and every day.

That was the problem with most of his peers, Stone thought. They didn't pay close enough attention to what was going on around them.

He, on the other hand, had a whole intelligence section sifting through the mountains of information that he and his people and his subsidiaries received every day, looking for and finding the patterns that allowed him to peer into the future.

And unlike most, he was able to do something about outcomes that he didn't like.

Neither the Republicans nor the Democrats would be able to agree on balancing the federal budget and reducing the nation's staggering debt. That was clear. The extreme Republican right and the Tea Party were too fringe—and, in his opinion, too unhinged—to appeal to enough people to have an impact. Palin, though shrewd, polled too many hard-core negatives to even be a successful spokesperson.

Nugent wasn't enough of a sure thing to warrant making bets on, although he would be easy enough to steer if he did buck the odds and get into the White House. Europe was a financial quagmire, and Stone already had several significant long-term bets going against the value of the euro, and nothing he saw now suggested changing his strategy or his timing.

And though they had an asset on the board against Obama, Stone knew that the nature of things wouldn't change, and that even a proven asset going against a sovereign wasn't a sure bet.

He needed another hedge, he thought, sitting back. He picked up the phone and dialed internationally.

"Señor Castelliano," he said when the call was answered.

***

Georgetown

Richard was locking his front door when the glass frame around the doorway exploded into shards.

He dropped to the ground a millisecond before another round blasted chunks out of the door, about where his chest had been. Cursing that he didn't have a weapon, he rolled down the steps of his stoop.

Damn, there goes the neighborhood.

In the seconds that this took, he realized that he hadn't heard a sound, which meant suppressed, subsonic rounds, not too far away. He dove into the bushes that lined the walkway to his front door and began scanning the street and the cars on the opposite side of the block.

Nothing. He pulled out his cell phone, dialed 911, and rapidly told the operator that shots had been fired, giving his address.

He was looking for the glint of sunlight off of a gun barrel when a car alarm went off right behind his Porsche. Suddenly, the windshield of the car two behind his exploded, and a line of shells walked up the block, shattering more glass behind the car whose alarm was plaintively wailing.

There was an eerie silence until he heard the sirens of police cars in the distance, approaching at high speed. Richard desperately wanted to get a look at that first car before the police arrived, so he crab-walked from beside his front stoop to the sidewalk.

So far, so good. Now he was behind the parked cars, which should shield him from the shooter, who was probably long gone anyway. He crab-walked in a crouch to the Saturn VUE parked behind his Porsche. The alarm had reset, but he noticed that there was a single bullet hole in the driver's side window.

That explained the alarm. It didn't explain the note stuck under the windshield wipers.

Richard managed to pry the note away from the glass with a pen and spread it open without touching it.

I USED TO HAVE A PRETTY GIRLFRIEND
TOO BUT SHE DEAD NOW

And below it was a pencil etching of a name that Richard didn't recognize, but thought it must have come from the Vietnam Memorial:

LANCE CPL WILTON STILES

He ran back and opened the passenger door of the Porsche and grabbed his Browning Hi-Power out of the glove compartment. The police sirens were louder now, and he scanned the areas across the street, looking farther and farther into the distance to see if he could see anything moving.

Ten seconds went by, then twenty. *C'mon.* Cops were two, maybe three blocks away when he spotted the truck moving in the distance, beyond the tiny little park that gave the neighborhood its bulletproof ambiance.

He fixed the image in his head, ran to the driver's side of the Porsche, jumped in, cranked it, and bounced it off the fenders of the cars boxing him in. He screamed out of the parking space a block in front of the Metro Police units, who squealed up behind him.

He drove parallel to the truck until he ran out of park and ran out of his line of sight.

Downshift!

He cranked the wheel right into a sharp turn, wiggling to avoid a double-parked red Prius, and then stomped on the gas, letting the RPMs blast up toward the red line as the car streaked past seventy-five in second gear.

He ate up the road bordering the park in seconds and then stood on the brakes and cranked into a left turn, onto the street that the truck had used to pass from sight.

He was doing 105 in third gear down a narrow Georgetown street, and he couldn't see the pickup in the distance. That was the problem with the Porsche, he thought, German engineering that made you think you could alter the laws of physics and gravity. The way he was driving was insane.

No pickup. That meant a turn, and he let the senses run in his head, and he then stomped on the brakes and cranked the wheel into a right turn and pulled the emergency brake as well so that the car's rear wheels lost traction and drifted perfectly into the turn.

Nothing! There were stoplights on this road, but there was no truck.

The clock in his head ran down.

Left turn. By now, if he guessed wrong, he was screwed.

He saw taillights as the truck hung a wild right turn.

He followed, but this was a really narrow street, and the truck managed to squeeze by a garbage truck just before it blocked the street.

Richard swung onto the sidewalk, sending trash cans flying and nearly giving an old lady walking her poodle a coronary.

He cut back into the street via a driveway, but he had to kill all of his speed to do so, and the truck disappeared around a curve in the road.

He stepped on the gas and felt the car settle back on its haunches as the g-forces depressed the back springs and pressed him deeper into the contoured racing seat.

He was rolling so fast by the time he hit the gentle curve he was afraid the suspension was going to let him roll the car and that would be it—game, set, and match.

But there was the truck and brake lights again, and then he saw the driver bail out, carrying a weapon.

A rifle.

Richard squealed to a stop twenty yards behind the truck, which had left two ugly streaks of muddy tire tracks across someone's manicured lawn.

He was out of the Porsche in a heartbeat, the gun up and pumping rounds at the man's fleeing back, but his target was juking and jiving so much that Richard knew that he hadn't even come close to mussing the bastard's hair.

Richard got off a string of shots, and he saw the figure go down.

Gotcha! Richard began crab-walking forward. The man had gone down in a field of high grass, and he couldn't see what the hell he was chasing.

Then he heard the shots—soft, little thuds—and a breeze whizzed past his face. He went to the ground as quickly as he could.

The truck alarm went off as the shooter peppered it with silenced rounds. Once the shooter found the gas tank, the truck exploded with a muffled *whuumphf!* and flaming parts began landing in the grass around him.

Richard crawled forward, but he knew that he was likely to be losing ground.

Another fusillade over his head convinced him that he was no match for the bastard with the long gun.

Not today.

He turned over and listened to the stolen truck cooking bits of plastic and lubricating oil until he was convinced that the shooter had gone away.

He went back to his car, climbed in, and left just minutes before the police cars arrived with tires screeching.

***

Alan Christiansen was pacing and looking at his watch when Richard Whelan finally pulled up to the FBI forensics lab. He quickly made his way through security and joined the FBI director in the ballistics test bed laboratory.

"What the hell took you so long?"

"Gunshots. Could have killed me, but didn't."

"Gracious. A drive-by?"

"No. A message. I'm going to get the first note back from Moynihan. You still have profilers, right?"

"Yeah, but they usually need more to go on than a note."

"OK. Were you serious on the phone?"

"Yup," Christiansen said as they entered the lab. The lab technician was waiting for them.

"Richard, this is Paul Regnan, the technician who did the bench tests on the rifle that was sent to you."

The two shook hands. "From what I know, matching a weapon to a crime involves matching the reference marks on the recovered round to those on a test round fired from the weapon," Whelan said.

"That's essentially correct. That's the only way to conclusively match a gun and a crime."

"So let's see the results."

"OK." The technician pulled out some photographs of the test bullet that he'd fired that morning. "As you can see, on this round the markings are consistent with the reference marks. Consistent with what you'd expect from a Remington product, and I don't think the weapon has been tampered with since the rounds in your case file were fired."

"Tampered with?" Christiansen asked.

"Mmm hmm. Your shooter could have replaced or distorted the barrel to change the way the gun marks a round that's fired from it."

"OK. What if I said this was a pretty old gun?"

"Wouldn't matter. This weapon is in great condition. And if this is the original barrel, then I'd say that there haven't been too many rounds fired through this weapon in its lifetime."

Richard said, "Show me the reference rounds from the case file."

Regnan pulled out a piece of paper that was a copy of a copy. "These are the markings that were recorded on the rounds recovered from the victim, in this case, an M. King."

Richard looked at Christiansen, who shook his head, and looked at the photo of the spent round. The photo wasn't dated, but it was marked M. King with a case number.

The markings were indeed very close.

"They're not completely identical."

"That's because a round changes when it hits the victim. The distortion is consistent with others that I've seen, and consistent with rounds that I fired at a hard target to simulate the damage these bullets suffered.

"If this is from your crime, this is your weapon," he concluded.

"Would it help if you had the actual rounds from the crime scene?"

"It's more conclusive, yeah, but I can confidently say this is a match."

Christiansen said, "Are you thinking from a chain-of-evidence perspective, Richard?"

"Sort of. There's no proof that this case file is actually related to this particular case. It's just a piece of paper in a folder with other pieces of paper."

"That's OK. I'm not interested in reopening the case," Christiansen said.

"But you are interested in continuing to investigate this, right?" Whelan asked.

"True, and we have more than enough to do that."

"OK. I'm going to call Moynihan."

Bettina Freeman was in her office when her assistant appeared in the door.

"Yes, Cordelia?"

"You have a phone call."

"OK. Why not use the intercom?" And then Bettina looked more closely at her.

"What's wrong, Cordelia?"

"Your phone call. He said I didn't know him, but he knew me. Told me what I was wearing. And his voice, it sounds weird. Electronic."

Bettina looked at the blinking light and instinctively placed her left hand over her stomach.

"Alert security, Cordelia." She picked up the phone.

"This is Bettina Freeman."

The voice on the phone was obviously being distorted through an electronic device.

"Talk to your boyfriend lately?" the voice said, a hint of a laugh behind the words.

"No, why?" Bettina said, frightened.

"Because I said I was gonna kill him, and I am. Just not today. Good-bye, bitch."

And then the line went dead.

"Mr. O'Shay, Richard Whelan."

O'Shay knew Whelan from his brief time served on the president's protection detail and from the past as well, before he'd started working for the president.

Odd that he would call me—doesn't he work with Treasury now? O'Shay thought.

"Something I can help you with?"

"Possibly. I should have waited and gone through the channels, but I'm not sure this can wait. Frank Moynihan has informed President Obama about the recent threat on his life, hasn't he?"

"Yes, yes, he has. Has something happened that the president needs to know?"

"Yes. One of the more outlandish claims by the would-be gunman appears to check out. That means this is no longer in the realm of some sort of kook."

"Why isn't Moynihan making this call?"

"Because the FBI is handling the forensics on this, and they just got the results."

"What forensics?"

"Are you sitting down?"

"Cut the crap, Whelan. What are you going to tell me—that there are aliens who helped defeat the Japanese in World War II?"

O'Shay looked sharply at the phone as he heard Whelan sigh.

"Something like that. And no, I'm not kidding, Mr. O'Shay. The threat was accompanied by a rifle. Which now appears tied to the killing of Martin Luther King."

Richard finished the call with O'Shay and dialed again.

"Frank Moynihan."

"Richard Whelan."

"Yeah—look, I heard from Bettina, and I understand she's pretty shook."

"Bettina?" Something flopped in his stomach. Bettina and the baby...

"Yeah. You haven't talked to her?" Frank asked.

"No."

"She got a weird phone call. Sounds like someone's watching her."

"What?"

"Yeah, look, I'll do what I can do, but—"

"There were shots fired at me this morning, Frank."

"Excuse me?"

"There were shots fired, and the asshole left me a note that talked about how the shooter used to have a pretty girl too, but now she's dead."

"Uh-oh. I think we should get you a protective detail, Richard."

"They wouldn't have saved me from a hail of bullets, Frank."

"But they may give Bettina some peace of mind."

"I'll talk with her about it. But here's the thing...What if I told you the ballistics of the rifle check out?"

"Check out to what?"

"The killing of Martin Luther King. Alan pulled the FBI files, and there was a copy of the ballistic markings on the round that killed King in it. We compared it to the rifle I was sent, and it's a stone-cold match."

"You're sure?"

"Alan and I are at the lab now. I've seen it with my own eyes."

"OK, OK. I'll update the president as soon as I can get on his schedule."

"I took the liberty of talking to Chuck O'Shay. I didn't want to overstep my boundaries, but I thought someone in the president's inner circle should know about this."

"So you called O'Shay."

"Hey, Frank, I'm sorry."

"Look, Richard, you have to maintain the protocol. Like it or not, the entire Service is in this with you, and if something about this doesn't check out, we all look bad."

"Understood, Frank, understood," Whelan said, not surprised that Moynihan would focus on the politics of the situation as opposed to the threat.

"We also need the original note that was sent to me."

"Sure, why?"

"The shooter this morning left me another message. I want the FBI profilers to take a look at both."

"OK, just get Alan to tell me who to fax it to, and I'll have a copy of the first note faxed over."

"He'll call you directly. Look, Frank, you have to convince the president to cancel his speech."

"I'm not sure that anyone is going to convince him to do that, Richard. The man senses that he's close to sealing the deal for a second term. This is when he launches the electoral juggernaut that is going to carry him through to the election. And he's pretty wound up about the symbolism too, an African American making a stump speech at the site of the 'I Have a Dream' speech at the Lincoln Memorial within days of the anniversary of King's speech. I'll never get him to reconsider."

"You're going to have to. The note, the craziness with the gun, and now shots fired at me—someone is determined to take a shot at the president. And you can't secure any site one hundred percent. You know that, Frank."

"Of course I know it. But the president won't see it that way. He'll ask me what the likely threats are, and I'll have to tell him that he's at risk for some sort of attempt coming from inside the crowd at the memorial, and he'll respond by forcefully suggesting that I keep him safe. And that will be the end of that discussion."

"Look, let's talk about it ASAP. There has to be a way to dissuade him from doing this."

"We can try. But I've worked with the man through a number of these so-called credible threats. He expects us to do our jobs."

"But this—"

"Is too incredible to be believed. And Oracle won't believe it."

"I disagree. This is the rifle that killed Martin Luther King, Frank. Obama will see the symbolism. He has to."

"Fine, I will try. But do me a favor. Let me assign you and Bettina a protection detail."

Whelan said nothing for a moment. Perhaps he was wrong about Moynihan not being on the up and up. "OK. We'll take a protection detail," Whelan responded, hoping that Bettina would go along.

"OK." Moynihan paused. "King, huh?"

"Yeah. After all these years."

"Damn. So do you think the rest of it was true?" Moynihan asked.

"You mean about Dallas?"

"Yup."

"I don't know. But I can't discount it right now."

CHAPTER 19

Earlier on Wednesday, August 24, 2011

The workbench was in a shed at the rear of the property, and he kept it padlocked. The Kid backed the rented SUV up the driveway until the back bumper was only a couple of feet from the weathered wooden door, then got out and opened the rear hatch.

He unlocked the shed door, pushed one of the doors inward, and then entered himself, making sure that the space hadn't been disturbed. There was a workbench and a wall covered with tools and racks that held various rifles and parts. The Kid pulled a pry bar from the tool rack and went back out to the SUV, which was still idling in the driveway.

The crate was heavy, and he had to drag it out of the bed of the Chevy Blazer and drop it on the ground, half in and half out of the shed. He quickly repositioned himself and pulled the crate inside the shed, just in case someone was looking at him through field glasses. Even though it was very early in the morning, he didn't want anyone to get a glimpse of the Cyrillic characters on the crate.

He finished dragging the crate into the center of the interior space and used the pry bar to work around the lid until he could pull the wooden slab back and reveal the contents.

The gun looked OK, but he wouldn't know until he completely stripped it down to its components and checked every single piece of iron and pin. And he didn't have time to do that now, he thought, glancing at his watch. He just had to hope that there were no surprises hidden in that crate.

He went outside to kill the ignition on the rental and get some breakfast.

After breakfast he returned to the shed, still chewing the bacon that he'd grilled for himself. He pulled the chain on the single naked bulb that presided over the center of the floor where the crate sat, the lid halfway off. Parts of the gun were packed in excelsior, and he lifted the packing out and placed the sections of the disassembled rifle on his workbench. He also pulled a box of shells from where he'd stored them, although the shells would be worked on last.

When he was done emptying the crate, he inventoried the parts that he had against what he knew should be there and was satisfied that he had the parts for a complete, working long gun mechanism. The bluing wasn't particularly thick, and he thought that the pieces had felt solid, but he'd have to work them with oil to see if he had any problems.

He went back inside to bring out a pot of coffee and a hotplate as well as his ax, so he could bust up the crate, take it into the Maryland countryside, and burn it to ash.

The contents of the case were, in effect, a custom-made super gun. A gunsmith had taken the action off of an old Soviet PTRD antitank rifle and custom-fitted an American barrel to it, thus allowing the heavy rifle to shoot Soviet 14.5-millimeter ammunition.

PTRD stood for *Protivotankovoe Ruzhe Sistemy Degtyareva.* The sights were offset to the left because it was a single-shot weapon whose barrel recoil popped the bolt and prepared the weapon for the next round.

The old barrels were lousy. American steel and a new tactical scope would allow him to use the 14.5-millimeter ammo. He had a case of type BS-41s, a 994 grain armor piercer. Muzzle velocity was somewhere around 3,300 feet per second, and the round itself was nearly twice as massive as the .50-caliber rounds that he had considered for the job.

He knew he was trading a certain amount of accuracy for long-range stopping power, because none of the ammunition that he'd been able to find was boat-tailed, which would have given it much greater downrange accuracy. But hitting a flesh-and-blood target with a massive armor-piercing shell was death on a stick, and he knew that nothing—no Kevlar podium, no phalanx of Secret Service agents, nothing—would stand up to these rounds.

Nothing.

It took several hours to clean the parts and inspect them closely. He went back and double-checked his work, compulsively touching the parts of the firing mechanism that would have to perform flawlessly, until he was satisfied that each part appeared to be in decent shape. This was the first, most important hurdle, because although he had a rudimentary metal shop here in the shed, he couldn't possibly create meticulously machined parts, and he doubted that any fabricator could have done so and met his Friday deadline. He wiped the sweat from his forehead and glanced at his watch—nearly 10:00 a.m., and he had hours of work still to do. He had to have the weapon ready to test fire tomorrow evening, only a day before the president's speech, because he refused to go into the field with a weapon that he hadn't fired. And he would have to do it at night. He would have to do it in a place where the roar of the huge Russian rifle's ammunition detonating wouldn't wake the dead.

Unpacking the smaller box that had been hidden in the crate, he picked up the tactical sniper scope that he was going to have to mate to the big Russian rifle. Here was the first hint of trouble—the scope had a broken lens, pulverized to powdered glass.

He would have to go back to his sources to get a replacement, and he simply didn't have the time to do that.

But this contingency was why he hadn't killed the dealer yet, he thought.

CHAPTER 20

New Jersey, February 1968

"Dad," Richard Whelan said to his father as an earnest seventh-grader, "there's a thing at school today."

Alfred Whelan was reading the paper and sipping his morning coffee. Mabel was lying down with a "headache."

"I have a heavy schedule today, son," Doctor Whelan said, thinking about how he planned to go to Brooklyn in the afternoon and how he'd already cleared his office schedule to make it happen.

"I volunteered to do something today, Dad. I just wanted to tell you. I didn't want you to come or anything."

"Son, we've been over this. I just need some advance warning. You know I'm a doctor. Patients get sick, and they won't wait."

Richard reflected on the phone calls late at night from his father's answering service, emergencies that required him to leave the house and go to the hospital.

For a second he flashed on that day five years ago when he'd thought his father had gone to Dallas to "fix" the mortally wounded president of the United States. His father was always too busy to do simple things with his son, and his sister was a ho, pure and simple.

"Uh-huh," Richard said eventually in that spooky way he had. "I just wanted you to know that we're collecting signatures on antiwar petitions today."

"You're what?" the elder Whelan said, thinking that going to a white private school had already turned his son into a hippy, like Roy Wilkens had said.

"Collecting signatures. At a shopping center. They said I should get my parents to sign a note saying it was OK."

"Did you ask your mom?"

"She said she had a headache. She said to talk to you."

"Are you against the war, son?" Alfred asked.

"Yes. The war is wrong."

"The war is wrong. Hmm. Why?" he said, more out of idle curiosity than anything else.

"Because the president isn't trying to win it."

Alfred Whelan put down his newspaper. "Excuse me?"

"I'm doing a school project about the war. I've tracked all of the battles."

"And?"

"I don't think we're trying to win."

"So what does your petition say?"

Richard pulled it out and slid it across the kitchen table.

WIN THE WAR OR GET OUT OF VIETNAM
We, the undersigned, urge the president of the United States to make a concerted effort to win the war in Vietnam or retreat instead of wasting innocent lives. Make the generals tell the American people how to do it or end the war NOW.

"Who the hell put this into your head?" Alfred asked, angered.

"What do you mean?"

"What teacher is putting you up to this?"

"None of them."

"Then where did you get this idea?"

Richard hesitated for a moment, as if the question made no sense.

This damn kid is really spooky, Alfred thought.

"It's my idea. I did a timeline of the war in Vietnam and compared it to other wars. I have a map in my room where I plotted all the battles. And I have a scrapbook of as many articles as I could find about the war."

Alfred Whelan shook his head. This was the kid who had written an essay about the Cuban missile crisis when he was, what? In first grade? Now he was trying to change foreign policy as a seventh-grader.

"I don't think I can approve this activity, son."

"Why not?"

How could he explain that he didn't want his son to get noticed by anyone? What would Roy Wilkens say if he found out his son was running around saying we aren't killing the NVA efficiently enough?

"The war is unjust," Alfred Whelan said, the irony of having to take the hippie position not lost on him.

"It's stupid, Dad. That's what I think. It's just dumb, and mine is the only petition that says that."

Alfred Whelan shook his head. "I'm sorry, Richard, I can't allow this. Your ideas are...odd, to say the least."

"Odd?" Richard said, and Alfred could see a surprising level of hurt in the young boy's eyes.

"Yes. I'm sorry, son," Alfred said, looking at his watch. He had rounds in forty-five minutes at St. Barnabas. "Are you ready? We have to go."

Richard nodded, carefully folding the parental consent form into its original rectangle and placing it in his school notebook. His father went to get his coat, and Richard grabbed his ballpoint pen, pulled out the parental consent form, and signed it himself.

He said nothing when his father came back into the kitchen for him.

Early February 1968

They were in a military airlift jet over the ocean on the way back to the States when Raoul told him that the target was Martin Luther King.

What? "When?" was all he could ask.

"We're looking for the right moment. Bobby Kennedy is definitely going to run, because we think Johnson is going to bow out of the race."

"LBJ? No way."

"He doesn't have the stomach for it anymore, Kid. And he doesn't want to get taken out of the Oval Office in a pine box, like they did Kennedy."

"Why would they do that?"

"Because he's thinking about trying to end the war. Our patrons can't let the war end just yet."

"So you think Bobby has a chance once LBJ quits?"

Raoul nodded.

"And you're afraid that he'll find out the truth about Dallas."

"A little. We're more afraid he'll find out the truth about Vietnam."

"And that truth would be?"

Raoul just shook his head. "Mook's favorite expression—FUBAR."

"Yeah. It's FUBAR all right."

"You know Mook was pissed about the setup in Dallas, don't you?" Raoul asked, deftly changing the subject.

"I got the sense that he wasn't pleased."

Raoul shook his head. "Politics and factions. Difficult to control when you have a large group, all of whom have to have their hands equally dirty to prevent anyone from ratting the rest out. It was a screw job, plain and simple. You were never supposed to be in the spot you were put in, and for that I'm sorry, Kid."

He said nothing for a moment, looking out the window and imagining the A Shau in the fog and Dallas in the sunshine.

"Why did you take me, really?" he said, looking at Raoul.

So Raoul told him.

He concluded his story by giving him a telephone number.

"Keep in touch. I'll tell you when we think it's set."

The Kid nodded, not wanting to say anything.

"Oh, and Kid?"

The Kid looked at him.

Raoul put two fingers up to his eyes.

"We're watching you. No games. The next time I have to find you, I'll just kill you."

Raoul dropped his hand. "This time it's just us. No groups, no politics, no factions. Just you and a gun, and a target we want you to get lethal with, boy, OK?"

***

Texas, Late March 1968

The Kid went to his aunt's house and retrieved his rifle. She was drunk, and there was no point in talking to her about his father. Her vacant

131

face didn't react when he showed up at her door. He took note of the deterioration of the neighborhood. This was Texas, after all, and there was oil, oil people, and everything else.

As he was leaving with the long box in his hand, he threw some bills on the table, hoping that she would use the money for some food. She reached for him and took his chin in her hands, studying his face like he was a prized animal or something. Her quivering, wizened fingers finally let him loose, and he worked his jaw to get the circulation back.

"You no damn good," she said, the only words that she would say to him on this last time he would ever see her. "You just like you daddy, a damned disgrace. Get outta my house."

The Kid left all right, the weight of the sniper box even heavier, so heavy his shoulders began to sag. The last time he'd held this particular weapon—**Weapons free! Take him down!**—he'd still been a kid, and now he was a much more terrifying man.

***

Richard came home from school to find his parents arguing. His father was packing a small suitcase.

"I'm sure that bitch is gonna be there, isn't she?" his mother said to his father. She looked at Richard as she said it, as if daring him to react to her language.

"Roy asked me to make this trip," his father said, keeping his voice low and calm as he continued stuffing clothing into the overnighter.

"Roy, my ass, Alfred. It's that bitch who you're going to see."

"No, Mabel, and certainly not in front of the boy."

"He doesn't care about people, Alfred. All he cares about is his models and his maps, and all that other crap he plays with, locked up in that damn room of his."

"Mabel," Alfred Whelan hissed, "how can you talk like he's not even here?"

"Because he doesn't matter, Alfred. He's a freak, and your daughter is a little whore. I hope your other family turns out better, since you spend so much time with them."

"Dammit, Mabel, this is not the time to talk about this. I'll call you from Memphis."

"Oh, come on, Alfred. Roy Wilkens did not ask you to go to no damn Memphis to talk to no damn Martin Luther King. I don't give a crap how high you think you are in the goddamned movement, that is just nonsense, and I don't care if your little brainiac here hears it or not."

"Mom?" Richard asked.

"What the hell do you want?" she screamed, but Richard didn't even flinch.

"Can I have Beef-a-Roni for dinner?" he asked.

"Haven't you heard a word we've been talking about?" she said, disgusted.

Richard just nodded, and then he shrugged. "So I'm not like you," he said as casually as he could, because he had a theory that he could hurt her back if he acted like he didn't care. "But I am hungry."

His parents looked at him in wordless shock.

"Don't worry," he said, "I'll get it myself."

Memphis, March 24, 1968

Raoul met him near the Holiday Inn where Martin Luther King usually stayed when he was in Memphis. The Kid had hopped a freight train to get here. He looked at the building and didn't like what he saw. There was nothing that guaranteed that he would ever get a shot at the target.

"This is the spot. What do you think?" Raoul asked him.

"I think it stinks. Maybe if he has a room on this side, I could find a place to set up and take a shot, but there's no way to guarantee that. Is there some reason why it has to be in Memphis?"

"We have friends here who can help."

"Like you had in Dallas?"

"Dallas and New Orleans, yes."

The Kid looked at Raoul and thought about him raping and cutting Ming's throat and then leaving evidence that his alter ego had been responsible for the gruesome crime. He wanted to kill Raoul more, much more than he wanted to kill Martin Luther King.

In fact, he felt guilty about having to shoot a man who most of his buddies in 'Nam had admired. He'd had a lot of black friends humping the bush in the A Shau. That place was so messed up that the primary racism that existed among the grunts was against the Viet Cong.

"Then if it has to be in Memphis, he has to be staying someplace else. Unless you want me to take him in a public place?"

Raoul shook his head. "Too difficult to control the spin afterward. We need a fixed place to take him so that we can lay down the patsy at the same time."

"You mean you have another Oswald."

"Yes, we have another Oswald. I've been working with this one for a while, and he's going to come to Memphis shortly."

"Didn't I read that King was someplace else?"

"Yeah, but he's going to come back."

"OK, look, if we have to do this here, then I'm going to need some special equipment."

"You mean like a rifle?"

"No. The rifle I have. And make sure your patsy has one that's similar—a Remington bolt-action 700."

Raoul took out a tiny notepad and jotted something down.

"What else do you need, Kid?"

"A helicopter."

***

They found a place where he could test fire his rifle. They started out plinking cans in a big field from thirty yards, and the big bolt action felt good in his hands. In Vietnam, he'd been using a variety of weapons. In fact, he favored a shotgun for close-in work, but the fact of the matter was, if the enemy got that close to him, something was seriously wrong, and he was likely to die. Only one of his hides had ever been overrun, and he'd barely escaped with his life. He still remembered cutting some poor Cong dude in half with his pump gun.

He and Raoul had a couple of beers, and then he moved out to one hundred yards, carefully watching the wind and the flight of his bullets. The Remington was a beautiful weapon, and even after sitting in his aunt's attic for five years, it still fired true.

He pulled another set of shells from the box and began moving farther out.

"Where the hell you going?" Raoul called, not wanting to walk with him farther out into the scrub grass.

"You stay there and set up the beer cans," The Kid called without looking back, because he was keeping track of his steps. It was some minutes before he calculated that he was one thousand yards away from the log and Raoul and the beer cans. They were tiny from this distance, even through the higher-power spotter scope. He'd banged an NVA colonel from nearly a mile away in '66, and the sumbitch never knew what hit him. They had never figured out where the shot had come from. It was a magic trick, and he figured that getting a shot at Martin Luther King at the Holiday Inn in Memphis was going to take a little more magic.

He settled into his position, making sure that he was solid against the ground and as still as he could possibly be. When he had the stock of the rifle firmly seated against his shoulder, he slowed his breathing and tried to remember how it had been in 'Nam when he was providing fire support for reinforcements dropping into a hot LZ. He took a breath, remembering the choppers running in from overhead into a clearing like the one Raoul stood in with the beer cans, the rippling small-arms fire and the chatter of M-16s on full auto as his marine platoon opened up to give the newbies a chance to get on the ground in one piece. One time a group of F-111s dropped a stick of napalm behind his target just as he was about to take a shot, and the bright slash of flame had so distracted him that he couldn't tell if he'd hit the bastard or not.

He took another breath, imagined the noise and the chaos of shooting into concealed enemy positions in 'Nam, and squeezed the trigger.

He plinked the beer cans off the log, one by one, his calculations for the amount his shots would drop and the drift the wind would cause, all done in his head, were all perfect.

It was only when he was done with the cans that he put the cross hairs on Raoul and pulled the trigger on an empty chamber.

Your day will come, bastard, The Kid thought.

CHAPTER 21

Wednesday Afternoon, August 24, 2011

Richard Whelan went to his office in the Treasury department. He'd moved some months ago, once his assignment as the liaison with Treasury had solidified, but he rarely came into the office. He unlocked his office door, went in, and turned on his computer. He lifted the telephone receiver and called the Secret Service dispatch office to inform them that he had released his protection team when he'd walked into the building.

He logged into the White House system, opened an intranet government directory, and looked up a phone number for the Pentagon's central recordkeeping archives.

He pulled the piece of paper with the name that he'd copied from the SUV's windshield and spread it on his desk.

He dialed.

"Archives."

"Hi, this is Richard Whelan with the Secret Service. I need access to an old service record, and I was wondering if records from this era were available electronically."

"This is someone who served in the past?"

"Yes. I believe this person served in Vietnam."

"Sir, a request for electronic access has to come from your supervisor to the Pentagon and be processed by the Joint Chiefs' staffs. I can e-mail you the forms, or you can retrieve them from the Pentagon website."

"Uh, OK. Would it help that I'm a Gulf War veteran?"

"Sir, I only work in the archives office. I don't handle requests for access."

Hmm. Was there anyone on the Joint Chiefs' staffs that he could call to put in a good word for him?

Wait—there was a guy. What was his name? Worked for the Defense Intelligence Agency? Sounded like the board game company. What was his rank? Major. Major Milton Hadley.

He got the number from the online directory and dialed.

Hadley answered and was free enough to take a meeting. Whelan glanced at his watch and decided to head over to the Pentagon now in the hopes of expediting things.

***

Moynihan had sent over the first note Richard Whelan had received with the gun, and Alan Christiansen had sent the second note from Richard's house to the psych group that agents used to profile unsubs, or unknown subjects. Clay Martino was in Christiansen's office going over his results, such as they were.

"Sir, with all due respect, there isn't much to go on. What an unsub writes is useful in the context of a crime scene, and given the crime scenes this guy is talking about, I'd say this is all nonsense."

"He shot up several cars at Whelan's house."

"So he's a teenager hopped up on marijuana and hormones."

"The gun that accompanied the first note checks out as a murder weapon."

"Then get me a case file, and I'll work it from that angle."

"Not possible, Clay. Let's just say that the unsub is a sniper with at least one kill to his credit."

"OK, but that could imply almost anything, depending upon the weapon. How far away was the shot?"

"We don't know, and we can't verify it via any forensic evidence."

"Well, Alan, look. The one thing I can tell you that doesn't make sense is that from the little we have to go on, this guy, and we're assuming it's a guy because of the weapons, is playing games."

"Meaning what?"

"Meaning he's a fairly well-educated person who's trying to seem like he's uneducated, but in fairly obvious ways."

"Couldn't the notes have been written for him?"

"Could be, but not from the contents. His English is good, even to the point that he tries and almost succeeds in making convincing mistakes in his use of language. In the first note, he says 'We killed Kennedy in '63, blah, blah, blah.' Which is ridiculous, but that's neither here nor there. Then, in the second note, he leaves out the apostrophe *S* in 'She's Dead.' He wrote 'She Dead.' Someone who was badly educated would make more mistakes, or less obvious mistakes, and the mistakes would be consistent from note to note. There's too much in these notes that is flawless English for the mistakes to be credible."

"So what are you saying?"

"That this guy is toying with you, and he wants you to find certain pieces of the puzzle. Otherwise, why leave an etching at the scene of the shooting that so clearly looks like it came from the Vietnam Memorial, and contains a name to boot? He's got your attention, and he's leading you by the nose."

CHAPTER 22

Memphis, March 27, 1968

"Put an *X* on the Holiday Inn Rivermont, then draw a circle out to one mile!" The Kid yelled at the pilot while the engines were winding. They were still on the ground, and the chopper's turbine was nearly deafening. The pilot did not seem to understand, and The Kid pointed at the map and traced a circle, and then mouthed "one mile."

The pilot got it. He took a marker and drew a circle around the hotel one mile in diameter. They both looked at the landmarks that were on the side of the hotel where they thought King's room was. There was a water tower that would provide an easy point of reference. The Kid pointed at it, and the pilot nodded.

The helicopter lifted, and they began to fly toward the water tower. The Kid checked the big Remington, although he knew that he had a round in the chamber, and he knew that round would fly true. If he had a target. King had come back to Memphis, and Raoul was supposed to tell them via radio when the civil rights leader was in the hotel and what floor he was on.

The Kid closed his eyes, remembering a day in the A Shau Valley. He could recall the sun, the smell of the fertilizer in the rice paddies, the way the rain had gone, and the way the sun had slanted into his eyes from his hide. He and his spotter were bored after twenty straight hours without any targets.

Ricky "Motown" Johnson was a heavyset black man who'd gotten into the marines on a dare to pick his service before the draft took him into the regular army. Motown, from Detroit, had taken the gangly white boy under his wing once he saw that the honky could shoot.

"Hey, Kid," Motown whispered, motioning toward the rice paddies. There was a woman with a big conical hat tending the fields. She was perhaps a thousand yards away.

"She ain't a target."

"I know, man, but I bet you could put a round through her hat, and she wouldn't even know it."

The Kid chuckled. Motown was smokin' weed or angel dust or something; he was so completely screwed up in his thinking.

"C'mon, Kid, you ain't man enough to put a hole through her hat?"

"I was man enough for your momma, Detroit."

"Oh, please, white boy, my momma'd laugh at that limp white noodle you got. C'mon, man, take the shot. She won't feel a thing."

"Hell no, Motown. Somebody spots us, and then we up to your ugly ass in Viet Cong."

"Kid, they ain't been a gaht-damned bumble bee up in this bitch for damn near a day. What you think, the Cong layin' in their caves waiting for you to let off a round? Take the shot."

"I think this is a bad idea, Mo," The Kid said as he slewed the rifle around the hide. He put his spyglass on the woman, calculating the range as she stood up and stretched her back. She was wearing black pajamas, and the black ooze from the paddy was up around mid-calf.

At a thousand yards, his round would drop approximately thirty-five feet, and there was a tiny puff of breeze moving from left to right all the way down the range from the movement of the trees in the distance. Then the woman bent over, working the muddy soil.

"Screw it, Mo, I'm not messing with it."

"Go on, man, take the shot. Maybe she'll feel it and start swatting at it like it's a bee."

"Yeah, right."

"C'mon, man, lemme watch her eyes go all wide as she takes the hat off and looks at the bullet hole and runs back to her hootch and tells her Viet Cong nigger that some Yankee bitch shot her hat!" They both were laughing louder than they ever should have been when they were in a hide. Motown Ricky Johnson pulled his gun around and pushed The Kid into position.

Chuckling, The Kid put the cross hairs on the woman's conical hat and then pulled the sights up to adjust for the pull of gravity on the round. He'd done this a million times, it seemed, and he never missed. That was the great fun of it, wasn't it?

Mo shut the hell up as he watched The Kid get down into his shooting thing. His breathing slowed down, and his position got as hard as a rock as he braced himself and the stock of the big Remington.

He closed his eyes as the picture from Dallas came back to him, and Raoul's voice over the Hendrix song, but this was OK, today he was just funnin'. His breathing dropped low, and he squeezed the trigger.

It was bad round, with a slight imperfection in the way the gunpowder was packed into the shell. There was a gap in the packing, a tiny gap that reduced the energy that propelled the shell by a tiny amount. The round tumbled, dropping ten inches more than he'd calculated by the time it traveled the thousand yards to the woman in the paddy. It smashed into her face and ripped brain and skull out of the back of her head, leaving a round, red hole where the back of her skull had been and a face so destroyed that the only thing that kept her hat on her head was the bloody string that ran under her still-intact chin. She tumbled backward into the mud of the paddy as he watched in horror.

"Oh, craaaaaaap" was all he could say, but Mo was laughing like it was funny. He lit a joint and passed it to The Kid.

"Either the bitch was Cong, or she was screwing the Cong, or she was feeding the Cong, or she knew somebody who was Cong," Mo said. The hell with that old stupid bitch, The Kid thought, just another piece of old ass the Cong wouldn't be banging anymore.

And then he and Mo got quiet. The Kid waved off the second joint, afraid that he was going to get emotional.

Either the bitch was Cong, or she was screwing the Cong, or she knew somebody who was Cong, he kept repeating to himself. He looked at Motown, but Mo just looked away.

Within the hour, they'd abandoned the hide.

And within a couple of minutes, the helicopter was over the water tower in Memphis, hovering.

Ralph David Abernathy, Martin Luther King, and Doctor Alfred Whelan were in King's hotel room in the Holiday Inn, arguing about the planned march the next day.

"Roy Wilkins send you down to screw things up, Doctor?" Abernathy asked, the hostility in his voice just below the surface. King knew that Whelan was a prominent New Jersey physician and one of the driving influences of the NAACP's criticism of his stance against the Vietnam War. Abernathy was a big man with a gentle nature, but he had little patience for infighting. King, on the other hand, was acutely aware of how his stature in the movement had slipped after the disaster in Chicago and his criticism of the war.

"The NAACP is against more of these grandstanding freedom marches, Dr. Abernathy. With respect, we think the potential for violence is just too high."

"Violence?" Martin Luther King said, as if contemplating the word for the first time. "There may be violence, Doctor Whelan, but if there is I can assure you that it will be the exclusive province of the police."

Doctor Whelan shook his head. "Are you trying to turn Memphis into another Birmingham, Reverend King?"

"No," King said, although the reference to King's fading glory was there if he wanted to see it. The SCLC had failed to create tension and change in a disastrous Chicago march. King and the SCLC had been stoned out of Cicero, Illinois, a suburb of Chicago, by locals determined to fight them and had left without meaningful accomplishment amid negative headlines.

Worse, he had angered Lyndon Johnson with his stance against the war in Vietnam, a stance that his Nobel Peace Prize, as much as his conscience, had compelled him to take. Without the White House, without an effective capability to bring off operations outside of the South...

"Tell Roy Wilkens that the SCLC has yet to set off a single bomb in a black church, or turn a single fire hose on its own marchers. You tell the NAACP that nonviolence is the reason why there hasn't been mass slaughter in the streets, Doctor Whelan."

"What do you call Watts in '65? Or the summer of '67? I was in Newark when it burned, gentlemen. Where was your nonviolence then?" Whelan had fled Newark when the Central Ward burned. Fled the city for the suburbs and a nice white private school for his son, a private school where he was one of the few blacks in the entire school and where the white kids routinely asked his son if he carried a gun or a switchblade.

"Does the NAACP blame us for the unrest last summer?" Abernathy asked.

Whelan responded, "No, but more violence contributes to the view that the Negro is a backward, violent race unfit for the very reforms that you trumpet. And now we risk more violence, more hatred, and for what? Garbage workers? Do we risk alienating the whites who support us for trash collectors?"

"Are you suggesting that these 'mere' sanitation workers aren't worthy of our support, Doctor Whelan?" King asked, surprised that Wilkens would send an emissary with that particular message.

"Reverend King, what I am suggesting is that this is a misguided adventure, just like the Poor People's March on Washington is going to be a misguided adventure. Neither will accomplish anything, and for this occasion, I'm suggesting that you call off your march and regroup."

Abernathy started to answer, but he looked to King to respond.

Yes, King thought, Whelan was all concern and no heart, a good-faith Negro sent here to keep him in check. The Poor People's March was something that he didn't or couldn't focus on right now because he wasn't sure what it was going to be or what format it would take.

And he was in Memphis in tacit response to the radical elements of the movement, the Black Power secessionists who wanted to carve out a little piece of the country for their own private ghetto hell.

Sanitation workers, indeed. Because this was about economics, not about segregation on the buses or in the lunch counters in the South. It was important for all the reasons why Whelan wanted to stop him, important to keep the movement from flying apart into a million warring factions that the establishment would pick off one by one by one, important because the Negro was as much an economic slave as a political one.

"No, we cannot. We are committed to the local movement. If we don't honor our commitment, then SCLC's credibility will crumble all across the South. Perhaps Roy would like that, but we're not going to let that happen."

"Your credibility with the White House has already crumbled, Reverend King. Johnson has been a staunch supporter of the movement. Your grandstanding isn't going to restore your glory, and I wish you'd reconsider."

King shook his head and then smiled. "You think this is grandstanding? Marching for sanitation workers? This is the movement, Doctor Whelan. This is where the movement lives. Not with the educated Negroes, not with the Black Power Negroes, not with the separatists or the Muslims. *This* is the movement."

King turned to Abernathy, and his grin widened. "Actually, we'd like you to march with us, Doctor Whelan. Show the people of the South that you northern Negroes understand the plight of your southern brethren."

Abernathy was stunned, but he knew King enough to simply keep quiet and go along.

Whelan shook his head. "I'm not authorized to participate. I was only asked to come here to deliver a message."

King looked Whelan in the eye. "Then, Doctor, I'm asking the messenger to separate himself from the message and see for himself. Join us—join us in the front or join us in the rear, but join us. You expect violence, then we will show you how nonviolence works. Either be a witness yourself, or take the message back to Roy Wilkens that sanitation workers are as good a cause as any and that marches still work."

Whelan hesitated. The force of King's personality was difficult to resist, the power of his voice compelling even in conversation.

He went to the window to look out, trying to frame an answer.

In the chopper they hadn't heard from Raoul. The Kid put the spotter scope on the hotel, looking at the rooms facing them, trying to pick up King, maybe standing in a window or about to go into the bathroom to take a crap.

But in the spotter scope, the hotel looked like a beehive of a million rooms, and it was difficult to see anything, much less pick out the silhouette of a black man that he could be sure was his target.

"Get Raoul on the radio! I can't see a damn thing!" he yelled to the pilot, and the pilot got Raoul on the horn.

"Try the fifth floor!" Raoul said, and The Kid began looking at the fifth floor, but hell, was the ground the first floor? And how many rooms

144

were there on a floor? Especially when half of them had their curtains drawn?

"Screw it," he said. He pulled the rifle into the sling he'd devised and asked the pilot to hold the chopper as steady as he could.

"Screw it," he said again as he began looking down the scope, looking for some big black man to kill, but he didn't see a goddamned thing no matter how hard he tried, and he knew that they were going to be conspicuous hovering over the water tower.

Then he saw someone—looked like it could be the fifth floor—a someone who was more shadow than human. His finger tensed on the trigger of his rifle as he sighted down the scope and put the cross hairs on the man standing in a sliver of the window looking out. Definitely black, definitely in the cross hairs. He took some more slack out of the trigger as he adjusted to the gentle swaying of the helicopter.

He's black, he's on the fifth floor, and he's in the window.

"Whatcha got, Kid?" his earphones squawked, and The Kid ignored Raoul's voice as he looked down the scope through the distance of the Memphis day and the sway of the chopper. He saw the man looking out, but he couldn't tell if it was King or not. And he remembered the old woman in the rice paddy whose face he'd blown off, and although he took more slack out of the trigger, and more slack, he wasn't sure. He knew that the nigger deserved to die just for being in the wrong place at the wrong time, and he waited for the chopper's sway to time out to where he could put a bullet in the man's brain, thereby teaching him not to stand in hotel windows.

But he couldn't. The curtain dropped, and the tiny sliver of a target disappeared.

He made a slashing move across his throat to the pilot and then called it in to Raoul. The Holiday Inn might as well be a fortress. Helicopter or not, they were not going to kill King if he stayed there.

In the Holiday Inn, Doctor Alfred Whelan stepped away from the window, letting the drape fall back into place, unaware how fortunate he was that he'd only peered out through a sliver of the drapes. He turned back toward King and Abernathy and smiled.

"I'll take you up on your offer, gentlemen. I'm going to march."

King and Abernathy smiled thinly, trying to look pleased.

Raoul wasn't happy, and this nonsense with the helicopter was making him even unhappier. He was going to have to call Director Hoover in a minute to say that they hadn't punched Zorro's ticket, and Hoover probably wasn't going to be happy.

Hoover clearly hated the niggers, but Raoul didn't know too many people that the sociopath did like.

Which was probably the source of his power. The pilot was someone that Hoover had arranged, and Raoul didn't know if he was FBI, military, or CIA, and it didn't matter. Hoover had that way of asking for things, like "Gimme a pilot," that made people nervous—like, does that son of a bitch have pictures of my wife humping the gardener? And then Hoover would just wait for any hint of an objection, and people would think about the Black Panthers getting blown away in "shootouts," and they would think about Malcolm X dead in a hail of bullets in New York, and they would wonder if what they had heard about Dallas was true, and then, poof—out would pop a pilot.

But this whole long-range thing was screwed, and Raoul was going to have a leftover pilot to waste when it was done, because when Hoover asked for a pilot, he wasn't suggesting that the person supplied was necessarily coming back.

Damn, he hated calling. Hoover would be pissy. He put the radio away, because someone was knocking on his door.

Raoul answered it, and the tall skinny man standing there was holding a package.

"Oh, it's you," Raoul said, opening the door wide.

The man began unwrapping the package that he was carrying, and son of a bitch if it wasn't a rifle. Raoul grinned and then looked more closely at the weapon.

Dammit! It was the wrong kind of rifle.

"I said a Remington 700!" Raoul screamed at James Earl Ray. "You'll have to go get another gun. A Remington 700 this time, like I told you," Raoul said, shaking his head. Just as well The Kid had failed, he thought.

***

J. Edgar Hoover put the phone down and thought that maybe this turn of events would be to his benefit. He needed to make some phone calls, and he needed the King section to put together some "not for attribution" remarks for the press and people he knew he could count on in Congress. They had two problems—one was that King was headed out of Memphis after his grandstanding march, and two, he was staying in a fine hotel that didn't allow the forces of justice to kill his black ass.

He'd sold his people on killing Zorro to send a message to Bobby Kennedy, but to Hoover, and the friends he had in the shadows, killing Bobby would be easier than killing his brother had been, and they would probably enjoy it more. In truth, Hoover wanted Zorro, and he wanted Zorro bad.

But the delay.

Well, maybe Bobby deserved to get some funnin' out of it after all.

Memphis, Tennessee, March 28, 1968

King awoke on march day in the Holiday Inn, with Ralph David Abernathy asleep in the next bed.

King got up and went to the bathroom before Abernathy began stirring.

In minutes, Abernathy knocked on the bathroom door.

"Martin, are you ready yet?" Abernathy asked.

"Almost."

"You think this Whelan is going to join us today?" Abernathy asked.

He heard King chuckle. "Sanitation workers. Perhaps not high enough in the upper crust for Wilkens and the talented ten-percenters."

Abernathy snickered. "They mean well, Martin."

"Some of them are worse than the whites. Their dream is for the Negro to be more white and earn his freedom." King splashed water on his face and came out of the bathroom.

"Sanitation workers, David!" King said with a big smile, calling Abernathy by his middle name, as was his custom.

Alfred Whelan showed up in a cab around the same time King and Abernathy arrived at the head of the procession. The crowd was large and restless and stretched back from the leaders as far as the eye could see, some of them dressed in their Sunday best, some of them in sharecropper worst. More than a few American flags were in evidence, along with the unsmiling presence of the Memphis police.

"Doctor Whelan," Abernathy greeted him with a smile. Whelan nodded, glancing over Abernathy's shoulder at the crowds.

"Is everything going to be OK?" Whelan asked.

"We have organizers that will help control the crowd, Doctor. Everything will be fine."

Whelan nodded and began walking back into the thick of the marchers.

"*Can* we keep things under control?" King asked Abernathy, but the organizers answered in the affirmative and began moving through the crowd. King remembered the freedom marches and the dogs and the fire hoses and the signs in protest of the segregationist Jim Crow policies of the South:

Khrushchev Can Eat Here, Why Can't We?

King glanced back again at the large crowd, hearing the periodic catcalls, as he looked for someone to link arms with once the march began. Coretta, his wife, wasn't in Memphis for this one, and Abernathy was cajoling the leadership to keep things cool and to remember the doctrine of nonviolence. King thought of the sanitation workers and grabbed someone dressed in his sharecropper worst with a straw cowboy hat that hadn't been washed since the Great Depression. King asked him to stay in the front and link arms with him when the march began.

Doctor Whelan, farther back in the crowd, came across someone wearing a distinctive Levi jacket, the trademark of the Invaders, a group sometimes enlisted to provide security for Doctor King on the marches.

"What's your role in the march, young man?" Doctor Whelan asked.

The man opened his jacket and showed him a pistol stuck in his waistband.

"Security. They better be cool with us, or we gonna jump bad right in their faces."

"Good Lord," Whelan said, taking a step back as the crowd around them began to inch closer. He looked toward the front of the throng, seeking one of the organizers.

148

The Invader grabbed him by the lapels of his suit jacket.

"You Uncle Tom, you think I'm gonna let the police take a club to my head and just start singing 'We Shall Overcome'?"

The man then turned to the crowd.

"They come for us, we gonna fight back, ain't that right?" he yelled, and some people in the crowd murmured assent.

He turned back to Whelan and pushed him backward. "So go on, little man, and preach that stuff someplace else. We know what we're doing."

But Doctor Whelan broke the man's grip and seized his throat in a surprisingly vice-like grip.

"You ignorant bastard," Whelan said under his breath. "You think you know anything about guns?"

Alfred Whelan hunted as a hobby and had a collection of rifles and pistols in his house. He'd been schooling his son on the proper use of weapons even though the boy was still terribly young.

The Invader reached up and clamped a hand around Whelan's wrist.

"You think you know something about Memphis, asshole?" he whispered just as fiercely.

Other organizers encountered similar people dispersed through the growing thong of people waiting to march. They'd never seen anything like it. A few of them, when they were able to compare notes, thought about calling the march off for fear that things might get out of control and embarrass Doctor King.

But there were too many people, and the organizers feared that calling off the march would be certain to induce an unruly response from the restless protesters.

"Are we ready?" Abernathy asked at the head of the crowd. The leadership nodded, and Abernathy nodded to King.

Martin Luther King looked back over the crowd for a moment and began marching through the streets of Memphis with seven or eight thousand people behind him.

The Memphis police, still stone faced, looked on, appearing to nod to some of the people in the crowd—people who had stones or bricks or bottles hidden in their clothes. A police captain on the scene pulled a note out of his pocket.

Hoover says pick up the pace. Somebody is gonna have to die.

They had gone three blocks when Doctor Whelan saw someone hurl a bottle into a storefront window, and it was like a signal. Other bottles began flying out of the crowd. Whelan ducked, scrambling forward as a cry went up from the crowd and more trouble began almost immediately.

Some storefronts were smashed and goods grabbed even before the marchers arrived, and along the route, the destruction continued even though Abernathy sent organizers back to quell the unruly.

Doctor Whelan was shaking his head as the Memphis police finally waded in, sticks high and swinging. The melee was on. Some of the marchers fought back against the brutal tactics of the Memphis cops, many of whom were terrified that this many blacks would overwhelm and kill them.

At the head of the march, the sounds of the mob became impossible to ignore. Whelan, the NAACP representative, was nowhere to be seen, and Abernathy began getting scattered reports from organizers about how bad it was along the march's route.

When they heard the distant crack of a gunshot, Abernathy's mind was made up. He looked at Reverend King, shook his head, and told one of his people to bring a car around.

King, who was still linked with the old man in the straw cowboy hat, looked back at Abernathy as the cry rose from the mob behind them and realized that they had, somehow, lost control.

Sanitation workers, he thought, angry at the lost opportunity to support them.

But Abernathy was there, breaking King's link with the sharecropper and pushing him toward a waiting car. As King got in the back seat of the late-model Olds, he saw the Memphis police officers pointing at them, their jaws working. One of them had a camera and snapped their picture just before the car sped away to the Holiday Inn.

Raoul, The Kid, and Nick, their pilot, listened to the police reports on a police radio that Raoul had arranged for them to "borrow." They heard that King had bugged out of the march as things went south, and Raoul raised an eyebrow at The Kid, wondering if they should try the chopper again.

"Did anyone report the helicopter the other day?" Nick asked, and Raoul lied and said no, no one had noticed the helicopter over the water tower. The Kid simply shook his head. They needed King in the open, and in a different place. "I think it's a no-go right now, Raoul, I gotta tell ya," The Kid said, and Raoul nodded, because he'd said the same thing to Hoover.

And Hoover had listened.

By the time the march was over, one protester had been killed. The press, as well as the moderate black leadership, blasted King over the failure of the march in Memphis and questioned the wisdom of the Poor People's March, scheduled for Washington DC in the next month.

By the end of the day on March 28, a set of talking points appeared among the press, which decried both the failure of the march and King's "posh" lay-about at the Holiday Inn, especially when there was a fine Negro-owned hotel, the Lorraine, on the other side of Memphis.

"Obviously," the mysterious briefing materials said, "supporting black business is something that King preaches but doesn't practice."

On March 29, as The Kid and Raoul were flying in the chopper, Raoul produced the first of several newspapers blasting King and the failure of the Memphis march.

"Hover, and keep it as motionless as you can!" The Kid shouted into his headset microphone.

When the pilot obliged, The Kid pulled out his rifle and began sighting on ground targets, trying to get used to the noise and the vibration.

Raoul tapped on his shoulder. "You can't be serious about trying to take a shot at him from a helicopter," he shouted, "because this sucks! You won't hit a thing."

That's what Mook said in Dallas. "You just get me a target. I need to know what room, and maybe we send him some flowers or something so he's moving toward the door."

"Doesn't help if the blinds are drawn," Raoul said.

"Then have the maid make sure the drapes are open," The Kid said.

"You're reaching, Kid," Raoul said.

"We need to catch a break here," he replied.

"Might be a no-go. Let's see if King stays around," Raoul said, eyeing the Memphis newspaper.

But Martin Luther King didn't remain in Memphis. He left some-time on March 29 as the press campaign against him picked up. In the coming days, King was lambasted in the nation's capital by Senators Byrd and Strom Thurmond for his planned march on Washington, given the violence and the death in Memphis, and he was also criticized for planning a layover in a "posh" Washington hotel while his marchers would be terrorizing Washington.

Over the next several days, Ralph David Abernathy and Doctor King talked about the march and their failure in Memphis. Roy Wilkens called and blasted Reverend King, based in part on the report from Doctor Whelan about the troublemakers in the crowd. Wilkens said that he was going public with his criticism and that the SCLC should abandon non-violence and the upcoming Poor People's March on Washington.

"And leave the sanitation workers where, Roy?" King had asked, but Wilkens had no answer to that one.

Abernathy was agitated when they hung up the phone. "We should be focusing on the Poor People's March," he said. He saw a cloud pass over his good friend's face.

"I have to go back to Memphis, David," King said, as usual calling Abernathy by his middle name.

Abernathy began to protest, worried that future events would suffer if they didn't focus—but King only tossed the newspaper down on the table where they were sitting.

"And this time, let's stay at the Lorraine Motel," he said, and Abernathy reluctantly agreed.

CHAPTER 23

Wednesday, August 24, 2011, the Pentagon

Richard Whelan walked into Milton Hadley's office and waited while he was announced. Hadley looked up from his phone call and smiled, waving Whelan inside. As Richard settled into a chair, Hadley concluded his phone call.

"So, Mr. Whelan, what can we do for you today?"

"I need some assistance. And I don't want to wait to jump through official hoops to get it."

Hadley smiled. "Yeah, I know some people in the Secret Service who think pretty highly of you."

"So can you help me?" Richard said, worried that Hadley's good humor was going to turn into a run-around.

"I think I can. You want to get a look at someone's file from the archives, right?"

Richard nodded, and Hadley consulted a notepad. "You said a marine, Lance Corporate Wilton Stiles, whom you thought was KIA'd in Vietnam."

"Yes. That's the one."

"Hmm." Hadley opened a desk drawer and pulled out a manila jack-eted file.

"This is the hard copy of his records. I went down to the archives section and threw my weight around a little bit. The full files from this period aren't digitized and never will be. So this is his jacket."

Richard glanced at the folder in Hadley's hand. "So can I see it?"

"That's where it gets tricky, Richard. What I have in my hand is classified as top secret. From what I can gather, you aren't cleared for this kind of material in your current assignment."

"This is a matter of national security, Major," Richard said.

"I understand that, but if you get this file and something comes out of it that you shouldn't have known, then I'm the one who gets roasted."

"This involves the security of the president of the United States."

"So? Let me tell you, Richard; I've never seen the military establishment in this amount of uproar, and Obama doesn't have a clue about the depth of negatives he inspires. Libya, Iraq, Afghanistan, hell, and all the while he's sucking up to the Arabs? Your boss has a Nobel Peace Prize for trying to appease the people who would destroy us. And now you're suggesting that he is at risk, from what?" Hadley tossed the file on his desk. "From this guy?"

"I don't know. All I know is that shots were fired at me, and that this person appears to have something to do with it."

Hadley said nothing.

"Look. If there was some sort of real threat and you did nothing to stop it, would you have done your duty? Or are you going to sit there and let your feelings for the president let a technicality get in the way? Which is it? Are you a patriot only when the person in the Oval Office does the things that you like?"

Hadley fished a pack of cigarettes out of his pocket.

"I'm going out for a smoke. Please don't remove anything from my office."

Whelan waited until Hadley left and then picked up the file.

Lance Corporal Wilton Stiles had enlisted in the Marine Corps on November 25, 1963, claiming that he was eighteen. His enlistment photo showed a kid who looked a lot younger, tall and gangly and awkward, with a shy smile and a face that was half turned away from the camera.

Richard grabbed the pad from Hadley's desk and began taking notes:

Enlisted only days after the Kennedy assassination

Eventually, the young man had requested assignment to Vietnam, and his request had been readily acted upon. Compared to Oswald, who had been identified within minutes of Kennedy's assassination, Stiles had a much better résumé as a killer.

His jacket contained a number of instances where he'd been recommended for commendations and medals, yet Stiles had turned all of them down, serving three combat tours in country. He was a sniper, humping the boonies of the A Shau, usually with a spotter.

Where were you November 22, 1963? Hundreds of people had been standing around in Dealy Plaza that day, yet Oswald was immediately identified as the killer. In part, because someone had found his gun in the Texas School Book Depository. In part, because he'd supposedly killed a Dallas police officer within an hour of killing Kennedy. In part, because he'd gone to a movie, and supposedly entered without paying.

Right after he'd gunned down two people in cold blood, one of them the president of the United States.

And Stiles enlists in the Marines Corps two days later and becomes an accomplished sniper.

Whelan skipped forward to the end of the file. Stiles died in February 1968.

A few months before Martin Luther King was killed in Memphis.

With a gun that someone sent me, even though James Earl Ray had been convicted of killing King.

Oswald was identified as Kennedy's killer within minutes of the assassination, yet FBI agents couldn't identify a single suspect in the bombings that plagued blacks in Birmingham months earlier, or the killers of Freedom Ride activists. Oswald, who had claimed to be a patsy.

Oswald, not a particularly noteworthy shot, kills Kennedy with a crappy rifle and deadly, rapid-fire shooting.

Stiles, a sniper who ends up in Vietnam, enlists within days of the Kennedy killing, requests Vietnam, stays for three tours of duty, and then conveniently dies before King is gunned down in Memphis.

And who used to have a pretty girl too?

CHAPTER 24

Washington, DC, April 3, 1968

FBI Director J. Edgar Hoover got the note from his secretary and glanced at it for a second before thinking about his next phone call. Although it was just a phone call, he wanted to be careful that the recipient got the message.

In the end he just decided to say what he felt and instructed his secretary to place the phone call. The note said

ZORRO back in Memphis ready to fall on his sword

He was quickly connected to Robert Kennedy.

"Bobby, J. Edgar Hoover here."

"Director Hoover, what can I do for you?"

Hoover toyed with the note in his hand.

"Bobby, I just wanted to tell you that these are dangerous times. You understand that, don't you?"

"I understand that times are changing, Director, and the country has to change with them."

"There are a lot of people who don't want the kinds of changes that you liberal boys want. They particularly don't want the Negroes riotin' in the streets of the capital like they're doin' in the South."

"The American Negroes have legitimate concerns. While I don't condone all of their methods, theirs is a cause whose time has come, Director, whether you and I like it or not."

Hoover sighed. *Nigger-lovin' liberal bastards.* "Bobby, you don't seem to be gettin' my message here. There are people in this country who don't want to see another Kennedy in the White House, and who think your candidacy is the height of foolishness. Before you protest, Bobby, let me tell you something. There are men of action in this country, men who will stop at nothing to preserve and protect the Union.

"These are men that you should listen to, Bobby, because your brother, Jack—he didn't listen to them, and now Jack is dead. I don't want the same thing to happen to you, Bobby. But I'm afraid that if you continue, we're gonna be pickin' your brains up out of the street, just like we did your brother's in '63."

"Why you, you—"

"Now Bobby, don't be getting upset with the messenger; you just have to listen to the message. I'm gonna give you some advance news, Bobby Kennedy. And you better listen to the message. Somebody gonna die soon, within the next day or two. Somebody you nigger-lovers think should run rampant over the good white people in this country, somebody who ain't nothing but a sex maniac in minister's clothing. Somebody gonna die soon, Bobby, and they gonna die because you need to know that if you run for president, they're gonna kill you too. Now I'm the director of the FBI, so I know things even though I can't necessarily stop them. And these men of action are determined, Bobby; they are determined not to have no nigger-lovin' liberal in the White House, and for better or worse, you are the very embodiment of everything they fear.

"So watch the news, Bobby Kennedy, and when some nigger dies, just remember that the same gun has a bullet with your name on it, and it's the same gun that killed Jack in Dallas in '63."

CHAPTER 25

Wednesday, August 24, 2011, Milton
Hadley's Office in the Pentagon

W helan read that Stiles was a "gifted" shooter based on his instructor's evaluation in basic training. There was a new sniper program being formed in the Marine Corps, and Stiles was a candidate because of his natural affinity for guns and his ability to make shots from a long, difficult range.

Whelan skipped further into the file and read from one of his commanding officers in Vietnam that Stiles had a "gift" for combat and that he thought the kid should get a medal for all the action that he'd seen. Even more curious, the CO remarked, was the fact that Stiles always underestimated his kills, kills that could be easily verified by other troops in the vicinity of his actions, and more particularly, kills that were verified by his spotter on sniper assignments.

Stiles' last CO had called him the most prolific sniper in the Corps, even though others were racking up triple-digit kills. This kid Stiles was a virtual killing machine who had re-upped so many times that they had started thinking he was indestructible.

Whelan paused to write *"What's he running from?"* before he got toward the end of the file. Sometime in late January 1968, something had gone terribly wrong with Lance Corporal Wilton Stiles. There was the brutal rape and murder of a Saigon prostitute while Stiles was temporarily posted there for an intelligence debriefing on his work in the dreaded A Shau Valley. The killer had curiously left the murder weapon, a knife with a plaque that said it had been presented to Wilton Stiles by his buddies in the 3rd Marine Division. The 3rd Division had been stationed in Vandergrift combat base, somewhere in the A Shau Valley, during Stiles's more deadly tours of duty.

The next day Stiles had had emergency orders cut, shipping back out to the A Shau to rejoin his unit, but he was reportedly killed in transit in early February by a stray round from ground fire as his chopper approached his forward fire base.

The report had been signed off on by Captain R. Sanchez, USMC.

Department of Defense letters of condolences to Stiles's next of kin in Arkansas, where Stiles was supposed to be from, had been returned "Addressee Unknown."

Whelan wrote:

He's from Arkansas but enlisted in Texas. Why?

And then Whelan stopped to think. If "Stiles" was fifteen at the time of the JFK assassination, he would have been around twenty when Martin Luther King was killed. Stiles, a shooter, and a good one at that, had been mysteriously killed in action within a day or so of a grisly murder of a professional girl that he was known to have visited in Saigon. Stiles, who had survived three campaigns without a scratch, conveniently died before he could be questioned about the girl's murder.

He sorted through the file again, looking for other references from this Captain Sanchez, who had signed off on the KIA report on Stiles. There wasn't a single other piece of paper in the file that mentioned a Captain Sanchez. He could have been relatively new in country and could have assumed command of Stiles's unit just before he was supposedly killed, Whelan speculated.

Whelan waited until Milton Hadley returned to his office.

"Thanks for the read."

"Find anything of interest?"

"Not really. One thing I'm curious about. There's a reference to a Captain R. Sanchez of the USMC. Could you pull a service record on him as well?"

Hadley sighed. *In for a penny…* "Sure," he said. "I'll call you when I get it from archives."

"Thanks," Richard said, and he left Hadley's office.

CHAPTER 26

Memphis, April 3, 1968

R obert Kennedy had his staff searching frantically for the where-abouts of Martin Luther King, and it took several hours before they were able to ascertain that King was in Memphis.

But he wasn't at the Holiday Inn. It took more time to locate the civil rights leader at the Lorraine Motel. Shortly before King and Ralph Abernathy left the room for the Mason Temple on the evening of April 3, a frantic Bobby Kennedy finally reached King on the telephone.

"Reverend King," Bobby said in his familiar Massachusetts twang, "this is Bobby Kennedy."

"Mr. Kennedy, how are you? And to what do I owe the pleasure?"

"Reverend King, I've had my staff spend the last several hours tracking you down."

Martin Luther King heard Abernathy in the bathroom splash-ing water on his face, getting ready to go. He thought about calling Abernathy out of the bathroom but thought better of it.

"Reverend King, are you aware of the FBI's efforts against you?"

"Mr. Kennedy, I'm not aware of anything that I can prove, but there are a lot of things that I think are clearly the work of the government, including the FBI, against me."

"Then please listen to me, Doctor King. I've just had the most extraordinary phone call from J. Edgar Hoover. He just about predicted that a major Negro leader was going to die, and soon. Doctor King, you are in the heart of the South, and you are at risk, sir, because we both know that Hoover and his people are not your friends."

"Perhaps Director Hoover was simply trying to scare you."

"He was trying to scare me, all right, but he has to know that I won't be intimidated. He said that the same gun that killed my brother in Dallas was going to kill a prominent Negro, and that if I didn't give up my campaign for the presidency, that same gun would have a bullet with my name on it, too. Now he said this under the guise of the FBI getting tips and threats and such, and that there was a limited amount that he could do about such things. But the way he said it, Reverend King—the way he cursed my brother's grave—leads me to believe that J. Edgar Hoover was not making an idle threat."

"I see." Abernathy was coming out of the bathroom.

"Reverend King? I'd urge you to leave Memphis at once and come to Washington, and I'll have some friends at the Justice Department arrange protection for you and your entourage."

"Martin?" Abernathy said. "Ready?"

"Reverend King?" Bobby Kennedy asked at the other end of the line.

If they wanted him, Martin Luther King thought, they would have him, one way or another, either this day or the next. Too many things had happened, too many bombs had exploded, too many workers in the movement had died or had been beaten senseless. So Martin Luther King looked at his friend Ralph Abernathy and smiled. He said quietly, "I'm sorry, sir, but you must have dialed the wrong number" and hung up the phone.

And in Washington, DC, Bobby Kennedy hung up his phone, furious and frustrated. He turned to his secretary and said in a low voice, "If anything happens to Reverend King, I will crucify Hoover when I'm elected president."

***

Martin Luther King stood to address the Mason Temple in Memphis on April 3, 1968, the phone call from Bobby Kennedy on his mind as he listened to Dick Gregory thank him for his work in the movement. He surveyed the crowd, expectant, looking at the American flags that stood in the limp air at the back of the temple. He thought about William Moore, a white postal worker shot and killed while marching to deliver a letter imploring Governor Wallace to end segregation during the height of the freedom marches in 1963; of Viola Liuzzo, a white Detroit housewife gunned down because she had given rides to freedom riders in Alabama. He thought of JFK gunned down in Dallas while his wife looked on in horror.

He thought of four little girls killed in a Birmingham, Alabama, church bombing while they attended Sunday school. He remembered leading the Selma march, with police and national guardsmen and helicopters overhead, and the people with their signs and American flags. He thought about the threats and the audiotapes, the FBI and their hatred of change, and of law enforcement and their hatred of the movement. Last, he thought of all the other people who had died, and those who would die, and he realized that as one of the leaders of the movement, he was liable to die as well, phone call from Bobby Kennedy or not.

Khrushchev Can Eat Here, Why Can't We?

As he heard the thrumming beat of a helicopter's rotors over the Mason Temple, he thought of the guns and the Air Cav in Vietnam. A chill went up his spine, because he had only the vision, the dream, and they had the bullets and all of the guns they needed. Of course he'd come out against the Vietnam War, of course he'd argued for peace, because he'd seen firsthand what his government could deploy against people of color.

The helicopter sounds faded as Dick Gregory concluded his opening remarks. King stood up, surveying the crowd, the hopeful faces, the expectant waiting audience of people, and realized that they would have to go on without him at some point, whether he died tomorrow or in a hundred years. And they would go on, he reasoned. The only thing that he could do was what he'd always done: give them his words, his vision of a new future, the future that he'd seen in the teeming crowds around the Reflecting Pool during the first march on Washington, during his "I Have a Dream" speech, the future that they would have to carry through the crackle of gunfire and the heated denial of their humanity. And so Martin Luther King stood, on the last full evening of his time on earth.

Once more the chill in his spine returned, even as his voice rose, and when the thrum of the helicopter's rotors passed again over the temple, as if the pilot were searching for something, he willed away the vision of men with guns far above, targeting him. He thought of a hymn that he hadn't sung in years:

> *Just as I am, without one plea,*
> *But that Thy blood was shed for me,*
> *And that Thou bidst me come to Thee,*
> *O Lamb of God, I come, I come.*

He thought again of Chicago and the failure of the SCLC to get results in a northern city. Could it be that his time was fading?

Could it be that he was sliding away into irrelevance, that his stance on the war and his alienation from the White House had relegated him to the backwaters of marches for sanitation workers? Could it be that he couldn't see into the future because the future was to terminate this very evening? *O Lamb of God, I come, I come.* Would the peace movement, the very essence of nonviolence, end in a gunshot? Would all his fears and flaws die with him in an instant?

And as King spoke of the mountaintop and the promised land, he understood, sadly, that for him it was quite possible that the pinnacle had passed, at least on this earth, and that violence would continue to be a part of the world even as he'd shown how unnecessary it was. That in fact the fear and hatred and loathing would always be a part of the world as long as it served somebody's purpose. In that moment of extreme clarity, to him the whistling of bombs from the open bays of B-52s sounded no different than the hiss of high-pressure fire hoses, and the inevitability of the sunset of the old day giving way to the dawning of the new would never be without casualties, without sacrifice. So many had died, and so many more would; it mattered not how the message of hatred was delivered, or to whom it was delivered. Triumph was a matter of faith, not of power. *O Lamb of God...*

As he ended his remarks to a thunderous ovation, King imagined that he would hear the shot that killed him if it was from someone in this crowd, like they killed Malcolm X, but in reality, he didn't hear a thing, not that evening—

-nor the next, when he died.

CHAPTER 27

New Jersey, April 1968

T he Whelans watched the world explode as word of King's assassination spread. Mabel Whelan said nothing as Alfred Whelan stared, a silent tear trailing down his cheek.

She handed him a tissue as Richard looked on, the wizard behind the curtain in all her booming glory.

"Please don't tell me you were in Memphis."

Alfred Whelan looked at her. "Roy Wilkens asked me to get Doctor King to cancel the march and the march on Washington later this year. Mabel, you don't need to believe it for it to have happened."

She stared at him. "And you never bothered to call me to tell me where you were or where you were staying."

Alfred Whelan looked away.

"So did she go with you?" Mabel Whelan asked, and Alfred said nothing. "You and your damn whore. Richard, you know your father has a girlfriend?"

Richard looked at her, knowing there was no response that would stop what was coming. Instead, he decided to shut her out and concentrate on the screen, where someone was throwing a Molotov cocktail at a police car. The screen said the pictures were somewhere in Detroit.

"Richard, I asked you a question."

He steeled himself for the insult that was likely to come next, carefully closing down every access that she had to hurt him. I don't care, I'm not like you, I'll never get married, he thought over and over.

"Richard, you goddamned little freak, I asked you a question."

On the television, whatever the rioter had thrown smashed against a police car and exploded in a gout of flame.

Richard looked at his mother and said, as clearly as a twelve-year-old could, "Mom, why are you being such a bitch?" She slapped him, knocking him off the couch and onto the plush carpeted floor so hard his head bounced and he saw stars.

I don't care, I'll never get married, Richard thought, because I don't know what love is, and I never will...

CHAPTER 28

Wednesday, August 24, 2011

Bettina Freeman was coming from the specialist's office humming a happy tune. The mood swings of pregnancy were nothing less than manic, and today was one of the days that she felt like she could float away, or, at least, solve the problems of mankind. Her OB/GYN checkup had gone great; the baby looked great. She knew, due to an amniocentesis that she'd had done without telling Richard, what sex the child was going to be, and she planned to spring it on Richard in as devilish a way as possible.

She was walking back to her car, swinging her keys, when she became aware of another set of footsteps echoing behind hers. Her doctor's office was in a midrise building surrounded by a concrete parking structure. She'd come in during the early afternoon when the closer spaces had been packed, so she had a bit of a walk to get to her silver BMW.

There weren't many other cars parked near her, and she quickened her step and began thinking about the pepper spray she had in her handbag. Or was it Mace? She was wearing flats, and she wasn't showing much, so could she run to her car?

The steps behind her increased their pace, seeming to gain on her. She chanced a look back and saw a man with a baseball cap pulled low on his forehead. He was looking down so she couldn't see his face. He was not thin, but athletic, and moved with a certain amount of confidence.

And she had about thirty yards to go before she got to her car.

She stopped and faced him, pulling her cell phone from her bag and dialing 911. He walked on, directly toward her, his face turned to one side.

"Metro Police Emergency," the 911 operator said in her ear.

The man walked past her, apparently headed to the only other car nearby, farther out than hers was.

"Never mind, operator. My mistake." She closed the phone and continued on toward her car.

Richard Whelan debated returning to his office as he waited for Hadley and any information that he had on this Captain R. Sanchez. It seemed like a waste to sit there and wait for the phone to ring, but maybe he could check with Moynihan to see if he'd been able to talk some sense into O'Shay about the president's speech.

His cell phone rang as he was wheeling his Porsche out of the Pentagon lot. He recognized Bettina's number.

"Hey, how was the appointment?"

"Fine. I've got a secret, though."

"Really? Are you going to let me in on it?"

"Maybe, if you buy me a really expensive dinner."

"Expensive, she says. What did you have in mind?"

"That new place that opened up in Georgetown, Grogan's."

"I don't know anyone who's been there for the food, Bettina."

"The food is cool. It's the movers-and-shakers atmosphere that I'm interested in."

"This must be some secret."

"You'll see."

"OK. What time?"

"Umm—" She hesitated. "That's odd."

"What?"

"I dunno. Car behind me is acting a little funny."

"Funny how?"

"I'm not sure."

"Is he following you?"

"Could be. He just blasted through a yellow light to stay with me."

"Where are you?"

"On my way home."

"I'm leaving the Pentagon. Can you drive in my direction?"

"OK. It'll take me awhile, because I'm already past the easiest route."

"Don't worry. I'll pull off the road right near the first lot entrance for the Pentagon."

"OK. See you in a few."

Bettina was driving fast but within the speed limit, programming the satellite navigation system in her BMW to take her to an intersection near Richard. She had to hit the overrides several times in order for the unit to let her do data entry while still driving.

When she finally had the location locked in and had the system calculating the best route, she glanced at her rearview mirror.

The black sedan that had been following her was no longer in sight.

Damn, she thought. Another false alarm. She cancelled the navigation and picked up her phone to redial Richard.

"Yeah, where are you?" Richard said as he picked up the phone. He jammed his Bluetooth headset against his ear and dropped the phone on the seat next to him.

"The funny farm, I think. I don't see the car I thought was following me anymore. Maybe I'm going through a mood swing."

"Either that, or it's a team that's following you," Richard said, regretting it the instant the thought left his mouth. A team would mean a conspiracy, just like the one that had killed Kennedy, and King, and—

"OK, Bond, what should I do?"

"Are you still coming toward the intersection I told you about?"

"Uh, no, because I cancelled the navigation system when I lost the sedan that was following me."

"Great. I think you should reprogram your little toy and get over here as soon as you can."

"Yeah, OK, but Richard, you know this thing doesn't like Washington."

That was certainly true. Because of the odd street patterns in the capital, Bettina's sat nav system had a habit of getting confused. He'd ridden with her when the damn thing had them literally going in circles.

"Give it a shot anyway. It shouldn't take you more than twenty minutes to get to me."

"OK. I'll call you…"

"Bettina?"

"Uh-oh."

"Bettina, what's wrong?"

"Now it's a tan minivan. Ran a light, two cars back."

"Once you get close, I'll pull out and drive toward you," Richard said grimly. He regretted having blown off his Secret Service detail to come to the Pentagon, thinking it would be safe. Clearly, Bettina needed protection too, but he'd deferred to checking with Bettina first before asking Moynihan to authorize it.

Worse, he realized that Bettina would always be a target for someone who wanted to get to him. Bettina, and their child…But who wanted him?

He accelerated, more intent than ever on reaching the intersection where he was supposed to meet Bettina.

The Kid was in the black sedan, which had swapped places with a tan minivan, which had handed off to a green Ford Explorer, which had then shifted the lead back to him.

It was fun having resources for a change, and he'd made it clear to the impromptu group of amateurs that he wanted Ms. Freeman to see them on her tail, which the succession of vehicles had accomplished easily.

By now she had probably been on the phone to her boyfriend, who would be coming toward them as fast as possible. This was always good, because he liked the notion of playing tag with someone like Richard Whelan.

He moved up until he was on the silver BMW's tail and flashed his high beams just to make sure Bettina saw him.

Her brake lights came on and then she sped up. *Yup, she saw me.*

"All units," he said into his cheap radio, "break off the pursuit. It's just me from here on out."

And then he smiled.

Richard's phone rang again.

"Dammit, Richard, it's the black sedan again, right on my bumper!" Bettina yelled, and Richard could tell she was on the verge of hysteria.

"OK, calm down, Tina, calm down. When we hang up, dial 911, and give them your location and direction of travel, OK? Ask them to send a marked unit out to escort you."

"OK," she said, still breathing hard but beginning to settle down.

"OK," Richard said. "I'm at the rendezvous point, so even if the police don't reach you, I'll cut the bastard off. Once I do that, drive to the nearest police station."

"Why don't I just do that now?" she asked, the fear creeping back into her voice.

Because I want to get a look at this guy, he thought but couldn't say.

The police scanner on the seat next to The Kid came to life, and he instantly became more alert.

"All units, vicinity of Rock Creek Park, silver BMW being pursued by unsub driving a black sedan requests an escort, all units vicinity of Military Highway please respond."

Well, well, The Kid thought. That would seem to be an invitation for gate crashers to come to their party uninvited.

He'd stolen the plates for this occasion, and it was good that they didn't have a better description of the car.

Bettina had turned right and was at a stoplight. *Aha—that should buy me a few minutes because she hasn't communicated her change of direction to the police yet.*

He pulled up behind her.

Oh no, Bettina thought, he's right behind me!

Just as the light changed, the black sedan lurched forward and tapped her bumper, and then it engaged and began pushing her into the intersection. Bettina's right hand flew to her mouth as she suppressed a scream just as the sedan disengaged and turned right, burning rubber as it pulled away.

She pulled the BMW over to the opposite curb and put her blinkers on. As she got out of the car, she pulled out her phone to call Richard and the police.

***

The Kid considered the afternoon's mission to be a success and retired to consider the problem of zeroing the new scope on the Russian rifle. He'd screamed at his supplier about the scope and had gotten a new one within an hour, no questions asked.

He'd paid off the people he'd used to follow Bettina in cash. None of them could be traced or could lead the police back to him. Amazing, he thought, what you could find in Internet chat rooms.

He chuckled at the consternation he was causing Richard Whelan and Bettina Freeman. *I used to have a pretty girl too.* He smiled, ignoring the darkness and the loneliness. *She used to be real damn pretty.*

He still had the persistent problem of testing the rifle and the scope, though. It was Wednesday, two days to go before the president's speech, and he needed to test-fire as many rounds as he could to zero the scope and the rifle. He could find some place in the woods and hope that he didn't bring down the law when he started plinking cans or bottles. From a couple of miles away, the 14.5-millimeter rounds blasting away from the muzzle would be a supersonic fist, rushing to put a world of hurt on the target and probably everything behind the target for another city block or so.

Or…he could have some more fun with the pretty girl.

And a wicked smile crossed his face.

***

Wednesday Evening

"Sprinter is entering the restaurant," the Secret Service agent said as Richard Whelan and Bettina entered Grogan's. He had a team of two, and he had specifically kept them around after Bettina's trauma this afternoon.

They waited while the maître d' scanned his list for their reservation.

"I don't get it," Bettina said. "He tapped me, didn't do any damage to my car, and then sped off. What was the point?"

"He likes attention," Richard said.

"I'll say. Maybe I should carry one of your guns," she said, glancing sideways at him.

"I don't have one that would fit in your purse."

"Damn."

"And guns are loud."

"Double damn."

"And pulling a gun in a fight means that you are irrevocably committed to using it. Otherwise, you run the risk that it gets taken away and used against you."

"OK, OK, Crime Dog. You've convinced me."

The maître d' consulted his seating chart and handed two menus to a hostess.

"Right this way, Mr. Whelan."

The hostess led them to their table.

The restaurant was filled with Washington's power players; Richard had seen at least three senators and two cabinet-level appointees of the Obama administration either at the bar or seated for dinner.

Bettina nodded to several people as they were shown to their seats.

"Ah, I forgot you were the power player, Ms. Undersecretary of State."

"I voted for Hil," Bettina said, chuckling.

"Very funny."

There was a flat-screen television with the sound turned down near their table that was showing one of the cable news outlets.

"Too bad you couldn't get us away from the Republican broadcasting company," Whelan said.

"Deerfields has always had a hard-on for the president," Bettina said.

"Yeah." Richard looked at the screen and did a double take. "Is that Minister Reinier they're interviewing?"

Bettina looked. "Yeah. Hmm. He must have said something they like."

Whelan shook his head. "Reinier hasn't been in the news much lately. Wonder what he said." The Nation of Islam had been relatively silent throughout Obama's presidency and hadn't been much of a media force for a long time.

Their waiter came, but Bettina shooed him away.

"What's the matter—can't decide on how many of the steaks you're going to need?"

"I am hungry, Crime Dog. Don't push your luck."

"I hear they have doggie bags the size of shopping carts here. So please, a multiple-entrée night won't even faze the platinum card."

Bettina just smiled as she buttered a roll.

"So what's the drama with being followed and stuff?" she asked. Whelan had been waiting for this and had carefully prepared his answer.

"Moynihan has agreed to put a team on you as well."

"Really?" Bettina said.

"You've now been threatened twice, even if indirectly."

"Yeah, but why? Who cares about me?"

"Someone does. Has to be related to the threats."

"OK," she said, skeptical, "but the question is still why."

"To push us to do something."

"Uh, *hello,* Crime Dog. To push *you* to do something."

"Oh," he said, suppressing a half smile, "what happened to 'we'?"

Bettina patted her stomach. "My job is to stay healthy and get fat with a kid, Crime Dog. That's as much 'we' as I can handle. The James Bond stuff is up to you."

The waiter came back, and they ordered. Whelan was surprised that Bettina ordered only soup and a salad.

"Are you gonna have a steak for dessert? If so, we better get them to drop the side of beef on the grill now."

"Nope. I am going to eat sensibly until the hormones tell me not to. So, since this isn't a particularly hormonal night, you get off easy."

"Maybe we should have you chased by strange cars more often."

"Goodness, Richard," she said, putting down the half-eaten roll, "you just really, really, really don't want to get laid tonight, do you?"

Later they exited the restaurant arm in arm.

"Everything OK?" the lead Secret Service agent asked as they left the restaurant.

"You might say that," Richard said, glancing at Bettina. "You feel like dessert, really? We could always try Balboa's, three blocks over." He turned to the Secret Service agent. "You know it?"

"Yeah, sure, I—"

And then his chest exploded, spattering them with blood and entrails.

"Get down!" Richard screamed, pushing Bettina to the ground.

This time he was packing, and the Browning automatic was in his hand in an instant.

The second agent was running toward them, having gone to get a cup of coffee.

Richard motioned to him to get down, but he heard a distant roar, like a cannon booming in the distance and then another roar, like an incoming artillery round's Doppler shifting to a higher frequency. The second agent's head disintegrated. Bettina started crying and screaming, staring at her hands that were covered in blood.

He went to her and pulled her close to a parked Chevy Equinox, hoping that the steel and mass of the car would protect them.

He hugged her, feeling the blood smearing his jacket as her arms went around his neck.

"Stay down," he whispered, checking the Browning to make sure a round was in the chamber.

He heard that sound again—the cannon booming—and a fist-sized hole appeared in the door of the Cadillac three cars down from them. Bettina screamed again as the car rocked back on its suspension.

Three successive booms came, and the Caddy's car door exploded off of its hinges, crashing to the sidewalk in a hail of broken glass and metal fragments.

"We have to get out of here!" Bettina screamed, and Richard began smelling gas. Gas, he thought, because the bastard shooting at them had dinged the Caddy's gas tank.

"We're running on three," he shouted, "OK?"

She nodded when the distant booming sounds echoed again. Flames erupted from the gas pooling around the ruined Cadillac until the gas tank *carumpfed!* and exploded, lifting the carcass of the car off the street and flipping it on its side.

Richard and Bettina ran, seconds before a fist-sized hole appeared in the door of the Chevy Equinox they had been hiding behind. Its windshield exploded.

Gunshots and crunching holes followed them down the block until they were out of breath.

The Kid whooped and hollered and prepared to move. Easily a mile away from the entrance of the restaurant, he quickly covered the smoking gun with the tarp lying in the bed of the pickup truck. Under the tarp, he collapsed the tripod that had supported the Russian rifle and laid the weapon flat on the bed of the truck.

He looked around, hoping there was no one in the vicinity; the truck was stolen, and he was wearing black. He got into the cab, secured his seatbelt, and chuckled once.

He cranked the engine and drove away.

CHAPTER 29

Late Wednesday, August 24, 2011

They were interviewed by the police for hours, it seemed, and Richard was unable to provide much in the way of details. He didn't know where the shooter had been, although he speculated that it had been a long-range shooter, with a very high-powered weapon. He started to speculate and then thought better of it, in part because he knew what a Barrett fifty-caliber rifle sounded like, and this guy's gun sounded different. And, given the results, that was scary.

***

Michelle Obama watched the news and saw the story about the two Secret Service agents being killed outside a popular Georgetown eatery and decided that she had put off talking to the president long enough. She picked up a white phone in the residence and had the operator patch her through to Chuck O'Shay.

"Mrs. Obama?" O'Shay answered.

"I need to speak with my husband tonight. Cut something out of his schedule and get him to the residence within the hour."

"Michelle, we're still talking about the comments from the Nation of Islam."

"They can wait. Did you see the news? Grogan's?"

"Uh, no. What happened?"

"Two Secret Service agents were killed. Tell the president, and tell him he and I need to talk tonight."

President Obama was making notes on an iPad when O'Shay came into the Oval Office without knocking. The president looked at his watch.

"I thought I had another twenty minutes or so, Chuck?"

"You did. But Michelle wants to talk to you and won't take no for an answer."

The president smiled the way only his wife could make him smile. "Who lost out to the First Lady?"

"Nothing important. It's getting late anyway. But I think you should know that your wife saw a news story about two Secret Service agents being shot to death outside of Grogan's in Georgetown. What with Moynihan changing your daughters' protection detail and the supposed threat, she's probably going to bend your ear about the speech on Friday."

"Given the Nation of Islam's comments, I think the speech is more important than ever, actually."

"No argument from me, Mr. President. But I've been hearing some rather strange things in the background."

"Like what?"

"Like a weapon has been recovered that has been implicated in the shooting of Martin Luther King."

President Obama settled more deeply in his chair and dropped the stylus he was using to take notes in the iPad.

"Moynihan's threat. Surely you're joking."

"No, Mr. President, I don't think I am. Frank Moynihan has been on the list to get into see you as well. Likely to tell you that bit of news himself."

"And you think Michelle knows this?"

"I doubt it. But now you're going to have to tell her."

"Thanks, Chuck. Thanks a lot."

"Hey, you're the president of the United States. The buck stops on your desk. The plans for limited nuclear war and the truth about Area 51 are yours for the asking."

"I'm going to need Secret Service protection to tell Michelle this, you realize that, right? And she will not be happy about me going through with the speech."

O'Shay shrugged, and he and the president shared a private smile. "We can always tell you about the aliens instead."

"Very funny. Any other platitudes?"

"Love means never having to apologize for trying to save the free world?"

The president sat down and picked up his stylus. "Get out, Chuck. Please tell Michelle I'll be up in ten minutes."

"OK. I'll make sure Secret Service is in the residence in five, locked and loaded."

"Not funny Chuck. This needs an FBI hostage rescue team too."

O'Shay chuckled. "Good night, sir, I'm heading home."

***

The Kid was back in his work shed, cleaning the rifle. The new scope was fine and the rounds he'd purchased were OK, but he planned on modifying them a bit. One of his shots had gone lower than he thought it should, which meant that he would repack the charge in each and every shell that he expected to fire at the president. It wouldn't take long and he'd budgeted the time, but he had to get the weapon into position. Given his demonstration tonight, it was much more likely that the Secret Service would cover the scaffolding around the top of the Capitol and the statue at the top of the dome.

It was going to be close, but he was confident that he would make it.

***

Richard called Alan Christiansen at home and woke him. Christiansen's wife answered the phone, recognized Whelan's voice, and passed the handset over.

"Sorry to wake you, but I think the president needs some unofficial help, Alan."

"Beyond the Service?"

"Things are developing too quickly. The president is likely in grave danger, and I can't stand aside and go through channels. I just can't."

Christiansen sat up in bed, searching for his reading glasses and a pen and pad of paper. "What happened?"

"Someone just took a dozen potshots at me and Bettina with what must have been a very large rifle."

"Large? Like a Barrett fifty?"

"I know what one of those sounds like. This was different."

"You OK?"

"Bettina is freaked, and I don't blame her. This is the second time today that she's been targeted by this lunatic."

"Really?" Christiansen said, and Whelan recounted Bettina's encounter with the black sedan earlier in the afternoon.

"Jeez. This guy has a hard-on for the two of you. Why?"

"I dunno. I'm clearly a target, but Bettina appears to have some weird psychological draw for him."

"What happened to your Secret Service protection?"

"Dead. Both of them. Blown directly into the crapper."

Christiansen was quiet for a moment as he said a silent prayer for the agents, who, after all, were part of the law enforcement fraternity.

"Do you want an FBI detail?"

"No. I'll stick with Frank's people."

"What does Moynihan say?"

"Dunno. Haven't been able to raise him yet, but his people are here because of the fatalities."

"Here as in a police precinct?"

"Correct. They just released us. I knew these guys, Alan."

"I'm sure you did."

"They were still wet behind the ears."

"You can't blame yourself, Richard."

"Yes, I can."

"One other question: Where was the shooter? How far away was he?"

"They don't know. The police say there's no spent brass anywhere nearby, and if you draw a circle around the restaurant, he could have been anywhere. There's a clear line of sight out to well over a mile. Because of the caliber of the rounds, it's not going to be possible to triangulate his shots because these mothers punched fist-sized holes through metal and glass and they were tightly bunched. Neither the police nor the Service seemed to know much about the weapon."

"If it was a distance shot, you're thinking that this opens up the possibilities for someone shooting at the president," Christiansen stated.

"That's what I'm thinking. This was a 'catch me if you can' demonstration."

"And so he targets Bettina and you?"

"He's claimed I'm a target from the beginning. And he keeps demonstrating it. I can't fathom the motive, but the means—yeah, big check mark."

"Are they replacing your detail?"

"Yes. And as soon as I get to Frank Moynihan, I'll ask him to put a team on Bettina as well."

"Is someone going to talk to the president?"

"I bet several people already have, but I'm going to try and make sure."

"You don't think he should go through with the speech then."

"No. But this is the president of the United States. The office, the man, can't hide behind a wall of agents forever. So whether he speaks Friday or in six months doesn't matter. Someone is going to make the attempt.

"And I'm not waiting on protocol to do whatever I can to protect him."

***

President Obama kissed his wife and told the steward that he'd like a light snack delivered to his office in the residence in forty-five minutes. Michelle waited patiently as the president removed his tie and unbuttoned the top two buttons on his crisply starched white shirt, and for a moment she imagined the fine cotton fabric stained with his blood. She turned away.

The president made himself a gin and tonic and motioned Michelle to join him on the couch in the main living area. They both ignored the television set muted in the background.

"Michelle," the president began, and she silenced him with a finger pressed to his lips and then kissed him on the cheek.

"We talked about this, Barack. What it would mean if you won, what it would mean if it looked like you would be successful in winning a second term."

"And nothing that has happened has been a surprise."

"Really? You had such high hopes after the election, and look at what's happened."

"I know, I know. But it's not so bad."

"Isn't it? Those idiots in the media wake up every day and demonize you in every way possible, in every way short of using the n-word, and there are wide swatches of the public who lap all of it up, every single lie.

"And God forbid that you make a mistake. God forbid that you do something unpopular. I know you think we will win again, but is it worth it?"

Barack Obama took his wife's hand. "There's something you need to know."

Michelle said nothing, her eyes widening.

"The Service thinks there may be a real threat against me, with an attempt possible at the speech on Friday."

"That's why they changed the protection rotation for the girls."

"Yes."

"And? Barack, I know that look. There's something worse that you're not saying."

"There appears to be a connection to the past. I haven't been fully briefed yet, but I didn't want to keep you in the dark on a technicality."

"The past?"

Barack Obama nodded. "Yes. The past."

"As in?"

"Martin Luther King."

"What?"

"I called Moynihan just before I came up. He confirmed what Chuck mentioned to me when he told me you wanted to see me. With the threat came a number of outlandish claims. And a weapon. A rifle.

"A rifle the paperwork suggests was the rifle that killed Martin Luther King."

***

Frank Moynihan was sitting in front of the television alone and didn't bother to respond to the ringing phone. Ordinarily, on the eve of a big speech, he would be working the phones and a pot of coffee, but not this time.

One of the cable news channels aired the shooting at the restaurant, and he sat back in his chair. He glanced again at the photographs his blackmailers had sent him and barely suppressed his anger. The phone stopped ringing for a second and then started again. Somewhere in his light jacket in his closet, his cell phone started ringing, and then his pager started going off. He muted the television, listening as his entire communications suite erupted in urgent ringing. He took a sip of warm beer, wondering if Biden would want him to stay on if Obama died. Maybe he could show good ol' Joe Biden the blackmail photo as a reference, he thought darkly. One by one, his cell and his pager and his home phone went silent, and then they started up again, one after another. Moynihan could practically conduct the sequence of rings from his chair like a conductor.

He'd already talked to the president, he thought. Gave him the news about the gun. Now he had to call the families of the two agents killed tonight.

Finally, he raised his beer to the blackmailer's photo and arranged his communications devices in front of him, wanting to close his eyes and pick which one he answered first at random.

Not that it mattered in the slightest. Next to the blackmail photo was the new message that he'd gotten today. It was one word:

FRIDAY

And he knew all too well what it meant.

***

Chuck O'Shay got home and turned on the cable news broadcast, noting that there had not been any new developments since he'd checked before leaving the White House. He could only imagine how the president was faring with the First Lady right about now.

His phone rang, and he picked it up, thinking it was the president.

"Chuck, it's Richard Whelan."

Oh, Christ.

"Yeah, Richard. What now?"

"Have you heard the news?"

"Yeah, I'm watching channel thirty-six now."

"They were shooting at Bettina Freeman and me."

Chuck O'Shay sat bolt upright. "What did you just say?"

"The shooter was using Bettina and me for target practice. That's why Secret Service was at the restaurant. My Secret Service guys are dead, killed by the sniper."

"Wait, it was Grogan's, Whelan. There were probably multiple teams in the vicinity—"

"The shooter killed them both right in front of us. Then practically chased us out of the area."

"Jesus, Whelan. You and Bettina…"

"We're fine, but Tina's pretty shook up."

"Good, that's good. Get back to her and take care of her, Richard," Chuck said, trying graciously to end the call.

"Chuck, you've got to get the president to cancel his speech. This at least establishes that the nut writing me notes is serious and deadly."

"Secret Service is all over the security arrangements, Richard. Let the protection detail do its job."

"Don't be stupid, Chuck. Two professionals were guarding Bettina and me, and they're headed for closed-casket funerals. I'm telling you, this guy is packing some kind of serious firepower, and the president is going to be in a heap of danger if he goes ahead with his talk."

"Moynihan hasn't said to pull the plug yet. He's still your boss, isn't he, Whelan?"

"Yes, he is, but this is the second time this unsub has used me for target practice. And Bettina was tailed this afternoon."

"Then maybe this is about you, Whelan."

"But then there's the rifle, Chuck. The rifle says that it isn't about me at all."

"Then what do you think it is?"

"This is some kind of decades-old grudge or something, or maybe the racist right is finally going to do what they can't seem to do at the polls, which is finish Obama off."

"Look, I don't know what you expect me to do, Whelan, but at the end of the day, it's the president's call."

"Yeah, Chuck, but let me ask you something. Is the criticism about the president simply about his job performance? Or is it something deeper?"

"What are you trying to imply?"

"That these people have an *agenda*. Do you or anyone else seriously believe that the conservatives and the Tea Party people would have gotten anywhere near the traction they've gotten if the president wasn't black? All this crap about his birth certificate? Sarah Palin?"

"Nation of Islam?"

"What—oh, come on, Chuck, you know that's just a splinter group with a bone to pick. Some of these news guys will say that if Obama got up on the left side of the bed, he should've gotten up on the right. And if he got up on the right side of the bed, they'll say he should have gotten up on the left. I've never seen anything like it, Chuck, and if you're honest, neither have you."

"What's your point?"

"He's vulnerable. The presidency doesn't let him call this environment what it is. He can't call them racists because of the weird racial politics in this country. But that means he's running blind, because if he can't call it what it is, then he won't understand how deep it runs. Think about it, Chuck—they sent me a rifle that tests out as the murder weapon of Martin Luther King. Do you understand the depths of what he's facing? The decades that this hatred has been building up? And the irony of killing him at the site of King's greatest oratory about the equality of people? Killing him so that he not only echoes King's words but his fate as well?"

"Sorry, I don't buy it. This is about a threat, not about race relations. In the end the Secret Service will do its job and keep the president safe. That's all that counts, conspiracy theories from the past notwithstanding."

"And that's exactly my point. *This is a credible threat.* This isn't business as usual; this isn't beef up the president's detail or have the president wear Kevlar. What I heard and saw tonight is a game changer, Chuck. If we don't start running scared, this thing will eat us and the president alive."

"Listen, Richard, I hear you, but the president is his own man. He's going to make the decision, and he's going to do it based upon what he thinks is right. He doesn't panic; he doesn't get flustered. And I tend to think a dusty old rifle isn't going to dissuade him."

"Then look at it this way, Chuck. JFK in 1963, Ford in the seventies, Reagan in the eighties. All of them were shot at—one of them died, and Reagan nearly died—despite tight security that tightened up after each incident. Despite reviews of Secret Service procedures that came after the fact and revealed critical flaws in the protection schemes or the reactions of the professionals. If Moynihan were straight, he'd tell you himself that no protection scheme can guarantee the safety of the protectee. The best bet is to keep the target out of harm's way whenever you detect a credible threat."

"So you're an expert on presidential security now? How long were you on the detail?"

"No, Chuck, I'm the guy who just got shot at by a maniac who just killed two people who weren't expecting the threat. Two professionals. I'm saying that the system is going to be loose, because it's been thirty years since an incident forced the review of their processes. This guy is going to exploit the 'business as usual' mode of operation that the Service has been in. Hell, he's probably expecting it. If the president gets up to the podium on Friday, he's going to get shot at, and if he gets shot at, he's going to get killed."

"Richard, you're obviously upset. Calm down, and we'll talk in the morning."

"Chuck, if you can't convince the president to cancel, get me in to see him. The note said we were both targets, and the nut has been all over me."

"OK, I'll see what I can do," O'Shay said as he hung up.

It might be up to Michelle now, he thought.

Michelle was listening to her husband calmly discuss the threat against his life, thinking that this was the very worst of a series of bad nightmares. The president was talking as if this were a threat to the presidency that had to be faced down, not as a threat to their children, and, not coincidentally, her.

For a few moments, she didn't allow herself to think about the past, about the shocking losses that the nation had suffered, between two Kennedys, King, and a host of other leaders. All lost to the guns of history and for what? The memories of a wounded nation, a family shrouded in black during a rainy funeral procession, and too many tears to quantify?

For what? For the bastards who weren't half the intellect the president was, or half the husband, or half the father, or half the leader?

The president wouldn't bow to the irrational fear that gripped her, because failure wasn't in his lexicon, and fear wasn't something that he could articulate, even if he were more intimate with what it meant.

No, she couldn't express what she felt, what terrified her, because the president would simply attempt to calm her down because he would think that he was right. This was his blind spot, his weakness, and of all the things that Michelle Obama feared, it was the one thing that she knew in her heart of hearts would get Barack Obama killed—his inability to account for the irrationality of others.

And what if it wasn't irrational? They had the gun that killed Martin Luther King, for goodness' sake. This was a page out of a playbook whose pages had been read and studied before. As she listened, she forced herself to step back and think about something besides the obvious, that it wasn't simply because of her husband's race but something deeper, more insidious, something about him that was far more threatening than his black skin and questions about his citizenship. *They didn't kill King because he was black. They killed him because of the power of his words. And a man with the same beliefs and the power of the presidency would be terrifying to some people.*

That meant, Michelle thought, that her husband was going to die. In that moment of absolute clarity, she looked around at the trappings of power, the residence of the White House, the knowledge that someone from the military was not more than twenty feet away with the codes that could commit the United States to nuclear war, and she realized that his was the illusory presidency, perhaps just the latest in a series of illusions.

"Michelle," the president said, snapping her from her reverie. "You just went somewhere."

"You don't want to know where I just went."

And Obama cocked his head at his wife. She's seen something, he thought. Some other iteration that he'd missed.

"You didn't buy a word I just said."

Michelle shook her head, treading carefully. "You think that no hill-billy with a gun is going to kill you. That isn't it at all—that isn't what we're looking at."

"What is, then?"

"These people presented you with a calling card that says they are serious, long-term thinkers. If they are to be believed, they killed a president and got away with it. They killed Martin Luther King. They killed Bobby Kennedy, or at least, maneuvered someone into place who killed him. This isn't some racially motivated vendetta against people of color, Barack. Parts of it, participants in it, may have been about color. But this is about power. They will kill you because you're in someone's way, dear."

"So you think I should cancel the speech."

And Michelle Obama looked in her husband's eyes and made the biggest gamble of her life.

"No, I don't think you should. They won't stop just because you deny them this opportunity. Now that we know, we have to smoke them out."

"How do you propose we do that?"

"Not us. Find someone in the Secret Service you can talk to. There must be someone who can look at this from a different angle, someone smart enough to get answers, if not Moynihan. There was that brilliant guy on your protection detail early on who rotated off into investigative work. Talk to him, if you need to get a fresh perspective."

CHAPTER 30

Early Thursday Morning, August 25, 2011

Richard dropped Bettina off, resisting the notion that he should spend the night. He assured her that there was a Metro Police unit right outside her door and then went back to the Porsche, seething inside that someone was using him for target practice.

Moynihan was still offline, and Richard hoped someone had told him that two of his agents had been killed. Richard felt horrible about that, felt horrible that he hadn't thought more about the Secret Service personnel who had stopped very large bullets for his benefit.

Worse than all of it, he was angry that he couldn't see the reason why the killer—or killers—would announce themselves like this, first with the shootings outside his house, then with tailing Bettina, and finally with the attack on the two of them at the restaurant.

And then it hit him.

How *had* the killer been able to track them so effectively?

***

Several Hours Later

The *Washington Post* was covering the preparations for the president's speech and the tight security that would be in place at the Lincoln Memorial. Richard Whelan was reading the piece, looking closely at the pictures, wondering how the assassin was planning to pull it off.

He went to his computer to pull up a map of the National Mall, recalling what Moynihan had said about the tight security and the metal detectors that would prevent anyone from getting close to the president with a gun.

Unless the assassin was suicidal, he had to be planning to get away somehow, yet the Mall was huge and flat and open, and he was sure that Secret Service agents would be working the crowds and the perimeters of the mall.

But there was no place to set up to take even a reasonable shot.

Richard shook his head. He was missing something. Something critical.

Why had the killer stalked Bettina and fired on them outside of Grogan's? Was he simply testing his gun?

He recalled the distinctive booming sound of the rounds as they zeroed in on the shooter's targets. He'd thought it was a Barrett fifty, but those sounded different.

He began pulling books from his shelves, looking at something that was even bigger than a Barrett fifty.

The White House

Chuck O'Shay knocked on the president's residential office and then stepped in.

Barack Obama was sitting at his desk, working on his speech with one of the senior speechwriters.

"Gill," O'Shay said, clearing his throat, "could you give us a minute?"

Gill nodded and gathered his materials.

"I'll be outside."

"Chuck?"

He looks ready, O'Shay thought. "Mr. President, did you by any chance see the news this morning?"

"Sure. Are you talking about the 'Obama's folly' stories, or something else?"

"I was really talking about the shooting outside Grogan's."

"Michelle and I talked about it. Suggested I talk to Richard Whelan for some perspective if I needed it. I thought about it, and I'd like to meet with him."

"Really?" Sometimes the man was just spooky, O'Shay thought.

Obama nodded. "I'm not going to postpone the speech."

"Really. Well, sir, I think it bears thinking about. Either delaying or changing the venue."

Obama shook his head. "This is where it all begins again, Chuck. I'm going to plant a stake in the ground that says four more years and dare the Republicans to come after me. This is going to be a game of catch me if you can. Assuming I start on Friday, the Republicans will never catch up."

"What if there is someone out there with the means and the intent to do you harm? This is what Richard Whelan believes, by the way."

Obama simply smiled. "That's why I want to meet Whelan. Because I assume he's right. And I have to believe that we have twenty-four hours to catch a killer, and Whelan is going to help us do it."

***

As he watched O'Shay leave the residential office, Barack Obama thought about letting it all hang out and telling like it is.

Or could be.

He looked at the phrasing and the structure of his remarks. He should call Gill back in and get to work on firming up the middle section. He was aiming to take no more than forty-five minutes—forty-five minutes to try and seal a second term.

He wondered why someone thought that he was worth assassinating. Was he a King, someone who could change the course of world history with the power of his rhetoric? Was he a Kennedy, someone who threatened the establishment by refusing to go along with Vietnam? Was he a Bobby Kennedy, someone who would run to bring his brother's killers to justice?

Or was it really about race, and Michelle was in denial? No, his wife had great instincts, and he trusted her first among his advisors. This was about something deeper, something more primal than his skin. He wondered if he would be able to find it in a day. Or, if he didn't find it, he wondered whether it would cost him his life.

CHAPTER 31

They were in the living room of the stately home his family had occupied for many years, sitting under a crystal chandelier within a few footsteps of his father's office.

"So what about Doctor King?" Richard asked, as anxious to break the silence as his father.

"We all killed him. The government. The FBI. The Negro conservatives who criticized him."

"I don't get it, Dad. You said Roy Wilkens sent you to Memphis to talk to him, not get him killed."

"That's true. Roy thought he was a grandstander, trying to get back on the stage after his time had passed. The 'I Have a Dream' speech was a fading memory by the time I met him, and he'd spooked the establishment blacks by blasting the Vietnam War. That was like blasting President Johnson, and when King did that, a lot of people ran for the exits. Roy sent me to Memphis to try to talk Doctor King out of having a march and out of his march on Washington that was planned for later that spring."

"What did you think?"

"I thought the march was completely out of control. Some little bastard threatened me with a gun, and I wasn't surprised at the violence that broke out during the march. There was widespread looting, and of course, the police needed no excuse to start cracking heads."

"But this was Martin Luther King, Dad."

"Yes, son, I know. But we were the black intelligentsia, and we looked at King with the same dismay that we looked at Stokley Carmichael and the black power boys. Kissing up to the white establishment, because we were the closest thing to the black establishment. We were 'Upstanding Negroes of Accomplishment.' But it was also 1968. The cities would burn again when King was killed; the memories of the long, hot summer of '67 and Watts in '65 were too fresh in people's minds. And then Bobby Kennedy was assassinated, and it seemed like the echo of gunshots would always hang over the country like a pall. Roy and the conservatives wanted no part of the controversy over Vietnam, and a lot of them privately said that Doctor King was killed because it was simply his time."

"What did you think when he was killed?"

Richard's father said nothing for a second.

"I was afraid, pure and simple. Afraid that one day they'd come for all of us. And what could we have expected when they did? Oh no, nigger, you wearin' a suit, you're OK? We were the house niggers of the movement, Richard, the conservative colored people wearing suits and content that we had ours."

So was it so surprising, Alfred Whelan thought, that his son was taking this one step farther and embracing a career in law enforcement, of all things?

His father looked at him, and Richard couldn't read his father's expression. "I'm urging you, Richard, don't join the Secret Service. The establishment has blood on its hands."

"Why? We've already had that discussion, Dad. I've already accepted the offer."

"Because I don't trust those sons of bitches, Richard. I don't trust them at all."

"But you said the conservative blacks were just as much to blame for King's death as whoever killed him."

"So?"

"So what does that have to do with my career choice? What are you trying to tell me—do as I say, not as I do? I'm not a 'programs for the poor' person, Dad. I believe in self-determination, and I believe in being strong. These are the things that I learned from you, and now, what? You want me to repudiate them? It's a little late for that, don't you think? A little late and a little unfair that you want me to make up for mistakes you think you made."

There it was, Alfred Whelan thought. His son had just pointed out the edge of the cliff leading to the abyss of his infidelity. The good doctor could do nothing but back away.

"Look, son, I'm telling you that too many people died in the movement, and too many of them were white. Your government turned a blind eye to their deaths. Your government, your FBI, your Secret Service let Kennedy die in a hail of gunfire. I don't *trust them, and I know there is no place for you in their ranks. You get in there, and you will find an establishment that's rotten to the core, and worse, racist—not because of hatred but because of convenience. We are the inconvenient truth, Richard, not part of this nation, and unable to separate ourselves from it. There is no revolution, son; the revolution died in Memphis, and it died in Dallas, and it dies in the ghetto every damn day at the hands of some racist cop. You mark my words, son. Mark my words."*

CHAPTER 32

Los Angeles, June 3, 1982

Officer Brad Hollister rolled over and waited to see if he was going to puke or not. He assumed the position, sitting on the edge of his bed with his head down between his knees and waited the customary thirty seconds to see if this was a gorge-rising morning or whether his stomach was stable enough to risk standing.

At the twenty-five-second mark, he decided that he was not close to upchucking and stood slowly, waiting for the world to stabilize and for his sense of equilibrium to return.

So far so good. He stripped off his tighty whities and went to the shower, calculating that he had about twenty minutes before he was at risk of being late for the morning roll call. God, how he hated being on days. It was almost as bad as being on nights. He adjusted the shower temps and stepped into the grungy tub, noting that he was overdue in cleaning the place up a bit. The kitchen didn't smell. That was usually the drop-dead signal to throw out the accumulated fast food and other crap that tended to pile up when he was on a semi-bender.

This time, though, he hadn't felt much like eating. For most of the last week, he'd been heavily into the whiskey, usually at Cobbs, one of the cop joints he frequented downtown near the Parker Center.

As he showered, he wondered about the application that he'd put in for the out-of-state gig he currently was pinning his hopes on. He was thirty-three years old, and he had no prayer of making detective in the LAPD. That meant that his career in law enforcement had to take a detour if he was to continue climbing the ladder. Assuming that's what he wanted.

Assuming.

He stepped out of the shower, his skin feeling raw and red from the needles and the heat, and wrapped a towel around his waist as he went to the kitchenette and started water boiling for coffee. He went back to the bathroom and began to shave, noting that he was still in good shape despite the binges and the junk food, although, with the appearance of a tiny roll around his waist, he knew that he was too old to continue like this before he began putting on the spread that would eventually mark him as middle-aged.

Screw that, he thought. *Forever young.*

He finished shaving and brushed his teeth and looked himself in the eye in the mirror. He held his hand at shoulder height to judge the amount of shakes he was exhibiting, which were minimal. If there was ever a voice in his head that told him to switch back to beer, he would take it, because the whiskey thing was not his cup of tea, and yet he was downing a hefty bottle of it every night.

He hadn't told his partner about his issues because his partner didn't care. Something was going down in the neighborhoods of South Central LA, something huge and ugly, but the official bureaucracy had yet to take note, and Hollister thought it would be years before it was noticed, if ever.

But whatever it was, it was ugly. And it would, if he was right, get really ugly before anyone began throwing rocks at it, and by then it would be a monster.

He slicked back his hair and looked himself in the eye again. You will get out of this OK, he said, even going so far as to mouth the words to himself and nod his head in agreement.

He was a survivor. Always had been. And he would get out before the demons on the streets of South Central LA made him eat his service revolver. Two guys in the last six months had already taken that road out.

So, he reasoned, this time his out-of-state shot would come through. He would count on it, he thought, and he would ignore the darker side of his mind that said he was going down with whatever was washing over South Central LA; that was his fate; that was his destiny.

He would check the PO box after his shift, he said to himself, promising himself that it was just time for a routine check, certain that if there was something in the box today, he would be man enough to take the outcome, whatever it was.

He checked his watch as he walked into the kitchenette to make his coffee. He still had just under ten minutes.

In fewer than five, his partner was banging on his door, wondering if he was ready to roll. He opened the door with a mug of coffee in his hand.

Which his partner took, drained a third of, and then handed it back to him.

"You still can't make coffee worth a damn." Timo Banks was a big guy, easily six-six, an ex-high school football star who had lost his scholarship to USC because he wasn't fast enough.

"I love you too. Gimme five seconds, and I'm ready to roll."

"You look lousy, Hollister. Better lay off the dope and the whores. You are one of LA's finest, part of an elite group of law enforcement professionals."

"And corrupt to the core."

"And damn proud of it. C'mon, I don't wanna be late for roll."

Hollister slurped the last of his coffee and dropped the mug in the sink after he rinsed it off. The roach scale was about a two on a critter scale of ten, so he was cool with it. He glanced back at his place and then locked the door, ready to face another day.

"Got some people I want you to meet," Banks said when they were rolling.

"Are they blonde, at least, with fairly impressive jugs?"

"No. Nor are they gay and looking for a good time. This isn't about your joint, Hollister."

"I figured that. Then it must be about money, Timo."

"Got it in one. You won't have to get your hands dirty, just some people you should know."

"Yeah, yeah, that's what you said the last time."

"What, you got complaints? Issues?"

Hollister didn't answer for a second. They had taken down a fairly big reefer dealer, guy with a couple of pounds he was distributing from some dump in the hood. It had been nothing but money and guns in the tiny apartment where he and his girl were bagging the stuff up for distribution. Guy's name was Henry, and when they had busted in on him from a tip, and he'd seen that it wasn't the cavalry with the heavy weapons, just two white guys in uniform, he'd been relatively calm. Narcs were a known stick up his ass. Patrol guys freelancing a takedown? *Sheeeeit.*

"Yo," he'd said, offering them a joint, "can we, like, talk for a minute?"

Timo had looked at the money and the weapons and the dope and immediately holstered his weapon and sat down. Hollister had been left standing like a statue, his gun still quartering the room like he was supposed to, still expecting a hail of bullets from somewhere. Timo had produced a lighter and fired the skinny cigarette up.

"What's on your mind, dude?" Timo had said between tokes.

"Look," Henry said, and his girl slid across the couch toward Timo. "We got us a situation here, right? You come in, OK, OK, I'm up to my ass in dope and fine women and money, and we can do this the official way, or we can do this the smart way, know what I mean?"

"Fine women?" Timo said. "As in more than one?" Henry's girl had one arm around him, and the way her shirt wasn't buttoned left nothing to the imagination.

"Yeah, we can work something out, if we can, y'know, address the larger issues here."

Hollister still hadn't said anything, but he dropped his weapon against his right leg.

"Are we talking a one-time pass, or a 'get out of jail free' card with some punches left in it?" Timo said. With his free hand he reached inside the girl's shirt, and they both giggled.

"Oh, well," Henry said, "I was thinking a 'get the hell out of Dodge' card, really."

"Why?" Timo said, fondling Henry's girl. "You got a good thing going here."

"Because the hood is changing. Nobody likes slinging weed anymore. They all into the new rock crap that's messing up everybody it touches. I'm thinking I need to move to Westwood, deal with college kids getting a monthly check from they mommas that get high so they can study better."

"What do you mean, this new rock stuff?" Hollister asked. It was the first time he'd spoken.

"Wow, so you can talk, huh?" Henry said. "Why don't you cop a squat and stop making everybody nervous, Officer Do-Right, OK?"

Hollister shook his head. "Tell me about the rock."

"It's coke, man, but it's cooked so that it's a deadly serious high. People take one hit and get strung, y'know? Big money, people selling their kids to get more once they get hooked. Don't tell me you blue shirts haven't seen it yet, right? C'mon, everybody knows what's going down."

Timo said nothing, head cocked at Hollister as if to say, "Don't."

"So the way I figure it, we just make a donation here to the policeman's ball or some such, and we roll back to a neutral corner, OK?" Henry said.

Timo had the girl's shirt off. She had some impressive breasts—and gaps in her teeth when she smiled.

"What are you, about fifteen?" Hollister asked, and Timo gave him the buzz-kill look.

She laughed. "I'll do you like I'm twenty, man."

Timo put his hands between the girl's legs, and she made to slap his hands away while reaching behind her, as if to unzip the denim skirt she was wearing.

Hollister pointed his gun at her. "Freeze!" he screamed, and before Timo could react, Hollister reached behind her and pulled out her hand, which now had a little pistol in it.

She laughed, and Henry shook his head. "Damn, Wendy, you done just jacked up the price I was tryin' to negotiate here, girl."

They had walked out with most of the cash and a load of pretty good weed—at least, that was Timo's assessment. Hollister had said nothing as they rolled away. The cash was still in the back of his closet at his house. He had refused a cut of the marijuana.

And now Timo wanted him to meet some people. Hands in another cookie jar, right, Timo? He knew the way it worked. You had to go along, or all of a sudden you didn't have backup in a firefight, or you rolled on a call alone into a Crips and Bloods shootout with heavy weapons and no shotgun—*surprise!*—in your cruiser, and if you got out of one of those with your life, you took the money, you turned a deaf ear, you became the see-no-evilest, hear-no-evilest, speak-no-evilest officer on the force, because there was nothing else for you but a hole in the ground and the scorn of your fellow officers for not getting with the program.

And it was killing him. Not because he was so pure. But because...

"Hey," Timo said as they rolled out after roll call. "I think I want a Happy Meal for breakfast. You look like you still need some coffee, amigo."

Just because...

They caught the call as they were finishing up in the McDonald's parking lot, some kind of dispute deep in the hood, and Timo was like screw it, let's wait for backup, but Hollister said no and called it in, and they were rolling as fast as Brad Hollister could stomp his foot on the gas and hit the lights and siren.

Near the 8700 block of Crenshaw, or thereabouts, shots were fired, and as they turned off the main drag, they could hear the popping sounds of rounds, and Timo cursed as Hollister bored in, getting the black-and-white as close as he could to the action.

Someone badly wounded was laid out on a lawn, leaking blood. Neighbors were shooting at each other from behind parked cars on either side of the street. Hollister let the cruiser roll to a stop against some trash cans, hoping the noise would get people's attention, and jumped out, gun clearing his rig like nobody's business, while Timo was working the radio requesting backup.

"Police! Hands up! Throw down your weapons!"

The response was a shot fired his way, high, and Hollister ducked behind the open door of the cruiser. He began moving around the back of the vehicle so that he could get a better angle on the shooter on his side of the street. Timo hadn't budged.

"I said, hands up! Throw down your weapons!" Hollister cleared the back end of the cruiser at a full sprint, handgun up and sighting the first shooter, who was now directly in front of him and behind a parked car, gun swinging toward him to engage.

Two shots—one in the shooter's leg, the other in the gun hand—and then Hollister was on him, slapping cuffs on the parts that weren't bleeding. "Shut up and we'll get you to a hospital," he practically screamed.

Once the perp was secured, he focused on the other guy.

"Last chance," he called out over the hood of the parked car. "Throw down your weapon, and come out with your hands where I can see them!"

There was no response, and Hollister peered over the hood. He's a rabbit, he thought, as he saw the man—medium build, black, with white sneakers and an oversized Lakers jersey that wasn't tucked into his jeans—sprint away from his concealed position.

"Let him go!" Timo said, but Hollister was up and running anyway, legs and arms pumping, his grip on his service revolver firm as he sought to run the suspect down, not caring whether he was running headlong into an ambush or not.

He was taller, he was fitter, and despite what promised to be a pounding headache once this was over, he overmatched the suspect stride for stride and finally caught him and tackled him two blocks away from the scene. There was a brief struggle, but the suspect was too winded to do much more than curse up a blue streak, and Hollister had his spare pair of cuffs on him.

As he was picking him up, four other black-and-whites screamed in from all directions. Because he'd fired twice, there would be a ton of paperwork and probably a shooting review, Hollister thought, but he didn't care.

Timo, when the first wounded suspect was being loaded into an ambulance, shook his head. "That was some John Wayne stuff, man."

Hollister shrugged. "Nothing scarier than 'Nam, man. Just another eight at the office, back in the day."

Timo looked at his watch. "Gotta make a call. Gonna be two hours before we get out of here. By then, I say we punch out for lunch so we can make my appointment. Cheer up," he said in response to the look on Hollister's face, "you're gonna be fine. These are connected people."

The meeting took place near the airport, at one of the Embassy Suites hotels near the 105 off ramp that led into LAX.

It was a big room, one of the conference rooms, and when they were all inside, someone in a dark suit closed and locked the door. Hollister had noticed another dark suit in the hallway, and he surmised that they were not only locked in but would not be disturbed.

There were maybe ten people there, and he and Timo were the only ones in uniform. The others looked like businessmen from what he could see, although several of them had had their backs to them when they had walked in and taken seats toward the front of the room.

There was one man who was clearly in charge. Medium build, decent suit, and youngish to be a don, so to speak, but clearly not a drug dealer or an organized-crime type. Hollister made him out to be a corporate type who probably chose this location because this was where he diddled his secretary so his wife wouldn't know.

"Are we ready to start?" the man asked. There was a quiet murmur of assent.

"OK," the man said. He turned to one of the suits in the room. "Have we checked to make sure no one has any recording devices? Nobody wearing a wire?"

At that a group of suits fanned out into the seated audience, and they were all frisked, and anyone carrying a briefcase had it searched. After a brief interlude, one of the suits nodded at Mr. Corporate, and he cleared his throat.

"What I'm about to tell you is highly confidential. The Regan administration would be incredibly embarrassed if any of this were to get out, and anyone who thinks they can make a name for themselves by releasing any of this information will be subject to immediate, and harsh, sanctions. Am I clear?

"With me is Emilio Sanchez, who works for the CIA. I'll introduce him to you in a minute. I also have John Bennigan from the DEA. They are not officially here, and this meeting didn't occur.

"Emilio has been working since the late seventies to support certain national security operations around the globe. If I were to tell you what he was working on, you'd understand instantly if you read the papers. I won't bore you with the details, but Mr. Sanchez dates his involvement with such people back to the days of the old anti-Castro movement in the 1960s.

"For my part, I work for an organization called Paradym Industries. We are corporate partners working with DEA and CIA and others to support the national security agenda. Our specialty is weapons and weapons procurement. Emilio?"

"Thank you." Sanchez stood up, and Hollister turned his face slightly away. Timo Banks glanced at him and the odd body language but said nothing.

"Since the late 1960s or so," Sanchez said, "the CIA and certain members of the DEA have been supporting an alternative funding model for certain…programs. That funding model requires certain, ah, compromises in the way that the agency does business, and now requires additional support from the business community as well as from a select group in law enforcement. You are here because someone invited you, and I think you will understand why you were invited once the details are laid out to you."

Mr. Corporate stood again. "And make no mistake about it: this activity, no matter how questionable it seems, is supported by the highest levels of the current administration and is vital to the security of the United States. The administration sees it as just as vital as the domino theory that led to the United States' intervention in Vietnam."

"So"—now it was Bennigan again—"we have developed a new 'black' funding source. We are actively working with a group based in San Francisco that has significant connections to the South American drug trade. That trade, specifically in cocaine, is now being expanded to include parts of Los Angeles."

Someone in the group asked skeptically, "Uncle Sam dealing drugs? You got any proof of this?"

Corporate answered, "There is a set of documents that you will be allowed to look at at the end of our discussion. You will not be permitted to take anything with you, however."

"Then why are we here?" another asked.

"Because we need people to protect the distribution organization in Los Angeles," said Bennigan. "Our connections are starting widespread distribution networks in the city, and we believe that it's a fair trade to sacrifice the lives of a few dopers for the country's national security priorities."

Just last week Timo and Hollister had taken a call to a single-family house that looked like it was inhabited by animals. The place was a wreck—there were roaches everywhere, and it smelled like something had died and been cooked in the oven for a week. Timo had glanced at the stove and the oven and held his nose.

"Damn, looks like they cooked the cat in there or something nasty," he'd said. Hollister looked at the dark-skinned man, who was cuffed to a bedpost and looked stoned out of his mind. The woman—his wife, girlfriend, or whatever—was dead, beaten to death or starved to death, Hollister couldn't tell, but she was in the Spartan living room half naked on the coach, and there was a pipe and a clear vial of something next to the body. In a case like this, you always looked at the male companion, hence the boyfriend/husband/significant other cuffed to the bed.

The neighbors had called because of the arguments and the smell, and Hollister looked again at the thing in the oven, wondering who could be so depraved to cook a cat in an oven, because that seemed to be a main source of the god-awful smell.

He went back to the bedroom and tried to rouse the man. "What you been doing here, huh? PCP? Angel dust? Weed?" The man was unresponsive. Crime scene people were en route, and Hollister just wanted to get outside and get some fresh air, because everything smelled like it had been lying in its own feces for a week.

They had one officer outside and yellow crime scene tape across the front door, and all of a sudden, there was a commotion in front, the female officer exchanging words with a young woman trying frantically to get past the yellow tape.

Hollister, glad to get out of the apartment, stepped over the tape into the hallway, where a few of the neighbors were standing, towels and handkerchiefs over their noses and mouths. "What's the problem?" he asked the deputy.

"She's freaking out. Says the couple in there was babysitting her daughter while she was down at welfare. Daughter's a newborn, and they haven't returned her, and she insists her daughter is inside," the deputy said.

And then it struck him just what was wrong with the thing in the oven, because it didn't have any fur and was too big to be a cat, and Hollister just managed to turn away before spewing the contents of his stomach in the filthy hallway…

Bennigan, the DEA agent, was still talking. "It seems as if people have developed a new form of the drug, similar to freebasing, where they cook the raw material down with ether into tiny particles, or rocks, which can be smoked and which deliver a potent amount of the drug directly into the bloodstream via the lungs. They call it rock or crack, and so far nobody seems to have noticed, since it's just the druggies killing themselves over this stuff."

Hollister raised his hand and asked his question without being acknowledged.

"Funding for what?"

Mr. Corporate cleared his throat and ignored the question.

"We need people in various areas to protect supply and distribution. Some of you in law enforcement will be asked to recruit others, discreetly of course, to help. Others are here to help ensure that we have secured means of transport and access to the city. Still others are going to be asked to provide security for shipments into the wholesale and retail channels."

Timo spoke up. "What's in it for us?"

Mr. Corporate pulled a duffel bag from beneath a table, opened it, and spread the banded stacks of greenbacks on the table. "A cut of the proceeds," he said. "You will be well compensated, and we will still be able to fund our programs quite nicely."

"What the hell have you gotten me into?" Hollister whispered to Timo.

"Didn't you hear? This is all sanctioned by the government. This is gonna happen whether the government is behind it or not. Look at the money, Brad."

Someone raised a hand. Mr. Corporate acknowledged the person.

"So is this some kind of payback agenda on the inner city? I've heard about this form of cocaine, but I gotta tell ya, it ain't in Beverly Hills."

Mr. Corporate shook his head. "Drug use is drug use, Officer. Regardless of where it starts, it spreads everywhere. Wait long enough, and you'll see it in Bel Air. But you'll see it regardless of who distributes it, or who profits from it."

There were a few other questions, and Mr. Corporate distributed a portion of the money on the table to the participants. Most, Hollister saw, went back into the bag. When he got his share, he stared at it and wondered what kind of misery this was going to bring to the people in South Central and debated whether he should care or not.

Eventually they were funneled into a line to meet the big guys, particularly Mr. Corporate, who shook their hands and looked earnestly into their eyes.

"Pleased to meet you," he said, taking Hollister's hand. "Officer Hollister," he said, reading the name on his uniform shirt, "glad you could join us."

"That doesn't get me your name, though, does it?"

Mr. Corporate smiled. "Smith is descriptive enough."

Hollister smiled and continued through the line.

Mr. Corporate turned to Bennigan and said, "That one bears watching."

Bennigan looked and saw a typical crooked LAPD cop. "Why?"

"Something about him," Corporate said.

Hollister came face to face with Emilio Sanchez. Sanchez shook Timo's hand and then gripped Hollister by the elbow.

"Mind if I talk to you, Hollister?" Sanchez said, his smile a little too bright. He didn't let go of Hollister's elbow and steered him away from the rest of the group.

When they were in a corner of the room, Sanchez smiled again, and Hollister remembered the cheap aftershave and the razor bumps that always had been a part of this man's look, back when he'd known him as Raoul.

"Hey, Kid," Raoul "Emilio" Sanchez said. "Been a long time since Memphis."

San Francisco, June 21, 1982

Secret Service Agent Richard Whelan was green as could be and had been assigned as a liaison to an active counterfeiting investigation as a way of getting some field experience. His supervisor had said that the San Francisco district was working on something hot and complicated, and they would need someone with good analytical skills to follow the money trail.

He'd been in Frisco for two weeks reviewing the details of the case. One suspect was Benito Menendez, who lived in the Mission Hill district and who had been passing bad twenties, the counterfeiter's bill of choice, all over the Bay Area.

On a lark he'd asked to spend some time on a stakeout of the suspect's house. He had been cooped up in the bakery truck they were using for about five hours while the FBI and Treasury agents took pictures of everyone that came or went from the suspect's home.

"Does this guy have a real job, or is he a full-time paperhanger?" Whelan had asked early on.

"Why?" Ramirez, the lead Treasury special agent, had asked.

"Because if this guy made his money as a counterfeiter, how'd he get such a nice house? The bills aren't that good, and he was sloppy as hell distributing them."

The FBI guys and Ramirez looked at each other. It was an obvious question that they'd neglected to ask.

"What do you think—drugs?"

Whelan shrugged, regretting his candor in front of more seasoned agents. "Maybe this guy is connected to a bunch of things, and the bills are a sideline."

"Crap," Ramirez said, "we better cross-check this guy with DEA."

"Hey," one of the spotters said, "we got a car approaching the house."

They all turned to the monitors as they tried to zoom in. Cameras with telephoto lenses were blasting away, taking pictures of the black Lincoln and its license plates and of the driver, who got out and approached the house. Ramirez was on the phone, alerting people in cars that they might have someone to follow when the black Lincoln departed.

Whelan watched closely as the man went to the front door. He was carrying a bag of some kind, and he shook hands with someone they couldn't see in the doorway, handed him the bag, and then returned to the curb, started the Lincoln, and drove away.

"You have people on the Lincoln?" Whelan asked.

"Yeah," Ramirez said.

"Didn't look like a counterfeit drop," Whelan said.

"Maybe, maybe not," Ramirez responded. "If it was drugs, it wasn't a large quantity."

"How soon can we run the plates on the Lincoln?"

"California DMV is running the plates now. When they pass the registration to our guy, we'll have it."

"OK, Benny is moving now—that's him, right?" Whelan said as Menendez walked slowly down the driveway to a battered Chevy. "That's his car?" he added.

"Yeah, why?" Ramirez said.

"Nice house, crappy car. Doesn't make sense. Does he own the house?"

Someone was flipping through the case file. "Yeah, no mortgage. Paid it off about a year ago."

"How much?"

"One hundred and thirty-eight thousand."

"What do you think real estate goes for around here?"

"What? Why? Are we working a case, or are you looking for a place to settle down?"

"Hear me out. I'm guessing housing prices are no more than three-fifty, right?"

There was a general shrug. It sounded about right to the people in the truck.

"So he bought the place with a pretty big down payment and then pays off the mortgage. But he still rides around in a crappy car."

"So?"

"So he had a one-time windfall. But he isn't making any money from what he's doing now. So he goes into the printing business to make a little extra cash."

"That would rule out drugs, wouldn't it?"

"From the windfall, absolutely not. From what he's doing now, yeah, probably."

"This guy a citizen, or a green card?" one of the other agents asked.

"Green card. From Nicaragua."

"Anyone know if he's been back there lately?"

"Last time was a couple of months ago. Stayed about three weeks."

"Then I'd put drugs back on the table. Lots of stuff coming out of South and Central America these days. I think," Whelan said, "maybe you want to talk to DEA about these guys."

It turned out that Benny was just going to the local store for groceries. Toward nightfall, Whelan, as well as the FBI and Treasury supervisors, left the truck to head back to the central office where they were coordinating the investigation. Ramirez stopped him as he was leaving the office.

"Hey. Good work today. Always good to have a new set of eyes on one of these. See you in the morning."

***

The joint task force had been put together to respond to numerous instances of counterfeiting and the suspicion that large sums of cash were trolling the streets of San Francisco. When Whelan arrived at the task force headquarters the next morning, Ramirez summoned him into his office.

"I showed the photos of the guy visiting our mark to a buddy of mine in DEA. He recognized him immediately. Says they have an open case on him that they've been working for nearly a year."

"What's his name?"

"Daniel Blancone. Also Nicaraguan. Seems he has a pretty large cocaine business here in San Francisco. DEA has been waiting to try and tie him to a supplier but hasn't been successful yet."

"They know about Menendez?"

"Yeah, but he's not a big fish. They think he does a little bit for Blancone, but nothing major, no weight."

"That's odd. Why would you have someone dealing small amounts of drugs for you?"

Ramirez shrugged. "I don't know."

"Then this is completely strange. Menendez has a nice house, but a lousy car. And if he's dealing drugs, he isn't dealing much. And he's a complete screwup as a counterfeiter. What are we missing?" Whelan asked.

"We may never know. Got a call from a higher mucky muck in DEA this morning. Told me to back off Blancone for fear of upsetting their applecart," Ramirez said.

"We ever look at Blancone for money laundering?" Whelan asked.

"No," Ramirez responded.

"Should we? I mean, if he's dealing drugs, he's got lots of cash he has to get rid of. Easy enough to distribute fakes into a network used to dealing with large sums of cash," Whelan said.

"I don't think I can touch this Blancone character. I think we stay with Menendez," Ramirez replied.

"OK. But we need to throw a blanket over him, twenty-four hours a day, seven days a week, wherever he goes," Whelan said.

"I've asked for more assets to do that."

"What if he gets on a plane for Nicaragua?" Whelan asked.

Ramirez shrugged. "We'll cover him there too."

Whelan shook his head. "There's still a big piece of this we aren't seeing. And if we don't figure it out, we're going to come out on the wrong end of something major if we're not careful."

Ramirez's phone rang. He picked it up, listened, and then banged the receiver down.

"Menendez is moving. Packed a suitcase in the car and hit the road. My guys have him on the 101 heading south. I'm going to get us a chopper for wherever he ends up."

"How far south does the 101 go?"

"All the way to Los Angeles and beyond."

"Hmm. Should I call the LA office to set up a liaison?"

"Not yet," Ramirez said, standing up. "Let's go see if we can catch our bird."

Los Angeles, June 22, 1982

Timo Banks was in street clothes with a radio strapped to his butt like it was part of his anatomy.

"Brad, you copy?"

Hollister was on the roof of one of the high-rises in downtown LA with a high-powered rifle and a scope peering down to the street level, focusing in on the corner of Hill and Seventh Avenue. *Helluva way to spend my day off.*

"Yeah, I copy."

"Radio check, dude. I got nothing so far, but I'll let you know when the mark comes out of the building, OK?"

"You sure you'll know who he is?"

"Yeah. Got a picture and everything. Also supposed to get a description of what the target is wearing once he leaves the meeting. We're cool; it's gonna be fine."

"Yeah, sure." *Easy for you to say, Timo. You aren't pulling the trigger.*

Since the meeting at the Embassy Suites and his unhappy reunion with the man he knew as Raoul, Hollister and Banks had been getting deeper and deeper into whatever the "operation" was. Once Banks had spilled to Mr. Corporate—whose real name was Philip Stone—and Bennigan about his prowess with a gun and supposed fearlessness, Raoul had pushed progressively more violent security and enforcement activities. Now here he was sitting behind a tactical scope looking for a target.

Just like old times.

Only he still had his exit strategy running. His appointment back east had come through, and his new identity had apparently held up to scrutiny. A couple more months of this, and Brad Hollister would simply disappear with a note and a resignation and no forwarding address into his new life. Just a couple more months, and he would skip.

Naturally, he had no doubt that Raoul would find him, but now he was certain that it would be the last time that he and the supposed CIA operative would cross paths. He still had fifteen years of payback pent up inside of him, and he intended to get his money's worth. *Just not now.*

"We have any idea how the meeting is going? I was only supposed to be up here a few minutes, and I don't want some asshole in a news chopper to start showing the whole world pictures of me on channel two."

"Few more minutes, bro. Few more minutes."

"OK."

***

Richard Whelan and Edgar Ramirez had followed their suspect, Benito Menendez, all the way into Los Angeles and into a nondescript building on Hill Street. They didn't dare go in, but they had agents all over the Chevy in the lot at Hill and Third as well as the building Menendez had gone into an hour or so ago. They were in a coffee shop at Hill between Sixth and Seventh Avenues, waiting for word of their guy reappearing.

Ramirez's radio squawked. "Yeah, looks like our guy coming out on the corner of Hill and Seventh, over. He's with someone."

"Get pictures and stay clear. Which way is Menendez coming?"

"Back toward his car on Hill. He's shaking hands with the other guy, and moving away, over."

"OK, stay on him, but stay loose. We have the car covered."

"No problem. I—"

Whelan happened to be looking at the tall, thin man as Menendez shook hands with him and moved away. He stayed on the other man, who checked his watch and was about to step off the curb to cross Hill when they all heard the big boom of a rifle, and while all the agents were diving for cover, Whelan, the rookie, stayed put long enough to see the tall man's head literally explode and his lifeless body crumple to the pavement.

"Oh crap! Shots fired; the other guy is down hard!"

"Where is Menendez?" Ramirez shouted. "I don't, wait—he's still on Hill, heading toward you. Looks like he's lighting a cigarette."

People were running, afraid that there would be more shots, unsure of what was happening until they saw the headless torso bleeding black blood onto the wide white lines of the crosswalk. Whelan took in the crowd and the confusion, and then swiveled to pick up their guy, who was calmly walking away, puffing on a cigarette, not a care in the world.

What the hell? Unless he had known…

***

"Yeah, Brad, the target is just about to cross Hill. You got him? He's all yours."

The Kid sighted down the barrel of the gun and put the cross hairs on the center of the back of the target's head, glad that the man wasn't facing him, glad that this wasn't Dallas or Memphis. He didn't hesitate, taking the slack out of the trigger, slowing his breath to nothing, and forcing himself to keep to a rigid line, holding himself, the weapon, and the ground frozen and immobile.

Just a second more…

And then he was back in Memphis, the nightmare that continued to haunt him, Reverend Doctor Martin Luther King there on the balcony at the Lorraine Motel, and there he was, half a mile away in a helicopter, pacing himself to the sway as the pilot conspired to keep the bird level in the gentle breezes, and him timing the rocking motion so that when he pulled the trigger the shot would run true.

And there he was, King in his cross hairs. He probably could hear the noise of the helicopter, and it seemed as if King was looking straight at him, and his mouth was moving—oh God, his mouth was moving, like he was talking to him, like he knew he was about to die.

And as the helicopter swung through one last arc and past the target point and then back again to the place where The Kid figured he had to pull the trigger and take the shot, he could see King's lips moving, and just as he pulled the trigger, he understood what King was saying, over and over again—

I forgive you, I forgive you, I forgive you...

And damn him, he pulled the trigger anyway, sending death at the speed of sound, managing to keep King in his cross hairs until the round hit and blew him backward, and he screamed at the pilot to get them out of there as he sat back and let the sling take his weight, his head turned so that the spotter wouldn't see his tears.

CHAPTER 33

Thursday, August 25, 2011

ichard Whelan's research had found a possible weapon for the sniper: a Russian-made antitank gun, a big-bore monster firing 14.5-millimeter shells capable of making a very long distance shot. The reference book recalled instances of antipersonnel sniping with the Soviet gun at distances of over two miles. Assuming that's what he'd heard Wednesday night, the real question was where the shooter was planning to set up.

He called Moynihan, who either wasn't picking up his phone or refusing his calls. It added to his anxiety that Moynihan had been queered in some way, and it meant that the president was in real danger.

He dialed Alan Christiansen instead.

"Got any pull with ATF?" Whelan asked, referring to the Bureau of Alcohol, Tobacco, Firearms, and Explosives, the federal law enforcement agency responsible for the investigation and prevention of federal offenses involving the unlawful use, manufacture, and possession of firearms and explosives..

"Why?"

"I'm looking for an arms dealer who has recently made a sale of a very large-caliber Russian super rifle."

Christiansen chuckled. "I can make that phone call. You think this is a recent purchase?"

"Recent or not, it would be memorable. It's a beast of a weapon."

"OK, gimme the details."

Whelan relayed the details to the FBI director.

"You think this is the gun you heard last night?"

"I don't know. I'm working backward from a weapon that could cover the distance needed to threaten the president. Moynihan doesn't return phone calls all of a sudden, and my girl and I are target practice for a lunatic with a gun that ain't exactly used for sport."

"What does Chuck O'Shay say?"

"I asked him to talk to the president."

"What's your next step?"

"Identify where the shooter is going to take the shot and try and get to the head of the president's protection detail."

"I hear Sam Redburn is the guy you want."

"Yeah, I know him, but not well. I'll give him a call."

Bettina was still in bed, still shaking from the sound of gunfire blasting echoes off the buildings on the street where Grogan's was located.

Weird.

She rubbed her stomach. Was this going to be life with Richard Whelan? Gunshots? Threats to her life? Creeps following her around?

Her phone rang, and she picked it up.

"Hey," Richard Whelan said.

"Superman Whelan. Well, well, how nice of you to call."

"Bettina, look, I wasn't the one with the rifle last night."

"Or with the black sedan on my tail yesterday."

"Right."

"Or on the phone, scaring the bejesus out of my secretary. And me."

"Why do I get the impression that this is a no-win situation for me?" Richard asked.

"Because it is! I'm still trying to calculate how much it's going to cost you."

"'Tina, look, I—"

"Don't go there, Superman. I'm not bulletproof. Just remember that, OK?"

"OK. See you later?"

"Maybe. I'll let you know."

***

Frank Moynihan had called Sam Redburn to his office to go through the protection plan for the president's speech one last time. Redburn took him through the protective sweeps that would begin well before the speech and the plan to transport the president from the White House. Then he went through the perimeter security and how far out the teams would be deployed.

Frank listened carefully, thinking about holes and how he could cover himself afterward.

"What about the scaffolding on the Capitol building?" he asked.

"It's two miles away from the Lincoln Memorial. We aren't planning to sweep it in the morning at all," Redburn said.

"That's it?"

"Yeah. And we aren't planning on having any units up there for the actual speech."

"I'd put two people up there in the scaffolding," Moynihan said.

"But if I do that, I'm a little short on my ground teams during the event."

"Then lose an entrance and a metal detector and double your people up at the remaining points of access. That way you won't slow things down too much by having one less entrance, and you'll have more than made up for the loss of two people sitting in the scaffolding during the speech."

"Might work," Redburn said, dubiously.

"Look, Sam, this is Protection 101. Cover the Capitol building and lose the extra entrance. He's expecting a standing room-only crowd, but you have plenty of points of access."

"OK. I'll make sure they're in place two hours prior to the event."

"Good. If you want, I'll check on them myself."

Redburn nodded.

***

Richard Whelan went online, looking at a map of the National Mall, checking the distances from the Lincoln Memorial to other places of interest. There really wasn't any place that would work that wasn't well over two miles out, which was just an impossible shot.

Idly, he clicked on the map and was rewarded with photos and related news links on the buildings that he was clicking on. There was nothing that convinced him that he had the sniper's perch.

Then he clicked on the Capitol building. A news story popped up about the cleaning of the Statue of Freedom on the top of the building and the extensive scaffolding that had been installed.

Richard sat up, reading closely. The cleaning was a regular occurrence, taking place like clockwork every two years.

He went back to the map. The distance was two miles from the Lincoln Memorial, but from the top of the Capitol building, the sniper would have a clear shot. What had Moynihan said when they discussed it?

"Because the nearest high ground is the Capitol building, and that's too far for a shot."

"Not even a heavy weapon, like a Barrett fifty?" Richard asked.

"Too far for one of those, even. Plus, a sniper would have to get a weapon up high enough to take a shot. Not easy."

But with the extensive scaffolding around the Capitol dome, and a big Russian-made weapon easily capable of delivering a killing round from two miles distant—if he was right—that would solve both the height problem and the distance problem.

And the shooter had just tested his weapon on him and Bettina.

He picked up the phone and called Sam Redburn.

"Redburn."

"Uh, hey, this is Richard Whelan, used to be on the president's protection detail."

"Yeah, Richard, I know the name. Hold on a sec," Redburn said, covering the headpiece and speaking with someone.

"Sorry," he said when he came back. "You've been working with Treasury for the last eighteen months or so, right?"

"Yeah," Whelan said.

"That's what I thought. Look, I'm kind of busy. What can I do for you?"

"Has Frank Moynihan mentioned the threatening note and weapon that I received?"

"Uh, no," Redburn said, sounding surprised.

"Well, the note said that the president was going to be killed, and threatened me as well. In the last couple of days, I've been shot at twice."

"Really?" Redburn said, signaling to his number two to pick up the line. Richard heard a click as the second agent picked up.

"When did you get the note?" Redburn asked.

"Sunday."

"Jesus, Whelan, today is Thursday. You know the protocol. What took you so long to call us?"

"Whoa—I told Frank Moynihan on Sunday when I got the package. And I've been trying to call him since someone used me and my girlfriend for target practice last night."

"OK, I'll check with Frank. Where are the note and the weapon you received?"

"I'm not sure about the note, but the weapon was taken to the FBI ballistics labs and tested. The tests confirmed that it was the gun that killed Martin Luther King."

There was a long silence on the phone, and Richard realized that he'd gone too far. They were probably busy labeling him a nutcase.

"I'm sorry," Travis said, "did you say the weapon was implicated in killing King?"

"Uh, yeah. Check with Alan Christiansen with the FBI, but I'm not kidding."

"OK," Redburn said. "Anything else you can tell us?"

"Just that I think the sniper may be planning a long-range shot from the Capitol building with an exotic Russian-made rifle."

"You think? What makes you think that?"

"Just from the nature of the gun that was used to shoot at me last night and from looking at a map of the National Mall."

"That's pretty specific for a 'hunch,' Richard."

"Look, I'm just doing my duty," Richard said, realizing that they now probably thought he was certifiable.

"Russian rifle, shot from the Capitol. You say Frank knows about this?" Redburn asked.

"Yeah. Has he been fully with it, by the way?"

"With it?"

"Yeah. He doesn't return my calls, so I was wondering if he was really involved with the protection scheme for the president's speech."

He probably thinks you're a lunatic, too, Redburn thought. "Well, yeah, I'd say so. He just recommended coverage of the Capitol building, Richard. So I would not advise you to try dragging a Russian-made rifle up there to take a potshot at the president."

"Look, it's not me—ask Moynihan!" Whelan said.

"Uh-huh. Damn, wasn't that you involved in the shooting last night? Grogan's?"

"Yes. That was me."

His statement was met with complete silence.

"Two good people are dead, Richard."

"Don't you think I know that? Large-caliber Russian weapon. Our people died because of this bastard, and I'm thinking he's looking to make good on his threat. So stop treating me like a nut, and talk to Moynihan, OK?"

"Will do, Richard."

CHAPTER 34

Los Angeles, June 22, 1982

"LAPD picked up the rifle. Whoever pulled the trigger left it on the roof of the building."

"Are they gonna share the ID of the victim?" Whelan asked. They were in the Los Angeles office of the US Treasury Department, trying to understand what the hell had just happened.

"DEA is still chewing my ass about Blancone. What's one more law enforcement agency being pissed off at me?" Ramirez said. He picked up the phone to call in a favor.

They had agents trailing Menendez, but Whelan was convinced that their target was headed back up to San Francisco. He'd been here for a reason, and that reason had concluded with the shooting victim lying dead in the street while Menendez had casually walked away.

So the meeting had been a setup, and Menendez had known the target was going to die. Given the nature of the target's death, Whelan suspected that an obstacle had been moved off the board, and either Menendez or someone else was going to move in and fill the void or continue with some larger agenda.

They could figure it out by process of elimination. If nothing happened with Menendez, he was just part of the lure to bring the target to that particular place so that he could be killed, and there wouldn't be much they could do with that.

But Whelan didn't like thinking like that. He believed in making bets in the vacuum of knowledge, as if by making a choice, he could force the universe to choose a particular state that either favored or ignored him.

And death by an assassin suggested money and organization. Something big, Whelan thought, and usually drugs were the big shadow passing over the law enforcement scene these days. Dope was everywhere, like a massive undetected planet.

So when in doubt, Whelan thought, it paid to bet on drugs and work backward from there.

If Menendez remained active in whatever had just happened, it stood to reason that his pattern would change at some point. Since the killing had taken place in Los Angeles, Whelan thought that meant that Menendez would likely be coming back to Los Angeles more frequently, or perhaps moving himself down here permanently.

But this wasn't some gang bust up in a lousy part of town. So if it was drugs, it was way above the level of street entrepreneurs slinging ganja or hashish. Why else would you pay someone with sniper skills to take someone down from afar, unless there was plenty of money to back the play?

What if there had been a change in the local drug market? Would that mean that Blancone, the man that DEA was determined to protect, was about to move up in the world and expand into Los Angeles?

If that were the case, why wasn't Blancone here instead of Menendez? And who set up the hit? Menendez felt like a guy closer to the street, so it wouldn't have been him. Blancone, if he was expanding, would have likely been here himself, unless he didn't want to get his hands dirty.

So if he were a betting man, he would bet that Menendez picked up the pace of his Los Angeles trips and that there was another major player associated with Blancone and Menendez who had set up the hit on the victim.

Now the question was, who could that be?

San Francisco, July 10, 1982

Whelan was back in the surveillance van watching Menendez's house. For the last two weeks, Benito had been as quiet as a church mouse and had been staying close to home. Ramirez hadn't been able to get anywhere with LAPD on the identification of the shooting victim in downtown Los Angeles; if the police knew who the man was, they were stonewalling for all they were worth.

"Hey, we got a car rolling up the street toward the house," one of the agents said.

"OK, black Lincoln. Bet we've seen that ride before," Whelan said, waiting for the others to confirm that the Lincoln had carried Daniel Blancone to Menendez's house several weeks earlier.

"Yeah, same one. Got a match on the plate."

This time the Lincoln pulled into Menendez's driveway, turned around, and then backed in so that the trunk of the car was close to the garage. Menendez came out of the front door and raised the garage door. Blancone got out of the car and went around to join Menendez at the back of the Lincoln.

"Dammit, anybody got an angle on what's in the trunk?"

"No, nothing. Can't see a thing."

Whelan was watching the back end of the car. Sure enough, as the two men stood behind the vehicle, Whelan could see the springs relax and the back end of the Lincoln rise ever so slightly from where it had settled when Blancone had backed it in.

"Whatever it is, it's fairly heavy. That's why he wanted to back it into the property. I bet they are transferring whatever it is to another vehicle if it's going anywhere. Anybody see Menendez's car?"

"In the garage, front in. Looks like the trunk is open as well."

"Then Blancone just passed Menendez some major weight. Bet Menendez is heading back to Los Angeles," Whelan said.

"How the hell can you tell that?"

"Powers of deduction, boys. Tell Ramirez that it's time for another road trip to LA, if he's up to it."

"I'm not calling anyone until you explain why you're so sure."

"Suit yourselves. But I bet this is the last time we'll see Blancone's Lincoln here. From now on, drops will likely be handled by someone lower in the food chain. Too much weight and too big a risk for Blancone."

They watched as Blancone shook hands with Menendez and got in his car and drove away. Within minutes, Menendez was in his vehicle, and the sole chase car they had on him confirmed that he'd gotten on the 101 heading south.

As they listened to the chase car describing Menendez's movements, Whelan wondered why Ramirez hadn't gotten them a chopper for the trip to Los Angeles.

The answer came in a few minutes. "Ramirez says he wants to see you in his office pronto," one of the Treasury agents told Whelan. "He says DEA wants to shut this whole thing down."

When Whelan reached Edgar Ramirez's office, he noticed two men sitting in the waiting area who looked so much like official US government types that he thought he was in Washington, DC.

Ramirez, his jacket off and his white shirtsleeves rolled up to his elbows, ushered him in.

"Hey, Edgar, what's going on? I'm pretty sure Menendez just moved to expand Blancone's drug business in Los Angeles. We need to get down there to see how it goes down."

"Have a seat, Richard," Ramirez said, and Whelan could hear the frustration just below the surface.

"What the hell is going on?"

"There are two DEA guys out in the waiting area. I'm pretty sure they're gonna politely tell me to shut the Menendez investigation down."

"What? Why?"

"I got a call from my boss. One of these guys has some major pull in Washington. He says people have gotten phone calls about this, like it's some sort of hush-hush CIA thing. If these people tell me to jump, I'm supposed to salute and ask how high."

"But we're about to find out that Menendez is a likely a major supplier into the LA market. I don't care who pursues it; we shouldn't let a lead like this get away. We could roll up a whole slew of mid- and lower-level dealers and get them off the streets of LA in one swoop and still leave DEA's pigeon alone."

Ramirez shook his head. "Let me have the receptionist show them in."

The men came in, and the temperature in the office dropped ten degrees. Both men were wearing dark suits with regimental ties. They shook hands and showed credentials that neither Ramirez nor Whelan bothered to look closely at.

"John Bennigan, DEA. This is Phillip Stone, who works in…the intelligence community."

"Whelan, Secret Service liaison to the Department of Treasury."

"Edgar Ramirez, and I'm sure you know who I am."

They all sat in Ramirez's tiny and now impossibly crowded office.

"Look," Stone began, "we can do this one of two ways. The easy way is that we make a request, you accept it and abide by it, and we walk away. The hard way is for us to generate a presidential finding that says that not only are we right but that the two of you should lose your jobs and never work for the government again."

Ramirez spoke softly. "You want us to leave Blancone and Menendez alone."

"Correct," Bennigan said. "Both are part of an ongoing sting operation, the nature of which I can't brief you on right now."

Try ever, Whelan thought but wisely didn't say.

"You realize that we've been all over Menendez for weeks. We think his status has likely been upgraded since he visited Los Angeles two weeks ago," Whelan said.

"We're sure you think you're onto something. But this is an active DEA investigation that has national security implications," Bennigan said flatly.

"You mean that you're aware that Menendez is now moving significant weights of drugs into Los Angeles for Blancone?"

"Let me reiterate what I mean when I say that we can approach this in one of two ways, gentlemen," Stone said. "We can play nice, recognize we're all part of the same team, or, we can make phone calls and put memos into each of your files."

There was a moment of silence that stretched to the edge of hostility before Ramirez finally stood up and said, "Thank you for your time, gentlemen. We will consider the Menendez investigation terminated as of this moment."

Stone and Bennigan both stood and shook hands all around.

Stone was slow to release Whelan's grip. "Take care, agent," he said.

Yeah, and up yours too, Whelan thought.

CHAPTER 35

Thursday, August 25, 2011

T he Kid had all the Secret Service deployment details and the timing of the crews that would be situated in the scaffolding that enfolded the statue sitting atop the Capitol building. All he needed to do, he thought, was get a heavy weapon to the top of the building after the security sweeps and prior to a team being posted in the tower to stop him.

For that he would need help. He picked up the phone and made a single, coded call.

Richard Whelan was surprised when Chuck O'Shay called him.

"Listen, Richard, the president appreciates your concern. That doesn't mean that he's going to cancel the speech. But he wants to hear it from you directly. The risks. I can clear a spot in his schedule later this afternoon, but you're going to have to be succinct, OK? He doesn't tend to have all day."

"You convinced him to talk to me?" Whelan asked, surprised.

"No. He convinced himself."

"Why doesn't he just cancel?" Whelan asked.

"He's billed this as the inauguration of his second-term campaign from the spot of King's 'I Have A Dream' speech. If he cancels, the lost symbolic opportunity and political fallout will be enormous."

"I don't understand that, Chuck."

"The conservative press will eat him alive. They will invent some lie to explain why he hasn't yet announced."

"I thought the press was speculating that it was too early for him to be talking about reelection," Whelan said.

"That's politics for you, son. Damned if you do, and damned if you don't. He's going to be at that podium Friday, so come talk to him about how you can help him be safe."

And this was such a tremendous breach of Secret Service protocol that Whelan nearly refused. *Be careful what you wish for.* As the silence stretched, O'Shay thought it was nerves.

"Look, you were on the detail for a bit. He's a very personable guy."

"It's not that, Chuck. I have to talk to my boss as well as the detail to tell them I'm talking to the president."

"Yeah, so?"

"They aren't going to like that I'm going directly to the man and bypassing them. Moynihan would be within his rights to fire me for something like that."

"Then get him on the horn and get it done."

"I can't get you to have President Obama talk to Frank, can I?"

"No time. Just be here at the appointed time ready to chat. Gotta go, Whelan."

"Guess what?" Richard said when he got Bettina on the phone.

Bettina had decided to go into her office because she was tired of sitting home and feeling terrified of the shadows.

"You're going to quit your job and become a live-in daddy."

"Nope. Going in to see the president today."

"Really. Frank OK with that?"

"Gonna call him now. But he hasn't been returning my calls. And the head of the president's protection detail thinks I'm some sort of nut job. So he won't be happy either."

"Man, you have a lot of relationship issues. Call me when you're done. You can start working off your bill," she said playfully.

Richard couldn't help but smile.

"You'll be in your office?"

"Yup. With the shades drawn and guns clicked and licked."

Richard chuckled. "That would be cocked and locked."

"Oh. Shades drawn and a Popsicle cocked and licked, then."

"Popsicle, eh? Girl, there's gonna be a lot of you to love."

"Excuse me? What did you just say?"

Oops! "I said there's gonna be a lot of you to love."

"And you were kidding, right?" And the way she said it made Whelan think that Bettina was sliding off the hormonal scale into a full blow-up.

Was I? "Jokes come from the heart. I'll call you later."

***

Obama was still in his study in the residence, looking over the eighteenth draft of his speech. It felt final, and he'd been over the cadences and the rhythms of it a thousand times in his head. As the consummate public speaker, he could deliver it in his sleep and dazzle his audience in a heartbeat.

Except in this instance.

I wonder if the manual has a protocol for making a speech under a death threat, he thought. Probably not.

If he really wanted to say something, if he really wanted to set the record straight, then maybe he should ignore the politics and tell the truth for once.

He wondered if the American people were ready for the truth. Not that he could tell it to them, but what if he could?

He grabbed a legal pad and began to write.

My fellow Americans, let me say that there are enough sorrows in the world that one could cry a river of tears from now until the end of time, until the tears had no meaning. I want to say that the notion of hope we had as a nation leaving the battlefields of World War II has long since been forgotten, and a new reality has sunk in as we are getting older. We face greater competition, and we are deeper in debt...

***

The trucking company knew it was a big wooden crate, it was heavy, and it was stenciled *Property of the Secret Service.*

The Federal Protective Services personnel at the loading dock of the Capitol building watched the special courier back into the loading dock with the characteristic beeping of a truck in reverse. They'd gotten a phone call to expect this particular shipment. The paperwork had been faxed over, and it was all in order.

The driver hopped out, holding a manifest on a clipboard.

"Yo," he said to the FPS guy he knew as Vinnie, "they tell you this was coming?"

"Yeah, they told us," Vinnie said, holding out his hand for the clipboard.

"It's a heavy sonofabitch. Wha's in it?"

"Jones, I could tell you, but then I'd have to jack you up," Vinnie said, laughing. He signed for the oblong box.

"Where you want it?" Jones asked, anxious to finish his route before rush hour bit him too deeply in the ass.

"Just offload it. We're supposed to take it from here."

Jones shrugged. He tugged open the tailgate of the truck and pulled the crate from the lip of the truck bed to the lip of the loading dock.

Vinnie looked at it and then winked at Jones.

"What?" Jones said. "That mean you gonna tell me what it is?"

Vinnie laughed. "Secret Service is gonna have people here in the scaffolding above the building for the president's speech," Vinnie said, hush-hush like. "We were told that it's a special gun for antisniper operations."

Jones whistled. "Special, huh?"

"Yeah, big mother with a lotta range."

"Sure it was Secret Service?"

Vinnie nodded. "Got the MOVE order right here. Signed off on by the head of the Service and faxed over half an hour ago. Called and confirmed and was told it was legit."

Jones looked at the authorization.

It was signed by Frank Moynihan.

Vinnie turned to his companion. "Let's get Dedrick from maintenance to help us get this thing in the scaffolding. Got a feeling it's gonna be one heavy son of a bitch to get up there."

***

The phone at his elbow interrupted his train of thought, and Barack Obama put the pen down after having furiously scribbled two pages on the legal pad. He thought about whether he could ever actually say any of it. At least, he thought, it had felt good to write it down.

"Yes," he said when he picked up the phone.

"Mr. President, I have Richard Whelan here. He's here for his appointment."

Obama sighed. He remembered Whelan from his brief time on the protection detail. He'd seemed very straight-laced and no-nonsense, almost as if something was missing from the man. He'd looked at his record though, and he had had a brilliant, if focused career. His gifts were in investigations, not protection, and he'd agreed with Frank Moynihan when Whelan had been shifted back into an investigative role. Not that he wasn't good with a gun or personable, Obama thought. It was just...well, other people less gifted could sign up to take a bullet for the president.

So here's to another form of protection.

"Send him up," he said.

CHAPTER 36

Los Angeles, July 26, 1982

B rad Hollister and Timo Banks were now working security for some of the major deliveries entering the Los Angeles area. They would meet a driver—they knew him as Benny—and he would have major weight in his trunk, like ten keys, or kilos, of cocaine, and Timo and Hollister would pick up the car as it came off the 101 in LA and escort it into the hood, where Benny did most of his business.

One of their stops was usually Henry, the reasonable marijuana dealer who had since changed his mind and his product line. He'd seen how crack cocaine was changing the face of the neighborhood, and he'd demonstrated a genius for large-scale distribution. Timo liked hanging around with Henry after their business with Benny was done, because Henry had large-scale preparation houses locked up in the hood, where there were plenty of naked girls cooking up the cocaine into the rock form that made it so addictive and so profitable. Nobody in the preparation houses was allowed to wear a stitch of clothing, because not a single ounce of the precious raw material or finished rocks was going to leave the house by any other means than Henry's retail distribution system.

Hollister didn't care for the prep houses, and once or twice he'd followed a batch of the rock to a so-called crack house, where addicts sat for days at a time smoking crack, because that's all they wanted to do. The houses were terrible pits of human degradation that Hollister could barely stand to be around. They reminded him of the little girl whose baby had died in an addict's oven. It had happened two months ago in actuality but light years away from where the black neighborhoods were now, it seemed.

And even as LAPD was inundated with the evidence of this new form of drug addition, shaking the ghetto to its very roots, there was no new guidance from their commanders about how to address the new threat. It was as if crack cocaine didn't exist, or that LAPD simply didn't care that it did.

"Where you think Benny gets the drugs?" Hollister had asked Timo one day.

"He's from Frisco. That's where his supplier is."

"Seems a little weird, doesn't it? We take down some guy and then out pops Benny with all the weight Los Angeles could want."

"That's the way of the jungle, my friend. Always another lion to eat the wildebeest."

"And you don't care."

"About the hood? Nah. If it wasn't Benny, it'd be somebody else and somebody else's payday."

"As long as the money's good, right?"

"That's what I'm talkin' about, kemosabe."

The worst days were when Raoul came to see him at his house. Despite the payoffs, Brad Hollister hadn't bothered to move because he was counting the days before he'd be gone. If Raoul noticed, he didn't say.

"Hey, you ever clean this dump up? Can't imagine you ever getting laid with the place looking like a pigsty."

"The neighborhood didn't start to go downhill until you showed up. What's on your mind?"

"Got a job for you."

"Not interested."

"Relax. This is really easy. Money drop. I need somebody good with a gun for security."

"Still not interested."

"Central America, amigo. Opportunity to see the world."

Brad Hollister stopped. "For how long? And when?"

"Couple of days, tops. Somebody requested you."

"Who?"

"The very top. That guy you call Mr. Corporate? He and his people are going to pay a visit to some people, and they want security."

"In Central America."

"El Salvador, if you must know."

"What's the route?"

"We fly into Panama separately and meet the principals there. From there, we have our own aircraft take us into San Salvador, the capital city, and make the drop. After that, back to Panama, and we disperse again. Simple. Easy."

"Weapons?"

"Supplied in Panama when we get on our charter."

"I need a passport, then."

"You have one. I checked with the State Department."

Wrong, Hollister thought. I have two.

"How much?"

"Two, three million."

Jesus, he just told me how much the drop is. "I meant for me?"

"Ten thousand."

"How many of us are there? Working security?"

"Five total."

"That's a lot for a friendly transaction."

Raoul shook his head. "It's a little bit complicated. Three-way deal. No need to worry yourself about it. But like always, Kid, you get the high sign from me, you start taking people down, no questions, no hesitation, OK?"

"This gonna be a regular thing?"

"Could be if you don't screw it up."

"Timo in on this?"

Raoul shook his head. "Timo is stupid and has a big mouth."

"When do we go?"

Raoul took a sheaf of tickets out of his jacket pocket. "Day after tomorrow."

Two days later Brad Hollister was at Los Angeles International Airport passing through security, hoping to meet Raoul and the others at the gate. He was flying some lousy little airline that he'd never heard of, even though the tickets had been issued by American.

He'd stopped to buy a candy bar at one of the concession stands near the gate when he spotted Raoul. Raoul was with Benny and another man Hollister didn't recognize.

Hollister quickly scanned the rest of the gate area. He picked out three Hispanic guys who looked like muscle of the sort that Raoul would employ for this kind of gig. These guys looked tough, like they would just as soon break someone's neck as speak to him.

He finished his purchase and headed into the gate.

He was surprised when Raoul motioned him to come over.

"You already know Benny," Raoul said when he reached him. "I want you to meet Daniel Blancone. He's from San Francisco."

Hollister did his best to keep his features neutral as he shook Blancone's hand, but in his head he was thinking that this was Benny's supplier. Which didn't make sense. Why would the supplier and the wholesaler be heading to South America together with a pile of money? Certainly not to secure more drugs. That was Blancone's job.

And why were they working security on a drug deal with so many people?

The "charter" out of Panama was an ancient DC-9 that screamed CIA to Hollister and had enough cargo space in the rear for several million dollars in small bills. There were seven of them arrayed uncomfortably around the cavernous space that wasn't particularly equipped for creature comforts. Hollister didn't inquire whether the money had come in directly from the States on the charter or by some other means. Raoul took the opportunity to familiarize the help with the weapons he was providing.

When he had given the others their weapons, he took Hollister aside and handed him a case that obviously held a long gun.

"Listen, Kid, I got plenty of muscle for the exchange. I want you to make yourself scarce and be ready to provide fire support for me if it goes sideways. You have good judgment, and I want you to take down the principals on the other side if you sense that things are not going right, you understand? This is a three-way deal, and I don't like it, so you are my insurance, OK?"

"How will I know the players?"

"The other guys will be dressed in military uniforms. Ignore any Americans that you see, OK? They're on our side."

"What's the play?"

"We're exchanging the drug money for guns. The Americans are on the arms side of things. The assholes in uniforms are involved in the guerilla war for Nicaragua. They may want to snatch the money and the guns and screw everybody."

"Why the hell do a three-way? Why not give the money to the Americans and have them deliver to the guerillas?"

"Because the guerillas are the link to the drug supply, stupid. They need to see the machinery at work so that they keep supplying Blancone and his mule, Benny."

"Sounds way too complicated, Raoul."

Raoul patted him on the back. "Yeah, and I'm gettin' too old for this stuff, Kid."

Phillip Stone waited in the heat for all the parties to show up, cursing himself for agreeing to appear at this particular juncture to ensure that everything went smoothly. But he had a military transport parked on the same airfield as the DC-9 loaded with weapons that his firm had sourced for the revolution. The money to be exchanged was a problem, because he'd have to launder it and make sure that the transactions never showed up in his books, but that was a good problem to have. He'd already talked to Blancone about a placement, and the beauty of it was that the money just turned over and over and over. *Guns, drugs, money. Guns, drugs, money.*

Hollister watched from a well-concealed hide about one hundred yards from the meeting point. He saw the corporate guy, Stone, and cursed. He saw Raoul, and wished he could pull the trigger on that asshole, but swept the gun toward the dope dealers, Blancone and Benny, aka Benito Menendez. The military guys were foolish-looking in their uniforms and the exaggerated medals on their chests, like they had actually been a part of a real war, even though Hollister had to admit that he knew nothing about Nicaragua and any military action there. He watched as Stone was shown the money. Stone pulled the flap up on a military flatbed and showed them a sample of the weapons that he had for them. At least, Hollister thought it was a sample, because there wasn't nearly enough tonnage there to justify the pile of cash that Stone was being given.

There was some discussion about that, as Stone spoke into a radio, hopefully to bring the rest of the shipment into the jungle at the meeting point. But Raoul and the generals were getting more and more agitated, and Hollister began to steady himself in earnest in case he had to separate someone's brain pan from their spine. He kept flipping from general to general, always aware that he had to keep Raoul out of the shot, but Raoul was slipping and kept queering the sight lines with his body.

Or maybe this was his way of making sure The Kid didn't shoot prematurely.

About five minutes after the argument started, Hollister could hear the rumble of trucks moving through the jungle toward the meeting point. Clearly Stone's shipment of weapons was being delivered to the meeting site to calm the generals down. But once a sniper, always a sniper, and Hollister pulled back from the rifle scope optics and began looking for anything out of place as the trucks began pulling up twenty yards from where the generals were still jawing with Raoul.

He nearly missed it in the first sweep. Three or four guys with machetes moving toward the trucks, trying their best to remain unseen from the high vantage point of the truck cabs. The drivers were going to be taken out and the trucks driven off, Hollister figured, so that the generals could cry no deal.

He had a radio that was on Raoul's frequency, so he clicked the mike twice, pulling the gun toward him and making sure that he could acquire all the machete men quickly should Raoul want him to react.

He didn't see Raoul put the radio to his mouth. All he heard was his response: "Yeah, Kid."

Hollister keyed his radio. "Four hostiles moving on the weapons trucks. These guys have steel, looks like they mean to hijack the merch and roll it out of here, over."

There was a hesitation as Hollister imagined Raoul thinking about what he was being told. Then:

"Take them out. Then cover me and the gringos if the Nicaraguans get nervous."

There you go, he thought. Just like being back in 'Nam.

He looked, making sure that the constantly updating target priority in his head represented the best opportunity to take all of them down before they reached any of the trucks. The calculus in his head completed, he steadied himself, put cross hairs on the first guy, squeezed the trigger ever so gently, and moved on to the second, third, and fourth targets, ignoring the boom of the unsuppressed rifle, because the noise was the point, and he imagined Stone craping his pants at the gunfire.

He was done in the time it took him to work the bolt three times, and then he swung the rifle around to pick up Raoul and the generals. He laughed when he saw Stone on the ground and the generals with their sidearms out, gesturing wildly to Raoul.

Hollister clicked his mike twice, and Raoul came back immediately.

"Four targets down," Hollister said.

Raoul looked at one of the generals. "It seems there has been a flaw in your perimeter security. One of my spotters saw four banditos trying for the trucks."

"What?" one of the generals said. "That's impossible."

"Perhaps I can show you the bodies?"

The general backed down. "No, that will not be necessary. That was the shooting? Your spotter?"

Raoul nodded. "You might want to wave. He probably has cross hairs on you right now, General."

Benny and Blancone, who had definitely hit the ground when the shots were fired, started laughing when one of the generals actually did raise his hand and begin to wave.

***

As the generals moved to take possession of the weapons, Stone motioned to Blancone to join him. Stone had a case full of money propped up against a tree.

Stone gestured to the money. "You going to give me your marker for this?"

Blancone smiled. "You know that I'm good for it."

"There's two million ready to be transferred to me. If you can complete the wholesale buys while we're here, we're talking ten to one, right?"

"Roughly. Particularly if LA can absorb the product in one shot. Cuts down on expenses."

"So, you just bought two million dollars' worth of decent but not top-of-the-line weapons for your contras with drug money, and now you expect to take the proceeds and make us both five times the profit, yes?"

Blancone smiled. "Yes. It's called leverage, Mr. Stone. We can continue to supply our comrades with arms, and by the time we're done, you will have grossed several hundred million dollars from recycling the cash proceeds back into a vertically integrated retail drug cartel."

"Assuming the Columbians don't get wind of this."

"There is plenty of territory to go around. And your country's Drug Enforcement Agency can help keep the Cali and Medalin cartels' heads down so they won't notice or care about what we're doing."

Stone smiled. "All for a worthy cause, right, Daniel?"

"Right, Mr. Stone."

***

In the end, it was bad luck that nearly cost Brad Hollister his freedom. The Panama airport was tiny, wrapped around a couple of fast-food shops and some duty-free shops. The gate for the Los Angeles flight was right next to the gate for the flight to Miami.

They were all going back on different schedules, so nobody was scheduled to be on the plane to LA with him. But Raoul wanted to talk.

"Hey, look, there probably won't be much of a need for this kind of op anymore. This was the first time, proof-of-concept kind of thing, OK?"

"Sure," Hollister said, looking at the proximity of the two gates. "When do you fly out?"

"In about an hour. Going to fly to Lima and then back to the United States."

"OK. They should be getting ready to call the LA flight. I'm gonna go cop a squat at the gate."

"You sure you don't want company, Kid? After action and all."

"Nope. I'm cool. Maybe one day you'll explain it all to me, Raoul."

Raoul shrugged. "Curiosity killed the sniper, Kid. You don't want to know any more than you need to know."

"Yeah, sure," Hollister said, but in his head he was thinking about a comment Raoul had made in Vietnam so many years ago.

> *They were in a military airlift jet over the ocean on the way back to the States when Raoul told him that the target was Martin Luther King.*
>
> *What? "When?" was all he could ask.*
>
> *"We're looking for the right moment. Bobby Kennedy is definitely going to run, because we think Johnson is going to bow out of the race."*
>
> *"LBJ? No way."*
>
> *"He doesn't have the stomach for it anymore, Kid. And he doesn't want to get taken out of the Oval Office in a pine box, like they did Kennedy."*
>
> *"Why would they do that?"*
>
> *"Because he's thinking about trying to end the war. Our patrons can't let the war end just yet."*
>
> *"So you think Bobby has a chance once LBJ quits?"*
>
> *Raoul nodded.*
>
> *"And you're afraid that he'll find out the truth about Dallas."*
>
> *"A little. We're more afraid he'll find out the truth about Vietnam."*

He watched Raoul wander off toward his own gate, and Hollister looked at the ticket and the passport that had him traveling back to Los Angeles, California. He shook his head.

That part of his life was over, he thought. He made sure that Raoul was far enough away when he went to the gate for the Miami flight.

"How long before boarding?" he asked the desk attendant in Spanish.

"Twenty minutes. Do you already have your boarding pass?"

"No."

"OK, can I see your ticket and passport?"

"Si," Hollister said, and he produced a second US passport with a different name that matched his Miami ticket.

"OK, Señor…" The gate agent struggled with the American last name.

The Kid merely smiled. "No problemo," he said, settling in to wait for the Miami flight to board, and leaving Brad Hollister behind *forever.*

CHAPTER 37

Thursday, August 25, 2011

Richard Whelan and the president regarded each other for a moment of strained silence. Finally, Whelan spoke up.

"Sir, I just thought I should do everything I could to tell you that I believe that there is a credible threat against your life. I believe the plan is to make an attempt tomorrow, at the speech."

Obama nodded. "It wouldn't surprise me."

"Really?"

Obama said nothing for a moment. "My wife thinks this isn't something as simple as a conspiracy, nor is it as simple as a race-based plot. This is something deeper if it's credible—which you, and she, believe it is."

"I think, at least, I know where the shooter is going to set up. And the weapon."

"Really. What does Moynihan say about your theory?"

"I haven't been able to get him. And your protection detail thinks I'm some kind of nutcase."

"So where and how?"

"The scaffolding on the Capitol Dome. A big Russian antitank weapon fitted for a slightly smaller but still lethal bullet."

"Good Lord. How did you figure that?"

"It's the only place that affords a shooting platform with a chance of escape. The weapon is the only thing that could deliver a lethal round from that distance."

"And if you're wrong?"

Whelan shrugged. "Anything closer would be tough with Secret Service working the crowds. The airspace over the memorial will be clear, and it is unlikely that an airborne threat would be seriously contemplated over Washington, DC. This is some of the most scrutinized airspace in the United States after 9/11."

"Should I get Moynihan on the horn?"

"No," Whelan said, surprising the president. "If something were wrong with Moynihan, alerting him to how much I know might be the same as alerting the sniper team."

"What makes you think—"

"Nothing. But he seems...off. I've known him since he joined the service, and he's been a star ever since he joined. Now he looks merely human. Which means he's either tired or compromised. Or I'm an idiot."

"Then what—"

"I don't know. I don't want to ruin his reputation by taking over. I don't want to become a pariah to the rest of the Service, particularly your protection detail, by going over everyone's head, particularly by going direct to the protectee. Bad business, that, particularly because of the race angle."

"Is that why you left the detail?"

"No, sir. But it made it more convenient to leave. There were some who were relieved that you and I weren't in a bar on K Street bumping fists on the weekend—not that that would have happened."

Obama smiled. "I always wondered about you, Whelan. The brilliant loner law-enforcement guy. Change something into a law degree, and you could be sitting in my chair."

Whelan took a moment to look at the trappings of the White House. "No, sir," he said, "I would have had to have different parents."

Obama cocked his head. "Is that it?"

"Probably a part of it, from what I've read about you."

"So what do we do from here?"

"The FBI knows that I'm looking at this. I'll get to Moynihan at some point, so let me handle the Service. Other than that, I want to stay out of the loop and off the radar as much as possible, if that's OK with you, sir."

Obama nodded. "OK, Mr. Loner. You got it."

"Say hello to Mrs. Obama, sir. I've always been a big fan."

"That I can do, Whelan. That I can do."

"And one last thing for Plan B, just in case things don't go precisely as planned. I want to take into account one possibility for why I'm being targeted too…"

***

The Kid was able to confirm that his crate had been delivered to the Capitol and had been dragged up to the scaffolding on top of the building. All he had to do was get in there and assemble the weapon and wait until the president made his speech.

And he could assemble the weapon in twenty minutes, tops.

That part of it was ready.

He looked at his watch.

Now he had to tie down the second part of the plan.

Richard couldn't wait to tell Bettina what Obama had said. He wheeled the Porsche over to the executive office building and was waiting at the curb when she came out. She was grinning, and he wondered if she was in another hormone-induced manic phase.

She opened the door and slouched into the low-slung Porsche.

"Gonna need an SUV when I'm big, Super Dad," she said.

"I'll make a note of it. How are we today?"

"Fine. With your debt, and my brilliant job performance, I'm a rich woman."

"OK," Richard said, and pulled the Porsche into traffic.

***

Everybody dies, Barack. The president finished rewriting his speech and contemplated burning it in the trash can beside his desk. He contemplated the speech as his potentially posthumous contribution to the State of the Union, but the people wouldn't have it. In the wake of his assassination, they'd call it the ravings of a crazy man. But he had heard things, rumors really, which he had begun to reevaluate in the last twenty-four hours.

Like, *this* is the way things work. *This* is the reason why nothing changes. Something deeper than bipartisan bipolar disorder. Something more sinister crawling around the walls of the capital, in the walls of the Pentagon and Langley and the FBI.

He wondered what Whelan knew, or thought. Probably just a fraction of what was really going on. Yes, a threat made the president paranoid, they would say, which was why he had to say what was written in those pages.

He pulled toward him a book of photos from the civil rights movement, and he came to focus on one that had always struck him as the most ironic photo from the movement. It was a sign, really, but in the charged atmosphere of the Cold War, it was a sign like no other:

Khrushchev can eat here, why can't we?

And now here he sat in the White House. And someone wanted to change that paradigm too in the most dramatic way possible.

But everybody dies, Barack. He took another sip of his club soda. *Everybody dies, but very few people get to pick the place and the time.*

***

Richard picked up on the black sedan following him as he was taking Bettina home to Georgetown. He watched it for a few blocks, not wanting to alarm Bettina. Then he saw it run a light to keep up with him, and that little part of him knew, just knew, this was trouble.

He was stuck in the middle of Georgetown where he couldn't exercise the Porsche's legs and lose this creep once and for all.

He turned toward Military Highway and Rock Creek Park.

Maybe I can lose him in the park, he thought.

Alan Christiansen sat in his office, contemplating a plot against the president of the United States.

He called Frank Moynihan and got him on his cell phone. He deduced that Moynihan was driving from the background noise.

"How's it going?" Christiansen asked.

242

He could almost hear Moynihan shrug. "As well as can be expected. Any other ghosts show up at the FBI offices?"

"The one we have is enough. What's scary is that the FBI establishment was probably a part of it. Or knew about it."

"What makes you think that?"

"Because I saw something in the old files."

"Really."

"Nothing conclusive. Just suggestive."

"Suggestive in terms of King?"

"No, this was a reference to JFK. Something about the Deep South and whether JFK was going to visit Birmingham, Alabama."

"But he didn't visit Birmingham."

"No. Just Dallas."

"Wow."

"Precisely."

"Has Whelan talked to you?"

"He's been trying to get in contact, but I've been pretty busy."

"He has a theory."

"Everyone has a theory."

"He's one of yours, Frank."

"Look, I'll make sure I talk to him. But he seems to have pissed off the president's protection detail. Say they heard from him, and he sounded like some kind of a nut job. He left the president's detail, and now they're starting to wonder why."

"That's crazy. Whelan is a decorated agent."

"Maybe so, but I'm just telling you what I'm hearing."

"It's still crazy. Talk to Whelan; ask him what he thinks."

"Like I said, I will talk to him. But what happens if the ghost is a figment of his imagination? What if he's out to become a hero and this is all somehow rigged to make him the good guy?"

"I have the proof about the rifle."

"So? What does the rifle have to do with anything except maybe as the reddest of red herrings?"

"But that's insane."

"Who got the package? Who the hell threatens a Secret Service agent?"

"Hey, Superman, driving kind of fast, aren't ya?" Bettina asked as Whelan began working through the gears in Rock Creek Park.

"Black sedan, been following us for the last couple of miles."

"Damn."

"My sentiment exactly."

He pushed down the accelerator and left the black sedan behind but was forced to downshift to sit at the next stoplight. The black sedan pulled up behind them, the driver's face obscured by the sun visor and his mirrored sunglasses.

"My gun is in the glove compartment," he said to Bettina.

"After last night, I'm sure his gun is bigger, hon," Bettina said.

Richard looked at her sharply. "It's not about size," he said as he accelerated away from the stoplight.

"When'd you dump your Secret Service team?" Bettina asked him.

"When I was coming to get you."

"Weird."

"Because he knew where we are?"

"Uh-huh."

"What if he's tracking you through the Secret Service personnel?"

"I thought about that. But that doesn't explain how he knew about your doctor's appointment."

"It's not like that's a state secret."

"But he'd have to know you were pregnant."

"No, he'd have to know that I was going to the doctor. Doesn't have to be pregnancy."

"So he could have gotten that from your secretary."

"Not likely, but possible."

Whelan slowed down for another light.

The black sedan pulled up behind him and then bumped them lightly on the bumper before pulling around and speeding away.

"Goddammit," Whelan cursed, reaching across for the Browning automatic pistol in the glove compartment. He pulled out to give chase.

"Oh, boy, Superman. Let me out at the next corner, and I'll take a cab home."

"Yeah, I'd feel better if you were out of the car."

He began shifting, trying to catch up with the fleeing sedan. He watched, incredulous, as it careened through a stoplight and nearly smashed into a cab. Richard screeched to a halt in front of the knot of traffic.

"Got your cell phone?" he asked Bettina.

"You want me to bail here?" she responded.

"Yeah. Before this gets ugly."

"OK."

Bettina hauled open the door and climbed out, watching as Whelan pulled away as soon as the door was closed.

She was about to pull open her cell phone to call a cab when one appeared, almost like magic.

"How convenient," she said to herself.

Whelan was pushing through the gears, testing the suspension. It was unbelievable that a late-model Chevy could keep him on his toes, but every time he started to close the gap, there was a slower-moving car that he had to avoid. His Browning was in the passenger seat that Bettina had just vacated.

After twenty minutes of spirited chase, they finally pulled onto a straightaway on 495, and he pulled parallel to the speeding black sedan. He motioned with the gun angrily, but the driver ignored him. He pulled slightly ahead and then feinted in toward the bumper of the other car, causing the sedan to fishtail wildly.

He dropped back to parallel with the sedan, and again he gestured with the gun.

The driver, wearing the characteristic black baseball cap and mirrored sunglasses, reluctantly pulled over to the side of the road.

Whelan pulled over and was out of the car in a flash.

"Get the fuck out of the car, now!" he screamed.

"Whoa," the driver said. "Dude, chill out!"

Just from the sound of the driver's voice he knew something was wrong. The door opened, the driver got out, and shit, Richard thought, he's just a kid.

He took the baseball cap off and put the sunglasses in his shirt pocket.

A pimply-faced kid.

A decoy.

He pulled his cell phone from his pocket and dialed Bettina's number.

It was answered on the first ring.

By a man.

"I used to have a pretty girlfriend, too," the man said, and then hung up.

CHAPTER 38

Thursday, August 25, 2011

W helan was frantic. He thought about calling the police, the FBI, the CIA, the Secret Service, the president, God, anyone. "Who hired you?" he asked the teenager. *Bettina's going to die because I can't mind my own damn business.*

"Some guy," the boy replied, shrugging.

Whelan grabbed the kid's T-shirt and practically lifted him into low earth orbit. He got in his face.

"You're going to have to do a damn sight better than that, son," he said, sticking the Browning's barrel into the boy's nose.

"I dunno, it was just a guy!" the boy screamed.

"What'd he look like?"

"Old."

Whelan twisted the T-shirt into a tighter knot around his fist. "How old?"

"Mister, don't hurt me! Said it was a goof, gave me some cash!"

"How old, you little prick?"

"Old—gray hair maybe. How the hell do I know?"

The kid was losing it and about to start crying.

Whelan responded by cocking the Browning. "One last time, kid. What did he look like, what was his name, and how old was he?"

"Skinny white guy wearing dark glasses and a baseball cap. Not quite as tall as you. Not real skinny, but not like a bodybuilder either. Gray in his hair, I think. Or maybe gray hair—don't kill me, man!"

"You get a name?"

"No. Found him in a goth chat room online."

"When?"

"Been a couple of weeks now. Said he needed a favor and he could pay for it, but he wasn't talking no gay stuff."

"How'd he ID my car?"

"Gave me the plate, told me where you'd be, told me to follow you. That's it, I swear."

"But no name?"

"No, man, no name. Please, mister, take the gun outta my nose. I thought it was a practical joke, that he, like, knew you or something."

"You live in DC."

"No. Spartansburg, Virginia."

"What the hell are you doing up here?"

"Making a quick two hundred bucks is all, I swear."

"Is this your car?"

"No. It's my mom's."

"Did he know you had a car like this in your family when he asked you for the favor?"

The boy shrugged. "I dunno. Maybe. Can I go now?"

Whelan took the gun out of the kid's nostril and eased the hammer back into position.

"Yeah, kid, get out of my sight before I change my mind."

Whelan got in his car and cranked the engine, then let his head slowly drop onto the padded leather steering wheel. His head was spinning.

Why take Bettina? To get him out of the way?

Why?

And how had he known where he was and what he was doing?

He called Moynihan and got voice mail at his office and voice mail on his cell phone. Richard wanted to throw the phone against the windshield in disgust, but he had to keep making phone calls.

He called Alan Christiansen at FBI headquarters. He was in a meeting, according to his secretary, who promised that he would get the message when he came back to the office.

He also called the major at the Pentagon who had gotten him Stiles's personnel file.

Hadley was in.

"Yes, Richard, what can I do for you?" Hadley asked, and Richard wanted to reach through the goddamned phone and choke the bastard.

"I was looking for the file on Sanchez. Were you able to pull his jacket?" Richard said through gritted teeth.

"Yeah, in fact, I was just about to call you. I have it right here."

"Can I swing by and pick it up?"

"Um, sure. This one isn't classified. I'll be here for another twenty minutes or so."

"Major, please make sure that I can get that file if I don't get there before you leave. Call me on my cell phone and tell me who you're leaving it with if you can't hang around until I get there. This is a matter of life and death right now."

Hadley replied like he didn't have a care in the world. "Fine. If I'm called away, I'll let you know."

"One question, Major."

"Shoot."

"Where is Sanchez now?"

"He turned in his papers in the late seventies, so he's out of the service."

"And you have no record of what happened to him after that?"

"That's not exactly true. Because of his training, the military kept tabs on him."

"So where is he now?"

"Dead."

"Dead when?"

"Within ten years of mustering out. It's all in the file, Whelan."

"Wait," Richard said, his mind still churning, "what about his training made you keep tabs on him?"

"He was an early spook. DIA/CIA, James Bond kind of thing. Technical name for it was Covert Action Group, or CAG. Guy was trained to do any and everything."

"What was he doing in Vietnam?"

"He wasn't over there for any length of time, and there's a lot in his jacket that just isn't there, which means it's classified and buried real deep, you know, big gaps in the timeline. But ten of these guys could have been dropped in Saigon and started walking north to Hanoi, and by the time they got there, the war would have been won."

"Hadley, that sounds like the biggest bunch of bull I've ever heard. If that's the case, why didn't we win the war?"

"Because we didn't want to," Hadley said, and Whelan did a double take at the phone. He remembered his 7th grade petition about the war and his father's shocked reaction to it, but he didn't follow up.

"How did he die?" Whelan asked.

"He was shot to death in civilian life."

"Anything in his file indicate that he has living relatives, people I could talk to?"

"Not since he mustered out. The military's trace on him was strictly to ensure that he didn't go freelance and become a mercenary. Once he was dead, they closed the jacket."

"OK. Shot to death—that in the file too?"

"Yeah, I think it is."

"Fine, I'll be there as quickly as I can."

It seemed like hours had passed when he arrived at the Pentagon and took the file from Major Hadley.

"Sanchez was a spook?"

"Correct."

"Can I get a list of people that he worked with?"

"All deceased."

"Including this Lance Corporal Wilton Stiles?"

"Yup."

"Whom I suspect might not be dead."

"What makes you think that?" Hadley asked.

Because he just snatched my pregnant girlfriend, you asshole! Whelan wanted to scream, but didn't.

"Because his jacket doesn't add up. And neither does the way that I got his name."

"Hmm. Then the only thing I can tell you is that Sanchez was killed in New Jersey in the mideighties. Maybe someone he knew was involved in his shooting."

"New Jersey, you said?"

"Yeah. Town of Willingboro, which I gather is in South Jersey. That part isn't described in any detail in the file, just that he's deceased and the date and the place."

Oh no, Whelan thought. "Are you sure it was Willingboro?"

"Yeah, why?"

"What date?"

"June fifteenth, 1985."

"Are you sure?"

"Yeah, you know something about this case?"

It was a notorious case from his adulthood. A shooting by a state police officer that had been ruled a justifiable homicide in a court case that had been ridiculed by minorities. Sanchez was a Hispanic male, and the judge had dismissed the case for lack of evidence, years before the "racial profiling" of minorities by the state police had been revealed.

He also knew the statie involved, because he'd checked his background when that decorated statie had joined the Secret Service to make sure it was the same guy. And it was.

The young state trooper had been none other than Frank Moynihan, who had left a fairly high rank in state law enforcement to join the Secret Service. He'd climbed through the ranks and been appointed head of the Secret Service by George W. Bush.

What the hell was going on?

***

Whelan was back in the Porsche heading home when he dialed the FBI director again.

"Alan Christiansen."

"Richard Whelan." Whelan thanked God that Alan was back in his office.

"What's wrong?"

"Bettina was snatched—by the guy who's been shooting up my house and the restaurant last night."

"What? Are you sure?"

"Positive. He had a kid chasing me, and I let Bettina out. The kid was a decoy, and when I called Bettina's cell phone, he picked up."

"Richard, let me ask you again—are you sure?"

"Alan, I'm positive. Do your FBI thing; see if you can trace her phone for me or something. All I know is that she was going to hail a cab near the park on Military Highway. That's all I know."

"OK, calm down and let me do some checking."

"I am calm. I called to ask a favor."

"Go ahead."

"How well does the FBI know local law enforcement?"

He could hear Christiansen thinking. "There's a loose fraternity of cops of all kinds, Richard, except maybe when it comes to the CIA. You know that. Though most locals think the FBI is pushy and jurisdictional, so there are limits. By the same token, there are people who leave the FBI and go into local law enforcement. Why?"

"Do you have any ties to the New Jersey state police?"

"I wouldn't know off the top of my head."

Whelan wanted to pound the dashboard in frustration. "Something's there, just beyond the edge of my consciousness, and I can't grab hold of it. Holloman in Memphis was ex-FBI. King gets killed on the day Holloman ordered one of the black cops protecting King off duty because of a Secret Service threat to his life that was never verified.

"Kennedy's car slows down in Dallas after the first shots are fired, and the Secret Service agent turns and looks at JFK and watches him getting his head blown off.

"Hoover was all over the civil rights movement in the sixties, and the FBI was all over any kind of black activists during that period. Hell, one of my earliest cases was in LA, and DEA and others were all over a bunch of drug dealers who they should have been arresting but didn't. What is it—what the hell is the connection that brings them all together? And now I find out that this Wilton Stiles character has a common link with—"

Richard stopped, realizing that he must have sounded delusional.

"Richard?" Christiansen asked him, but Whelan began to see bogeymen everywhere.

"You said Stiles has a common link with someone?"

"Forget it, Alan," he said, because some things were trying to click in ways that he couldn't and wouldn't believe. "Just find Bettina, OK?"

"But you were about to say something, weren't you?"

"No, I'm tired and scared. I'm going home to figure some things out."

He called Moynihan next.

"This is Frank Moynihan. I'm not available to take your call..."

Yeah, I'll bet.

Whelan decided to drive to Frank's house. He knew the address. It would take about forty minutes.

Alan Christiansen sat back in his office chair for some moments after his call with Richard Whelan ended. Whelan had asked him how well the FBI knew local law enforcement.

He also thought about his call with Frank Moynihan earlier in the day. Whelan was the linchpin, Moynihan had said, because all the threads involved him. And now his girlfriend was missing? Who did you look at when it came to domestic violence?

The boyfriend/husband, that's who. Good Lord, was Whelan going to hurt Bettina Freeman and blame it on aliens from Area 51?

Or was she already dead?

Oh, the undersecretary of State has been kidnapped by a lunatic who may somehow have killed Martin Luther King, Christiansen thought. Or, her boyfriend, the mysterious loner Richard Whelan, who was last seen with her, has somehow abducted her, and she's either dead or in harm's way.

Which one passed the Occam's razor test, Alan? C'mon, you like and respect Whelan, but is it time to close ranks? Is this the guy you want to trust with the Bureau's dirty laundry?

And what would happen if something bad went down at the president's speech tomorrow? Was he exposed? Did he need to sanitize anything?

Wait, wait, wait, Alan. This is Richard Whelan.

He thought for a moment and then picked up the phone and hit a button that connected him to his administrative assistant.

"I need you to call in some favors. I need the personnel file of one Richard Whelan at Secret Service. I also need to talk to Tennyson at Treasury and Zorn at DEA. Set them up in that order if you can, and if it's gonna take more than an hour, I'll take them as I can get them.

Clear my calendar and have one of my babysitters go to Starbucks for my usual. Got it? Thanks."

Bettina Freeman woke up in a shed of some kind, in the dark. She was groggy, which scared her, because she couldn't remember going home and getting into bed. And the mattress, what was the...

And then she remembered.

She had gotten in the back of the cab, and the doors had locked. The driver hadn't turned around or acknowledged her. The doors had locked, and then she began to feel sleepy, and then she'd blacked out.

She tried to stand up and then noticed that her ankle was chained to an eyelet sunk deep in the concrete floor. She had maybe a five-foot radius of mobility in the inky blackness, and as she moved around, she got the sense that she was underground. She couldn't hear anything; there were no street sounds, no night ambiance, no neighborhood noise—just silence.

Underground. She was claustrophobic, at least a little.

She reached up but could not touch the ceiling.

OK, that was something.

Maybe she would stand for a while, and if she did, maybe the walls wouldn't seem to close in on her, even as the silence did.

Whelan pulled up in his Porsche and surveyed the scene. Moynihan's house was a colonial, painted a pretty maroon color with white trim, and it looked empty. There were no lights on that he could see. He parked and got out of the car to have a look around.

He was conscious that it was a quiet residential street, and there wasn't much foot traffic about. He wondered whether Frank was a security nut and would have alarms and spotlights and infrared detectors going off if he set foot on the property, but there was nothing that he could do about that. He went up the front walk, climbed the porch stairs, and knocked on the door.

Nothing seemed to stir in the house.

Still, his sixth sense was such that he pulled the Browning from his waistband.

He stepped off the porch and began circling around toward the back of the house. He noticed the garage in the back and the shed adjoining the garage, but even from where he stood, he could see that the garage and the shed were padlocked and very secure.

He continued to the back of the house, thinking that he could check the garage in a minute. The back door was screened and locked.

For a minute he considered breaking in, but then again, he was black man skulking around a nice neighborhood with his gun drawn.

As he turned toward the garage, he heard a car engine on the street in front of the house. He peeked around the corner but could see only a set of wheels next to his Porsche.

The engine was idling, that much he could tell.

He started out from the rear of the property, thinking it was Moynihan—he didn't want Frank to see him skulking around like this.

As he came toward the front walk, he couldn't see the driver of the car, but he could see more of the car itself.

A black sedan. Moynihan drove a gray government-issue car that screamed *cop*.

Whelan broke into a run. As soon as the driver saw him hit the front walk, he peeled rubber and pulled away.

***

Chuck O'Shay was in his office, thinking about the future. O'Shay loved the Obamas, and he had been one with their agenda for a long time. But he had long thought about the lunatic fringe and whether Obama's risk increased as the Republican Party grew more splintered. A second-term Obama would have vast potential without the worry of a subsequent term. And Obama was a young man—young enough to have a second career in just about anything he wanted after a second term, or hell, after a first.

If he survived tomorrow. Obama was going to go through with the speech, and Michelle seemed to be on board with it all. That meant that he was at risk, and that meant that come tomorrow afternoon, there was a tiny chance that a new administration would be forming, and he—O'Shay—likely wouldn't survive.

Yeah, he was a prick for even thinking that way, but this was Washington, and the unthinkable was thought and war gamed every damn day. Besides, like a lot of people, O'Shay had been thinking about when the best time to bail would be, in terms of cashing in on his time spent in the White House. Emmanuel was now mayor of Chicago, he reminded himself, but he had been a politician of some gravitas prior to joining Obama's administration. But Emmanuel was a lesson to everyone that service to the administration was not an excuse to let grass grow under one's feet.

The problem was that Chuck hadn't been getting any feelers about opportunities. His ear had been to the ground, but he wasn't hearing the distant rumble of hoofbeats from anything close, or anything in China, for that matter.

He wasn't wealthy, even though he was frugal and he had savings. He wasn't going to get wealthy either, goddamn it, because he wasn't likely to pen a tell-all book and wasn't particularly newsworthy on his own. He was a very good functionary who kept the machinery running and who contributed to the strategy skull sessions run by others further into the president's inner circle. And he hadn't been on the job long enough to squeeze out a memoir about his time here. No, as he'd thought many times, he'd bet on a second term and a departure within the first eighteen months or so of it in order to cash in; timing, he thought ruefully, which wouldn't work if the unthinkable happened tomorrow.

He'd even been studying the Nixon presidency and what had happened to the people around Tricky Dicky as the only analogue to a presidency that ended prematurely. Probably a bad example, since Halderman, Erlichman, and Dean had all had their own serious legal problems as a result of their service to the president. Colson had found religion, and O'Shay was reminded of an obscure quote from the movie *Malcolm X*, where Spike Lee, in his cameo, had called Malcolm's religious conversion "the best religion hustle he'd ever seen."

Of course, Malcolm had replied something to the effect that it wasn't a hustle.

O'Shay thought that Colson's conversion had definitely been a hustle.

"Praise Jesus!" O'Shay said, trying it out.

Nah, he thought to himself. You probably needed a couple of years in a Club Fed to get the spirit, and O'Shay had no intention of going to that particular type of divinity school.

***

Whelan's Browning was up and out, and he nearly fired several rounds as the black sedan sped away.

Lights snapped on in several of the neighboring houses at the sound of the sedan's tires squealing on the pavement.

He jumped into the Porsche and sped off in hot pursuit.

The driver of the sedan knew the street patterns better and had a distinct advantage, even though Whelan had more car. Every time Whelan pushed the finely tuned German suspension to catch up to the sedan, his opponent pulled some trick out of his pocket, like a sharp turn onto a street that suddenly narrowed.

Whelan slammed his dashboard in frustration. He'd gotten close to parallel with the other driver, close enough to see that the other driver was alone.

Finally they hit an open stretch of county road, and Richard jammed a gear and pulled out into the opposing lane, coming up beside the black sedan. He hit the switch for the passenger-side window, and he had the Browning cocked and locked, with his other hand on the steering wheel and eyes alternating between the sedan and the road ahead.

They were coming up onto a hilly section. Whelan couldn't determine just what the next rise would mean in terms of oncoming traffic, so he beeped his horn and made an angry gesture at the other driver, who ignored him. All Whelan could see was a baseball cap and some dark glasses.

Ignore this! Whelan thought as he put a bullet through the driver's side rear window.

A Dodge Ram pickup truck crested the hill on Route 15 going north and took note of the Porsche coming toward him in his lane, and coming fast. The driver leaned on the horn in a panic, already starting to twist the wheel to run out on the shoulder to get past the screaming Porsche.

Whelan was about to pull ahead and put a bullet through the windshield when he heard and then saw the pickup. He was forced to stand on the brakes and drop behind the black car until the pickup whooshed by.

Screw it, he thought, and pumped a round through the back windshield of the black sedan.

That got no response either.

The two cars continued to race down the highway at absurd rates of speed. The pickup driver had notified the police of the crazy man driving on the wrong side of 15; county police were rolling as soon as they determined who was closer. One marked car entered the highway three miles behind the speeding cars and began accelerating.

In the black sedan, The Kid heard the call on his police scanner and smiled. Time to have a little fun, he thought. He pulled a rotating red flashing light unit from his car's glove compartment.

Whelan was about to pull out into the oncoming lane again when he became conscious of the police flashers behind him. And they were getting closer.

He either had to make a move now or simply run away. He didn't want to get caught with a weapon that he'd discharged—not in this county.

He hit the gas.

The Kid saw Whelan making his move just as the cop behind them told his dispatcher that he was closing on a suspect vehicle that looked like a Porsche traveling at an excessive rate of speed. He pulled his own gun out of his waistband, a Walther PPK automatic, and made sure that it was ready.

Then he stuck the red flashing unit to the roof of his car and turned it on.

Whelan's Porsche loomed large in his rearview mirror.

Whelan saw the red light on the car's roof but didn't make the connection. Why would he want to look like an unmarked police car?

The bastard slammed on his brakes, and Whelan fishtailed around him, just barely clearing the man's bumper before swerving into the opposite lane. He managed to pass the black sedan, swerving back into his own lane, just in time to barely miss being smacked by an SUV.

Blam blam blam! Now driver of the black sedan was firing at him, and cracks appeared in the Porsche's back window as he ducked to avoid the bullets.

Damn, this is Maverick, and I've got a bandit on my tail, and I've gone totally defensive, Whelan thought. He'd always loved the movie *Top Gun*.

He hit the gas.

The Kid picked up the microphone to the radio in his car as he increased his speed to catch up to Whelan.

"All units, all units, please respond."

"This is Black Eagle County Sheriff on Route 15 southbound in pursuit of a black Porsche, over," The Kid said before letting his finger slip off the "press to talk" button.

He waited only a second or two. "Suspect should be considered armed and dangerous, approach with extreme caution, over."

He paused, hoping the dome light on his roof would help sell the subterfuge.

He pulled the trigger on his gun a few more times, intentionally sending shells high over Whelan's speeding Porsche.

Do some of that pilot stuff, Mav, Whelan thought to himself. He stomped on the accelerator and watched as the black sedan receded into the distance.

Uh-oh, he thought as he saw a stoplight coming up. Route 15 was one of those semi-highway types that had occasional cross streets.

Right now the light was red.

Three cars back, a Pike County police cruiser heard the radio call and saw the unmarked car with the flasher on its roof. Odd that the sedan didn't have municipal or county government plates. Especially odd when he saw the blowback from…gunshots? From the driver's side window. And the back window was…gone?

He picked up his radio to transmit.

The light in front of Whelan was red, and there was a tractor trailer snaking across the cross street. He heard the loud blast of its air horn as it waited for a little old lady to make a left onto 15. The intersection was completely blocked. Whelan glanced at his speedometer and then shrugged.

Hell, 115? Piece of cake.

"All units, be advised, am in pursuit of black sedan with Maryland license plates Alpha Charlie Victor Niner Two Five Seven. Shots fired. Suspect vehicle appears in pursuit of a sports car and has a flashing red light on its roof but no government plates. Over."

The Kid heard the call just as he saw the semi blocking the intersection up ahead. He saw Whelan's brake lights come on and the car start sliding as Whelan turned slightly to fishtail around the rear end of the semi's trailer, but there were cars behind the rig as well.

He had no choice but to stand on his own brakes and see if the jam would break up.

The semi moved with glacial slowness as Whelan zoomed toward it. He had no doubt that the crash would make for a spectacular Viking funeral, because the tanker truck had FLAMMABLE written all over it. The black sedan behind him began dropping back, the driver no doubt standing on his own brakes to avoid skidding into the upcoming wreck. He also saw the police cruiser, its lights flashing, coming up behind. His Porsche was rocking into a slight right swerve, trying to negotiate a gap that wasn't there; the cars behind the semi didn't provide much of a gap that he could shoot through.

Well, Whelan thought as he stood on the horn, that's gonna have to change.

The driver of the minivan waiting behind the big rig saw the blur of Whelan's approaching Porsche and heard the bleating of its horn. Her kids were in the back watching the onboard DVD player. She looked at the sleek sports car and thought *drug dealer* and slammed the gear shift into reverse. She ignored the crunch of the minivan's bumper against that of the Jeep behind her and fed her car more gas as the gap between her minivan and the tractor trailer in front of her began to open ever so slowly.

The Kid saw the minivan heroically push into the Jeep behind it, trying to open a space for Whelan to squeeze through. He saw the tractor trailer begin moving as the little old woman finally executed her left turn and skidded away. Whelan's going to make it, he thought.

He hit the gas.

The policeman behind them saw the jammed intersection and the wreck about to happen. He slammed on his brakes, sending his cruiser into a skid, and then watched in amazement as he saw the black sedan actually speed up and head for the growing gap.

These sumbitches are crazy, the cop thought.

The Porsche cleared the gap, and Whelan managed to get it straightened out without too much difficulty. Gas, gas, shift, gas. He saw the rpms climb toward the red line.

The Kid miscalculated and clipped the back of the semi just enough to lose control and spin around in a hail of plastic car parts. His black sedan did a three sixty, ending up on the shoulder with the left front fender ripped apart and dangling from the frame. The Kid pounded the dashboard in frustration.

The local cop pulled up.

CHAPTER 39

Thursday, August 25, 2011

The Pike County cop skidded his cruiser to a halt and jumped out, his Glock service revolver drawn and ready. As he approached the car, he was accosted by the owners of the maroon minivan and the Jeep Laredo who had kissed bumpers getting out of the way of the lunatics using County Road 15 as a speedway. He waved them off as he approached the black sedan.

The driver was conscious and struggling with his seatbelt.

"Freeze, pal," the cop shouted.

The Kid looked at him.

"I'm law enforcement."

"Then lemme see some ID."

"Soon as I can get this seatbelt off, I'll reach in my pocket and get it, Officer."

The cop stood back, the gun still ready but now pointed at the ground. Finally he heard the seatbelt click and saw it retract.

The Kid hopped out of the car, pulled a thin leather case out of his back pocket, and flipped it open.

The cop looked and whistled. "Secret Service?"

The Kid nodded. "The guy in the Porsche is plotting to kill the president tomorrow."

The cop looked at the black sedan and noticed the scanner. The man had fired a weapon on a busy suburban highway.

"Stay right there for a second. Let me call this in."

The Kid nodded.

As Whelan sped away, he couldn't shake a nagging thought. Why had the black sedan been outside of Moynihan's house? How badly was Moynihan compromised? As he drove home, he began to formulate a plan. He prayed that he could get Bettina out of the middle of this, but he wasn't certain that he could.

The Kid waited, looking at his watch and glancing from time to time at the cop on his radio. After twenty minutes, his patience was just about exhausted.

The police officer exited his car, strolled over to him, and handed him back his identification.

"Sorry for the delay. Like I said, I wanted to check it out."

The Kid waited to see if the man would say anything else, but he didn't. He'd seen it before—you mention Secret Service or FBI, and the whole thing got "federalized" in an instant.

"Do you want us to put out an all-points on the Porsche?" the officer asked, now extremely solicitous.

"No, Officer. I'd rather not have my screw-up all over the state police band. Thanks anyway," The Kid said as he got into his car and sped off.

CHAPTER 40

Thursday, August 25, 2011

The Whelan file came first. FBI Director Christiansen had seen the case before, the Treasury investigation on the West Coast and the notes Whelan had sent in requesting information on a DEA agent named Bennigan and a supposed CIA operative named Phillip Stone. Neither name meant anything to him, but when he mentioned Bennigan and a case in the early eighties in a phone call to Dave Zorn, the sudden silence and chill made him sit up straight in his seat.

"Who's asking?" Zorn said finally after Christiansen had let the silence stretch uncomfortably.

"The head of the FBI, Dave," Christiansen said.

"Why now? That era has been dead and buried for a while."

"Because I've got a man who was involved on the periphery of something that smelled bigger."

"And where is this going? I swear, Alan, if some Congressional subcommittee of hypocrites is going to subpoena me, I'm going to tell everyone to kiss my ass."

"How much do you know?"

"How much do you know about the darkest parts of the Hoover regime at the Bureau?"

"Enough to be afraid of anything coming out in public."

"Well, this is the anchor chain that ties it all together, Alan. Don't tug on it unless you know what you're doing."

Alan Christiansen settled down with a yellow legal pad and a pen. "This is a secure line, Dave. Why don't we start with what you know?"

CHAPTER 41

Thursday, August 25, 2011

P hillip Stone was in Washington staying at the Capitol Hilton and planning to watch Obama's big coming-out party tomorrow on the grounds of the Lincoln Memorial. He had checked in with the assets he had in place and was satisfied that the hit was on track and on schedule. The wheels of history were repeating themselves, and the Silent Night file had been returned to the back of a very secure safe and would be burned one day, perhaps soon. The government was a misnomer now, and the transformation would be nearly complete with the elimination of Obama.

The rationale was simple, really. The arms dealers had decided in Vietnam that the war was good for business and great for profits. And then they had discovered the heroin trade in Southeast Asia, and how warlords had used dope to fund all manner of empire-building since the beginning of time.

Some think tank had done the first study and estimated that the profit potential was enormous, that drugs and guns were a money pump that would create nearly unlimited wealth and power for those capable of accessing both sides of the equation. Drugs financing guns financing drugs. It was brilliant; it was self-sustaining, a perpetual-motion machine if ever one had been invented. Vietnam was the crucial "in," the reason why Kennedy had to die, because once a foothold was established, there would be no stopping the men and women who were involved. Generations of wealth would be created just by allowing entrepreneurs to run around Southeast Asia under the cover of a winnable war that nobody felt like winning until the last bit of toehold had been exploited.

The beauty of it was the patriots got what they wanted—a campaign against communism and a secure funding source for all manner of covert operations too sensitive for the light of day. A funding source that made up for the competitive disadvantage of being in a democracy that required things like "oversight" and "disclosure." The communists had none of those disadvantages, the rationale went, but they had all the military might, all the missiles, and the will to use all of it.

Not surprisingly, the motives of some of those involved weren't completely pure. Killing Kennedy opened a Pandora's box to all manner of agendas, as the small cadre of powerful white men in suits looked at the nation in the 1960s with increasing dismay.

Phillip Stone could only speculate how much of the violence of the sixties had been a direct spinoff of the forces that gathered in '63 to assassinate JFK. His father had thought most of it, because it was difficult to underestimate the depths of the FBI with Hoover at the helm, and so many people had died.

Stone was a byproduct of that era, skilled in commerce, a money changer capable of washing dirty sources into pristine uses with more than enough left over in obscene profits to satisfy the most jaded plutocrat.

When the Cold War ended with the Soviets revealed as mere sock puppets in makeup masquerading as the evil empire, no one, particularly on Stone's side of the ledger, thought to walk away from the money machine that war by proxy had created in any number of fertile geographies. The money was amazing, capable of suborning whole sectors of the government and sweeping away resistance to policies that benefited the arms and drugs cartels, which now included some of the most influential names in global business.

When the Columbians began to raise their ugly heads, the administration conveniently declared a war on drugs, which in turn declared war on the cartels. Nobody cared about winning that war either, just as long as the wrong side didn't get a chance to get too far ahead of the game. The beauty of it was that it was the official policy of the federal government, and as such, places like Panama and people like Noriega could be invaded and arrested months or years after they had been hailed as allies—what was the difference when people soaked in ill-gotten gains controlled the horizontal, the vertical, and the on/off switch?

Who cared, as long as the money was fantastic?

And then came 9/11.

Iraq had oil. Gin up some hocus-pocus about terror and weapons of mass destruction, and voilà, Iraq had an American "liberation," and Stone could sleep at night because the profit motive aligned with the notion that Hussein had to go.

Afghanistan had poppies.

Libya had oil and poorly armed rebels.

So did Syria.

Obama refused to see the connection. The potential yields were astronomical and strategic. A matter of national security, if you liked, given the strategic petroleum reserve, like anybody gave a damn about that. The world could burn at both ends and in the middle as long as somebody made a buck; the logic was unassailable, the players global, the power almost absolute.

Almost.

If the rumors were true—that Obama would use a second term to get out of Afghanistan—then their nascent command and control and supply lines would be cut. Stone and his partners had invested heavily in players within the military and the Afghan government. They could not be withdrawn for the next three years based upon their calculations in order to solidify the money pump with the Taliban—drugs financing guns financing drugs.

So today, Obama had to die.

QED.

He was waiting at the bar for a late addition to his schedule. He looked at his watch, slightly annoyed that he had rushed through dinner to make this appointment, when he saw the man, heavyset but in an immaculately tailored suit, crossing the lobby to the lounge area.

Stone took a long gulp of his drink and then turned and waved to the newcomer, who smiled and walked over to him.

"Hugo," Phillip Stone said, shaking hands with Hugo Castelliano.

"Phillip," Hugo managed with enthusiasm.

"What can I get you?"

"Oh, nothing for me. It's rather late, and I appreciate you squeezing me into your day."

Stone nodded, waiting.

"I wanted to apprise you of an opportunity," Castelliano started, "an extraordinary opportunity that my patrons have stumbled upon. The woman behind it is a visionary thinker, because it will take at least five years to bring it to fruition."

"Are the cartels expanding beyond their traditional lines of business?"

"Yes and no. It's an ingenious extension and an expansion of territories."

Phillip Stone frowned. "You realize that may create sources of friction with some of our Asian counterparts?"

Castelliano smiled. "We have no wish to compete with the heroin trade, Phillip. But there are markets where we are underpenetrated. It's not that these markets are particularly robust for your consortium, either, by the way. And we have years to think about the ramifications either way."

"Then why approach me now?"

Castelliano signaled the bartender and asked for a glass of water.

"Because one day we will be having a conversation that is much more contentious. I wanted to plant a seed, Phillip, a seed to suggest that the world is big enough for competing agendas."

Hugo Castelliano raised his glass. Phillip Stone clinked his against it.

"To the future," Hugo said, and Phillip Stone agreed.

CHAPTER 42

Thursday, August 25, 2011

"**W**hat's your e-mail address, Alan?" Dave Zorn said. "I mean a private, secure e-mail address that you aren't going to open from a Bureau computer."

Christiansen gave it to him.

"I'm going to send you a trial transcript concerning two people from Whelan's mysterious LA case in 1982. This is the unredacted, real deal, Alan, and the file will be encrypted. I suggest you delete it as soon as you read it. It's been awhile since someone sniffed around it, but having it in your possession is not something you want to become public knowledge. OK? If the file isn't self-explanatory, I don't know what to tell you, because I will never answer another phone call about this particular case, and I cannot guarantee that equally hinky stuff doesn't go on elsewhere in our bright, beautiful world."

It took about thirty minutes for Zorn to send, via separate e-mails to different addresses, the file and the encryption password. Christiansen didn't know what to make of it, deciding to ask Whelan about it when he saw him next. The file contained just four pages of transcripts—the sealed grand-jury testimony of one Benito Menendez about his activities in Los Angeles during 1982 and 1983. He was introduced as a confidential DEA deep-cover witness in the trial of one Henry Washington Carver, a major drug dealer in the LA crack epidemic of the time.

Menendez: Yes, I was working for the DEA and a front organization that was funneling money to the Nicaraguan resistance, known as the Contras.

Prosecutor Gilbrand: And you came to know the defendant, Henry Carver?

Menendez: Yes. He was originally a customer of Juan Hidalgo but had wanted to move up to greater weight. I knew Juan casually and also knew that Daniel Blancone could supply weight to Carver.

Gilbrand: What happened to Hidalgo?

Menendez: He was shot to death in Los Angeles in 1982.

Gilbrand: Was the crime, to your knowledge, ever solved?

Menendez: No, but we all knew DEA had his head blown off so that we could move the business to me and Blancone.

(Defense objected and was sustained.)

Gilbrand: So you began supplying Carver.

Menendez: Yes. Blancone had introduced me to a small network in 1981, but since most of the money was going back to Nicaragua, there was no money in the weight that I was doing. So Carver was seen as a way of increasing my volume and providing enough money for me and the movement. Carver began moving major weight, because he figured out how to make freebase available to the masses. They called it crack. And the money was amazing.

CHAPTER 43

Early Morning, Friday, August 26, 2011

T
he president of the United States rose, showered, and accepted a glass of orange juice from the steward holding his breakfast tray. He gazed out of the residence, out over the grounds of the White House, and realized that today was the beginning of the end, either way. Either he would win a second term, and the pundits would trace this as the day the campaign began, or he would lose his bid for reelection, and the pundits would also point to this day as the beginning of his failed strategy.

And, if he were assassinated, Barack Obama thought wryly, it might be a matter of hours.

Michelle joined him, receiving her own glass of orange juice from the steward. She met her husband's eyes and held them for a long moment, oblivious to everything, the White House and all of its trappings, as she held her husband's gaze.

The look conveyed everything that she needed to say, and when she broke off, it was to read the *Washington Post* and the front-page story about her husband's upcoming speech.

My husband is not going to die today, she said to herself, and muttered a silent prayer.

Barack Obama glanced at his watch.

It was a little before 6:00 a.m.

***

At 7:00 a.m. Chuck O'Shay woke to his alarm at the same time as his wake-up call from the White House operator rang through. He picked up the phone, acknowledged to the operator that he was awake, and hit the snooze button on his bedside table. He stretched and sat up as he thought about the president's speech today.

Obama was ready, he had claimed, to give the speech of his life.

Now, if he could just get him to live through it.

He swung out of bed, thinking that he should probably check in with Moynihan or at least Sam Redburn, who was the head of the protection detail. Might seem a bit intrusive, he thought, but he was the chief of staff, and he needed to at least appear to be in control, whether he was or not. The question was: Which phone call would be the least intrusive and annoying? Well, he would talk to Redburn later and in depth. For comfort food, he would reach out to Frank Moynihan.

Always start at the top, he thought, and dialed Frank's number.

"Moynihan."

"Chuck O'Shay. Is the president going to live through his speech today?"

"God willing," Moynihan said, which O'Shay didn't particularly take a shine to.

"Look, Frank, I'll be talking to Redburn later as Obama gets ready to go, but we have everything buttoned down, right? No loose ends?"

"Sam Redburn is mad as hell. Someone in the White House leaked that Whelan was there and actually met with the protectee?"

Oh, crap, O'Shay thought. "Um, look, Frank, when the man asks, the man gets. And he definitely asked."

"And I suppose no one mentioned to Mr. Obama that Whelan had made a threatening phone call to Sam Redburn prior to that visit?"

"Threatening how?"

"Not important. It's an incredible breach of protocol for anyone from my staff to see the protectee prior to an event like this with a credible threat hanging in the balance. Now we don't know what Whelan knows about the protection scheme, but if he was the one trying to defeat it, he'd now have a lot more information than he did prior to seeing the president."

"Are you suggesting that *Whelan* is the threat?"

Moynihan took a deep breath. "If something goes down, I want the record to show that I strongly suggested that the president cancel, Chuck. Understand? I'm going on record for this one."

"Have you told the president?" O'Shay nearly shouted, but Moynihan had already hung up.

***

Frank Moynihan had already been awake when O'Shay rang him. He had not been able to sleep, and fatigue was all over him. He stirred creamer into his morning coffee and pulled a tiny green pill from a foil packet.

He hated working with stimulants, but he couldn't afford to be sleepy. Not today.

He debated calling Sam Redburn but decided against it. He'd call him from his car on the way in. He glanced at his watch and grabbed a light jacket and his car keys, patting his pockets to make sure that his cell phone was in his pocket.

Just as he was locking his front door, his cell phone chirped. He yanked it out of his pocket, grunting in surprise when he saw who was calling.

"Yeah?" he said.

"We have to talk," Richard Whelan said.

***

Bettina Freeman woke but had no sense of time. She was starving, angry, and terrified, but there was nary a sound from beyond the walls of her prison.

As her eyes adjusted to the dim surroundings, she noticed a tiny red dot glowing halfway up one of the walls. She went to it, finding a small rectangular box secured firmly to the wall.

Was it an intercom? she wondered.

But there was no button to press, no way to initiate communication.

She turned away from the mystery box, pressed her back against the wall, and slowly slid down to the floor, crying.

***

Moynihan had simply hung up in his ear.

Richard Whelan was pacing. He hadn't slept. He looked at his watch for the fifth time in the last half hour and decided that he could no longer sit around, even though it was just 7:30 a.m. He had to do something. How badly was Moynihan compromised?

He grabbed his keys and his Browning and went out to the Porsche. He would go to the Capitol building and hope that he could stop what he was almost certain was about to go down.

As he cranked the car, he fought against the shivers and shakes that suddenly wracked him, the tension of his fears for Bettina's safety and what he was going to have to do to get her back.

His cell phone rang, and he answered it without looking at the display.

"Richard? Richard Whelan?" the voice said, somehow familiar even though he couldn't place it.

"Yes, who's calling please?" he said as he pulled his car into traffic, balancing the phone against his shoulder as he shifted gears.

"This is Bettina's father, Richard. We met last Sunday."

Richard's heart soared. Had he heard anything?

"Yes, sir, what can I do for you?"

"I'm sorry to be calling you so early, but Mother Freeman and I are frankly worried. Bettina was supposed to call us last night, and we haven't been able to raise her, either at her house or by her cell phone. So I was wondering if you'd seen her?"

The worry in the older man's voice was palpable.

I used to have a pretty girl, too.

Richard swallowed and up shifted again, now accelerating toward the Capitol.

"No, sir, I haven't seen or heard from her since day before yesterday."

There was a hesitation on the other end, and Richard was finding it more and more difficult to drive with the cell phone pressed against his ear with his shoulder.

"Um, I'm not sure I understand. Her assistant said that she left with you yesterday after she finished up at the State Department."

Lord, now he had to lie. "No, whoever said that is mistaken. We were supposed to, ah, get together, but she cancelled."

"Do you recall when was the last time you spoke to her?" Bettina's father was sterner, getting closer to outright anger.

"No, but look, I've got to go. I'm driving, and I don't have a hands-free earpiece with me. I'm sure she'll turn up eventually," he said, disconnecting the call. He turned the phone off and threw it into the passenger seat of the Porsche in disgust.

***

At the National Mall, Secret Service Agent Sven Mikkleson surveyed the teams of agents sweeping the Lincoln Memorial and securing the immediate vicinity. It was early, and they'd had to chase only a few squatters out of the area as they set up the security perimeter and manned it with agents. Now his advance teams were checking every inch of the closed-off area nearest the memorial to ensure that nothing was hidden within the rope boundary that would give a potential assassin a weapon within a stone's throw of the president.

"Advance Two, this is Radius, come in please," Mikkleson heard in his earpiece.

"This is Advance Two, Sam. Go ahead," Mikkleson said to Sam Redburn, who was still at the White House and would be for some time.

"It's seven forty-five, and I need a sit rep, over," Redburn said.

"It's seven forty-five, and we're right on schedule, Radius. Perimeter's set up, and the advance teams are working the patch."

"Find anything?" Redburn asked, although the question was redundant. Protocol would have demanded that Mikkleson tell him if they'd found as much as an errant paperclip during the walk-arounds.

"Negative, Radius. Oracle's ETD?"

Mikkleson waited as Radius checked his watch and his timeline.

"Ah, Advance Two, be advised that we are plus one hour prior to Oracle's ETD. We are expecting an on-time departure."

"You expecting to do anything fancy on the way over, Sam?" Mikkleson knew Redburn would never answer the question over an open circuit, even though the Service's radios were encrypted. He asked just to needle Redburn, who he thought was taking the entire exercise way too seriously.

"That's a negative, Advance Two. Straight in, nothing fancy."

"Roger that, Radius. Next check-in time is in one hour. Talk to you then."

"Right. Radius out."

In the Secret Service office, Sam Redburn looked at the cold cup of coffee on his desk and tried to will his stomach to settle. Instead, the sight of the crusty mug, which hadn't been properly washed all week, turned his stomach. On a whim, he dialed someone he knew in the residence to inquire as to Oracle's health and state of mind.

One of the White House stewards picked up his call.

"He's just fine. Getting things sorted for the trip to Camp David later today and eating breakfast with Michelle and the kids."

"How's his mood?" Redburn asked, regretting asking the question but morbidly curious because he had so much riding on today.

"He seems the same as usual. The man has ice water in his veins, Sam. He's not like other presidents. Whether he's on his way to a state dinner or taking time off to shoot a round of golf, the man is cool and even-tempered. Why, you guys got something?"

"No. Just checking," Redburn said and hung up the phone. He then reached for the frequency chart to get the advance team at the Capitol building.

***

Richard Whelan arrived at the newly constructed underground visitors' center at the Capitol a little before 8:00 a.m. Naturally, the center didn't open until 9:00 a.m.; a curiosity even in Washington, where things were usually synchronized to business hours or staggered to museum time, which would imply an 11:00 a.m. opening.

Whelan parked, walked up to the entrance, and looked at his watch. It was 8:03 a.m.

"Advance Three, this is Radius, do you read?" Sam Redburn was using the main comms office to get a signal over to the Capitol, because

Advance Three, the two-man team covering the Capitol building, and more specifically the scaffolding around the Statue of Freedom atop the building, had not answered his calls from his body-mounted set. He figured it was a signal problem.

He clicked the microphone again.

"Advance Three, this is Radius, do you read?" he said and let the mike flop to his side.

Nothing but static.

Redburn looked at his watch: 8:07 a.m.

Frank Moynihan was in the Capitol building, having flashed his credentials a million times to get past the security checkpoints manned by the Federal Protective Services personnel. He was about to make his second trip up to the scaffolding above the dome when his cell phone rang.

It was 8:15 a.m.

"Moynihan."

"Frank, Sam. I, ah, was wondering whether you were planning to visit the counter sniper team at the Capitol building."

"Yeah, Sam, I am. Is there a problem?"

"No, not really. They missed a check-in, and I think there may be some kind of a comms glitch. I was hoping you were in the vicinity and planning to check on them."

Moynihan had just reached the elevator leading to the maintenance spaces in the building. He pushed the call button.

"I should be able to get back to you in a few minutes, Sam. Will that be sufficient?"

"Sure, Frank, sure."

"What's the matter? Nerves?"

"Well," Redburn said sheepishly, "yeah, kinda."

"It's OK. You've done this by the book. Nothing is going to happen, OK?"

"Right. Right. OK. Are you carrying your radio?"

"Nope. Just the cell. I'll call you as soon as I get up top."

"Right. OK."

Richard Whelan looked at his watch again: 8:30 a.m. Another thirty minutes until the visitors' center officially opened, thirty minutes before

Obama was scheduled to speak. He dialed Moynihan's office, got voice mail. He then tried his cell phone, which was busy.

Perhaps he could impress upon the FPS people to let him in early. He had his Secret Service credentials, and it wasn't like this was the Pentagon. He expected less security here than at the normal entrance.

He went to the rolled-down security gate and began banging on it.

It took several minutes, but he was rewarded with lights snapping on in the center and an FPS officer with a ring of keys making his way toward the entrance.

"We're not open for another thirty minutes!" the officer yelled from behind the Plexiglas façade behind the roll-down security gate.

Whelan pulled his wallet and showed his Secret Service credentials.

"I'm with the Secret Service, Officer! Here to secure the scaffolding," he yelled back.

"Their team is already on the premises. And the list only said three people!"

"I need to get into the maintenance elevator. It's a matter of national security."

"Then you can get your butt to the regular entrance. This area is closed till nine this morning."

Whelan pulled his cell phone out and called Moynihan as he watched the FPS guy walk away.

"Moynihan."

"Frank, Richard Whelan."

"Yeah, Richard, what can I do for you?"

"You need to get me into the Capitol building, you son of a bitch."

"I'm sorry?" Frank said.

"I'm at the Capitol building in the underground visitors' center. The FPS people won't let me in, and I need you to make a call, Frank."

"Sure," Moynihan said, with a chuckle.

Moynihan was in the maintenance elevator, heading up to the highest level of the dome. He switched to the external scaffolding elevator that would take him to the top of the dome. Once at the top, he entered the closed-off area where the Secret Service team was supposed to be waiting. He opened the plywood door and stopped cold.

Whelan tapped on the security gate again and watched as the FPS cop ambled into view. This time, the cop unsnapped the holster of his gun and waved it angrily at Whelan.

Whelan drew his own Browning from his waistband and showed it to the Federal Protective Services officer, who paled. "This is why I can't go to the regular entrance," he yelled. "Did Moynihan contact you?"

"No!" the cop said, eyeing the Plexiglas barrier behind the roll-down gate.

"Frank Moynihan of the Secret Service is going to get someone to authorize you to open up. This is related to the president's speech. Don't be alarmed."

But the cop was alarmed, and he picked up his radio to make a call.

Either this will be resolved in a couple of minutes, or I'm in deep trouble, Richard thought.

Moynihan noted the unopened crate and pried the lid off of it, checking his watch. It was 8:35 a.m. Two trips up and down, and he was cutting it close. He would have to make a phone call about Whelan in a hot second.

He looked at the weapon inside the wooden crate and inspected it carefully. He picked up the heavy gun and inspected the scope.

Everything looked intact. He pulled out the tripod stand and began setting up the weapon.

Now there were three FPS cops in the sealed vestibule of the visitors' center talking to Whelan.

"Contact the Secret Service, guys, that's all you have to do," Richard shouted.

The FPS guys were talking, and one of them was speaking into a radio. No doubt they were going to have someone on the outside of the building come put the cuffs on him.

One of the other cops went behind one of the counters and picked up a land line.

Sam Redburn picked up his phone, angry that an outside line had been directed to him now, of all times.

"Redburn."

He listened for a moment. Some nutcase at the Capitol with Secret Service credentials wanting to get into the visitors' center? No, and hell no, was his response.

"Yeah, sorry, I understand. Do you have this man in custody? Get him in custody now. Understand? I'm going to contact someone over there and have him meet you near the maintenance elevator on the visitors' center sublevel, OK? And this is very important—under no circumstances is this guy to get access to the inside of the building by himself, capisce?"

When the FPS sergeant had acknowledged that he understood, Redburn called Moynihan.

"Yeah, this is Frank."

"Redburn."

"Yeah, sorry, I didn't get back to you. The team over here is fine. I'm just helping them with the pregame stuff."

"OK, but I got another problem. There's a nutcase down at the visitors' center wanting to get in. Keeps claiming that the Service was going to authorize him to get access to the building. Can you get the advance team to check it out?"

"Yeah, sure. I believe it's Richard Whelan. I'll make sure it gets checked out."

Redburn let go a sigh of relief. "Thanks, Frank."

Redburn looked at his watch—8:40 a.m.

Moynihan looked through the scope at the Lincoln Memorial and then tested the weapon against the tripod. There was some give that he didn't care for, and he didn't want the weapon or the stand collapsing. He secured a wing nut, surveyed his work, and headed for the elevator to deal with Whelan.

He smoothed his jacket and checked the battery on his cell phone. He had a feeling he was going to need it.

He whistled an old Hendrix tune as the elevator descended, and he transitioned to the maintenance elevator in the Capitol building proper.

He was in the sublevel of the visitors' center by 8:46 a.m.

The FPS officer came up to Whelan with his gun drawn, and Whelan put his hands up. Officer Thomas relieved Whelan of his weapon and waited until the officers inside pulled the Plexiglas barrier and turned the key to raise the security gate.

"Did you hear from the Secret Service?" Whelan asked.

"Yeah," Thomas said. "There's someone here who's going to want to talk to you. So we're going to wait here until he arrives."

Whelan relaxed. Hopefully he could get Moynihan to listen to reason and help him. *Unless he's in too deep to pull out.*

Frank Moynihan came into the visitors' center and announced himself, holding his credentials high.

"Moynihan, Secret Service. What seems to be the problem?"

The FPS cops looked toward the sergeant to respond.

"We got a call from Agent Redburn, who said to detain this person who was requesting early access to the building through the visitors' center. Redburn requested that we wait until he could send someone, Agent Moynihan."

Frank surveyed the situation. Richard was not handcuffed, but Thomas was holding what had to be Whelan's Browning in one hand and Whelan's elbow in the other.

"I know this man," Frank said to the officers. "He's a member of my Secret Service team."

Whelan watched as Moynihan introduced himself. Frank and the FPS personnel had a brief conversation about Whelan's bona fides.

Moynihan was moving toward him when Whelan saw it.

Omigod.

Richard pulled away from the FPS officer but Frank, with his gun already out, turned and shot the sergeant and the other officer standing by the phone. Thomas had Whelan's gun in his left hand and was unprepared when Moynihan shot him.

Thomas went down, and Whelan's gun clattered to the marble floor. It was 8:48 a.m.

***

Whelan reacted instantly, sweeping Moynihan's legs from under him and diving for his weapon. Moynihan went down, a wild shot slicing the air over Whelan's head.

Richard scooped up his Browning and dove away from Moynihan, aiming for his head in the process. It was a difficult shot, but Whelan was a shooter, and he pulled the trigger.

And sent the hammer closing on an empty chamber.

Damn, the gun did feel light, he thought. Thomas must have taken the clip.

As he rolled he heard Moynihan open up, the shells whizzing past him.

Moynihan was down, cursing, as he tracked Whelan diving across the floor. His body sprawled, his aim settled, and he pulled the trigger as Whelan dropped the hammer on his empty chamber. He saw the Browning's clip in the partially open hand of Officer Thomas, and Frank Moynihan smiled.

Catlike, he snapped to his feet as Whelan scampered away across the marble floor.

Whelan dove behind the display counter just before it shattered with the impact of several nine-millimeter slugs. He covered his head with his hands as the glass rained down and continued scrambling as pistol rounds dug up the marble floor behind him. His hand closed on a paperweight, a glass etching of the Capitol, and he turned and saw Moynihan coming up behind him, aiming his weapon.

Without thinking, he chucked the paperweight at Moynihan and dove to his left as Moynihan pulled the trigger again.

The heavy paperweight caught the head of the Secret Service in the chest, forcing him to drop his gun to his side.

"Whelan! Give it up!" he yelled, but Richard Whelan had come back around behind him and snatched the clip to the Browning from the dead Officer Thomas's hand.

Moynihan turned, sensing that Whelan was behind him, and blindly squeezed off two quick rounds as Whelan jammed the clip into the Browning Hi-Power.

"Who's blackmailing you?" Whelan yelled, unwilling to bring the gun to bear on Moynihan.

Then he stumbled over the body of one of the FPS officers and nearly went down.

Moynihan turned toward him and saw him stumble.

"You wouldn't understand!" he yelled, fishing a fresh clip from his pocket.

Whelan recovered, retreating to a display recounting the construction of the underground visitors' center, Moynihan sending chips of plaster and marble at him as he continued firing.

"Try me, Frank! Someone's up there now, getting ready to kill the president! We can't let that happen!"

"They have me by the balls, Richard! Obama's doomed! I'm going to save myself!"

Whelan turned and shot, a clear miss, and ran toward the elevators. It was 8:49 a.m.

***

Sam Redburn debated calling the Capitol staff or Frank Moynihan back to see what had happened with the nutcase that Moynihan had suspected was Richard Whelan, but there was an incident with a homeless man on the National Mall that he needed to get locked down immediately. He was already at the memorial. He would not to ride with the president in the motorcade but would instead make a visit to the most critical sites before Obama took the podium. He did manage to make a note of the contact, and his suspicions about Whelan, in his case file before he and his number two saddled up to walk the grounds.

***

Whelan made it into the elevators and managed to get the doors closed before Moynihan could catch him. He had to get to the scaffolding, where the sniper was no doubt set up. Moynihan, compromised, had been sent to stop him; Frank had said as much.

At the top floor, he watched as the second elevator in the bank rose up—carrying Frank inside, and he scrambled to the construction elevator that would take him to the catwalk at the top of the dome. The entire dome of the Capitol was obscured by the scaffolding, but he imagined that there would be a long, thin walkway from the elevator to the Statue of Freedom.

He closed the wire gate of the construction elevator just as he heard a ping, and the second elevator from the visitors' center arrived. He hit the switch to go up just as the second elevator's doors began opening.

He leaned against the cage, safe for the moment because there was only one car and one way up. He checked his gun, wondering if he could surprise the assassin, thinking that he might have to take whoever it was down as soon as he spotted him from the elevator or on the catwalk leading to the Statue of Freedom. Then he would have to deal with Moynihan, but he thought he could convince Moynihan to give it up if he could stop the shooter. If he could stop the shooter, there was no point in going through with it.

Or so Richard hoped.

***

Moynihan waited for the elevator to come back down, knowing that he had no choice in the matter. Whelan had seriously outflanked him by reaching the high ground first. This was not good. He looked at his watch.

It was 8:51 a.m.

He checked the clip in his Glock and began consolidating his partials as he waited for the construction elevator to return.

***

President Obama was in the limousine on his way to the National Mall. He wanted to get there a few minutes early and survey the crowd to get a feel for its mood and whether the people would be receptive to his message today. He understood that Redburn was already on site, and he felt secure with the Secret Service agents in the car with him and in the accompanying Suburbans riding shotgun on the motorcade.

He noticed again that it was a nice day, beautiful, actually, with the sun shining and a nearly cloudless blue sky. There should be a big crowd, he thought, and his pulse quickened.

They were passing the satellite trucks from the various media outlets now, but he couldn't see the size of the crowds that were waiting for him. He spotted one network reporter who was apparently broadcasting live through his microwave uplink, and he tuned the TV in the limo to the station.

The picture fuzzed for a moment and then came in sharply through the aerial on the trunk.

"Julie, I'm here on the National Mall, just a few minutes prior to President Obama's speech, and I'm stunned at the huge turnout" the reporter was saying, and Obama's pulse quickened some more.

"How so, Marvin?"

"Well, if we can get a camera shot to pan on the National Mall, you'll see that the scene is virtually jammed, Julie. Johnny?" the reporter said, talking to his cameraman. The view changed to the mall.

The mob was huge and growing as Secret Service agents struggled to get people to form orderly lines to get access to the memorial. He could see that the security personnel manning the checkpoints at the gaps in the barricade, where people could pass through metal detectors, were rushing around like madmen.

"So, if you got that, Julie, you know that this is shaping up to be a major event for the Obama administration, with crowds the president hasn't seen since his 2008 campaign for the White House. One has to wonder, with the stakes this high, can the president recapture enough of the spirit of his election campaign to carry him back to the White House for four more years?"

The correspondent looked at his watch. "It looks, Julie, like we've got about five minutes before we find out if the president is punctual."

The studio anchorwoman shuffled papers, looking at her watch.

"With so little time left, is it your sense that the crowd has peaked, or are more people on their way into the site?"

"Oh, no, Julie, there are still busloads of people disembarking that we haven't even begun to deal with. I'm hoping to snag one of the Secret Service or security personnel to ask about their plan for the overflow. We'll check in in another two minutes with an update on the president's whereabouts and whether we will have a 9:00 a.m. start. Julie, back to you in the studio."

It was 8:55 a.m.

***

Whelan stumbled into the scaffolding surrounding the Statue of Freedom with the Browning held high as he quartered the area. He saw the bodies of the two Secret Service agents on the advance team. It was their blood on Frank Moynihan's clothes that had confirmed that Frank was dirty.

He saw the Russian super rifle set up on a tripod that looked like it could support the weight of a Russian Soyuz on one leg, much less three. He didn't need to look through it to know that it was perfectly zeroed on the president's podium set up in front of Lincoln's statue at the Lincoln Memorial.

But there was no shooter.

Moynihan made his way to the scaffolding, ignoring the top of the statue that protruded through the top of the scaffolding. He came in with his Glock at the ready, and his cell phone set to speed dial at the touch of a button.

Whelan was standing there, in the middle of the area, his gun down at his side, as Moynihan came through.

Whelan merely looked at him.

"Drop your weapon, Richard," Moynihan said softly.

Whelan looked at him.

"Tell me she's all right," he said, but he didn't drop the gun.

At 8:56 a.m., Chuck O'Shay took a phone call from Sam Redburn, who informed him that the crowd had so far exceeded the National Park Service's estimates that the Service and the additional manpower they had deployed was having trouble coping. There was no contingency plan for overflow areas because of the vast size of the area already occupied by the still-growing crowd.

"We could have a situation here if the president starts speaking before everyone's inside, Mr. O'Shay."

"What are you saying—delay the speech?"

"Or move the president from the outdoor podium into a more secure area, like a sound truck from one of the networks, and have him make the speech from there."

"Are you insane, man? The crowd wants to see Oracle."

"I understand that, sir, but should something happen I'd be more comfortable if the president was inside and in a place only we know about. We can still feed the image to the monitors that are already set up. It's just going to be an empty podium."

At 8:57, O'Shay called the president's body man and asked the aide to pass the phone to the president.

"Yes, Chuck," Obama said, his voice tinny and hollow-sounding on the cell.

"Mr. President," O'Shay said, "the Secret Service is concerned about the size of the crowd and crowd control. They are suggesting that you not make the speech at the podium but instead from one of the network sound trucks that's suitably equipped for audio and video, and they feed the image to the monitors set up for the crowd."

"Are they insane?" Obama asked, anger flaring. "They want me to speak over the image of an empty podium? The media will have a field day with that one, Chuck."

"Sir, I can only say that they don't feel the security arrangements are up to snuff for a crowd this size, and the news reports are saying that the crowd is growing."

By now the motorcade had parked and the doors to his limousine had been flung open, and Obama was on his feet and moving.

"Look, there is no way I'm going to take their suggestion, Chuck," the president said, but he was nearly drowned out by the Marine Corps band striking up "Hail to the Chief" as he approached the stage. "I will delay for a minute or so to let people coming through the security perimeter finish entering."

Back in the White House, O'Shay looked at his watch.

It was 8:59 a.m.

"Tell me," Whelan said, almost under his breath, "that she's all right."

Moynihan pulled the cell phone from his pocket, and Whelan snapped the gun to arm's length, pointing it directly at his midsection.

Moynihan showed the phone to Whelan, then flipped it open and pressed the send button to the speed-dial number he'd already programmed.

In a basement, somewhere in Bethesda, the red light on the intercom box above Bettina Freeman's head blinked, and a sound like a telephone ringing got her attention.

"Hello?" she said to no response.

Moynihan held the phone out so Whelan could hear the tinny voice from the handset.

"Bettina?" Whelan said.

And he heard her voice, choking with fear, answering him back.

Phillip Stone watched the news coverage and the crowds and wondered about the aftermath. The president shot dead, a state funeral, Michelle and the girls in black, and a whole magazine's worth of images that would play on the American psyche forever. He had not heard from the asset in some time, but he wasn't concerned. He'd been reliable, used in a variety of situations through blind drops and anonymous contacts once his bona fides had proven out.

If the president didn't die today, there would be other times, other places, and other opportunities. He and his counterparts were masters of the patience that long-range thinking required, and to him, the daily course of events was just an entertaining sideshow.

He guessed, as he saw Obama approaching the stage waving and shaking hands, that the country had about two minutes before the machinery of violent governmental succession kicked in.

Moynihan's cell phone had a hands-free speaker option. He held it out so Richard could hear Bettina's voice.

"Richard," she said, "Richard, I want you to know..." Whelan could hear the tears choking her voice. "I want you to know that no matter what, I love you. And...it's a boy, Richard. Our child is a son."

And then Moynihan pulled the phone away.

"You have a choice, Richard," Moynihan said as he closed the phone. "You can kill me, and she dies, or you can stand down. No negotiations, no nonsense, understand? You'll never find her if you kill me, and

I'm the only one who knows where she is. That phone call was false-switched all over the country before it connected with a tiny little box in the dark basement where she is. I die, she starves to death. And so does your boy." The things we do to our children, Moynihan thought.

Richard had the gun up, still pointing it at Moynihan.

"Then it *was* you in Dallas?" he asked, his voice trembling.

Moynihan said nothing and glanced at his watch: 9:00 a.m. The president would appear at the podium at any moment now. He raised his gun.

"We can either do this easy, or we can do this hard, Richard."

He saw Whelan's finger tighten on the trigger.

"Why?"

In 1968, so long ago, they were on a transport headed back from the bush, when The Kid asked Raoul why they had wanted him in Dallas. He thought that if he understood why he'd been abandoned at such an early age, it might help him deal with the demons that haunted him.

Raoul lit a cigarette and took a deep breath that was not audible over the drone of the plane's engines.

"Why me?" The Kid had asked him, and Raoul decided that he would tell him the truth.

"It wasn't you that we were interested in. It was your father. He had something on Jack Ruby. Something that let us own Ruby without any doubts. So we took you to get him to blackmail Ruby when it went down. Without Ruby, we couldn't close the circle around the patsy. And without a dead patsy, we wouldn't have done it."

At 9:01 a.m., President Barack Obama took the podium in front of an expectant, jubilant crowd on the National Mall. He stood in front of Lincoln's stately repose and cleared his throat, thinking that he'd made the right decision.

He cleared his throat and started to speak.

"Your choice, Richard. The president, or your girlfriend."

Moynihan knew that time was ticking away. He would simply have to take his chances if Whelan didn't give up the ghost. Just like Dallas, he thought.

Obama began, "My fellow Americans, let me say that there are enough sorrows in the world that one could cry a river of tears from now until the end of time, and, in fact, until the tears had no meaning. I want to say that the notion of hope we had as a nation leaving the battlefields of World War II has been deferred and frayed by a contentious social and political reality, and this new reality has come as we understand that we are getting older, we face greater competition, and we are deeper in debt. In no time in recent history has the blank check of promises America has made to its people seemed more in question as we struggle to provide adequate health care, to fund retirements, to provide the backbone the economy needs to prosper, as we the people confront limits to everything, including our regard for each other..."

It wasn't a choice. Whelan refused to think of it as a choice that any sane person could make.

Your duty or your child—who could choose between the two? One life or two? This was a choice? Whelan recalled the sermon from last Sunday, about being in the wilderness, about being forced to confront that which he alone could not control.

Just as I am, O Lamb of God.

He looked at the gun and at Moynihan, and he knew in a heartbeat of intense clarity that he didn't love her, because he didn't know what love was, and he had never known. What he and Bettina had wouldn't exist at all without the child growing inside of her.

He knew duty, not love. That's what his parents had taught him, and he was hesitating because he had a higher calling, and that meant that he had no choice but to let Bettina die.

Her and his child—himself, really—and all the self-hatred and bitterness of his choices pushed gorge into his throat, that he should be forced to make such a choice— that he was making such a choice...

Then Moynihan tackled him.

Obama continued, "But today I want to echo the words of Martin Luther King as I announce my candidacy for a second term as your president of these United States. King, as you know, made his famous 'I Have a Dream' speech from this very venue, but whether we like it or not, many aspects of his dream remain unfulfilled, even though we have the power to make change a reality. Doctor King knew this, and, sadly, died for it. And in reality, the dream, as Doctor King called it, is no longer an American invention; it is not limited to an American ideology spoken with the fervor of an American minister. We are seeing the desire of all people to live in a world that respects their humanity, whether that humanity manifests itself in the streets of Beverly Hills or the slums of Calcutta..."

They traded punches, but as Obama started speaking, Whelan hesitated, and in that moment Frank Moynihan acted, a nasty overhand right that stunned Whelan and allowed Moynihan to disarm him. Moynihan kept his pistol and handcuffed Whelan's right wrist to one of the scaffolding supports to the right of the super gun.

Then, Moynihan holstered his Glock and moved to the super gun. He pulled on the special gloves that he'd prepared for this very moment and turned to Whelan, showing him the tips of the fingers of the gloves.

"Your fingerprints, Richard. Taken from your Secret Service files."

Obama continued his speech. "Around the world, people are protesting repression by governments bent on suppressing their freedoms. Our challenge is not simply to meet this repression with the barrels of our guns, because we have seen in Iraq and Afghanistan that even we cannot restore freedom within an armed camp without terrible cost.

"Nor can we sit idly by while the rule of despots and criminals goes unchallenged and disclaim responsibility to the chagrin of generations that are losing opportunity. We must realize when we look at those protesting in Egypt, in Libya, in Tunisia, that our freedom is inextricably bound to theirs, that we cannot remain unmoved by other people's oppression..."

Moynihan pressed Whelan's prints on the gun, carefully making sure that there would be no doubt who the shooter was. That he'd gotten away with it sickened him, but he'd been sick for a long time. He'd been sick since that day in Dallas, when Mook's voice had condemned him to the twilight zone, a twilight zone of an impossible shot that only he could have made that fateful day, sick that day in Memphis, and sick in Los Angeles, as the drug epidemic swept through a community that he'd not stopped but had actually helped progress. It was a special sickness, a special darkness, his own river of tears, he thought, which had allowed him to come up with the plan to implicate Whelan as the patsy, from sending him the package with his old rifle to kidnapping Bettina so that he would have no choice when he confronted him here, in the sniper nest, as he used Whelan's prodigious intellect against him to get him into position.

Obama was speaking: "But freedom has a price. The cynics and the pundits would have you believe that America is somehow paying a price for transgressions against what they claim is the American way, but, quite frankly, their American way is rooted in the wealth and power of the privileged, and their American way is about maintaining a status quo that in other countries has led to protests in the streets, and their status quo has too often resulted in the demonization of those we deem our enemies. The fact is, we are all in this together. Not just as Americans, but as a global people bent on enjoying the reasonable fruits of our labors. If we are to make a meaningful move forward, we all must move forward because we will recognize in each other kindred spirits driven by hope.

"If we were to tell the truth, we would have to speak about our complacency, the abstraction with which we've viewed those less fortunate than ourselves. If the past several years of economic trials have taught us anything, however, it is that the line between the 'us' we thought we were and the 'them' we knew we weren't has been crossed by too many people too many times, for reasons that we can and have done something about.

"It's just that we need to do more. Not because the government can solve all our problems, but because the check that King talked about fifty years ago needs to be made good on, not just for minorities, but for all of us who have ever lost a job, have ever had a health problem, or have ever been insecure about where our next meal was coming from. This was a basic tenant of the economic dream Martin Luther King talked about; this is the promise we, as a nation, as well as the community of nations around the world, have failed to keep.

"This is why I'd like to continue as your president. But in doing so, I want us to understand that our greatness isn't because we deny these things, but because we confront them, that we will always confront them, that in the confrontation of our weaknesses we grow stronger, and the movement King started is as alive and well in Cairo as it was in Birmingham.

"I am aware many of you here today are experiencing economic tribulation that was unthinkable except to the generation that survived the Great Depression. My fellow Americans, you are experiencing this loss of economic viability just as the doubts about the ability of the government to keep its promises to you are at their highest.

"I say this to you with the understanding that the world, our world, must strive to serve both the powerful and the powerless, not with equal care, but with the sense of meeting unmet needs. I speak not with the platitudes of politicians promising all things to all people, because I do not want you to underestimate the struggle, sometimes with ourselves, to achieve these ideals. I speak not just of hope, or of dreams, although we as a people live lives of brutish irrelevance without both. I speak of action, of changing the course, of making a difference. I speak of realizing the promise laid out by Martin Luther King and others; I speak of victory over uncertainty, not because we all agree but because we disagree with mutual respect, because it is in that mutual respect that we can find the will and means to govern and move forward.

"I say to you today, my friends, that even though we face the difficulties of today and tomorrow, I still have a dream. It is a dream deeply rooted in the American dream, but it is a dream that is not limited to Americans..."

Moynihan remembered Raoul, face down in the high grass bordering some obscure roadway in New Jersey, turning and looking up at him in his state trooper's uniform and laughing, laughing because—

"We didn't even care that you could shoot, Kid. Mook put you on that retaining wall to keep you out of the way. Good thing you could, though, because if you couldn't, Kennedy would have lived, and we would have been screwed. Now ain't that some shit." He laughed again.

And he'd stepped back to avoid getting blood on his uniform and to make it seem less of an assassination than a righteous police shooting, and he gripped his service revolver in both hands like the professional he was and remembered Dallas and the bloody A Shau and the proficiency that he'd acquired in killing people. He stepped back and put a bullet in Raoul's heart. Heard his breath catch in the new hole in the center of his chest and watched the light drain from his eyes. He waited there for a long moment. He waited and waited, because he was praying that maybe, just maybe, Raoul would get up so he could kill the bastard again...

Moynihan had Obama in the cross hairs. He adjusted for the prodigious drop of the bullets as they traversed the two miles to the target.

He centered himself behind the gun and let his breathing slow. Whelan was beside him, a comforting presence somehow.

Whelan was chained down with a view of the distant Lincoln Memorial. He could hear the boom of the sound system as the president stepped to the podium. *I'm sorry, Bettina. I really am sorry that I don't feel more than I do.*

Richard remembered the last time he'd seen his father, the reluctant hug they'd exchanged because his dad was going into surgery that he would never recover from. He remembered his grief, which was not so much about the words unspoken between them but about the fact that in the end they'd had nothing to say and hadn't for a long time.

And now he had a son in harm's way, and he'd hesitated just long enough for a killer to get the drop on him.

Obama continued, "When I came into office, I had those dreams, and I have them still. I am a candidate for the presidency of these United States, and if you will have me, I will continue to pursue those dreams for Americans and for the oppressed and marginalized people around the world, and I will do so not just as a dreamer, but as a determined man driven by the audacity of hope that I have for us all."

Moynihan stood there, taking pressure out of the trigger, his breath slowing—slowing, slowing—aware of nothing but the sight in the cross hairs and the thought, *Have some death,* which took him back so many years and so many killings ago.

At 9:06 a.m., Frank Moynihan pulled the trigger.

CHAPTER 44

9:06 a.m.

P hillip Stone was watching the news coverage, which naturally alternated between camera shots of the growing crowd and a frontal shot of Obama at the podium.

He saw Obama look up into the distance, not missing a beat from his speech, and then there was a sound like a jet engine roar, and the hard shell podium exploded.

Sam Redburn was relaxed, watching the huge crowd. He happened to glance toward the Capitol and the scaffolding atop the dome.

And saw a flash, then another, and another, and another...

He ran instinctively toward the president and the podium but was at least a heartbeat too late as the shells impacted, and the podium exploded, and time seemed to slow.

Whelan had a throwaway weapon at his ankle, but as he saw Moynihan working the weapon, he didn't think he could get to it in time.

Time for Plan B, he thought, and managed to fish a mirror out of his jacket pocket and point it so that the flash would be seen by President Obama if he was looking at the scaffolding like they'd agreed, because, as he'd said to the president, *The only way this makes sense is if I'm the patsy.*

And Whelan prayed that he was looking.

Barack Obama was in full cadence, now nearly six minutes into his speech, but he kept looking toward the point of maximum threat, just as he and Richard Whelan had agreed, and then he saw it.

Son of a bitch, the flash of a mirror. Obama bailed from behind the podium just as the first shot was fired.

Sam Redburn tackled him and landed on top of him as the terrible booms continued racking the stage where the president had just been standing. Three times the explosions and a sound like incoming artillery shells came in, seemingly one on top of the other.

Whelan pulled his clutch piece and pointed it at Moynihan, who looked back at him as he fired the last round, a look of sad triumph on his face, and then, was it resignation, as he saw Whelan pointing the snub-nosed revolver at him. Before Moynihan could turn back to the weapon, Whelan shot him, the tiny crack of the revolver almost comical compared to the massive cacophony of the big weapon. Moynihan, stricken, went down, and as Whelan watched in horror, rolled to the edge of the scaffolding.

Moynihan, hurt, could have stopped himself as he approached the edge, but as he got to the edge, he twitched just enough to fall into space, free-falling toward the ground.

As if I could pray for anything!

And he looked to the stage and found, at last, a small measure of peace before he died.

On the stage, Obama, buried under the weight of the much heavier Sam Redburn, saw the mirror flash again from the direction of the Capitol. That was the signal that Whelan had told him would mean a downed sniper.

"The next time you want to dance," he said ironically to Redburn, "Just ask nicely."

And then they were hustled to their feet and taken off the stage amid the pandemonium of the crowd.

296

***

There was no delay in the footage that went out all over the world. So many cameras had been focused on the president behind the podium, and there were so many angles that it was impossible not to show them all and repeat them nonstop. Within minutes, though, there was more news and more footage as CNN's Atlanta anchor came back on air.

"This is CNN with continuing coverage of the breathtaking assassination attempt on President Barack Obama. The president's condition at this moment is unknown, as officials are refusing to say anything until the scene is locked down. But from the footage we've replayed, it does not appear that the president was hit.

"In addition, the Secret Service is now reporting that the gunshots were from the Capitol building and that the sniper was in the scaffolding surrounding the Statue of Freedom at the top of the dome. Repeating— the Secret Service is reporting that the sniper took the shots at President Obama from the Capitol Dome in the scaffolding built to perform maintenance to the Statue of Freedom atop the…"

The world watched as the Atlanta anchor hesitated, listening to the director in her earpiece.

"OK, please bear with us, because we have new video of the scene where the shootings took place—this is from our helicopter that is over the scene now. Let's listen in to their live broadcast…"

Whelan pulled his cell phone from his jacket and called Alan Christiansen as the helicopters whirled overhead.

"Christiansen!" the FBI director yelled as he answered the phone.

"Alan, it's Richard Whelan. Is the president OK?"

"Where are you?"

"At the scene, in the scaffolding."

"Then that's you that's all over CNN," Christiansen said as the CNN helicopter settled in to hover over the area and send back pictures of the tripod platform and the huge gun it supported.

"Yeah, but is the president—"

"He's fine and en route to the White House. They're saying it's a miracle that the shooter missed."

"Not a miracle, Alan. A mirror. But Bettina's still missing, and Frank Moynihan was the shooter all along. You have to get every resource you can looking for her, Alan, because she's trapped somewhere, and I don't know how long she can survive. Tear Moynihan's life apart, tear his phone records apart, but you damn sure have to find her, Alan. Do you understand? Find her."

On CNN, a newsreader looked up from the printout of Obama's speech and, ignoring the teleprompter, spoke directly to the camera, a tear falling from one of her eyes.

"Who," she said, her voice breaking, "who would want to kill a president trying to deliver that kind of message to the world?" before a frantic director called for them to cut to a commercial.

EPILOGUE

*Sunday, August 28, 2011, the forty-eighth anniversary
of Martin Luther King's "I Have a Dream" speech*

I t was an obscure church in the Virginia countryside, and she noticed the man immediately when he walked in. Tall, good-looking, and dressed down as if he had decided to do so on purpose. She was an usher, and, deciding to sit next to him, she gave him a smile on a bright and sunny Sunday morning, a smile that was acknowledged with something approaching shyness. The reverend closed his Bible and began to preach.

"Scripture tells us the Holy Spirit drove Jesus into the wilderness, because the man in Jesus needed to be tested. When the Holy Spirit came upon him after the baptism, he was entering a new chapter in his life. His human dimension was coming to an end, and his divine dimension was about to take hold. God drove him out there to show him he was ready for Galilee and to show us the way to an intimate relationship with God.

"It is from the wilderness that our salvation is born. It is from the wilderness that we truly learn to love, and I mean really love. It is from the wilderness that we learn to go to work with joy, and to come home with joy, in jobs that are impossible.

"It is from the wilderness, from the harsh places of living, that we are liberated to be the servants of Christ. God is driving us there. In those forty days, God wants us to meet him, through prayer and fasting. Yes, through study and reflection. Yes, but also through actions that will invite people to impugn your motives—that invite people to talk behind your back and to tell lies about you—but it is from the desert that we gain the strength to walk tall through it.

"God did not call us to be comfortable," the preacher said, his voice rising. "God did not call us to be relaxed every minute of the day. God did not call us to squander the fruits of our mother and father's struggles. God has placed us here to use us. In order not to get weary, you must meet him in the wilderness.

"You must know that it is not for you that you live, but for Him. The doors of the church are open…"

The woman looked toward the man and smiled again, hoping that he would go forward and give the preacher his hand, even though he hadn't bothered to stand up when they had asked all the visitors to stand.

He smiled back at her, although there was something distant in his eyes, and his clapping seemed forced. As the congregation stood, he made his way toward the aisle, barely brushing by her in the crowded pew. For a tall man, he was surprisingly agile. She looked forward after he passed to see if anyone was going to accept the preacher's invitation to become part of the church, and then she glanced back to see if she could catch sight of him before he left.

They had found Bettina Freeman barely alive, after the most intensive manhunt in FBI history. Finally, in the forty-ninth hour, they had identified the hiding place and pulled her out of the root cellar that she'd been in without food or water for several days.

As he left the church, Richard Whelan thought about his doubts, about his past, and about his future. The story about his role in stopping the assassination of President Obama was slowly being unraveled by the press.

The president's reelection campaign had, as well, enjoyed a remarkable but predictable bounce from the attempt. Obama had, in fact, offered Whelan a more senior position in the administration, a kind of "name your own price" sort of job as gratitude for saving Oracle's life.

But then, Whelan reflected on the main part of the minister's message:

"You must know that it is not for you that you live, but for Him."

And he thought not of God, nor of Obama, but of his unborn son.

ACKNOWLEDGEMENTS

There are many people who have analyzed the events fictionalized in this book. For those interested, please refer to the comprehensive works by Robert J. Groden, including *The Killing of the President* and *High Treason* (by both Mr. Groden and Harrison Edward Livingstone) as well as *Orders to Kill: The Truth Behind the Murder of Martin Luther King,* by William E. Pepper, and *Murder in Memphis: The FBI and the Assassination of Martin Luther King,* by Mark Lane and Dick Gregory.

The story of the drugs for Contra weapons financing in Los Angeles and elsewhere is told by a reporter, Gary Webb, in his book *Dark Alliance.*

The sermon concerning Isaiah 40 was inspired by many sermons that I have heard, particularly the words of Reverend William Howard, pastor of the Bethany Baptist Church in Newark, New Jersey, although I alone am responsible for any theological errors.

The Birmingham News story about the probe of the "Negro Lie" in Chapter Nine is based upon the actual story that ran in the paper that day.

Music buffs will also know that Jimi Hendrix's song "Manic Depression" actually postdates the fateful events of November 22, 1963. Similarly, geography buffs will understand that there is no such place as Spartansburg Virginia, and that the highway and the police chase toward the end of the novel are set in a completely fictional area near Washington.

As to the veracity of conspiracy theories, please note that any body of evidence supporting a conspiracy theory is most convincing when presented without the evidence that contradicts it.

The reverse is also true.

ABOUT THE AUTHOR

Eric James Fullilove is an MIT graduate, a CPA, and a published author. His novels have been published by Bantam Spectra and Harper Collins. He currently resides in Los Angeles with his lovely wife.

Follow him on twitter at @FulliloveEric, as well as his blog at ericfullilove.wordpress.com.